CRUISE SHIP
MURDERS

A MURDER MYSTERY BY

CLARK SELBY

Library of Congress Control Number: 2025914188

ISBN
979-8-89641-091-1 (Paperback)
979-8-89641-092-8 (eBook)
979-8-89641-090-4 (Hardcover)

CRUISE SHIP
MURDERS

Table of Contents

1

Life After Retirement

Sonny Cousins, and his best friend, Gene Simpson both retired from, the Kansas City Police Department on the same day. They both joined the police department on the same day twenty years ago.

They had spent so many hours working overtime on the job that they both had accumulated more than two years of comp time.

Comp time is giving to police officers, instead of being paid overtime for hours worked beyond their normal eight hour shift. Since police officers weren't paid for overtime work, they are given credit hours for future time off.

So for the next two years Sonny and Gene would be getting their full pay checks every two weeks, just as if they were still on the job.

Truth be known, they probably had another two years worth of overtime, but they were only allowed to carry over a maximum of two years of overtime hours.

The other thing it did for them was to give them credit for two more years of service, to add to their retirement pay.

The two of them decided several years ago, they would take their wives on a cruise around the world. This was to make up for all of the time they weren't there for their wives when they needed them to be there.

Now, two weeks after they retired from the police force they were at the airport getting ready for the first leg of their trip, flying from Kansas City to San Francisco to board their ship two days later.

They booked an around the world cruise on the Golden Supreme, the flagship of the Supreme Line.

This trip would take them to all seven Continents, being gone for so long, their wives were really worried about their kids, even thought they were now all in college.

Sonny and his wife, Jane had two boys and Gene and his wife, Susan had a daughter and a son.

Sonny and Gene both had told their wives, you raised them to be independent, so now let them be independent.

They told their wives that they were sure their kids would get along just fine and besides you're able to keep in touch with them by email while they were gone.

If any one of them had a major health problem while they're gone, they could always fly home to be with them.

Then Sonny said, "They better be really sick, if we have to cut our trip short, because if they not. I'll have to killing them myself."

The wives didn't think that was funny at all.

The four of them arrived in San Francisco and took a taxi to the Hyatt Regency Hotel, there they had booked suites a friend of Sonny had connections through his travel agent to get them suites for the same price as a regular room.

When they were shown to their suites they were very impressed and Jane said, "Sonny are you sure this suite is the same price as a regular room?"

"Well, I would say it was, because we prepaid for them for two nights at $250 a night and when we checked in they gave us our paid receipts for $500, including taxes. I'd say old Charlie did pretty well with his travel agent for us."

"Sonny then saw a beautiful flower arrangement and a bottle of Champagne in a ice bucket just waiting for them across the room.

"Look Sonny, here's a note on the flowers."

Jane opened the note and read, "Bon Voyage, from Charlie and the gang at Charlie's Diner."

Sonny said, "I'll be darn, that was really nice of Charlie and the folks at the diner, don't you think?"

"I'd certainly think so. I think you and Gene must have drunk a lot of coffee at Charlie's Diner over the past twenty years."

"We spend a lot of time going over cases for a lot of years. I'm sure we drink a lot of coffee and had lots of meals there too, but it still awful nice of him anyway."

Jane agreed.

Gene called and said, "Sonny, did you and Jane have flowers and a bottle of Champagne in your room from Charlie and the gang?"

"We certainly did and we've just opened the bottle and we're having some now, do you and Susan want to come and join us or have you already opened your bottle?"

"No, we haven't, that sounds good. We'll bring our glasses and come over to your suite and we can split our bottle with you guys later."

Before Sonny could tell Jane, that Gene and Susan were on their way to have some Champagne. He heard a knock on the door.

Sonny opened the door and Gene and Susan came in and Gene said, "Hey is this joint with the free booze, we brought our glasses."

Jane said "This is the joint with the free Champagne, bring your glasses over here and I'll fill them."

Jane filled their glasses and the four of them sat down and Gene looked around the suite and said, "This is a lot better than looking at corpses and looking for clues, don't you think Sonny?"

"It's a lot nicer, and there's hardly been any blood been spilled here so far.

"Jane hasn't punched me or anything."

Jane screamed, "Sonny!"

Sonny looked at Jane and said, "Well you haven't."

Sonny and Jane met while students at the University of Kansas. Jane was from a small town called Selby on the Bay, Maryland, just south of Annapolis.

She just wanted to get away from the East Coast, where she had lived all her life.

Jane had heard the people in the Midwest had a totally different outlook on life as compared to the people on the East Coast.

It seemed to her the people on the East Coast were always trying to do better; better than their parents; better than their neighbors or better than them self.

They were never satisfied being who they were.

She thought no one ever seemed to just be happy with their lives living there.

Jane's father worked in Washington D.C. for the State Department.

She was never exactly sure of what he did, but she knew it had something to do with coordinating between the State Department and the CIA.

He advised the diplomats of potential threats to US citizen's traveling and working in these countries. He was responsible to know of any potential threat to our country and our citizens traveling to these countries.

Before he worked at the State Department. He worked at the CIA as an analyst of conditions in these same countries.

However, he would never discuss what he did or anything about his work.

Jane was born in Boston, where her father was a professor at Harvard University teaching Eastern European History.

He had spent lots of time traveling those countries while studying them in college as he was working on his doctoral degree.

Before she started to school, her father was recruited by the CIA to work for them and was told the CIA needed his expert knowledge on these countries and he agreed to help them if he could.

Her father didn't want her growing up in Washington, so he found them a home in a small town away from Washington and a room that he could stay in Washington during the week, so he only came home on weekends.

However, if there was some type of crisis going on in one of his countries, then they might not see him for several weeks.

Selby on the Bay was a very small village on the Chesapeake Bay and they had one of the best homes in town, plus it was away from Washington.

It could have been a million miles away for the difference in life styles.

When she was looking for a college, she thought one in Kansas would be about as far away from the East or West Coast that she could get.

So she picked the University of Kansas, but she would have never considered that she would live most of her life in the Midwest.

There she met and fell in love with Sonny Cousins, so she was hooked on living in the Midwest, because she knew Sonny would never leave it.

Sonny was born and raised in Hutchinson, Kansas, he attended school there and always lived there and since both of his parents went to the University of Kansas, they wanted him to go there too.

His folks were both lawyers and had their own law firm.

Sonny's grandfather had been an attorney as well, another KU grad and practiced law for over fifty years in Hutchinson.

Jane always said, "According to Sonny if it didn't happen in Hutchinson, it never happened.

"Movies where made there, well three movies were actually made in the area, but if you listened to Sonny, you would have thought Hutchinson, Kansas was really, Hollywood Central."

She did have to admit Hutchinson had a lot more going for it than Selby on the Bay, but it was a long ways from being where everything happened.

Not only had Jane met Sonny at KU, she also met and became friends with Gene and Susan there, the four of them became best friends.

They did everything at school together and continued to stay together after they graduated.

Gene was another Mid West product growing up in one of the western suburbs of Chicago, Downers Grove.

He got to KU by being a good basketball player and had a four year scholarship to play basketball for KU, one of the best basketball schools in the country.

However, he got hurt in his freshman year and wasn't able to recover to be a player after the first game he had as a freshman.

Tough luck for him and KU, no million dollars pro offers would be coming to him in the future.

Susan was another woman from the East Coast, New York City was where she was born and raised.

She wanted to go to college somewhere that wasn't New York City, no worry she found it, because Lawrence, Kansas, certainly wasn't New York City.

After graduation the two couples had a joint wedding ceremony in Lawrence, where they had all met.

After a short honeymoon, the two new husbands went to FBI School before joining the Kansas City, Missouri Police Department.

Because they both had college degrees, the police department chose them to attend the FBI School before they went to work in the department and then they were to be assigned to the detective division.

The new police chief wanted to get better educated police officers and he advanced them through the department quickly.

However, after they finished the FBI School, they had to take additional training in riot control and then sharpshooter training.

Then they were assigned to the detective division, there they were not well received by the other officers.

These officers resented their quick jump from patrolman to detectives without ever spending one day on the street as a police officer.

All of the other detectives had to work the streets as patrolmen for several years, before they were promoted to detectives, so they didn't want these college boys to succeed in their new jobs.

None of these men had college degrees or had graduated from the FBI School.

Despite them having to work with people who wanted them to fail, they were soon accepted, as just another detective trying to do their job.

They also had Captain Jackson, who was in charge of the Detective Division and understood why the new Police Chief wanted to improve the department with better educated police officers.

So he also helped to smooth the way for Sonny and Gene by giving them some of the worse assignments the detectives could have; such as working the 11 p.m. to 7 a.m. shift and stake outs, watching houses for wanted criminals.

Jane and Susan had jobs with an accounting firm in a new division to prepare income tax forms, at a low cost and by providing quick service. The two brothers who owned the company called this new division H & R Block.

Jane and Susan's job were to train the people to become the trainers. These trainers would be the ones training all of the staff that the company would soon be hiring to staff their locations all over America.

It was an exciting time for all four of them.

Jane and Susan retired after working for twenty years with H & R Block.

At the time of their retirement, they were the National Staff Directors for the USA.

Jane was in charge of the Western USA and Susan the Eastern USA.

The country was divided by using State Line Road in Kansas City, which ran between Kansas and Missouri. This road became the dividing line between the Eastern and Western United States.

The four of them took several tours of San Francisco over the two days they were there.

They decided they all loved San Francisco and thought one day they should come back and travel all around the San Francisco area.

The following morning it was time to board the ship for their 154 day world cruise.

When they arrived at the port, they were very impressed with the look of the Golden Supreme. She looked to be a beauty.

They were able to board with very little problem and soon made their way to their staterooms.

They were on deck eight of a ten deck ship and their staterooms were next to each other and near the elevator.

Sonny and Jane were assigned stateroom 8051 and Gene and Susan had stateroom 8053.

Sonny opened the door to suite 8051 and saw it looked pretty small compared to their home and said, "Jane, do you think we can live in this tiny room for 154 days?"

"Look it was your idea to get the min suite and it is pretty small, but I'm sure we can make it all right."

Gene and Susan opened the door to their stateroom and Susan said, "Well it's small, but it not too much smaller than our first apartment in Kansas City."

Gene replied, "Well it certainly cost a lot more for five months, than what our apartment cost."

Susan said, "Well our apartments never went anywhere and we didn't get fed three times a day or more of you wanted too.

"Unlike our apartment this ship will be moving most of the time taking us all around the world to see seven continents."

Gene replied, "True, very true. So let's go find some of that food as soon as we put our things in our room."

Susan telephoned Jane and Sonny stateroom and said, "Gene's hungry, do you want to go with us find something to eat?"

Jane answered, "Sounds, good to me.'

Then she said, "Sonny, put all of our stuff in our cabin and let's go to lunch with Gene and Susan."

They put their things that they had carried onto the ship and put them in their room then the four of them took the elevator up to the ninth floor to go to the Grand Buffet for lunch.

2

Going to Sea

After they finished having way too much lunch at the Grand Buffet, they returned to their staterooms to begin organizing where they were going to put everything away.

When they returned to their staterooms, they found the crew had delivered their suitcases and left them near their stateroom doors.

The women were happy to see their bags and knew that they now had all of the clothes that they planned to have for their trip.

Sonny and Gene soon had their newly arrived luggage inside their rooms and begin taking all the clothes out of the suitcases and laying them out on the bed.

They heard an announcement that all passengers must take their life vest and attend a safety drill at 2:30 p.m. in the Main Show Lounge.

All passengers were required to attend this drill or the ship couldn't leave the port until all passengers had been recorded as attending the safety drill.

No exceptions, all passengers must attend the drill as it is the US Coast Guard regulations.

The four of them made the trip to the drill and after the staff demonstrated how to properly put on your life vest each of them actually had to put on their life vest and be checked by a crew member to be certain they could put the vest on correctly.

The drill took about 45 minutes before it was finished. Since some of the passengers didn't coming directly to the drill as they were told to, over and over.

Some of them didn't arrive until a crew member went to their stateroom and brought them to the drill.

Sonny said, "Isn't it amazing that some people believe that the rules don't apply to me. I don't have to do what the regular people do. Rules aren't made for me. I'm far too good.

"I can do what I want, but then these same people would be the ones causing others to drown, because they didn't know the proper way to put on a life vest."

Eventually all the passengers were accounted for and had at least put on their life vest.

After the crew had completed the drill and they were sure all of the passengers on the ship had attended the drill, the drill ended and the passengers were told they could return to their staterooms.

The four of them went back to organizing and arranging things in their staterooms and then they rearrange everything again and again.

Finally, both Jane and Susan were satisfied with the way they had their staterooms were now arranged.

Sonny said, "OK Jane, do you know it's almost time for dinner. We have to get ready for dinner; do you know what you are going to wear?"

"Yes I do and it won't take me long to get ready."

By five o'clock. Jane and Sonny were ready to go to dinner.

They walked out of their stateroom and met Gene and Susan who had just closed the door to their stateroom.

The four of them took the elevator down to level five and started walking to the dining room and were soon shown to their table for ten people.

They were soon met by two other couples, both couples were from England.

Then a man who was problem in his early forties, maybe late thirties, who looked like a movie star and dressed like a model for GQ Magazine joined them at their table.

Jane and Susan looked at him and then at each other and smiled like they knew something that no one else knew.

The man bid them hello and said his name was, Lucky Jordan from Madison, Wisconsin.

Last to join them was a woman, who looked to be about forty years old, dressed in designer's clothes and introduced herself as Linda Goodyear.

Linda took a seat between Lucky and Sonny, and then Sonny introduced himself and his wife, Jane from Kansas City, Missouri.

Next, Gene introduced himself. Then he introduced his wife Susan and said they were also from Kansas City, Missouri.

Followed by the man seated next to Susan, who said he was Reggie Churchill and his wife Elizabeth from London, England and said, and no I'm not related to Winston.

That remark got a laugh from the rest of the dinner guests.

The next man said his name was Charles Stairs and his wife's name was Barbara and they were from Bath, England.

Which got them back to Lucky Jordan, he repeated his name again, and said as I told you before I am from Madison, Wisconsin and before you ask, Lucky is my nickname.

"I've been called that for so long. I hardly remember my given name, which I think is still Vernon, now you know why I go by Lucky.

The last person at the table said, "I'm Linda Goodyear, from Beverly Hills, California."

After they had dinner, they had a show to go to in the Supreme Main Show Room.

The show tonight was by the Supreme singers and dancers.

The four of them really enjoyed the show and as they were on their way back to their rooms, they saw Lucky and Linda having a cozy drink in the cocktail lounge.

On the way up in the elevator Jane said, "It certainly didn't take long before Linda latched onto Lucky did it?"

Susan replied, "No, I guess she knows a good thing when she sees it. I think Lucky looks something like a young Robert Redford or Paul Newman. What do you think Jane?"

"I think you got it right. I can't decide if he looks more like Redford or Newman or something in between."

"Whichever it is, he's one good looking dude."

Sonny said, "Gene, I think we should ask for a different table for dinner tomorrow, so our girls can eat their dinner without dripping their food from their pretty mouths down the front of their pretty dresses. I'm sure it must be hard chewing your food with your mouth open and drooling over Lucky. What do you think Gene?"

"I'll tell you based on my many years as a detective, my believe is, it is very difficult to chew food having your mouth open going gag-gag over some good looking man.

"Ladies, that's a fact, because you will have food dripping down your mouth and on your clothes every time if you're chewing food with your mouth open."

Jane replied, "Well, I've personally had the opportunity to see a couple of detectives with their mouths hanging open, looking at some good looking girl with their breasts hanging half way out of her blouse or their dress was so short it was barely above her watering hole."

Sonny replied, "It was all in the line of duty, my dear we had to know if we would have to book them for incident exposure."

Gene added, "Yeah, we wouldn't have wanted to cite them if there was any chance the judge would let them off and run our record for getting convictions, isn't that right Sonny?"

"Absolutely Gene, we wouldn't have wanted to ruin our conviction record, which was about 90 percent."

Susan said, "One of them lies and the other one swears it's the true."

Jane said, "These boys wouldn't know the true if it smacked right in the face."

Then the elevator door opened and that ended their conversation.

They got out of the elevator and made their way to their staterooms, where they soon said goodnight.

After they went inside their stateroom, Sonny said, "You girls are really hot for Lucky aren't you?"

Jane replied, "My darling, you know I never wanted anyone but you. However, I'll have to say Lucky is one good looking guy."

"OK, you remember the rule you give me when we got married, you can look but don't touch."

"No problem, you just watch yourself with Linda. I think that gal's got the hot's for any guy, who's got the equipment that she doesn't have."

"You are pretty quick to come to that conclusion, don't you think?"

"Gals like Linda coming on a world cruise by herself is looking for only two things, a husband or stud to fill her desires."

"Wow, I think you should have been the detective, if you can tell that much about someone by just having one dinner with them. So what do you think about your dreamboat?"

"I think he's here to find and make every woman on this ship that goes for him or to find one who's got enough money to support his life style."

"You know Jane, I think you been living with a detective for so long you think everybody has something else in mind from what they seemed like their doing.

"So what do you think, I really wanted to take you on this around the world trip for?"

"To get me all alone, so you can have your way with me and you better get started, because it getting late. I might fall asleep before you do."

3

Things Begin to Happen

The next morning the four of them made their way to breakfast around nine thirty at the Grand Buffet and got an announcement that tonight would be a formal night and prior to dinner everyone was invited to the captain's sail away cocktail party.

The day went by pretty fast and it would soon be time to go to the captain's cocktail party.

Jane and Susan had discussed what they would be wearing tonight and decided on their choice for the first of many captains' cocktail party and formal dinner.

The women had purchased several new outfits for the formal nights and their men had a couple of new tuxedos, plus some regular suits for these special nights.

It took them all about an hour to get completely ready and when they were ready each of them had to look in the mirror once more to decide if they looked pretty darn good.

The four of them made their way down to the Main Show Room. They were looking forward to seeing Captain Morehouse, since they hadn't see him yet. They had only heard his name.

The girls had decided he probably would be a very nice looking man and would look very distinguished in his white uniform.

They were met by several of the Captain's staff, when they arrived and made their way to meet the captain and then they discovered Captain Morehouse wasn't a man but a woman.

The captain certainly wasn't exactly what Jane and Susan had pictured in their minds on how their captain would look.

Not only was the Captain a woman, but she was beautiful with a peaches and cream complex; she had slim trim figure. She was wearing a wonderful looking white uniform that she filled out to perfection.

The captain was greeting everyone and shaking hands with and when Sonny's turn came, he looked at the captain and said, "Donna Jean, is that you?"

"Sonny Cousins, how in the world are you?"

Jane, Gene and Susan stood in disbelieve, they looked first at the captain then at Sonny.

Sonny said, "Captain Morehouse, I had no idea you were a captain of a cruise ship, the last I heard you were the captain of navy aircraft carrier."

"Sonny, that's right. That was my last command before I retired from the navy after my twenty plus years of service.

"Sonny, we need to talk later, right now we're holding up the receiving line and we're keeping my passengers from getting their Champagne."

Sonny replied, "Yes, I'm looking forward to doing that very soon captain."

Then the four of them made their way to a table and took a seat.

Jane, Gene and Susan couldn't wait to hear how Sonny knew Captain Morehouse.

Jane spoke first, "Just how do you know our captain, Sonny?"

"You mean Donna Jean?"

"I don't mean Santa Claus."

"Well I have known her since we were babies and we starting kindergarten together."

"You're telling me you went to school with her in Hutchinson."

"Yes, we went to school together, until we graduated from high school.

"Then I went to Kansas University and Donna Jean went to the Naval Academy in Annapolis and made a career of the Navy."

Jane said, "Sonny, I can't believe you never said one word about her to me during all the years we've been together."

Gene said, "I can't believe you never said anything to me about a good looking woman like our captain in all the years we've worked together."

"I guess it never came up before and it's been a long time. Since I've seen her or heard much about her."

Jane asked, "Did you every date her?"

Susan said, "I'm really interested to hear the answer to that question."

Sonny replied, "We dated all through Junior High and Senior High School."

Jane asked, "So how come the two of you stopped dating."

"Easy, we went in two different directions. I went to KU and Donna went to the Academy.

"She planned to have a career in the Navy. I didn't know what I was going to do.

"At KU, I met Jane and fell in love with her and never had any other communications with Donna."

Jane questioned, "You said you heard she was in command of a carrier, how did you know that?"

"I'm sure my mother must have told me sometime when I was talking with her.

"Mom and Donnas' mother are very close friends and they know everything about what the two of us are doing."

Gene asked, "So how come you didn't know your friend Donna was the captain of our cruise ship?"

"I don't know, I guess my mother didn't know it or she never thought to say anything about it to me.

"We need to drink our champagne. It's almost time to go to dinner.

"I'm sure the girls can't wait to see what dreamboat will be wearing tonight."

That ended the conversation about Donna. They drink their champagne and headed to the dining room for dinner.

When they arrived at their table, the two English couples were already seated at the table and not long after that the four of them sat down.

Lucky Jordan joined them, looking splendid in his tux.

Sometime went by and Linda never came to dinner.

Sonny asked, "Has anyone seen Linda Goodyear today."

Everyone said, "No, they hadn't seen her."

Lucky said, "We had a drink together last night and we talked for a long time. I'm sure it must have been after midnight before we said goodnight.

"We talked about getting together for lunch today, but she never showed up.

"I tried to call her room, but never got an answer, the phone rang a long time, but no answer."

The dinner was excellent and after they finished dinner they went straight to the Supreme Main Show Room.

This night the show featured a singer doing all of Frank Sinatra's hit songs.

The young singer did a great job performing Sinatra's songs and the girls loved it.

After the show they passed the casino bar and they saw Lucky and a good looking young woman deep in conversation.

Jane said, "Well I see Lucky has found a replacement for Linda Goodyear.

"As they say, you snooze you lose."

Gene replied, "You didn't think it would take long for Lucky to find another gal did you?"

Susan said, "No, I think he will have a lot of busy nights on this cruise."

Jane added, "Probably days too."

Sonny said, "I don't think he's that young to be able to be a twice a day man anymore."

Jane replied, "Speaking for yourself are you?"

All of them started laughing at Jane's statement.

"No more two times a day for us old guys.

The four of them reached their staterooms and said goodnight.

As soon as they got inside their stateroom Jane said, "Sonny, I can't believe you never said anything about dating Donna Jean Morehouse."

"I guess I never thought it was important enough to talk about it.

"Donna Jean and I were best friends for almost all of our lives before I left for KU and she went off to the Naval Academy.

"Then we just lost touch with each other.

"I met you and Donna had a whole different life in the Navy, so we never had any communications with each other.

"My mother didn't have much to say about Donna and I never asked mom about her."

Jane said, "Man, once you're out of your life a little while. It's like you never existed.

"As long as we've been together, I really can't believe that you've never mentioned Donna, did you two have a big fight when the two of you went in differ directions?"

"No, we just kissed goodbye and wished each other all the best."

"Did you ever love her?"

"Sure, I loved her. She was my best friend. I still love her, but I never felt the way I did about you."

"Did you every have sex with your best friend?"

"No, we had plenty of hugs and kisses, but that's as far as we ever went."

"You know Sonny, somehow I believe you. Even thought I can't understand you, never telling me about her.

"I would think anyone else would have said something about Donna, because they were still so much in love with her, but you, I believe. To you, it wasn't important enough to talk to me about her. Why you never thought it wasn't important enough to talk about your best friend growing up. I'll never understand it."

"Sorry Jane. I guessed it never crossed my mind to talk about someone you never knew. I didn't think you probably cared about my child hood friends."

"Come on Sonny, anyone who was that important in your life. I certainly would have liked to have known about them. I would have thought you would have wanted to keep track of your best friend all your life. You know that old says, *"my wife doesn't understand me"* it's true. I can't understand how you can just toss away your oldest best friend? Sonny, I love you, but on some things. I can't believe the way you do things. Come on my love, let's go to bed. I'm getting very tried."

"Jane, I guess you know now. I'm just not a very good friend."

"You could be, if you ever wanted to be, but I love you anyway, God only knows why."

4

What Will this Day Bring

Sonny was up, showered and getting dressed before Jane woke up and he leaned over and gave Jane a kiss and told her good morning.

She put her arms up and stretched as far as her arms would go and said, "Sonny what are you doing up so early. We got four more days until we get to Hawaii?"

"Don't know. Guess I had all the sleep I could stand. So I had to get up. I'm ahead of you getting ready for the day."

"Sonny, that's no news, you are always up and dressed before I am."

About that time their telephone rang.

Sonny said, "Who in the world would be calling us here, the police department knows I'm retired."

Jane asked, "Why don't you answer it and find out?"

"That a novel idea, anybody could do that."

Sonny picked up the phone and said, "Hello."

The voice on the other end of the line said, "Sonny, this is Donna Jean. I have a problem and I think you might be able to help my security officers, since you worked as a homicide detective for a long time."

"OK Captain. I'd be glad to help you if I can."

"Great, will you meet me at stateroom 7073 in about ten minutes?"

"Sure Donna. I'd be happy to do that."

Sonny hung up the phone and Jane said, "Just what was that all about Sonny?"

"I'm not really sure. Donna called and asked me to meet her in stateroom 7073 in about ten minutes."

"So why did she want to meet you in stateroom 7073?"

"Well she said it was because I worked as a homicide detective. So I have to think she believes someone in that room must have been murdered."

"It certainly didn't take her long to find a way to get to see you alone, did it?

"If you two didn't keep in communication, how did she know you were a homicide detective?"

"My mother talks to her mother."

"Oh I forgot her mother and your mother are close friends. So I'm sure your mother kept Donna informed through her mother on what you do, regardless if she didn't let you know what Donna was doing."

Sonny gave Jane a kiss and said, "I'll be back as soon as I can love."

Sonny made his way to stateroom 7073 and the captain and two security officers were standing outside the stateroom with her.

Donna said, "Gentlemen, this is Sonny Cousins, he's recently retired as a Kansas City Homicide Police Captain.

"I've asked him to help us with this investigation.

"Captain Cousins, this is my head of security, Jack Taylor and his assistant, Bob Ford. Jack, would you open the door please."

Jack opened the door and let them into stateroom 7073.

Sonny went in the room first and saw a woman in the bed covered with blood from her vagina.

Before he took another step in the room he asked, "Who's been in this room from the ship's company?"

Donna answered, "No one has actually gone into the room. The room steward opened the door and saw what you saw and called security.

"Jack and Bob came to the room and did the same thing, than they called me. After they called me, I called you and asked you to meet us here."

Sonny said, "Captain, please have one of the photographers come here as soon as possible.

"I want him to take lots of pictures of the crime scene before we touch anything."

Donna said, "Jack, use your radio and have one of your people bring a photographer up here ASAP."

"Yes madam."

Jack contacted his office by using his radio and asked one of his people to bring a photographer to stateroom 7073 ASAP."

Sonny said, "Captain, get some of your maintenance people to build a screen of some kind around this door, so no one can see in the room from the hallway.

"Then would you have someone contact Gene Simpson in stateroom 8053 and ask him to come and meet me here as soon as he can get here.

"Donna you don't know Gene, but he's also a recently retired homicide detective and we can us all the eyes on this that we can get. Captain, we're going to need your doctor up here sometime soon, to see if he can help us with the time of death of this victim."

"Sonny, I'm going to go to my office and make arrangements to have a screen build to cover the view of the doorway of the stateroom from the hall and I'll contact the doctor. I'll be back as soon as possible."

"Thank you captain, in the meantime, we'll keep this door closed, as much as possible to keep people from looking into the room."

Donna left to go to her office, while Sonny; Jack and Bob waited for the photographer and the maintenance people to come to the stateroom.

Short time later a security officer brought one of the ship's photographers to the stateroom to take pictures of the murder scene for Sonny.

Before Sonny opened the stateroom door, he asked if the photographer could take picture of a dead person with a lot of blood all around her without getting sick or something.

The photographer said, "I worked for the San Francisco Police Department for a few years as a police photographer. I got tired of taking pictures of dead people, so I thought I would try the live ones for awhile. Do you know what, the dead ones never complained about how they looked in their pictures, unlike how the live ones do."

Sonny, Jack and Bob laughed a little.

Sonny said, "I never had a dead one complaint about anything that I ever did either."

Again, there was a little laughter from all of the others.

Before Jack opened the door to the stateroom, a maintenance crew arrived with a screen that would block anyone from having a direct view into the stateroom.

Jack waited until the maintenance people finished sitting up the screen, before he opened the door.

Sonny said, "Jack, would you and Bob stay back by the door, until we get the pictures we need. If my associate, Gene Simpson arrives, please have him come in as soon as he is here."

Jack replied, "OK Captain Cousins, well stay by the door and if your friend comes, we send him right in."

Sonny asked the photographer what his name was, and he was told it was Ted O'Shea.

Sonny said, "Ted, I'm Sonny Cousins, so please take me lots of really good pictures of the victim and the crime scene for me will you please."

Ted began taking pictures of the victim and after a few shots, Gene Simpson arrived.

Gene asked, "What's going on here, oh my God that's Linda Goodyear. Wow, someone really done a number on her."

Sonny asked, "Gene, do you have your trusted note pad with you?"

Gene reached in his back pocket and replied, "I'm ready when you are Sonny."

Sonny said, "I'm going to begin by listing the abuses to this victim, OK Gene. Here goes: Champagne Bottle inserted into the vagina. I would say multiple times, enough to cause excessive bleeding of the vagina; throat has bruises indicating the victim has being strangled; the victim has a pair of pink panties stuffed down her throat; both of her wrists and ankles shows evidences of a rope or some type of restraint used to tie the victim to the bed that she was found in. That's about all I can observe without a medical examination of the body."

Gene asked, "Do you have any idea of how long she has been dead?"

"No, I'm hoping the doctor can tell us something when he gets here."

Just as Sonny finished speaking Captain Donna and the doctor arrived in the room.

Donna said, "Gentleman, this is Dr. Sam Spears. Dr. Spears, this is Sonny Cousins and his associate, Gene Simpson."

The doctor shook hands with both of them and asked what he could do for them.

Sonny said, "We would like for you to tell us how long this woman has been dead if you can?"

Dr. Spears replied, "I'll do the best I can." I would say just by looking at her she appears to have been dead for quite awhile."

The doctor took out his thermometer and took a reading and did some calculations and said, "I'd guess from the little information I can get she been died over 24 hours.

"I'm sorry. I can't do any better than that."

Sonny said, "Doctor Spears, since you have on plastic gloves. Could you remove the Champagne bottle as carefully as you can from her vagina and drop it into this plastic bag, try not to touch the bottle anymore than you have to."

Dr. Spears careful took hold of the bottle with just the tips of his fingers and slowly eased it out of her vagina as Gene held a plastic bag open.

Gene got the bag as close to the body as he could and the doctor careful slipped the bottle into the bag.

Then Gene closed the bag and labeled the bag with the date and time of the removal of the Champagne from the vagina of Linda Goodyear by Doctor Spears.

Sonny than asked Doctor Spears if he could take some blood samples to see if she had any signs of drugs in her system.

The doctor told them he could do that and drew several vials of blood.

He told them they had limited abilities to do a lot of drug analysis on the ship, but he would preserve some vials for future testing in Honolulu.

Sonny asked, "Doctor, do you think having the panties stuffed into her mouth and down her throat would be enough to kill her?"

The doctor thought for a moment and said, "I'd say from the look of her throat she died from strangulation, the panties might have contributed to her death, but I think it's highly unlikely it would have been the cause of her death."

"Dr. Spears, would you please write up a report of your findings and give a copy to the head of your ship's security, Jack Taylor. Doctor Spears, thank you for taking taken time to come and help us."

As soon as Dr. Spears left the stateroom Sonny asked Ted, if had enough pictures of the crime scene?"

Ted replied, "I certainly think so. I should have them ready for you in an hour and half."

"That's good Ted, thank you."

Captain Morehouse said, "Ted, don't be posting them on the ship's picture display or Face Book."

"No worry captain, they will only be in Captain Cousin's hands."

"Thank you, Ted."

Sonny said, "Donna, sorry pardon me. Captain, do you have the information available on the ID of the victim?"

The captain replied, "It's all right Sonny, just so the folks here understand, Captain Cousins and I have been friends, since we were born.

"We went all through school together, until we graduated from Hutchinson High School in Hutchinson, Kansas.

"Our parents were close friends and we were both only children, so every since we were babies, and born only one month apart, of course he's older, so we were always together.

I don't know any person on earth better, than I know Sonny Cousins.

"Sonny, this is the information we have on Linda Lavern Goodyear, she was 38 years old and her address is 35 Beverly Hills Drive, Beverly Hills, California and her occupation was a designer of women' clothing.

"Her emergency contact is her mother, Dorothy Goodyear, of New York City.

"Apparently her father belonged to the Goodyear family, the ones who started the Goodyear Rubber Company."

Sonny said, "I guess we know she probably never had any money problems in her life, so she wasn't likely turning tricks for cash."

Gene said, "Not likely."

Sonny added, "We knew one of our table mates told us he was with her until almost twelve o'clock night before last.

"We know that, because he told us that last night, when she didn't show up for dinner. We also saw him with her in the bar after we left the show, which would have been around, what about eight o'clock, Gene?

"If the doctor's right with his time of death of more than 24 hours, she must have died sometime around 3 or 4 o'clock yesterday morning.

"What do you think Gene, do you think someone broke into her room and killed her or was she entertaining someone who did it?"

"Sonny, if I had to guess. I would say it was someone she invited into her room.

"How did we find out she was dead?"

"I don't know. Donna, how did you find out she was dead, who found her?"

"Her room steward reported opening the door to make up her room and saw her body lying on the bed.

"He said he quickly closed the door and called his supervisor, who reported it to security, who then contacted me."

"Donna, I think we need to talk to the room steward."

Jack said, "I'll get him, he still doing rooms just down the hall."

Bob said, "I'll get him sir."

Bob walked down the hall and found the room steward and brought him back to talk with Sonny and Gene.

Bob said, "This is the room steward, he's from India, his name is Constantine, he was the one who found the body."

Constantine looked at Sonny and said, "Sir, I will be happy to answer any questions."

Sonny said, "Thank you Constantine, what time did you find this woman?"

"Sir, it was a little after 8 o'clock this morning."

"Did you see her anytime yesterday?"

"No sir, she had her sign on the door."

"The sign that says, *Privacy Please?*"

"Yes sir, that's the one."

"Was the sign still on the door this morning?"

"Oh no sir, we never go in rooms with the sign on the door."

"You mean if I put my sign on the door for a week and just left it on the door you would never open the door."

"No sir, we never open doors with sign on them unless we have been told the passengers had finished their cruise and left the ship."

"How many times yesterday do you think you passed the door with the sign on the door?"

"Many times, the last time was around eleven o'clock last night."

"Thank you for your help Constantine, oh, one more question did you see anyone go in or out of her room?"

"No sir."

"Thanks again for your help; we better let you get back to your work."

"Thank you, sir."

Sonny said, "That means the killer wanted us to find her body or he would have left the sign in place."

Donna asked, "Why do you think, he would have wanted to have her body found."

"Good question, I have no idea. We need to get a complete list of all passengers; along with their room numbers and with as much information you have about them as soon as you can get it to us.

"One other thing we need to have Linda's body moved into one of your coolers, so when we get to Honolulu they can do an autopsy on the body.

"We need to let passengers know that one of your passengers passed away this morning from a heart attack, so we don't have too many people getting upset and worried there's a killer on board the ship. I'm sure you don't want everyone getting off the ship on a world cruise in your first port of call do you?"

"No, that would never do. Do you think it's possible that some serial killer has decided to take a cruise to find his victims?"

"Donna, the odds are when most people are murdered, they're murdered by someone in their family or one of their so called friends or at least they know the person. Not always, but between 80 to 90 percent of murders are done by these people."

"OK, we'll put out a notice that Miss Linda Goodyear died this morning from an apparent heart attack."

Sonny thought for a moment and said, "I think you better say it was a blood clot in the brain which caused a massive stroke and get to your doctor to say that was the cause of her death, if someone asked him. If someone one does ask him. I want to know who it was that asked."

Donna said, "Sonny, I'm going to go to my office to prepare a statement that I'll read at noon, that's when every day I give the information on our current position; our speed and the distant we've traveled. Then I'll include my statement on the death of Linda Goodyear on my announcements."

"OK, Donna that sounds good."

Then Donna left to go to her office to prepare her announcement.

"Jack, you should talk to Constantine to tell him not to talk about what he saw in room 7073."

"No problem Captain Cousins, we'll do that."

Sonny asked, "Who will be in be responsible for taking care of moving Linda's body to the cooler?"

Jack replied, "I will be, with the help of people from the medical staff."

"Jack, what about the room, do you have any way of searching for fingerprints or semen?"

"No, I'm sorry we don't have any type of equipment for collecting that kind of evidences. You have to understand our primary function is to provide security for our passengers and the ship. Investigating crime is not our job. We are here to keep our passengers and ship safe from everything from bringing on illegal materials onto the ship to defending the ship from pirates and keeping them from boarding the ship."

Gene said, "Jack, you mean there are still pirates who ply their trade in this day and age?"

"I'm afraid so, in fact when we get to the area between Thailand and until we passed through the Suez Canal we will be on the alert for pirates. In fact when we get into that area, you and the crew will be undergoing pirate drills."

Sonny said, "You've got to be kidding."

Jack replied, "No joke, we are required to hold these drills every time we enter these waters. One thing you should know is that the latest information on pirate activates over the past few years is way down. So we should be safe."

Gene said, "OK, Sonny who's going to be the one to tell the girls about pirates?"

"You win Gene. You get the honor because right now the girls think I'm not believable."

"Jack, we need to lock this room up and not allow anyone in the room after the body has been removed. We'll see when we get to Honolulu, if the police can go over the room for any kind of evidence that would help us find who killed Linda Goodyear. Another thing Jack, when the medical people pick up the body have them take care not to touch anything in this room except the body. We don't want to disturb any potential clue."

"I'll watch them to be sure nothing is touched, except the body, you can count on me, Captain Cousins."

"Thanks Jack, we'll see you later.

"Wait before you leave this room have maintenance change the code on the door, just in case the killer has a key card that would open the door."

"Roger, will do."

Sonny and Gene made their way to the their staterooms to see if the girls had already had breakfast and if they did they would ask them to go with them while they had theirs and the girls could have another cup of coffee or something.

Sonny opened his stateroom door and Jane and Susan both rush to the door to met him.

Before they had time to ask him any questions Sonny said, "Gene, your wife's in here."

Gene turned around to go back to Sonny and Jane's stateroom.

Sonny waited for Gene to come to the door before he went in and as soon as both of them were in the room.

Jane said, "Did it take two of you to talk to Donna this morning?"

Gene replied, "There wasn't much talking with the captain.

"We had our hands full trying to investigate the murder of Linda Goodyear."

Susan said, "Oh my God, did someone kill her?"

Sonny replied, "Yes, someone certainly did. The doctor thinks she was murdered sometime around three or four yesterday morning."

Gene added, "You two better stay far away from Lucky, as far as we know he's the last one who was with her."

Sonny said, "However, he told us last night that he left her Monday night a little past midnight. Then he said they planned to have lunch on Tuesday and she didn't show up for their date. If the doctor's right on the time she was murdered, she was killed early Tuesday morning. This is Wednesday, isn't it, since we been on this ship. I can't keep track of the days of the week. When we were working it wasn't a problem for me to know what day it was, here every day seems about the same."

Jane replied, "Its Wednesday, but Sonny when we start going on the tours in all of the countries, then all the days won't feel the same."

Gene said, "Whatever the day is, let's go have breakfast."

The others agreed and the four of them left to go to the Grand Buffet.

5

Working with Honolulu Police

Four days later, their ship arrived in Honolulu and when they arrived in the port there was an ambulance and team of police detectives waiting at the pier for them.

Captain Morehouse notified the Supreme's home office and explained that there had been a murder on the Golden Supreme and she requested help from the Honolulu Police Department with an autopsy of the body and help with checking the stateroom for clues in the murder case.

Jack Taylor, Security Chief met the Honolulu Police Detectives and the ambulance attendants at the gang way.

He introduced himself and his assistant Bob Ford to the detectives and then asked Bob to take the ambulance attendants to the cooler, where the body of Linda Goodyear was stored. They would take the body to the morgue for an autopsy.

After the ambulance attendants left Jack took the detectives up to the captain's office and introduced them to Captain Morehouse, Sonny Cousins and Gene Simpson.

The Honolulu detectives introduced themselves to Captain Morehouse and her associates, the detectives names were Sergeant Troy Allen and Sergeant Robert Blake.

Captain Morehouse, thanked them for coming and said, "Gentlemen, I appreciate you coming to help us with the investigation of the murder of one of our passengers, Linda Goodyear. I also wanted to tell you Sonny Cousins and Gene Simpson are both recently retired homicide detectives from the Kansas City, Missouri Police Department and have been helping with the investigation of the murder of Ms. Goodyear."

The four detectives shook hands and Troy Allen asked, so how long have you two fellows been retired.

Sonny said, "Include the trip from San Francisco to here four whole weeks.

"To bring you up to speed on what we've done so far on this case:

- We had the doctor on board check the body to see if he could tell how long the woman had been dead. The best he could do was to say it was over 24 hours. We also asked the Doctor to draw blood from the victim, which you can get vials of blood from him to check for drugs.
- We had the body moved into cold storage; there the body would be kept about the same temperature as what it would have been in the morgue.
- We had the stateroom where she was killed, sealed off with no one going in or out.
- We had one of the ship photographers take plenty of pictures of the crime scene. They're very good pictures, since he was an ex police photographer for the San Francisco Police Department.
- We collected statements from the stateroom attendant. He's the one who found the body and the two security officers, who you have all ready met of their actions after finding the body.
- We had Doctor Spears remove the Champagne bottle from the victim's vagina as carefully as possible and bagged it for evidences. However, I asked the doctor not to remove the panties from her mouth or throat, since I thought there might some clue on them.

"What we haven't been able to do, for lack of equipment, we couldn't dust for fingerprints or look for DNA or semen.

"Let me show you the pictures and you will be able to understand why I think these will be important clues."

Sonny pulled out a larger folder filled with pictures of the crime scene and as soon as Troy and Robert saw the pictures.

Troy said, "It certainly looks like a sex crime scene to me. What do you think Robert?"

"One thing I think for sure is, whoever did this is one sick son-of-a-bitch he must really hate women."

Troy asked, "Can we go to the stateroom now, so we can get started trying to see what kind of evidence we can turn up?"

Captain Morehouse said, "No problem. Jack will take you to stateroom 7073 where Ms. Goodyear was murdered.

"Please let me know as soon as you have removed Ms. Goodyear's body from the ship, so I can allow passengers off the ship."

Troy replied, "I think her body has already been take off, let me check for you."

Troy took out his cell phone and called one of the ambulance attendant's number and when he asked if they had loaded the body in the ambulance yet, he was told they were ready to leave for the morgue now.

He asked the ambulance attendant to also go to sick bay and find the doctor and get the vials of blood the doctor had drawn from the victim and have them taken to the lab for testing for drugs.

After the captain was told the body had been removed from the ship, she gave the all clear for the passengers to disembark for their tours or whatever they wanted to do in Honolulu.

Soon passengers were streaming off of the ship and Jack had taken the Honolulu Police Detectives to stateroom 7073 to begin their search for clues in the murder of Linda Goodyear.

Sonny told Donna, let's see what kind of clues these fellows come up with, but in the meantime we are scheduled to go on a couple of tours with our wives.

Donna said, "I want you both to know how much I appreciate you taking some much of your time helping with this investigation.

"Please tell your wives. I hope to make it up to them for taking you away for so long."

Gene said, "We will certainly do that."

Sonny added, "We're glad we were here to help you. Just let us know if we can do anything else."

"I know Sonny, you were always there to help me with any problem I ever had when we were growing up. I still love you my big brother."

With that she gave Sonny a kiss on his cheek and a big hug.

Sonny said, "You always have a place in my heart, little sister. I love you too.

"We'll see you after we return from our tours, to see what the detectives have to say."

Sonny and Gene hurried to meet their wives in the lounge where their tour was leaving from; they made it just in time.

Their first tour was a driving tour of Honolulu and they were surprised as to how much area the city covered.

Their second tour was the one Sonny was most interested in. On this tour they visited Pearl Harbor and saw a well done movie on the attack on Pearl Harbor on December 7, 1941.

After the movie they were taken to the battleship Arizona Memorial. It was honoring the sailors and marines who died on this ship. The ship was still leaking oil after all these years.

The battleship Oklahoma lay next to it on the bottom of the harbor, along with some other battleships that were anchored there on that awful day.

Visiting there was so moving that most of the people in their tour group had tears in their eyes for the Americans lost on that faithful day.

After leaving the Pearl Harbor site the tour moved just a little ways away from where the Battleship Missouri was anchored and they saw marked on the deck where the unconditional surrender by the Japanese was signed, ending World War II.

This visit to the Battleship Missouri was very moving, Sonny thinking back to the thousands of Americans and Japanese people who died in the war.

He thought war was such a tragedy whichever side you were on.

Japan couldn't keep any of the territory they took, and in the end. They paid the ultimate price with the deaths of hundreds of thousands of their people.

He knew America had no choice but to fight back after Pearl Harbor and after losing so many people.

Sonny said to Gene, "We spend a lot of our lives trying to catch people who killed just one person, how would we deal with the lost of hundreds of people a day?"

"I'm glad we never had to deal with that kind of thing."

They returned to their bus, which then took them on a tour of the downtown area of Honolulu.

It was much more enjoyable seeing people busy living their everyday lives in a wonderful paradise.

Instead of remembering the one faithful day in 1941 and the years that followed that day when the war finally ending on the deck of the Battleship Missouri.

It did seem appropriate to Sonny that the icons of the beginning of World War 11 for the Americans and the ending of World War 11 were just across the waters of Pearl Harbor from each other.

The sunken Battleship Arizona and the Battleship Missouri, they represented the beginning and the end of the war.

When the tour ended, the bus took them back to the Golden Supreme and as they were getting back on board.

Sonny thought how small the Battleship Missouri looked today, compared to the huge cruise ships that took over 6,000 passengers.

The world was always changing to bigger and better, at least that what we were all supposed to believe.

Sonny was not so sure everything always changed for the better.

As soon as they were back on board the ship said, "Gene, we need to talk to Captain Morehouse to see if she's heard anything back from the Honolulu Police Department."

Jane said, "You two didn't stay retired very long did you, one little murder and you're right back in your element."

Sonny replied, "No, we're not back in our element, we're just trying to help the captain and her security people solve a murder and catch the killer."

Susan said, "OK you two, go play detective like you've been doing for twenty years, you both know you love it."

Gene replied, "Yes dear, we love playing detective, don't we Sonny?"

"Absolutely Gene, that's what we love to do."

Jane added, "Sonny, how come you started calling Donna Jean, your best friend and now you call her Captain Morehouse?"

"Just respect for her position, you know she's had to work hard to obtain a job like the Captain of a cruise ship.

"How many women have you ever heard of that was a Captain of a cruise ship?"

Jane and Susan both replied, "None, so how come we got one?"

Gene replied, "We're just lucky, bet there not another Captain of a cruise ship that were ever a Captain of a Naval Aircraft Carrier task force.

"In the navy that's a big job, Donna Jean may have been the first woman to hold that position and maybe the only woman to have done it.

Sonny said, "OK girls, we see you as soon as we can.

"We need to find out if Donna Jean has heard from the detectives, OK?"

Jane said, "I hope you two make it back in time to get dressed for dinner."

6

The Report from the Honolulu Police

Sonny and Gene went to find Captain Morehouse and found her in her office, talking on the telephone. She waved them on into her office as she continued talking on the phone.

Listening to one side of a telephone conversation doesn't let you really always get the full understanding of what's going on.

When Donna got off the phone she said, "That was the Detective Troy Allen with the Honolulu Police telling me what the autopsy report said.

"The coroner confirmed Linda Goodyear cause of death was due to strangulation.

"Detective Allen told me that they found some finger prints in the stateroom and they would be running them to see if they could get a hit on any of them.

"He also told me the lab hadn't had enough time yet to do all of the tests on the blood.

"Detective Allen told me they didn't find any semen on the panties or anywhere in the room and the coroner reported no semen in the victim's vagina.

"The last thing he said was he would send a complete report of theirs and the coroner's report to me by email."

Sonny said, "I'm surprised they didn't find any semen either in the vagina or in the room. I would have bet whoever killed Linda would have raped her before or after he killed her."

Gene said, "Maybe the guy couldn't produce enough semen to eject it, due to being too old or he had some type of medical problem.

"You know we had a case like that once when we were working rape cases along with our homicide cases. "

"You remember that cases don't you, the guy almost walked, because we didn't have enough evidence to charge him, but then after we took his DNA we had him. You remember he's the one who claimed he never met the woman and had never been in her apartment. Then we got his DNA from a water glass, than he confessed to raping her."

"Yeah, I do remember that case, he had something medical wrong with him that he couldn't produce semen, but his DNA nailed him."

Donna asked, "Do you two every have a normal conversation?"

Sonny replied, "No, not really, we spent so much time working cases together, we seldom took time for chit chat, isn't that right Gene?"

"I guess that's right, we never spend a lot of time talking about the weather, but every once in a while, we did talk about our kids and wives, but not often."

Donna said, "Sorry, I have to go, because we are scheduled to leave Honolulu at six o'clock tonight'

"I need to make sure we have all the passengers back on board the ship and that our harbor pilot is with us, so that we leave port on time.

"When I get all of the reports from the Honolulu Police Department, I let you know.

"I'm having our staff put together all the information we have on all the passengers and crew for you.

"I think we will have all of that information for you tomorrow."

Donna got out of her chair and headed to the bridge to direct the ship out of the harbor and on its way to Tahiti.

This segment of the trip would take seven days at sea before arriving there.

Sonny and Gene left Donnas' office and went up to their staterooms. They would have just enough time to get dressed for dinner.

By five, the four of them were dressed and ready for dinner and made their way to the dining room.

Arriving there they found a very long line of people, who apparently had the same idea of arriving early for their five-fifteen dinner time.

They got into the back of the line and promptly at five-fifteen the line began to move. Then it didn't take long before they were seated at their table.

Arriving first, they had their choice of seats, however being creatures of habit. They all sat down in the same seats they had been sitting in ever since the first night of their trip and every night since.

One thing different, they had more room between the chairs, since one chair was missing. Linda Goodyear's chair had been removed from the table.

When the rest of their table mates arrived, they all noticed the increased space between the chairs, but no one said anything, until Lucky Jordan sat down and said, "It doesn't seem right about poor Ms. Linda, it so hard to believe that she died so suddenly."

Reggie replied, "Well she certainly looked healthy enough to me, what do you think Sonny, about her dying so suddenly?"

The question caught Sonny by surprise. He hesitated for a minute and Reggie said, "Sonny, did you hear me, what you think about poor Ms. Linda dying so suddenly?"

This time Sonny replied, "Well I sorry to say Linda isn't the only person I've know that looked as healthy as a horse and fell over dead in my arms from a blood clot in the brain.

"My own mother died like that when she was forty years old. We had been playing a basketball game called *horse.*

"You never know when something like that can happen to you, you just never know when your time on this earth is up.

"So as our preacher says, everyday you better be ready to meet your Lord."

Reggie replied, "Amen, to that brother."

Jane, Susan and Gene looked at Sonny in complete surprise, since all of them knew Sonny's mother was as alive as any one of them sitting at the table.

One thing certain, it stop the talk about Linda and there was no more questions about her, as their head waiter brought them the menus of tonight's offerings from the chef.

The conversation now, was on what everyone was going to eat tonight and what the show was going to be in the Supreme Main Show Room.

The Chef always had several new items on the menu every night and their menu always had certain items available every night.

Sonny normal always picked something from the every night portion of the menu, because he wasn't one who liked to try a bunch of new dishes with names he never heard off, or did he have any idea what was in them.

The other three were game for whatever, as Sonny called it. Some nights, Sonny was quite sure the dishes served were certainly whatever.

Five days later, Donna called Sonny in his stateroom and asked him and Gene to come to her office she had some information for them on Linda Goodyear.

Sonny and Gene arrived at Captain Donnas" office and knocked on the door and was invited in. When she saw who was there she said, "Have a chair and I'll go over what I just received from Detective Allen of the Honolulu Police Department."

Sonny and Gene sat down in a couple of chairs across from Donnas' desk and she began reading the report.

- Linda Goodyear was killed by strangulation and after she was dead the assailant repeatedly inserted a Champagne bottle into her vagina causing massive blood loss and destruction of the vagina.
- 'Her blood test showed prior to her death she had been drugged with some type of drug causing her to become sleepy or unconscious.
- The blood test and other tests of her body gave no indication of being a drug user.
- DNA samples of several people where present in the room indicating several people having been in the stateroom. Most of the DNA samples were from women.
- Honolulu Police request DNA samples be taken from all known persons who had entered the stateroom and the DNA samples had been be sent to them.

- Linda Goodyear appeared to be in excellent health prior to her death by strangulation.
- Fingerprints taken at the crime scene where ID from Linda Goodyear and the stateroom attendant, Constantine, no other fingerprints were found in the stateroom.

Sonny said, "I find it pretty strange that the detectives found DNA from several people in the stateroom, but only two people's fingerprints."

Gene replied, "Very strange, very strange."

Donna asked, "Could the killer had wiped off their fingerprints, in the movies the killers always wipe their fingerprints off, so the police can't ID them."

Sonny replied, "It's possible, but highly unlikely. If they had time to do all of that, they certainly weren't in any hurry to get out of the stateroom after he killed her. It's more likely the killer worn rubber or plastic gloves, so they didn't have any reason to wipe off fingerprints. I would like to talk with her room steward, what's his name?"

Donna and Gene replied at the same time, "Constantine."

"Thank you, you know I can never remember names.'

Donna said, "I'll have him found and brought up here to my office, so you can talk with him."

"Thanks Donna Jean, but when he comes. I think you should go out of the room, having you here might intimidate him, you being the captain."

"Your problem right, very few of the crew has ever been in my office. When he comes, I'll go up to the bridge and check on our progress to Tahiti."

Donna picked up her phone and contacted the head of hotel operations and asked her to have the room steward, Constantine brought to her office to help her fill out a report of him finding the body of Linda Goodyear.

It took about twenty minutes before the head of the hotel operations knocked on the Captain's door with her room steward, Constantine.

Donna got up from her desk and went to the door and kept her office door almost completely closed and told Barbara White, "Thank you Barbara for bringing Constantine to my office. I promise I won't keep him very long."

"No need of you staying here. I'm sure you have lots of other things you need to be doing and this is just a routine form I have to submit to our home office anytime we have a passenger or crew member die on board our ship."

Barbara replied, "I didn't know that. I've been working cruise ships for thirteen years and I have never been on one where either a passenger or crew member died until this cruise."

Donna said, "Well, I guess it's like Russian roulette, you keep working cruise ships then something that never happened before, does.

"Thank you again Barbara, Constantine won't be here very long."

"OK, captain I'll leave him here in your hands."

While all of this was going on, Constantine stood by wondering what this was all about.

Barbara left and Donna opened the door and asked Constantine to come into her office.

They both went inside and when Constantine saw Sonny and Gene waiting in the office, he knew what this would be about.

Sonny and Gene both said, "Hello."

Then before anyone else said anything Captain Donna said, "I need to go up to the bridge. I'll be back in a few minutes."

She turned around and went out the door.

Sonny said, "Constantine, please sit down. We won't keep you very long, we just have a couple of questions to ask you about when you opened Ms. Goodyear's stateroom door and saw her body.

"Did you go over to her body and touch anything?"

"No sir, just like I tell other policemen. I just open door and see Miss Goodyear body with all that blood and the bottle in her body. I shut the door and called my supervisor, that's all."

"OK, Constantine. When you last cleaned her room did you wipe off all of the furniture and really clean her room?"

"Yes sir, just like I do, every time I clean room."

Gene asked, "Did anything in the room look different than it normally did except for poor Ms. Goodyear's body, you didn't see anything changed in the room?"

"No sir."

Sonny asked, "Have you said anything to anybody about finding Ms. Goodyear's body?"

"No sir, no body."

"Thank you for coming to talk with us and answering our questions, but if you think about anything else, please contact us and tell us. Thank you for your help. You can go back to your work and if anyone asks about your visit to the captain's office. Please just tell them it was about finding the body of Ms. Goodyear for the captain's report to the home office, OK?"

"Yes sir, no problem. I go now."

Constantine left the room leaving Sonny and Gene alone in the captain's office.

Sonny said, "The captain has a pretty nice little office here, nicer than I thought it would be."

Gene replied, "Not bad for a floating palace, you know I never notice that door behind her desk, it's made to look like it just part of the walls, where do you think it leads to?"

"I don't know Gene, maybe that's her bedroom?"

Before either of them was able to get to their feet, Captain Donna opened the office door and came back into her office.

Donna asked, "Sonny, did you get answers to all of your questions from Constantine?"

"Yes we did, we just wanting to know if he wiped down the furniture and everything in the room every time he cleans a room and he said he did.

"That's why there wasn't any fingerprints found in the room except his and Linda's and it also confirms to me our killer worn gloves.

"Donna, Gene and I have a question that has nothing to do with this murder case, does the door behind your desk led to your bedroom?"

"Yes it does, would you like to see my quarters?"

Gene replied, "We certainly would."

"Come on then. I'll show you my secret hideaway."

Donna went behind her desk and opened the door and bid them to follow her.

What they saw surprised them, when you went into her quarters you entered a small sitting room with a large TV; this small room led them into a small dining area, about large enough to seat four people at her table: then there was a door that opened up into her bedroom and bathroom.

The bedroom had a Queen Size bed and another TV mounted on the wall, where she could watch TV in bed.

Last her bathroom had a large tub and a separate shower stall, a nice size sink and toilet stool.

Everything was sparkling clean in her quarters; the other thing in her bedroom was a large wardrobe and full size dresser.

When they went back into her bedroom she opened the doors of her wardrobes and they saw all of her uniforms neatly hanging up in a row including at least two of her dress naval uniforms complete with numerous ribbons.

Donna said, "I do have a guest bedroom with its own bathroom, it's off the sitting room."

Gene said, "If you would like to change your suite for mine, it would be OK?"

Donna laughed and replied, "You have no idea what I had to go through in my naval career to earn these quarters."

Sonny said, "No Donna Jean, we don't really have any idea of all the things you had to go through during your naval career.

"I'm guessing you never had any quarters liked this."

Donna replied, "Some of my quarters were pretty awful, but my last command as the captain of the carrier. I had some very nice quarters. There's no way to compared it to the quarters I had coming up through the ranks.

"Many of the ships I was assigned to, never had quarters for women, so they had to provide me with makeshift quarters. Some of those were pretty sad I don't know how I made it through some of those assignments.

"Sometimes, I was the only woman on board the ship, which certainly always got me lots of attention.

"The attentions were sometimes good and sometimes not so good.

"Lots of the older officers resented have women coming up through the ranks and be assigned on combat ships.

"So I normally drew the worst duties that could ever be assigned to an officer, but I stuck it out and made it up the ranks to captain, it wasn't easy."

Sonny said, "Donna Jean, if there was any woman who could have made it, it would have been you. I always knew one thing, if you made your mind up to do something, nothing or nobody could stop you.

"I certainly hope you are very happy with your life, you've certainly made yourself a wonderful life and I hope without too many regrets. I've always wanted the best for you."

Donna responded, "As the old song goes, *regrets I've had a few, but too few to mention.*

"The one real regret I have was not having any children, my mother and dad would have loved me to have children, and so would I. It's a little late in life now."

Gene said, "Well, I could give you a couple."

Donna laughed and said, "No thanks. I'm afraid I'll have my folks to look after pretty soon. I certainly will be happy to do it, because I love them. I just hate the fact they're getting to the age someone will have to do it. It not something they would ever want, but that's the way life works. It's just because, I'm going to hate the fact they could no longer take care of themselves."

Sonny said, "Gene, we better make it back to our staterooms before Jane and Susan file missing husband reports."

"Sonny, I guess you're right. However, as many times as we've been missing before, they never did."

"Well Gene, we've never been on a ship before, they may think we've been thrown overboard."

Donna smiled and said, "I think you two best fine your way back to your staterooms before Jane and Susan thrown me over the side of the ship for taking up all of your cruise time helping me with a murder case."

7

Cruising the Might Pacific

The next morning Sonny said, "You know Jane we are on the biggest body of water on earth, it's so big it is larger than the entire total land mass on earth."

"So where did you hear that?"

"I didn't hear it. I read it in one of the brochures the Supreme Cruise Line put out about our world cruise."

"I guess I missed that. I was more interested in the excursions offered in all of our ports. You know Sonny, we haven't signed up for very many of them and I want to see all of the sites they offer while we're on this world cruise."

"OK love, I'll leave the excursions picking up to you and Susan, if that's OK?"

"OK, but I don't want to hear any bitching from you and Gene about the ones we pick. One question are you sure Gene will be OK with us girls picking the excursions?"

"I don't know, maybe we better ask him at breakfast, speaking of breakfast are you about ready?"

"Of course I am. I just need to finish my hair and put on my make-up."

Their conversation was interrupted by a knock on their door.

Sonny opened the door and found Captain Donna standing there.

Sonny said, "Good morning Captain Donna, won't you come in?"

"Certainly Sonny, we need to talk."

Donna came into their stateroom and Sonny closed the door.

As she came into the stateroom she said, "Good morning Jane, how are you this morning?"

Jane replied, "I'm just fine captain, a little slow getting around this morning."

Donna responded, "Well I certainly know all about that. The older I get the slower I get in the mornings.

"Jane, I want to have the opportunity to really get acquainted with you during this trip. Then we can compare what's different from a grown up Sonny, to the guy I knew all my life.

"I'm pretty sure what we will find is, Sonny the same person today, as he was growing up."

"Captain Donna, I would like us to be good friends. I think it would be a good thing for both of us."

"OK Jane, but please just call me Donna.

"Since you're the wife of my best friend, I would love it if we were too."

This conversation went on like Sonny wasn't even in the room.

Finally, Donna and Jane realized Sonny was indeed standing next to both of them.

Then Donna turned her attention to Sonny and said, "Sonny, I have the list of all of the passengers and crew members who were on board when Linda Goodyear was killed."

Donna handed the very large computer print-out to Sonny.

Sonny took one look at the volume of computer paper and said, "It looks like you have brought us a best seller."

"I don't know if it's a best seller, but it's as much information as we have on every passenger and crew member on this ship."

Sonny asked, "How many passengers are on board?"

"Without Linda Goodyear, three thousand two hundred and twenty-five."

"And crew members?"

"One thousand eight hundred and eighty-nine crew members."

"Wow, you are responsible for five thousand one hundred and fourteen lives?"

"You math is as good as it use to be in school. I had to use my calculator to add those numbers up."

"Sorry, all I had to do was look where you added the numbers up and wrote down the answer on the front of the print-out."

"Sneaky, aren't you Sonny?"

"No just observant."

"OK Sonny, you and Gene have fun reading the latest best seller."

"Donna, on that print-out is the name of our killer, it may not be his really name, but it's on this document.

"Now all Gene and I have to do is figure out who did it?"

"Good luck figuring it out. I don't need to lose any more passengers."

"OK, Donna we'll do our best."

"Jane, remember what I said. I want us to become very good friends. I would like to invite you, Sonny and your friends, Gene and Susan to dinner tonight at the steak house about seven thirty, if that's OK?"

"Great Captain Donna, oh Donna, I forgot. I will accept your invitation on behalf of all of us, right Sonny?"

"Whatever you say dear?"

Jane and Donna both laughed and Donna said, "Right Sonny, whatever your wife says is right?"

"Of course it is."

Jane and Donna laughed louder this time and Jane said, "You do know him, don't you?"

"All of my life."

With that being said, Donna opened the door and said, "See you tonight."

Sonny knocked on Gene and Susan's stateroom door and Susan opened the door and Sonny asked, "Are you guys ready for breakfast?"

Before Susan could answer, Gene said, "We certainly are, I thought you guys were never going to be up and ready."

The four of them made their way up to the Grand Buffet and started through the line of other passengers who had the same idea.

One by one each of them had a plate of breakfast goodies. Jane was the first one finished getting her food and found a table for the four of them.

After all four of them were seated Sonny said, "Gene, after we finish breakfast we need to get started going over the information Donna Jean brought to our room this morning with all the information she has on the passengers and crew members."

"What does it look like Sonny?"

"I don't really know. I've hadn't had a chance to have a look at yet. She just brought it as we were getting ready to come over and meet you guys for breakfast."

Jane said, "I'll tell you what it looks like, it's pages and pages of computer print-out."

Gene asked, "How many passengers are on the list?

"Three thousand two hundred and twenty-five not counting Linda Goodyear and one thousand eight hundred and eighty-nine crew members.

"That's a total of five thousand one hundred and fourteen people."

"Wow, that's a lot of people on this ship."

Jane said, "By the way, we four are invited to dinner tonight with Donna at the steakhouse at seven thirty."

Susan asked, "Now you are calling our Captain, Donna and she's invited us for dinner, what gives?"

"Well she told me this morning to call her Donna and that she wants us to become very good friends, since Sonny is such a big part of both of our lives."

"Jane, are you sure she want Gene and me to come to dinner with you and Sonny."

"I'm sure she does, she asked for you and Gene to join us for dinner."

"OK then, we'll be glad to join Donna and you two for dinner then, won't we Gene."

"We certainly will. I like Donna, she a great person. Besides we're trying to help her find a murderer.

"Right now, Sonny and I better get started on this giant print-out."

Sonny replied, "I think that's a great idea, do you want to work in our stateroom or your?"

"Yours, I'm sure the girls can find something to do."

"Jane said, "We certainly do have something to do. We're signed up for the crafts and it starts in about an hour."

Susan and Jane went into Susan's stateroom and Sonny and Gene went into Sonny's stateroom.

Sonny said, "Gene, I think we better bring the table from our deck for one of us to use to go through these documents.

"I think we should divide the passenger's information up first and go through it before we think about looking at anything to do with the crew. When we look through this information, I think we should first look for single men traveling on the cruise or two men traveling together."

"At least, I would think that's the most logical person who would be our killer. What do you think Gene?"

"I think that's the right approach, you would think whoever this is must really hate women, the way they left Linda Goodyear body.

"They certainly weren't happy enough just killing her, they had to tear her insides up after she was dead."

Sonny said, "OK partner, let's get started, because somewhere in this list of names is the name of our killer."

Sonny opened the door to the deck and Gene and him picked up the table and sat it down in the stateroom, then Gene brought in one of the chairs from the deck.

Gene said, "OK Sonny, I'll work on this table and use the deck chair and you can use your table and chair to work on."

Sonny opened up the list of passengers and laid the whole document on his table and opened it up to make two equal sections out of the document.

Next he took a pair of scissors and cut the document in two sections.

Sonny handed Gene one section of the split document and kept the other half for him.

Gene took his section to his table, sat down on his chair and began reading through the list of names; stateroom numbers; sex; single, married, widowed, home addresses; telephone numbers; passport numbers and anything else recorded on the document pertaining to that individual.

Sonny sat down and began going through his half of the document.

Sonny said a little while later, "I've got some paper and pens for us to make a list of all of the single men or couples of men traveling together."

Sonny handed Gene a packet of paper and a couple of pens to make his list on.

After two hours had gone by Sonny asked, "Gene, are you finding a lot of single men on your half of our document?"

"No, so far I think I only have two single men traveling together, not one single man in a stateroom by himself, how about you?"

"The only single man I have in his own stateroom is our table mate, Lucky Jordan and I've got two men together in two other staterooms. That's it."

Sonny then said, "I've got Lucky Jordan in stateroom 7061 and Bobby Brown and Walter Johnson in stateroom 8020 and Toby White and John Townsend in stateroom 6005.

"So what's your men's names Gene?"

"Josh Taylor and Sid Jenkins, they are in stateroom 7825.

"Gene, it sounded like a good idea looking for men traveling alone as our suspect, however, one of these guys could still be our killer, what do you think, Gene?"

"Sonny, right now the only think I know for sure is that if our killer is a passenger then he had to board the ship in Los Angeles."

"Why do you say that?"

"Our steward told me our ship had just been fitted with all new beds and had been out of service for a week and they had no passengers on board."

"That makes senses, so everyone on board this ship boarded in LA."

"Yelp."

"So how about the crew, did they all board in LA?"

"Same story, they all came on board the day before we boarded the ship."

"That means everyone except the four of us, are suspects?"

"Yelp!"

"Great, so we only have five thousand one hundred and ten suspects after I subtracted the four of us."

"You got it Sonny."

"Gene, I guess the odds of finding the killer is better than we had in Kansas City with our metro area of over a half million people."

"Right Sonny, it ought to be no problem of us finding the killer with the odds like that in our favor."

"OK Gene, let's see what we know about each one of this men, first we know each one of these men hold a US Passport. We know how old they are and where they come from in the states.

"I'm not sure, but I think we may be able to forget about any of these men over the age of say, seventy-five."

"Sonny, I think that would depend on how good a shape they're in."

"Really Gene, we're only in our fifties and I don't think in another twenty or twenty-five years we're going to have a whole lot of interest in the opposite sex."

"Speak for yourself, John Alden."

"OK, I guess it would depend on how good their health is and their physical condition."

"Sure Sonny, don't you remember seeing pictures of Charles Atlas when he was ninety something years old.

"I'm telling you for sure he could still do his thing with the women."

"OK, I give up. Forget the age; all of these men are our prime suspects."

"OK then."

"Sonny said, "Some of these men maybe be couples and living in today's world, hell they maybe even married."

"Yeah, what a world we live in now."

"Gene, it's certainly not the world we grew up in."

"That's for damn sure."

Next, they began to look where the men lived according to the print out.

Bobby Brown and Walter Johnson were from San Francisco, California and were oil field workers.

Toby White was from Chicago, Illinois and his roommate, John Townsend was from Washington, D.C., both were lawyers.

Josh Taylor was from Boston and Sid Jenkins was from New York City and they were both investment consultants.

Sonny said, "These guys are not exactly what we would pick for our normal suspects in a murder case.

"Especially as gruesome as this one is but maybe one of the oil field workers might fit the bill, but I'd doubt it."

Gene said, "We're right back to Lucky Jordan, where is he from, and what kind of work does he do?"

"Lucky Jordan is from Madison, Wisconsin and it says here he is retired."

"Sonny, what do you think he's retired from?"

"I have no idea, maybe from some rich widow's money."

"I think you got it Sonny, he probably knocks off the husband to get the widow and her money."

"To tell you the truth Gene, I don't think he would work that hard, knocking off husbands.

"Besides, you might get your hands dirty, knocking off husbands. I doubt that he's ever got his hands dirty doing anything in his life.

"Gene, it seems to me Lucky is more interested in making love to women, then killing them.

"I'm pretty sure he knows his way around their bodies well enough, but somehow I don't think he would ever consider hurting them, he seems to like them way too much to want to hurt them.

"Which leads us back to nowhere?

"It's getting close to lunch time, lets break and take another look at what little we have so far, in a couple of hours, OK?"

"Sounds good to me, let's find the girls and go to lunch."

"I'm right behind you, Gene."

They found Jane and Susan in Gene's stateroom right next door and when Gene opened the door Susan said, "I hope this means you two are ready to go to lunch."

Gene replied, "We're ready and waiting for you two to come out that door."

Jane and Susan got up from the couch and were soon out the door joining Gene and Sonny.

The four were soon going around the Grand Buffet gathering up food for their lunches.

When they sat down Jane asked, "So how's it going?"

Sonny replied, "We've been going through the information Donna Jean brought us this morning and so far we don't have a clue.

"I had one idea, but right now I would say we have so little to go on it's going nowhere fast."

"Is that about the way you see it Gene?"

"Yeah, nowhere is the path we're on."

After lunch, Sonny and Gene went back to studying the information Donna had provided them and around four thirty.

Gene said, "Partner, I think we've looked at these documents for so long now, if we found a clue in them we wouldn't know it if we found it.

"Let's break for today and get ready for our dinner with the captain and start looking over this stuff again tomorrow. My eyes are getting so all I can see is bleary letters."

"I agree, let's get ourselves ready for dinner and for tonight show, someone said there was a beautiful singer on tonight and she can sing too."

"Sounds great, a beautiful woman that can sing and a steak dinner bought by the captain. Sounds like a winner to me."

Gene left to go back to his stateroom and a short time later Jane returned to theirs.

Sonny said, "Hello my Jane how was your day?"

"From what Gene said I'm guessing is was a lot better than yours."

"So what did you two do?"

"We went to the talks on the ports. We will be calling on during this segment of our around the world trip. I think we will love seeing these places that we've never been too before. They sound wonderful."

"Good, I'm looking forward to seeing them. I'm really looking forward to seeing all the places that I just heard about or read about in the past.

"Jane, it's going to be a wonderful trip."

The four of them got all dressed up in their formal wear with Sonny and Gene wearing their new tuxedos. They had never worn them before and the girls looked wonderful in their new party dresses.

They made their way to the steakhouse and found Donna had a private dining room for the five of them.

Donna was dressed in her dress white navy uniform with all her medals and ribbons on it, she looked regal and beautiful like she was royalty.

Donna greeting them as they were all her very old friends and gave each of them a hug and asked them to please sit down as their waiter began pouring champagne.

After everyone was seated Donna said, "I want to raise my glass to my oldest and dearest friend, Sonny Cousins and his wife, Jane and his friends, Gene and Susan.

"It's been a long time since the two of us have shared a meal together. When we were growing up we had a meal or two together every day until our lives took us in different directions. I hope this is the beginning of new era, where the five of us can share many meals together."

Donna put her glass to her lips and slowly sipped her champagne as the others followed her example.

During dinner, Donna told all of them about her years in the navy and that she had been engaged to marry a navy pilot, but he was killed during the Gulf war.

She said after that, she spent all of her time doing her job in the navy and never considered dating or getting married again.

When asked about the man she was going to marry.

She said he was from Overland Park, Kansas and they went to the Academy together and he was in the class ahead of hers.

After dinner she told them they had to go see the woman singer, Sammi Opal Smith, who was staring in the Supreme Main Show Room tonight.

Donna said "Sammi joined the ship in Honolulu and will be leaving us in Tahiti."

They all thanked Donna for a wonderful dinner and she said she would go down with them to the show and introduce them to Sammi.

It was a big stir when the five of them entered the show room as everyone was starting at Captain Morehouse dressed in her white navy dress uniform wearing her many ribbons and medals.

Donna asked one of the folks working in the show room if they would see if Ms. Smith had time to come out, so she could introduce her to her friends.

When the captain of a ship asked if someone had time to do something for them, as far as everyone was concerned, it was an order.

Sammi Smith was no different she came directly out with the attendant and was introduced to the captain's friends, as soon as she had been introduced to them.

The captain told her, she appreciated her taking time to come out to meet her friends. Then Sammi was on her way back stage to her dressing room.

Cruise Director, Frank Baylor was soon introduced to open tonight show and he came bouncing into the spotlight and yelled, "High HO Everybody!

"We've a special treat for you this evening. We have the winner of TV's, *Who's Got Talent Show*; this young lady has been voted the USO's entertainer of the year, five years in a row."

"She's been given a nickname by the USO naming her the SOS Gal, because when they need someone to perform for the troops anywhere in the world."

"They just contacted her, and she there for them, so here is the SOS Girl herself, Miss Sammi Opal Smith."

Sammi came out into the spotlight and the audience gasped, they had seen her on TV, but she was even more beautiful in person and her voice, well it was like honey. Sammi was the real thing, a rising star.

What Gene had heard about Sammi was correct, she was as good a singer as she was beautiful and she put on a wonderful show and her audience loved her.

After the show was over they left the show room together and Sonny and Gene said they were going to stop and buy Sammi's CD's as a reminder of their wonderful evening with the captain and seeing Sammi's show.

Sammi was there signing her CD's for all the people who were buying them and although the line was long. Sonny and Gene stayed until they both got signed CD's by Sammi.

She was very gracious when she saw them again and signed their CD's to Sonny and Jane and to Gene and Susan.

Then she drew a happy face, just below her signature and wrote *"Any friend of the captain is a friend of mine."*

She gave Sonny and Gene each a kiss on the cheek when she handed them her CD's.

Sonny and Gene both thanked her for the special kindness she had shown them and bid her goodnight and told her they looked forward to her next show later in the week.

The next two days while they were at sea, Sonny and Gene spent pondering over the computer printout and found nothing they thought would help them with their case.

8

A New Day a New Victim

Sonny heard a knock on their stateroom door and he made his way to the door.

Jane was still in the bathroom and Sonny had just finished dressing and was ready to go to breakfast.

Sonny wondered who was knocking on their door, since he had the *Privacy Please* sign on their door.

He opened their door and there was Donna.

Sonny said, "Oh no, don't tell me, not again?"

Donna answered, "Sonny, someone has killed Sammi Smith, her steward just found her when he was bringing her morning coffee."

Sonny reached out to Donna and took her into his arms as she was standing there shaking and looked like she was about to start crying.

Jane opened the bathroom door and saw Sonny holding Donna in his arms and Sonny said, "Jane, someone has killed Sammi Smith."

Jane then put her arms around Donna too.

Jane said, "What happened, Donna?"

Donna tried to straighten herself up and said, "I don't know Jane, they just told me her steward found her.

"I told them to close the door and don't touch anything, until Sonny and Gene have time to investigate the room."

"Oh Donna, what a nightmare to have someone murdered on your ship, now a second person murdered.

"Sammi was such a beautiful young talented woman and to be killed like that it's awful."

"Sonny you and Gene have got to find out who's doing this, you've got too."

By this time Donna had regained her composure and said, "Sonny, I guess you better let me stand on my own two feet now, but it felt like my big brother was looking after me again and after all these years."

Sonny released the hold he had on Donna and said, "Donna, as long as I can do it. I will always be happy being your big brother."

"Thank you Sonny. I love you too."

"Donna, I better get Gene and the three of us go take a look at the crime scene and you better get your security men, Jack and Bob to meet us there."

Donna picked up the room telephone and told the operator this is Captain Morehouse. Please contact Jack Taylor and Bob Ford and have them meet me in stateroom 3023 right away.

As Sonny and Donna were going out the door, Sonny said, "Jane, you and Susan might as well good ahead and have breakfast.

"Gene and me, well we will get something when we can."

Sonny knocked on Gene's stateroom door and when Gene opened the door and saw Sonny and Donna standing there he said, "Don't tell me we've got another one?"

Sonny replied, "Not only another one, but its Sammi Smith."

"Oh God not her, she was a really a special gal!"

"Yes, somebody killed her."

"Damn, that no good son-of-a-bitch, I hate him and I'll tell you one thing we've got to get him."

Donna said, "Oh I hope you can, this has to be one of the worse things that every happened on a Supreme Cruise Liner."

Sonny said, "I don't know how Donna, but we'll get him some way, won't we, Gene?"

"We sure as the hell will."

When they arrived at stateroom 3023 Jack and Bob were waiting for them in the hallway.

Jack asked, "Captain, do we have another victim?"

"Sorry, Jack we've got another one. Go ahead and open the door. Let's see what we've got."

Jack unlocked the stateroom door and opened it and they saw almost the same crime scene as it was with Linda Goodyear.

The five of them went inside the room and closed the door behind them.

Sonny and Gene approached the body and found the same brand of champagne bottle stuck in Sammi's vagina, as it was in Linda Goodyear.

She too had a pair of panties stuck in her mouth and signs of being strangulated on her neck.

Gene said, "Same story, second verse."

Jack said, "The police department in Honolulu gave us some equipment to take fingerprints and DNA. We've got them in our office, even though we have no idea how to use them."

Gene said, "Get the stuff they gave you. We'll see if we can use them."

Bob Ford left the room to get the kits the Honolulu Police Department had given them to get fingerprints and DNA.

Sonny said, "Captain, I think it time you got your senior staff members together to discuss this problem and try to get some help finding this killer."

"OK Sonny. I'll check everyone schedule and try to have a meeting with all of them this afternoon."

"Captain, when you get your people together. I'll explain what they need to do to help us catch this killer, OK?"

"Good Sonny, if you don't need me. I'll arrange the meeting and notify my home office, that we've had a second person murdered.

"I can tell you one thing; they're not going to be happy to hear it."

"Captain, I doubt if they can be any more upset then you are."

"Probably not, but they yell louder."

"I don't think they can hold you personally responsible for having some nut job killing your passengers."

"Guess not, but who knows what they think."

"Anyway, I'm going to my office to get the information to them and sit up a meeting for the senior staff members this afternoon. I'll try to sit it up for two o'clock."

Donna turned and left the room.

Sonny asked, "Jack, can you get your photographer to come and take more pictures and have your doctor come and try to determine a time of death and examine the body for us."

"OK, Sonny I'll go and see what I can get done."

Jack left the room and Sonny and Gene were now the only ones left in the room except for the body of Sammi Smith.

Gene said, "I can't believe someone would kill Sammi, she was such a sweet young woman and she was so talented and so beautiful.

"I could understand guys wanting to have sex with her, but to kill her, unbelievable."

Sonny responded, "Gene, there are some really sick people in this world, but I wouldn't think one of them would be on a world cruise."

Bob came back with the kits for fingerprints and DNA.

Gene went to work dusting for fingerprints.

He was able to gather several sets of prints while Sonny was trying to find DNA samples.

As they were both working on their assigned tasks, the photographer arrived and began recording the crime scene in photos.

When Ted O'Shea finished taking his pictures and was ready to leave. The doctor arrived to help establish the time of death and determine how Sammi was killed.

The doctor confirmed first, that Sammi was dead and he estimated her time of death was around two or three a.m. this morning.

He also confirmed Sammi was killed by strangulation.

Sonny asked the doctor to check the vagina to see how badly it had been damaged, since there was very little blood present, unlike when they found Linda Goodyear's body.

Sonny said, "Let's get some good copies of the fingerprints you found and have them sent to Kansas City and ask them to run them, to see if they can get a hit on any of them. I guess we better take the fingerprints of the room steward, to send along with the ones you found."

Gene replied, "Sure, I can do that.

Gene then asked, "Bob, can you get the room steward for us, so I can take his fingerprints?"

Bob replied, "I can do that, but all Supreme Cruise Ship employees have their fingerprints on file. I can just make a copy of them and give it to you."

"That's great Bob, if you have a copy of his fingerprints we won't need to take them again. Thanks."

Sonny said, "I didn't do too well with the DNA samples, but I did get a few and we'll have to send to Kansas City from our next port."

Gene replied, "We better send the prints to the police chief and ask him to have them run for us, otherwise it might not ever get done."

"I'm surprised at you Gene; you really think our fellow cops wouldn't do something for us."

"They would, if we were there looking over their shoulders and asking them if they had done what we had asked them to do.

"You know Sonny, they always had good intentions, but what they lacked was good attention."

"Gene, for once you're right on. We'll send the prints directly to the Chief."

Bob left to get a copy of the fingerprints of the room steward for them and as he was going out the door, Jack returned.

Jack said, "I talked with the captain and she asked me to tell you that the meeting with the senior staff is set for two o'clock at the Supreme Main Show Room."

Sonny replied, "That's good we need to get the staff on board, so they know what's going on and see if one of them could provide us any clues about these murders."

Jack asked, "What do you think we should do about Miss Smith's body?"

Sonny said, "I think we should do the same thing we did the last time, have her body taken to one of the coolers, until we can get to somewhere that we could have an autopsy of the body.

"Jack, do you think when we get to Papeete, Tahiti, the police there could help us with an autopsy?"

"I don't know, but from what little I know about Tahiti. I would feel better taking Miss Smith's body on to Auckland, New Zealand for an autopsy.

"I can contact our man in Auckland and have him make arrangements for them to pick up her body and take it for an autopsy.

"There we can also make arrangements to have her body returned to her parents in the states."

Sonny asked, Jack do you know what arrangements were made for Linda Goodyear's body left in Honolulu?"

"Yes sir, our agent there had her body taken to New York City; this is where her mother lives and when it got there Supreme paid for her funeral."

Sonny said, "Do you have any idea what kind of relationship Linda had with her mother?"

"No, I haven't any idea. I did hear from one of our people who met with her mother in New York that the mother said "My baby has finally found some peace."

Gene said, "That's a kind of a strange thing to say about your dead daughter."

Sonny replied, "It's strange, but maybe Linda had lots of problems in her life and her mother thought she was never happy about her life and had kept searching for happiness."

Jack replied, "The one thing we know for sure about Ms. Goodyear was she never lacked for money in her life, her family had billions.

"I know that because the New York City newspapers ran a story about her death and said her family was one of the richest families in New York."

Sonny said, "Money doesn't buy happiness."

Gene piped up and said, "Well, it can buy about everything else."

This caused a few seconds of laughter, even if they were in a room with a murder victim.

Sonny said, "Jack, please make arrangements to move Miss Smith's body to one of the coolers."

"I will do that, Sonny."

Sonny said, "Jack, you can have housekeeping go ahead and get this stateroom cleaned up. I don't think we can get any more clues here."

"Yes sir. I'll have the room cleaned as soon as we have Ms. Smith's body out of here."

"I'll also take the champagne bottle and place it with the other bottle we got from Ms. Goodyear's room."

Sonny and Gene left and made their way up to their staterooms to talk with Jane and Susan.

Jane and Susan had already had lunch and were getting ready to go to their craft making class, so Sonny and Gene went to the Grand Buffet and had their breakfast and lunch.

A few minutes until two they met Captain Morehouse at the Supreme Show Room, and promptly at two o'clock. Captain Morehouse took a microphone and said, "Ladies and Gentlemen most of you are not aware that we have a serious problem on our ship."

"I have asked two of our passengers, Mr. Sonny Cousins and Mr. Gene Simpson, who are recently retired homicide detectives from the Kansas City, Missouri Police Department to help us with this problem. Now I'm turning the meeting over to Captain Cousins to discuss the problem we're having on our ship."

Captain Morehouse turned to Sonny and motioned him to take the microphone from her.

Sonny took the microphone in his right hand and said, "We have a major problem here and the problem is we have someone killing people on your ship."

"So far, we've had two people killed on the ship since we left Los Angles."

Sonny paused as he could see a light bulb had just been turned on in the audience's brains.

Sonny continued, "The first victim was, Ms. Linda Goodyear who was killed before we reach Honolulu and last night, Miss Sammi Smith was killed."

Now there was a gasp in the audience and words spoken like *"Oh my God"*.

Sonny continued, "It is our opinion, both mine and Gene Simpson's, with our experience of working homicide for almost twenty years that we believe this is a work of a serial killer and we don't think he intends to stop until we find him."

"This meeting was called to make you aware of what's happened so far and to ask for your help, along with that of your staff to try to help us find the killer."

"We need you and all of your staff to keep your eyes and ears opened and observe what's going on and report anything you think is suspicious or passengers who act strange."

"Yes, I know many of your passengers are strange, but I'm talking about ones that have quirky habits."

"In the past some of the serial killers talk to themselves all the time and others who talk about someone from outer space controlling them."

"Some of them act very normal, until they suddenly started saying the same thing over and over, about someone trying to hurt them or making them doing something they don't want to do."

"You are never to do anything about them, your job is to report the information to the captain or your supervisor and they will contact us, then we will investigate them."

"You need to talk with your staff and explain what is going on, so they will be aware to help watch people as they work around the ship."

"We will be holding a meeting with all the passengers tomorrow and informing them about what has happened."

"This meeting will be held in the muster stations at two o'clock tomorrow afternoon."

"I will tell you after this meeting, you are going to have a lot of very nervous passengers, so it very important to stress to your crew to keep cool and carry on just the same as they have before."

"Try to give the impression that they have nothing to worry about."

"If anyone has any questions, please raise your hand and I will try to answer your questions the best I can for what we know right now."

One person in the front row raised his hand and Sonny asked, "What's your question sir?"

"Why do you think this is a serial killer?"

"Since the clues at both the crime scenes are all the same."

"Can you tell us what these clues are?"

"No sir, not at this time."

One woman in the back row asked, "Because I'm a woman and he's killed two women do you think. I'm in more danger than the men?"

"Honestly, yes, I do."

You could hear several women suddenly became very upset hearing that.

Sonny said, "The lady asked a question and I wouldn't lie to her, my advice to all of you ladies would be don't be going into men's staterooms after midnight, or letting some man into your."

"We know both of these women were killed around two or three o'clock in the morning and they were in their own staterooms."

Another lady asked, "Did the killer break into their rooms?"

"There was no evidence that their staterooms were broken into, it appears the killer was invited into their room."

The captain got up from her chair and said, "I want each of you to remember you are professional cruise officers and you will perform you duties on this ship the same way as you do on every cruise."

"Keep your cool, do your job and let the detectives and our security people do theirs of trying to keep everyone safe and finding the killer of these two women."

"One last thing before you are dismissed to go back to your duties, none of this is to be discussed with the passengers until we have our meeting with them tomorrow."

"This meeting is finished and the company is dismissed."

As soon as all the staff cleared out of the room Donna said, "Sonny, we never discussed having a meeting to advise the passengers about two people being murdered of this ship."

"No Donna, we didn't but you know you have to tell people about what's going on."

"I'd guess before we have the meetings with the passenger's tomorrow afternoon half of the people on this ship will know all about the killing by then."

"How many people were in the meeting this afternoon?"

"I don't know for sure but more than a hundred."

"Information we just told these people and next they are going to have a meeting with all of their people, so you will soon have over 1,500 people know what's happened."

"You can never keep that many people from talking with their friends or their favorite passengers and telling them what's going on."

"OK, Sonny I have to let my home office know that we will be advising our passengers tomorrow of the murder of two people on my ship."

"I hate to tell them, they may have people flying out here to take over the investigation."

"Good, let them. I'm sure they have people in the home office that's had lots of experience handling murder investigations."

"OK, Sonny. I'll go send the information that we will be telling all of the passengers and crew members about the murders of two people on my ship tomorrow."

"Donna, you can also tell them you have two detectives on board with almost twenty years experience investigating homicides who have advised you for the protection of your passengers to warn the passengers of how not to become victims of a serial killer."

"OK, Sonny I'll do that."

"Donna, you seem so worried that you're going to lose your job because of people being murdered on your ship. Don't you have a very nice pension check coming every month retiring as a captain in the navy?"

"I do, it not the money, it's the fact I'm one of the first woman to ever have command of a cruise ship."

"I don't want to screw up and keep other qualified women from becoming captains."

"You never screwed up anything in your whole life and you're not doing it now, no captain of a cruise ship has probably ever had very many people murdered on their ship."

"Donna, what could you have done differ to prevent these women from being murdered?"

"I don't know of anything I could have done, nothing I guess."

"No, you couldn't have done anything to stop some crazed killer from killing someone."

"Here some advice from your big brother, take care of your job as commander of this vessel and keep as many of your passengers as safe as you can."

"Gene and I will do the best we can to find and stop this killer, can I guarantee we can find or stop him, no."

"All we can do is to do the best that we can, based on the evidence we have. Which I hate to say it, but the truth is we don't have much to go on so far. But we'll keep trying, and that's the best we can do."

Donna said, "As my father always told me, *Do the best that you can do, Angels can do no more!*"

Sonny asked, "Well Donna, are you doing the best that you can do?"

"Yes, I am."

"Angels can do no more."

By dinner time that evening the word was out that Linda Goodyear and Sammi Smith had both been murdered. The story spread so fast that by now everyone on the ship knew about it.

The mood of the passengers and crew was mixed as they were both excited and afraid at the sometime.

Sonny knew as soon as the all the crew knew about the murders, the news would spread through the passengers like wildfire and it did.

Sonny sought out Captain Morehouse and suggested she make an address over the loudspeakers about the meeting at two o'clock tomorrow afternoon of all passengers in their muster stations.

All passengers are required to attend and their attendance will be recorded.

Donna took Sonny suggestion and made the announcement of the meeting.

After the announcement the conversations on the ship really began to become even more excited and louder.

A little while after the noise began it came more subdue, as the waiters began taking the passenger's dinner selections.

All of the table mates at Sonny's table were talking about the news about Linda and Sammi being murdered.

Everyone was talking except for Sonny; Jane; Gene and Susan, when suddenly Lucky Jordan said, "What do you think about these two women being murdered, Sonny?"

Sonny said, "I think it's terrible, that two innocent women had to die to make some nut job feel, well I guess, important."

Lucky said, "That's a strange thing to say. Why would you think the person who killed them would feel important after killing them, Sonny?"

"Oh, I've read about people who kill someone and they say they feel like they are God. They can either let you live or they can snuff out your life, just like God."

Lucky replied, "Well, I never heard anything like that before."

The conversation came to a halt as their waiter began sitting down the first course of their dinner.

9

The Investigation Continues

Gene emailed the copy of the fingerprints he found in Sammi's stateroom along with copies of her room steward's and Sammi's fingerprints, which Gene was able to get from the Supreme's employee files.

These he sent to the chief of police of the Kansas City Police Department and asked him to have the prints ran to see if he could get a hit on any of them.

Gene said in his email to the chief that there had been two murders on their world cruise and Sonny and he were helping the ship's captain and the security people with the investigation.

He also said in his email that when they reached their next port, Sonny would be sending some DNA samples he collected from the crime scene to see if there was any known DNA's that matched.

The day was going by pretty fast and it would soon be two o'clock, time for the captain's meeting with all of the passengers informing them about the two murders on the ship.

The crew members assigned to each of the two muster stations were at their positions, as the passengers made their way into their muster stations.

Each passenger, attending the meeting had their ID's scanned into the ship's computer system by using their passenger ID Cards, to be certain every passenger on the ship attended the meeting.

The captain, Sonny and Gene would make an appearance in both muster stations and their talks would be broadcast through the ship.

They started in muster station "A" and the captain introduced Sonny and Gene to their audience by saying.

"As most of you know by now, that we had suffered two homicides on our cruise since we left San Francisco.

"The first victim was Ms. Linda Goodyear and the second victim was Miss Sammi Smith.

"We're lucky to have on board two recently retired homicide detectives, with more than twenty years experience investigating homicides with the Kansas City Police Department.

"I want to introduce to you, Captain Sonny Cousins and Captain Gene Simpson, who are helping us with this investigation.

"I have asked Captain Cousins to say a few words of advice for your safety on this voyage: Captain Cousins."

Sonny got up from his chair and said, "Ladies and Gentlemen. I'll try to keep this as short as possible, so you can get back to the reason you're on this cruise, to have fun.

"The most important thing I can tell you is that these murders are not some kind of terrorist attack, like you hear about everyday on your news. This killer seems to know his victim, well at least well enough for them to let him into their stateroom."

"I will tell you like your mother told you long ago, don't invite anyone into your stateroom. Keep your eyes and ears open for anything you may think is suspicious, if you do, please report it to one of the ship's staff member."

"We are doing everything possible to solve this case as quickly as possible."

"Captain Morehouse and her crew will do everything possible to insure each of you have a safe and fun trip on this wonderful world cruise."

Sonny sat down and then Captain Morehouse got up and said,

"We would be happy to answer any questions you might have, please raise your hand to be recognized and we'll try to answer your questions."

One older lady in the back raised her hand and Donna said, "Yes, what is your question?"

"Captain, do you think we should leave the ship and go home at our next port?"

"No, I don't think you should let what's happened to these two women scare you from completing your world cruise."

The next question from the audience was, "Captain, are you concerned about your own life being on this trip?"

"No, I'm not afraid of course I have served in places where people were shooting at us and having men dying while serving in the Gulf War."

"My advice to you would be to follow what Captain Cousins told you, don't let strangers in your stateroom and pay attention to what you're doing and who you are doing it with."

"If there no more questions we need to go meet with the folks in Muster Station B, thank you for joining us and we'll let you know if there is anything new in this investigation."

Captain Morehouse; Sonny and Gene made their way to Muster Station B.

Arriving there Donna went through the same speech she gave in Muster Station A and Sonny followed her with almost the same speech he had made before.

The questions were almost the same as in the first presentation, except one person asked if they got off the ship in Sydney if Supreme Cruise Line would give them back a full refund for their tickets.

Donna handle the question as graciously as possible and said, "I don't believe they would, but they might consider give you full credit for your cruise if you wanted to take the same world cruise next year."

That ended the presentations and everyone seemed to be calmer after hearing what the Captain and Sonny had to say about the murders.

Two days later they arrived in Bora Bora and most of the passengers went on tours of the island, including Sonny; Jane; Gene and Susan.

They did the drive around the island and made a stop at Bloody Mary's Restaurant which was made famous in the play and movie "*South Pacific*".

They each had the restaurant's famous drink, which was of course, the Bloody Mary.

All in all, they enjoyed being off the ship and seeing the beautiful island.

They learned the island totally depended on tourists, since other than fishing and making some local crafts they had no industry and little in the way of natural resources.

Education on the island was limited to the eighth grade to get a high school education required the student to go to the island of Tahiti.

They learned very few student ever did, they seemed to be happy just living the way they did.

When they returned to the ship, Captain Morehouse was looking for them because she had received a message from the Kansas City Police Department.

As soon as they got on the ship, Sonny and Gene were taken to the bridge where Captain Morehouse was waiting for them.

Donna handed the message to Sonny and he saw the police chief's report that they had a hit on one of the fingerprints.

Sonny and Gene quickly read the email the police chief sent saying only one fingerprint didn't either match the room steward or Sammi Smith's fingerprints and that the one fingerprint was a match to a US Army record belong to a Tony Longstreet.

The police chief said in his email, Tony Longstreet was in Special Forces and had served in both, Iraq and Afghanistan.

It said, Tony had served two tours of duty in Afghanistan and one tour in Iraq and left the army after eight years of service with the rank of sergeant.

His current address was unknown. No criminal record and only one minor traffic ticket for speeding, when he was seventeen years old.

Tony grew up in California, were his father was in real estate, owning large tracts of land near LA.

Tony had no record of ever being employed, except in his father's company and there he was listed as Senior Vice President.

Mr. Charles Longstreet passed away last year and the company was sold by his son, Tony Longstreet to a group of Saudi's.

Sonny said, "It looks like we have a real lead, a mister Tony Longstreet."

Donna said, "Except we don't have a Mr. Tony Longstreet listed as a passenger."

Gene said, "What do you mean, we have a fingerprint of Tony Longstreet at the scene of the crime and we don't have him as a passenger?"

Sonny asked, "Could that fingerprint still be present if he had been a passenger on an earlier voyage?"

Donna answered, "I guess it could be, but I doubt it, our steward's keep our staterooms pretty clean and they are dusted every day."

Sonny said, "Then he must be traveling under another name."

Donna replied, "I don't know how he would have gotten a passport, under some other name. The US government is pretty strict on positive ID to get a passport."

Sonny said, "They maybe, but if you've got enough money, you may be able to get a fake passport made.

"Donna, tomorrow I want all of the men's passports, so Gene and I can go over them to see if we can spot a possible fake passport."

Donna replied, "I'll have my people go through all of them tonight and have all of the men's passports ready for you in the morning.

"I'll also contact our home office and see if Tony Longstreet was ever booked on this ship. I think they can do it pretty quick, all they need to do is run his name through our computer system and see if Tony Longstreet was ever a passenger."

Gene said, "I'll contact the police chief again and see if he can send us any pictures of Tony Longstreet."

Sonny said, "That's a great idea, then at least we will have some idea what the guy looks like.

"I guess we need to check how many women on this ship have staterooms by themselves.

"I believe they would be the natural target for our killer, not sure our killer could handle two women at the same time."

Gene replied, "I think that's a good idea, then maybe we could have some kind of watch on their staterooms using the ship's staff."

Sonny asked, "Donna, do you know if your video people have some TV monitoring equipment that we could set up in the hallways?"

"I don't think so, even if they did. I don't know if we could power them and I'm not sure corporate would let us monitor our hallways."

"Donna, if you have the equipment, we should use it, it might save some woman's life, you know it's always better to ask forgiveness, than to ask permission."

"Sonny, where in the world, did you ever hear such a thing?"

"Easy Donna, I worked in the police department for over twenty years.

"There you can never ask permission to do anything, because the answer is always the same, no!"

"Gee I thought the navy was tough sounds like the police department has more rules than the navy."

"I don't know about having more rules, but in the police department saying "no" is easier than thinking about the question.

"This is the way it works Donna, you have a good idea and it works and then they tell you, "great idea, now don't ever do it again.""

"What if it doesn't work?"

"Then you say, gee I thought that would work, and they say, "Don't ever do that again.""

"Sonny, in the navy and you have a good idea and it works, they may give you a promotion."

"What if it didn't work?"

"Well they might give you a reprimand or demote you, either way you lose."

"Well Donna, I think you win. The navy is worse than the police department for having ideas."

The following morning, after having breakfast with the girls, Sonny and Gene made their way to the captain's office.

Sonny knocked on her door and heard Donna say, "Come in."

Sonny and Gene went into the office and Donna said, "Good morning, happy to say no new reports of any murders this morning.

"Gene, you do have an email from your chief of police along with several pictures of Tony Longstreet."

Donna handed the pictures to Gene.

Donna continued, "Sonny, I have all of the men's passports for you."

Sonny replied, "Great, with the pictures we have of Tony Longstreet and all of the passports we should be able to ID Tony."

Sonny and Gene looked over the pictures of Tony Longstreet and Sonny said, "He looks pretty young in these pictures.

"This picture of Tony Longstreet, in his army uniform, looks like he was eighteen, certainly no older than maybe twenty years old."

Gene replied, "Well all of the pictures we've seem to have been taken about the same time.

"We should still have a chance to ID him from these pictures, don't you think Sonny?"

"A chance, but he may have changed a lot from when these pictures were taken. I don't think it's going to be easy, no I don't.

"One thing, it's the best chance that we have to ID him."

The two of them divided up the passports and sit down to begin searching through the passports looking for Tony Longstreet.

They began to sit aside passports that they though the pictures looked somewhat like what they thought Tony Longstreet would have looked like today.

They spent almost seven hours without a break going through the passports and the two of them had set aside seven passports.

They made a list of the passengers they considered looking like what Tony might look like now. They listed:

1. Lucky Jordan, stateroom 7061
2. Bobby Brown, stateroom 8020
3. Walter Johnson, stateroom 8020
4. 3Toby White, stateroom 6005
5. John Townsend, stateroom 6005
6. Josh Taylor, stateroom 7825
7. Sid Jenkins, stateroom 3007

Sonny said; let's see what we know about these men."

"We'll start with our table mate, Lucky Jordan. His passport says he was born in Beverly Hills, California on August 19, 1977, which makes him 40 years old.

"It says he is single and his home address is 6066 Madison Ave. Madison, Wisconsin.

"His emergency contact is his mother, Ida Jordan, 2500 Beverly Hills Drive, Beverly Hills, California and her email is Ijordan@aol.com.

"We also know Lucky was the last one seen with Linda Goodyear when she was still alive. He told us that himself."

Gene said, "You wouldn't think if he killed her, he would have volunteered that information."

Sonny replied, "Well at the time he said that, we were only his table mates, not detectives looking into her murder."

"I think he's our number one suspect in this case."

"Well he does look something like the pictures of Tony Longstreet. I'll have to give you that Sonny."

"OK, but let's keep working on the list of men we have put their passports aside as possibly being Tony Longstreet.

"Who's next Gene?"

"Bobby Brown, stateroom 8020. His passport says he was born in Tulsa, Oklahoma on January 2, 1975, so he's 42 years old. He is single and his home address is 8721 South Oak Street, Dallas, Texas.

"His emergency contact is his sister, Betty Johnson; address is 1801 Oak Circle, Dallas, Texas. Email Bjbrown@gmail.com

"Next is, Walter Johnson, stateroom 8020. His passport says he was born in Dallas, Texas on January 22, 1973, so he's 44 years old. He's married and his home address is 1801 Oak Circle, Dallas, Texas.

His emergency contact is his wife, Betty Johnson, her address is."

Sonny said, "Never mind. I know her address and email address."

"OK, then next we have Toby White, stateroom 6005. His passport says he was born in Colorado Springs, Colorado on July 13, 1971, so he is 46 years old. He's married and his address is 751 Boulder Drive, Colorado Springs, Colorado.

"His emergency contact is his wife, Marie White."

Sonny said, "OK, I know, 751 Boulder Drive."

"That's right Sonny.

"OK Gene, who's next on our list?"

"His roommate, John Townsend, and his passport say's he was born in Denver, Colorado on September 9, 1947, so he is 70 years old."

"Whoa Gene, let's look at his passport picture again, we surely don't think he looks like an older version of Tony Longstreet."

Gene took another look at the picture and said "Well he doesn't look like he's seventy, but I don't think he looks like what we would think Tony would look like today."

Gene handed the picture to Sonny and he had one look and said, "Man that guy doesn't look that old, but I should have looked at his birthday before I put it into our pile.

"Let's throw it back into the "no way it's him pile" and get on to the last two."

Gene picked up the next passport and said, "The name is Josh Taylor stateroom 7825, born in Lubbock, Texas on March 20, 1973, so he's 44 years old, single and his address is 8752 Lone Star Drive, Houston, Texas.

"His emergency contact is his brother, Tyler Taylor; 3431 Grand Blvd. Jackson, Wyoming, email address is ttaylor@gmail.com.

"The last one is Sid Jenkins stateroom 3007, born in Miami, Florida on May 2, 1970, so he's 47 years old, single and his address is 8700 West Key Drive, Key West, Florida.

"His emergency contact is his father, Ben Jenkins; 22 Ocean Drive, Miami, Florida, emails address Bjenkins@aol.com.

"That's all of them Sonny."

"I'm glad. I don't know about you, but that's about all that I'm good for today on this case.

"After going through all of those passports, we only have six suspects left.

"We should have copies made of those six passports for our file on this case."

Donna opened her office door and came into the room an asked, "So, how are you two doing?"

Sonny said, "I think we've about had it for the day, Donna can you have someone make us copies of these six passports for our files?"

"No problem Sonny. I'll have someone make your copies for you and leave them on my desk for you.

"Did you two ever leave this office today?"

Sonny replied, "No, we didn't."

Donna said, "You didn't even have lunch or a bathroom break."

Gene answered, "No, to both questions and right now my bladder is complaining, since I stood up."

Donna said, "OK, you two get out of here and get your bathroom break and get ready to have a big dinner, it's your captain's order."

Sonny replied, "Yes, my captain."

Donna smiled and said, "I finally have the opportunity to boss my big brother around."

Gene replied, "You're pretty good at giving orders, captain."

"I had lots of experience, ordering men around as the captain of a carrier task force."

Sonny added, "But you do it with such poise, my captain."

"Practice, my son, practice, now you two get out of my office before I have you thrown in the brig."

Sonny and Gene just smiled and both saluted Donna as they hurriedly made their way out her office door.

Gene said to Sonny, "Do you think she would do it?"

Sonny asked, "Do what?"

"Have us throwing into the brig."

"She just might.

Then Sonny laughed and Gene gave him his biggest smile as they made their way to their staterooms to get ready for dinner.

10

One New Clue

The next morning as soon as they finished breakfast with their wives, Sonny and Gene made their way to the captain's office to see if they had any new information from the Kansas City police chief or maybe from some crew member.

They met with Captain Morehouse and she told them she had the copies of the seven passports on her desk for them.

She also told them they hadn't received anything new from the Kansas City police chief.

Last thing she said was she had checked with her video people and they didn't have any equipment that could be used as monitors in the ship's hallways.

Sonny and Gene wasn't sure what they could do next.

Donna said, "I have an idea for you two, why don't you take your wives and go on one of the tours here in Tahiti.

"I'm sure they would enjoy seeing you and it's a wonderful Island to see.

"I'll have one of my officers taking the DNA samples Sonny gathered at the crime scene to be sent to your police chief by DHL.

"We have much better service from them then the post offices, your chief should have the samples in two or three days using DHL."

Sonny said, "Donna, I think you're right. It would probably do us some good to get away from the ship awhile and let us think of something else.

"I'm sure our wives would think so, that we actually got to go with them to see somewhere we've always wanted to go."

Donna replied, "It would do all of us some good to have time to do something besides thinking about people being murdered.

"I need to do some captain's stuff before we set sail to Auckland, it's hard to think about anything else, but I have to, and it's good I have a great staff to help us stay on schedule."

Gene said, "OK Captain. We'll see you later."

Sonny and Gene went directly back to their staterooms and when they got there Sonny opened his stateroom door and Jane said, "What are you two doing here.

"I thought you two were busy playing detective?"

Sonny replied, "First, we're not playing detectives, we are detectives and our captain gave us the day off, right Gene."

"That's right Sonny. The captain suggested, well actually she ordered us to go with our wives and see this beautiful island."

Jane replied, "Damn nice of her. Susan and I were beginning to think we would be doing this whole world cruise by ourselves, while you two would be spending all your time with the captain."

Susan had already came into the stateroom when Gene was talking and she said, "Hooray for the captain, we get to spend a day with our husbands."

Nothing else was said, the four of them made their way down to join the people going on the same tour they were going on.

Their tour would take them all around the island and give them the opportunity to see how people lived in paradise.

One thing they didn't expect was the traffic in the city was as bad as it was in Kansas City, perhaps worse, since the City of Papeete was a lot smaller area than Kansas City and the population was more dense.

One thing Kansas City didn't have was the beautiful Pacific Ocean all around it.

They made a stop at the spot were the first European explorers landed in Tahiti, here there was a monument with all of the explorers names on it.

Their next stop was at the home of James Norman Hall, one of the authors of the book, *"Mutiny on the Bounty"* his house was still occupied by one of his decedents.

They found that James was in Tahiti during World War II and he and his friend, Charles Nordhoff decided after the war they would come back to Tahiti to live and write books together.

They both married local island women and had families and stayed in Tahiti for the rest of their lives.

One thing Sonny found very interesting was that James Norman Hall had served in the French; English and America's military during the two world wars.

The house had a room with his pictures in his various uniforms and medals from all three countries, unbelievable.

He also won an Academy Award for filming *"Butch Cassidy and the Sundance Kid"*.

They made their way around the island on their tour and Jane saw some of the floating bungalows at the big hotels and said, "Someday, I want to come back here and spend a week staying in one of those."

Sonny said, "I've heard those places cost a thousand dollars a night. We could take a river cruise in America for two weeks on what that would cost and that doesn't include what it would cost us to flying here."

"OK, so I was just dreaming of spending a romantic week with my good looking husband in one of them."

Gene said, "Oh Jane, does that mean you're dumping Sonny and getting a good looking new husband?"

"Gene, I'm talking about Sonny, he's my good looking husband."

"Well, if you really think so."

"I certainly do, he's my good looking husband."

"Everybody is entitled to their own opinion."

That certainly made the four of them, laugh.

The tour took them back to the ship and as they were checking back onto the ship, the man who was checking them in said, "Mr. Cousins, the captain wants to see you in her office."

Sonny and Gene left to go up to the captain's office.

When they arrived at the captain's office, Donna was just on her way out but stopped and said, "Come in, I have some information for you."

The three of them went into her office and she asked them to sit down.

"What I want to tell you is that one of the women who works in the Casino Lounge came to Jack Taylor this afternoon and said, "She didn't know if it was important or not, but she said she saw Sammi having a drink with one of our passengers about one o'clock in the morning the night she was killed.

"She told Jack she hadn't come forward with the information before because she didn't want the nice man to get into trouble."

Sonny asked, "Does she know who this nice man is?"

"Yes, she did because he signed his bar tab and his stateroom number."

"OK, Donna who was it?"

"It was a man by the name of Lucky Jordan, in stateroom 7061."

Gene said, "I'll be damned if that not the second woman who was killed after having a drink with him, just before they were killed."

Sonny said, "You know he told us he had a drink with Linda the night after she was killed."

Donna asked, "When did he tell you that?"

"Lucky is one of our table mates and he told us at dinner the evening after it was announced she had died from a blood clot in the brain."

Donna asked, "Wonder way he didn't say anything about having a drink with Sammi?"

Gene answered, "Well, I would think he wouldn't wanted to admit having a drink with Sammi after it was announced she had been murdered.

"Especially after finding out two of his table mates were investigating the murders of Linda and Sammi.

"Actually, he probably wouldn't have wanted to admit having a drink with her, even if he didn't commit the murders."

Sonny said, "Well, we're certainly going to have to have a conversation with him to hear what he has to say."

Gene said, "Yes we are, the sooner the better. As you have said before, he is our number one suspect."

Sonny asked, "Donna, could you have one of your staff ask him to come to your office, because you would like have the opportunity to meet with him?"

Donna picked up her phone and called Jack Taylor and said, "Jack, this is Captain Morehouse, would you please find passenger Lucky Jordan, who's in stateroom 7061 and bring him to meet me in my office."

Jack replied, "Yes captain, I'll find him and bring him up to your office as soon as I can."

"Thank you Jack, it's appreciated."

The three of them tried to make some small talk while they waited for Jack to find and bring Lucky to her office.

It wasn't working too well, because their mind was on the task at hand, waiting to talk with Lucky Jordan to see if they could decide if he was the one who murdered two women.

Finally, after about fifteen minutes passed they heard a knock on the captain's door."

Donna waited a minute and said loudly, "Come in."

Jack opened the door and said, "Go ahead Mr. Jordan."

Lucky walked into the office and saw Captain Morehouse along with Sonny and Gene sitting there waiting for him.

Lucky was cool, he said, "How do you do, Captain Morehouse. I've seen you on the stage and in the meetings, but haven't been this close to you before.

"I must say you are a very beautiful woman, captain"

Donna reached her hand out to shake hands with Lucky and he said, "I'm sorry, I'm have flair up of an old skin condition. I can't shake your lovely hand right now."

Lucky held out both of his hands in front of him and they could all plainly see he was wearing a pair of white gloves.

Donna, a very clever girl and asked, "Is this something that happened to you a long time ago or was it something that happened to you recently."

"I'm sorry to say it was caused when I was in the army special forces over in Afghanistan."

Donna said, "I'm sorry to hear that it happened a long time?"

"A day is too long sometimes. However, I did two tours of duty there and was wounded the last time and couldn't get medical treatment right away leading to my skin problem.

"I don't understand it, but apparently it's a virus or bacterial infection the doctors say it was probably something in the dirt over there that caused it to get into my wound and it flairs up sometimes. Sometimes it last for weeks, other times it's gone in a few days."

Donna said, "Well let's hope this time it gone in a few days."

Lucky said, "Hope springs eternally."

Sonny said, "That's very poetic, Lucky.

"However, we would like to ask you a few questions concerning your relationship with Miss Smith."

Lucky replied, "Certainly, I'll try to answer any questions you have."

"OK, how did you happen to be having a drink with her?"

"After Sammi's second show, I was having a drink in the bar and as she was walking through the bar.

"I congratulated her on her show and asked if she would like to have a drink before going to her stateroom and she said, yes, that would be nice.

"So I got up from where I was sitting at the bar and moved over to a small table in the corner and we sit down there to have a drink.

"She ordered a scotch and soda and we talked for some time. I told her I had see her USO show when I was in Afghanistan and how much we all appreciated her come into that hell hole.

"She remembered doing the show for only about 150 people when she was there.

"She told me the conditions she was put through to do that show was the worse she ever encountered. They had to fly her in and out to do the show using a chopper and it was just her, and her keyboard player that could come to us.

"On the way back from doing the show, she said they lost power on the chopper and it had to make an emergency landing before they could get back to Kabul.

"She told me they went down in the middle of a bunch of sheep and the people who owned the sheep where not happy and begin throwing stones at the chopper and hitting the windows of the chopper with their staffs.

"She said she thought they would have done more if a truck load of MP's hadn't come rushing to our aid.

"She said, they put me in the front seat of the truck and her keyboard player had to sit in the back of the truck with his keyboard, while a group of the MP's stood guard over the downed chopper."

Gene said, "It sounds like you two had quite a conversation, so what happened after you finished your drinks?"

"Sammi said she needed to get some rest and thanked me for the drink and listening to her tale of woe about being in Afghanistan.

"She left me and was going to her stateroom. I had another drink and called it a night."

Sonny asked, "Lucky, what time would you say it was when she left you?"

"I'm not actually sure, but I'd guess it was about twelve-thirty maybe twelve-forty-five."

"When she left you, did you see anyone following her?"

"I do think, so it was pretty quite. I don't remember see anyone around.

Sonny asked, "What outfit were you with, when you were in Afghanistan?"

"The way things were there we kept be assigned from one company to another, but it was all Special Forces."

"What was your rank when you were there?"

"Rank didn't mean much there, but I was a Second Lieutenant, a platoon leader."

Sonny asked, "How did you get wounded?"

"My platoon was ordered to hold a mountain pass and suddenly we were surrounded on all side and hit by some heavy fire.

"We radioed for help, but I guess from our location the radio signals couldn't get through back to our company.

"Several of my men were killed when the fire fight began and we keep being pushed back in a tight circle at the top of the mountain.

"One of the men near me was hit and I pulled him to as safe a place as I could get him and attended to his wound the best I could.

"Some of my men managed to break through and get away from the top of the mountain, but my wounded man was hurt too bad to make a break for it.

"So we were left behind, while the remnants of my platoon escaped.

"I was under fire for some time, as I kept trying to keep my wounded man alive and keep fighting off the enemy at the same time.

"Because I held the high ground the guys trying to kill me just couldn't make it up to my position before I could get them.

"One finally shot me in the back before I killed him. Then it was a standoff, so they decided just to wait and keep us up there until we died.

"We were there for four days, before my company came back in force and wiped out the rest of the men that had kept us trapped up there."

Sonny said, "What about your wounded man you stayed with?"

"I had managed to keep him alive and he made it back to the states at the same time I did.

"The army doctors keep me supplied with medicine and gloves to treat the virus and they say because it's so rare they have very little experience treating it.

"It cost me my career in the army and I was discharged and receiving a life time disability."

Sonny brought a chair over to Lucky and he took a seat.

Lucky said, "Guys, I'm sure you're going to ask me why I didn't say something about having a drink with Sammi the night she was killed.

"To tell you the truth, to begin with I was shocked that two women that I had had drinks with were murdered after I had just met them a few hours earlier.

"Then when I found out that my table mates, Sonny and Gene were ex homicide cops. I was sure you would have me down as the killer, because I was one of the last people to see the women alive, right?

"So I blow it. I such have said something to you about it the night after I heard Sammi was murdered.

"Sorry, but I've had enough trouble in my life to go around looking for more of it."

Sonny asked, "Why do you say that?"

"Well I went to college to become a doctor and then my father died and I needed to help my mother, because she then became ill with cancer.

"So I dropped out of medical school to help take care of her and got a job to help paying our cost of living and for her medications.

"Happy to say my mother got better and married one of her doctors and I was on my way back to school and I found I just couldn't keep up working and school at the same time.

"So I dropped out of school again and joined the army.

"I really liked it in the army, because you never had to plan your future, they did that for you, but after I was wounded and got the infection and they discharged me with my small pension.

Gene asked, "Lucky have you ever been married?"

"No, I was engaged once, but she decided the day before we were to be married she found she was in love with someone else, so that was it."

Sonny said, "You seem to like the women and they certainly like you, so have you had a lot of lovers?"

"A gentleman doesn't discuss such matters and I am a gentleman. The congress of the United States said so when I was made a Lieutenant in the US Army."

Sonny said, "That's pretty funny Lucky, but you still need to answer our questions."

"OK, I have had been involved with several women during my life."

Gene asked, "Sonny, do you really like women?"

"Now that's a really strange question to ask me, what you think?"

Gene said, "Were you ever involved with a woman who was so jealous that she might want to kill some other woman that you liked?"

"No, maybe some might have wanted to kill me, but normally if I had a relationship end, we still parted friends."

Sonny asked, "Have you had any woman on this trip you have became involved with, other than the women who have been murdered?"

"No, and I wouldn't exactly called being involved with either Linda or Sammi, by just having a drink with them in a very public bar."

Sonny said, "Lucky, thank you for coming to talk with us and thank you for answering our questions. I don't have any more questions at this time, do you Gene?"

"No, thanks Lucky, we'll see you tonight at dinner, OK."

"Thank you and I'm sorry I didn't tell you about having a drink with Sammi before.

"Captain Morehouse, I hope I have been able to answer all of the questions concerning Linda and Sammi.

"Do hope to see you sometime, when it just to have a nice conversation."

Donna replied, "Mr. Jordan, thank you for answer our questions and I do hope you have a very pleasant time for the rest of our cruise and hope your rash clears up for you very soon."

Lucky got up from his chair, turned around and left the office.

Sonny said, "Well he certainly seemed to be able to answer all of our questions and he's either the best liar we probably ever interviewed or he's telling us the whole truth."

Gene replied, "Well he certainly didn't show any signs of making it up as he went along, still for me he's still our prime suspect."

Sonny said, "The sad truth is he's our only suspect, we don't have anyone else to even consider at this point.

"One thing when he came in with those white gloves on I was pretty sure we had our man and that he had guessed we had his fingerprints.

"Then he told us about being in army in Afghanistan. I knew we had him.

"What he had to say about being there kind of covered the reason why he was wearing the gloves.

"It's also so easy to check with the army to see if Lucky Jordan was in the army and in Afghanistan and if he came home wounded and receives a pension that has to be true."

Gene said, "Right, I will send the police chief the information on Lucky Jordan and asked him to check with the army if that all true."

Gene send a message to the Kansas City police chief and ask him to request information on Vernon Jordan, with the nickname "Lucky" who was a Lieutenant who had served two tours of duty in Afghanistan.

Donna received a message from her home office while they were all there that read: Tony Longstreet has never being a passenger on a Supreme ship.

11

Arriving in Auckland

Two days later the Golden Supreme arrived in Auckland, New Zealand. Here, Sammi's body would be taken off the ship and her body would have an autopsy before been sent back to her home in the USA.

They wouldn't have any information back from the autopsy for several days and they would be in Auckland for only two days.

Sonny and Gene were surprised when they found out that several of the passengers were only doing portions of the world cruise.

They would be having passengers leaving and new people joining the ship in Sydney; Hong Kong; Singapore; Dubai; Venice; Fort Lauderdale; Rio de Janeiro; Lima and in San Francisco.

Jane and Susan had signed them up to do two tours during their stay in Auckland.

Their first tour would take them on a tour of the City of Auckland and would be making stops at a large park where they would be able to look down on to the City of Sails, as Auckland was called, due to all of the sail boats based there.

Their last stop on this tour was at the tallest building in New Zealand, called the Sky Tower.

There they would have lunch and spent an hour in the casino in the Sky Tower.

Then they would be taking back to their ship, the Golden Supreme.

No big wins at the casino, were made by any of them.

Sonny said as they were leaving the casino, "OK, we've made our contribution to the New Zealand economy, so we can leave the country now."

On their second day tour they would visit one of the many beaches located all around the city and visit a park where they could take a walk through the bush to see examples of the various trees and plants.

Last, they would visit a museum, where they had displays of rocks from all around the earth, plus some rocks from the moon and outer space.

They enjoyed both of their tours and found the people in New Zealand warm and friendly.

The girls liked the museum best there were lots of rocks and jewelry for sale.

Each of them bought necklaces and earrings. Well they bought them, but when it was time to pay, they handed them to Sonny and Gene to actually make the purchase.

At the end of their last tour as they were boarding their ship and checking back onto the ship.

Sonny was told that the captain wanted him to come to her office as soon as he came back on the ship, as she had some new information for him.

Jane and Susan made their way back to their staterooms, while Sonny and Gene went to meet with the captain.

Sonny and Gene arrived at the captain's office and Gene knocked on the door and they heard Donna say, "Come in."

They walked into her office and when she saw who it was she said, "Glad you two made it back.

"I have a message from your police chief with information about Lucky Jordan that you asked him to get.

Donna handed the email to Sonny and he sat down and began reading it out loud, "The email is from Chief Jones and he says he checked with the US Army Records Department regarding, Lt. Vernon (Lucky) Jordan.

"Lt. Jordan served for eight years in the Army seeing combat service for one tour of duty in Iraq and two tours in Afghanistan.

"In Afghanistan he was wounded and sent back to the United States to recover from his wounds at Walter Reed Hospital. He had two bullet wounds in his back and an unknown skin infection.

"Lt. Jordan was awarded the purple heart; silver star and two bronzes stars and giving a disability award after his treatment for his wounds.

"Prior to his release from the Army, Lt. Jordan received a promotion to Captain.

"He continues to be treated for his unknown skin infection, which will likely continue for the rest of his life."

When Sonny finished reading the report from Chief Jones he said, "Damn, there goes our number one suspect.

"Donna, under the circumstances we need to take the fingerprints from our other five passengers that we flagged as possibly being Tony Longstreet.

"We need to take their prints, so we can compare them to the print belonging to Tony Longstreet that we found at the crime scene."

"Sonny, we can do, but I thought you had seven passports of men you thought might be Tony?"

"We did Donna, but we don't need to take Lucky Jordan's prints because we knew he's not Tony, since we know for sure who he is.

"We dropped John Townsend from our list because we found out he's seventy years old.

"Now, we only have five men left on our list that we think that could possibly look like what we've guessed, Tony Longstreet might look like today."

"OK, I can make arrangements for you to take their fingerprints, as captain I have the ultimate authority when were at sea.

"I could even have you shot if I thought you were in endangering my ship, of course I'd probably lose my job with Supreme as they frown on having passengers shot."

Sonny said, "Well then I hope it doesn't require shooting a passenger for us to find our killer.

"I really doubt that he would put up much of a fight if we could figure out who he was.

"Men who kill women the way this man does, normally doesn't put up much of a fight when their caught, they are usually pretty much of a coward."

Donna said, "OK, give me the names of the five men and their stateroom numbers and I'll have them brought to my office and you can take their fingerprints.

"First, though I need to get us out of the Auckland port, even though we have a pilot on board.

"I still have the overall responsibility for getting the ship safely out of the harbor and everywhere else we go.

"As soon as we are out to sea, I'll have all of the men on your list brought to my office and you can take their fingerprints.

"Just leave me the list and I'll let you know as soon as I can, when you can come back to take their fingerprints.

"Right now, I have to go to the bridge to oversee our exit from the port."

Donna got up from behind her desk and left to go to the bridge.

Gene took out his notebook and wrote out the names of the five men and their stateroom numbers, they were:

- Bobby Brown 8020
- Walter Johnson 8020
- Toby White 6005
- Josh Taylor 7825
- Sid Jenkins 3007

Some two hours later, Sonny received a telephone call from Donna telling him she had the first two men on their list in her office.

Sonny knocked on Gene's stateroom door and Gene answered the door right away and when he saw Sonny.

Gene turned and said to Susan, "I'll see you as soon as we get the fingerprints from our five suspects."

Gene blow Susan a kiss and away him and Sonny went to fingerprint their five men.

When they arrived at the Captain's office, they saw Donna talking with two men and Jack Taylor and Bob Ford were also in her office.

Donna said, "Mr. Brown and Mr. Johnson.

"I want to introduce you to Sonny Cousins and Gene Simpson; these are the two detectives handling the investigation of the murder of Linda Goodyear and Sammi Smith.

"You've been asked to come to my office, so Detectives Cousins and Simpson can take your fingerprints to help them clear both of you from having any involvement in this case.

"I'm sorry to ask you to do this, but you fit a profile of the man suspected of committing these crimes.

"You can refuse to cooperate in this investigation; however as captain of this ship. I have the power to demand you to submit to us taking your fingerprints.

"Do either of you have any objections to cooperating with our investigation by letting us take your fingerprints?"

They both answered, "No."

Donna said, "Good, let's get started, so you both can go back to having fun on your cruise."

Gene took the fingerprint kit supplied by the Honolulu Police Department out of its box and set up the special ink pad and a fingerprint card.

Sonny took the right hand of Bobby Brown and placed his thumb onto the ink pad and then placed his thumb down onto the ID card.

Sonny took each finger on the right hand and did the same, until he had all five fingers on the right hand fingerprinted.

Then processed to do the same thing with Bobby's left hand and then gave him a special cloth to clean the ink off of his hands.

Sonny said, "I hope this didn't hurt too bad Mr. Brown?"

Bobby replied, "Only my pride. I'm not use to being a suspect in a murder case."

Sonny said, "No sir, I'm sure you're not, but we need to be able to clear you as a suspect in this case.

"I'm pretty sure you'll be happy to being taken off of our list.

"We'll let you know as soon as we can, that you are no longer on our list."

Bobby asked, "Can you tell me how we came to be on your list in the first place?"

"I'm sorry. I can't at this time.

"We will be through with your roommate in a few minutes and you may either wait here, while I take his prints or you can leave."

"I'll just wait for him."

Sonny said, "OK, Mr. Johnson you know how this works, so let's get started with your right hand, OK?"

Gene placed a new fingerprint ID card on the desk where Sonny had the ink pad and Sonny beginning taking Walter Johnson's fingerprints.

Gene wrote Bobby Brown's name of the fingerprint ID card that Sonny had just used to record his fingerprints."

One by one Sonny pressed each finger of both hands of Walter Johnson on the ink pad and then onto the record card.

Sonny was soon through with Mr. Johnson's fingerprints and gave him the cleaning cloth to get the ink off of his fingers.

Sonny thanked them for their cooperation and they left to return to their stateroom.

One by one they went through the same routine until they had four of their suspect's fingerprints.

The last one of their five men objected to having his fingerprints taking and of course, it was Mr. Sid Jenkins, an attorney and he said he resented being a suspect in a murder case.

Captain Donna said, "Mr. Jenkins. I'm sorry to say this to you, however if you refuse to cooperate with providing your fingerprints.

"I will have no choice, but to have you locked in the brig until you decide to cooperate with us.

"As an attorney, I would think you would want to be cleared of being a suspect in a double homicide case as soon as possible."

Sid Jenkins replied, "All right Captain, you people can take my fingerprints.

"However, I'm telling you now, when we return to San Francisco. I will be filing a lawsuit against you personally and the Supreme Cruise Lines."

Captain Donna replied, "I'm certain you can do that.

"However, you might want to consider the fact you would have to do it under Maritime Law, because your complaint happened on my ship in international waters.

"Failing to comply under a Captain's order is something the Maritime Law is very plain about.

"I do believe you might want to reconsider filing your lawsuit and just let Mr. Cousins take your fingerprints and then you can go back to enjoying your world cruise.

"That is unless you're the man who killed two women on my ship."

Sonny quickly took Mr. Jenkins' fingerprints, using as much pressure as he possible could as he pressed down hard on each finger on the fingerprint ID record card.

When Sonny finished taking his prints, he gave him a wipe up cloth to get the ink off of his fingers and said, "Thank you Mr. Jenkins for cooperating with us in our investigation."

Captain said, "Again, I want to personally thank you for cooperating with us and I do hope you have a very pleasant journey for the rest of your trip with us."

After Mr. Jenkins left the room Sonny said, "Donna, I think it might be a good idea if you sent each of these men a bottle of champagne to make up for their inconvenience."

Gene added, "In Mr. Jenkins bottle maybe a little rat poison would be appropriate."

Donna; Sonny; Jack and Bob all began laughing.

Sonny said through his laughter, "Gene, you say the most perfect thing anytime it called for."

Which made everyone laugh even more?

Sonny then said, "Gene, I guess we better study these fingerprints to see if we can tell if any of them match Tony Longstreet's printers."

Sonny and Gene spent an hour studying the printers they had just taken from their five suspects, but they couldn't see any of the prints they made, that matched the one they found at the crime scene."

Gene said, "I don't think any of these match our man."

Sonny replied, "No, I don't think so either, but maybe we should send the copies we made of our suspects to Chief Jones in Kansas City and have him run them though the FBI file."

"I know their machine can do a better job of matching prints then we can by just looking at them, but I'm pretty sure there no match with our five guys."

Donna said, "I'll have copies of their prints made and send them to your friend, Chief Jones."

Sonny said, "Thanks Donna, we better go and see if we can still get some dinner somewhere."

Donna replied, "I will sent each of our suspects a bottle of champagne to see if that will pay them for coming up here to take their fingerprints.

"However, I'll make sure that Mr. Jenkins bottle doesn't have any rat poison in it."

Sonny and Gene left to see if their wives had dinner yet and if they did the two of them would go to the Grand Buffet to eat, since they were too late to have dinner in the dining room.

When they got to their rooms, they found notes saying they had eaten their dinner in the dining room and were now in the Main Show Room.

So Sonny and Gene made their way to the Grand Buffet and had dinner by themselves.

After dinner they returned to their staterooms and found Jane and Susan waiting for them in Jane room.

Jane asked, "Well did you two have any success finding your killer?"

Sonny answered, "I'm sorry to say that none of the fingerprints of our five guys who we thought might be our killer matches the fingerprint of the one we found at the crime scene."

Susan said, "Too bad. I wish you could find the guy, so you could enjoy our world cruise more and not have to worry about the guy killing some more women."

Jane said, "We know several of the women in our activities have said they were really worried about continuing on the trip. Some have said they were thinking about leaving the ship when we get to Sydney."

Sonny said, "I sure hope they don't, it would be a shame to give up on their world cruise after just getting a good start.

"If they leave the ship, I'm not sure they could get any of their money back if they just did a portion of their cruise."

Susan added, "I think some of them are just afraid they might be killed and said they would rather lose some money than their life.

"Come on guys, you're the super homicide detectives, so why don't you solve this case?"

Gene answered, "I guess it because we don't have a lot of clues to work with and whoever is doing them in, is very good at not leaving any clues."

Sonny said, "Normally in a homicide. We have people that are relatives or friends who turn out to be the killer.

"This case we don't have anyone on the ship who was either a friend, relative, lover or boyfriend of the victims, they might have had some of these, but as far as we know none of these people are on the ship.

"We've got one piece of evidence and that is one lone fingerprint and it isn't a very good one at that, and it our only clue we have to work with.

"Gene and I are very good detectives but we're not magicians, we can't just invent clues in a murder case, we have to have something to work with."

Jane said, "It sounds to me like you two have about decided to give up trying to solve this case."

Gene replied, "Not in a pig's eye have we given up, somehow we've got to solve this case, right now we just don't know how."

12

Sonny Has an Idea

The next morning as the four of them were having breakfast together in the Grand Buffet, Sonny said, "I got an idea on how we can get Lucky Jordan's fingerprints."

Gene asked, "So how are we going to get his fingerprints, when he is always wearing those white gloves and why do we want them anyway, we know who he is?"

Sonny said, "Gene, maybe we have given up on the wrong person, what if the killer was our first suspect, Lucky Jordan.

"We confirmed using the information Lucky gave us that what he says was true, but the information being right doesn't mean the man we have here is Lucky Jordan.

"We haven't been able to take his fingerprints to prove he's the man he says he is, the question is, is it really him?

"Maybe Tony Longstreet is Lucky Jordan and he's got us confused by him knowing all of the facts about Lucky.

"We've got to get his fingerprints, to prove who he is."

Gene asked, "OK Sherlock, how do we do that?"

"Well unlike, when we were working in Kansas City, we've got the suspect in one place, on this ship.

"We also have people going in and out of his stateroom at least twice a day and he surely has to take off those gloves to take a shower or to wash up.

"Maybe he has them off when he brushes his teeth and when he rinses his mouth and uses a water glass.

"In addition, we have a captain who could order her people to collect his water glass and lots of other things in his stateroom to get his fingerprints from."

"Great idea, Lucky surely has to take off those gloves sometime in his room."

"You know Gene this might actually work to get his fingerprints. We should be able to get his DNA too."

"That's a great idea, and then we should be able to really have a positive ID of Mr. Lucky Jordan."

"Gene, let's go up to the captain's office and talk with her about helping us get his fingerprints and DNA samples from Lucky's stateroom."

Sonny and Gene told the girls they would be back in a few minutes. They had to go talk with Donna about getting things from Lucky's room to get his fingerprints and his DNA.

When they arrived at the captain's office, Sonny explained to Donna what they wanted the room steward to do to get these things for them from Lucky's stateroom.

Donna called the Head of Hotel Operations and asked her to bring the steward who takes care of stateroom 7061 to her office as soon as she could.

Donna didn't explain why she wanting them to come to her office.

After she hung up the telephone, Donna thought they would be worrying about what in the world they had done wrong to be called to the captain's office.

It didn't take the two of them very long before the Head of Hotel Operations was knocking on the captain's office's door.

The captain said, "Come in."

Barbara White, Head of Hotel Operations and Room Steward, Romeo came into her office.

Ms. White said, "Yes Captain, you wanted to see me and the room steward for stateroom 7061.

"Captain, this is Romeo and he takes care of stateroom 7061."

Captain Donna said, "Thank you both for coming here so quickly.

"I wanted to introduce you both to Mr. Cousins and Mr. Simpson.

"These are the detectives who are investigating the murder of our two passengers.

"They have asked me to have your help in gathering some evidences in these murders."

Sonny said, "What we need is for Romeo to gather some of the water glasses from stateroom 7061 for us, we are looking for fingerprints on these glasses.

"You could do it just like you do every day, except we don't want you to touch the glasses with your hands.

"Romeo, here how you would do it."

Donna had an empty glass sitting on her desk and Sonny took a ballpoint pen from his pocket and put the pen inside the glass.

Sonny had brought a small paper bag with him from his stateroom and picked up the water glass with his pen and then by holding the glass at an angle he careful slipped the water glass inside the bag.

Then Sonny pushed the top of the bag inside the glass and handed it to Romeo.

"This is how you can pick up the glass without touching it with your hands."

"Romeo, the other thing I want you to do is to see if you can find a loose hair or several of them in the shower or the bathroom.

"Then careful pick them up and put it into one of these plastic envelopes that I'm giving you.

"Do you understand what I want you to do Romeo?"

"Yes sir, but why do you want me to do this?"

"We want to make sure that this man wasn't the one who killed the two women."

Romeo asked, "Sir, would I be in any danger doing this?"

"No, I'm sure you wouldn't be in any danger doing these things for us."

"How long do I have to do this?"

"Maybe only one time, we won't know until we see if we can get good fingerprints from the glasses."

"OK, what do you want me to do with the glasses and the sample of hair if I find some?"

"Just take them to Ms. White and she will bring them to the captain's office for us, OK, Romeo?"

"OK sir, I'll do my best."

After Ms. White and Romeo left the captain's office, Sonny said, "I hope this works, so we can find out if Lucky Jordan is really Lucky Jordan or not."

Donna asked, "Why don't you think he isn't, Lucky Jordan."

Sonny replied, "Well actually, we hope he is. We're concerned that he may be Tony Longstreet using Lucky's name and ID.

"As you know he was the last one with both of the women who's been killed and they were with him only a short time before they were killed.

"That's why he has always been our prime suspect.

"We like Lucky a lot, we'd hate to think he's the one who killed our two women.

"Lucky is a real American hero, saving one of his men while fighting off the enemy while he's got two bullets lodged in his back and holding out for four days all by himself.

"It takes some kind of man to do that.

"It's really hard for me to think a guy like that would be killing defenseless women."

Donna replied, "Well let's hope he's who he's says he is then."

Later that day Captain Donna called Sonny and said, "Ms. White had brought up two water glasses and some hair from Lucky Jordan's stateroom."

Sonny replied, "Gene and I are on our way up."

When they arrived in Donna's office, Jack Taylor was already in Donna's office with the fingerprint kit for them to see if they could get any prints from the water glasses.

They carefully examined the glasses for prints.

Nothing was what they found, no fingerprints at all.

Sonny said, "I'll be dammed either Lucky wiped his prints off these glasses or he was wearing his gloves all the time he was in his stateroom."

Next, Sonny and Gene looked over the hairs Romeo had collected from his stateroom and Gene said, "These should give us all the information we need to be sure he's Lucky or not."

Sonny replied, "The only problem we have is we have to send them to Kansas City, before we can get any answer if it's Lucky Jordan's DNA."

Gene said, "Well, it's more information about him then we have be able to get, even if it takes a week or more to get an answer."

"That's true, Gene.

"Donna how many days before we arrive in Sydney?"

"Three days."

Sonny said, "Donna, do you know Gene and our wives are leaving the ship in Sydney to make the trip to see Uluru, you know what use to be called Ayers Rock.

"I've always wanted to see it and before I got there they even changed its name, but I told Jane, Gene and Susan. I wasn't coming to Australia if I didn't get to go there.

"I was glad Supreme Cruise Line offered it as one of the tours in Australia."

Donna said, "When I was in the Navy. I've never got to go there even with all the trips I made to Australia.

"Just never had enough time off to make the trip, but I've heard it's worth the trip.

"Hope you guys have a great trip and I'm sure Supreme will do it up right for you. I have to say, they normally do a great job with their tours.

"So when do you come back to the ship?"

Sonny replied, well, we leave the ship in Sydney and take a short tour around Sydney to see the Harbor, the Sydney Opera House and the Sydney Harbor Bridge.

"Then we are flying to Uluru, that afternoon and stay there for two nights and then fly to Cairns on the third day to rejoin the ship."

Donna said, "Well that sounds like a wonderful trip and when you get back I'll make arrangements to have the four of you for dinner and you can tell me all about your trip and you can show me your pictures."

Sonny replied, "That's a deal. I'm sure Jane will have a million pictures of Uluru to show you when we rejoin the ship.

"She always has her camera in her hand ready to take another picture."

Donna said, "I hope all of you have a great time and when we're in Sydney I'll have the hair samples from Lucky Jordan's stateroom DHL to Chief Jones in Kansas City.

"Sonny, do you want to write him a note telling him what you want."

"Certainly, I have it ready for you in the morning."

Sonny wrote a note to Chief Jones, asking him to please run the hair samples to see if they could ID who the hairs belonged to. Then let us know as soon as possible.

Then Sonny took the note up to Donna's office and gave it to her.

Donna said, "Sonny, I'm sorry these murders are messing up your world cruise.

"I hope someday. I can make it up to you."

Then she gave Sonny a big kiss and said, "I've sure missed my big brother all of these years, no one has every meant as much to me as you have.

"I've always loved you.

"Sonny, try to have a great time on your trip. I'll see you all when you get back.

"Tell Jane, I'm looking forward to seeing all of her pictures of Uluru."

"OK, Donna I will.

"Bye, we'll see you soon and try not to have anymore murders while we're gone."

"Oh God, I hope not but maybe our murderer will leave the ship in Sydney."

"How many people are leaving the ship there?

Donna replied, "One hundred thirty people."

"Donna, Lucky Jordan is not leaving the ship is he?"

"I don't think so; let me check my passenger list."

Donna went to her computer and looked up Vernon Madison Jordan and found he was going from San Francisco to San Francisco.

"No, he's booked for the entire trip."

"Good, if he's our murderer. I don't want him leaving the ship, that's for sure."

Sonny gave Donna a hug and left to get ready to leave the ship with Jane; Gene and Susan for their trip to Uluru.

When he returned to his stateroom he found Jane had packed everything in one suitcase for both of them for their four day trip.

So they were all ready to go, they just had to wait until 9 o'clock. The time they were to meet in the Supreme Main Show Room for their tour.

13

This is Uluru

At eight forty-five the four of them headed down to the Show Room to meet their fellow tour members and found there were total of twenty-one people making the trip to Uluru plus the photographer, Tony Blair, who would be taking movies of their trip and their Supreme Tour Guide, Betty Lovejoy.

Betty checked off each one of the people with her list of people making the trip and gave each of them a plane ticket with an assigned seat numbers.

They made their way out of the ship, to a bus waiting for them which would take them on their short tour of Sydney and then on to the airport.

The Sydney Tour turned out to be a windshield tour, which allowed them to take pictures of the Sydney Harbor Bridge and the Sydney Opera House and as they drove along Betty pointed out several different buildings and monuments.

Two hours later they were dropped off at the Sydney Airport at the domestic flight terminal and Betty led them through to their gate for the flight to the Uluru Airport.

Everyone only had carry on luggage, so that made checking in for their flight much easier.

An hour and half later they boarded their plane.

The flight to the Uluru Airport took almost three hours and as they were in the final approach to the Uluru Airport.

Sonny could see Uluru off in distances, gee Sonny thought, it looks just like all of the pictures he'd seen of it all of these years.

After they landed they were met by a bus, which would take them to the resort, where they would be staying for three nights.

They had people at the airport who loaded their luggage into the luggage space, under the seating area of the bus.

The tour group then all loaded onto the bus and were asked if they would like to have some water and yes, they would and water bottles were distributed to each passenger.

The bus driver said, "The trip to the resort will take us about two hours, so sit back and relax.

"I will get you there as soon as possible."

The road was a paved two lane road that was just big enough for the bus and a truck to squeeze past without going off the road.

Plus, they were driving on the wrong side of the road as far as Sonny was concerned.

They couldn't see Uluru most of the time, just desert and lonely looking prairie and they only met another vehicle occasional.

It was a pretty boring trip to the resort.

Finally, they arrived into a large area with many resorts and a small village apparently one company owned all of the resorts, because later they found, there was a shuttle bus that would pick you up and drop you off at all of the resorts and into the town center.

When they arrived at their resort they were told their luggage would be delivered to their rooms as each of their pieces of luggage had a tag with their name on it.

When they walked into the resort main entrance there was a man playing an Australian musical instrument, called a didgeridoo.

It made a very haunting deep sound and was like nothing any of them had ever heard before.

The didgeridoo was made by aboriginal men, using a long stick that they hollowed out somehow by using fire, how they did it no one they talked knew.

Sonny guessed it was a secret process since they didn't tell everyone how they did it; they did have them for sale in the resorts gift shop.

Sonny thought of buying one, but decided he had a hard enough time playing the TV, so he figured there was no chance he'd ever be able to learn to play a didgeridoo.

They found their rooms weren't ready yet, but they were scheduled to take a tour over to Uluru in fifteen minutes.

The four of them sit down in the huge lobby to wait for their tour.

They didn't have too long to wait before a tour guide came and directed them to a small bus waiting for them in front of the resort.

The four of them climbed into the small bus and another young man came on the bus and said, "My name is Toby, and I will be your tour guide this afternoon to visit Uluru."

The bus had fourteen people in their tour group and as soon as the bus began to move they had a great view of Uluru.

As the bus drove along, Toby began to tell them about Uluru.

He said, "Uluru has been returned to the Aboriginal Tribe by the Australia Government.

"The Tribe that owns it, has a settlement next to the mountain which we will pass by as we drive around the base of the mountain, however, we are not allow to visit their settlement.

"The Aboriginal have lived in this area for centuries and you can see evidence of this from their wall paintings on the mountain.

"Uluru is taller than the Eiffel Tower in Paris and we can only see a small portion of it, the scientists tell us it is two times bigger underground.

"It simple rose up from underground at some time in the history of Australia.

"Uluru is an Aboriginal sacred place, we don't climb on it, however some people do, but it is disrespectful to the Aboriginals.

"It's difficult to climb and there are no facilities on it, so if you need to go to the toilet, well some people use it as one.

"The other thing as I said, it's difficult to climb there is a monument at the base on one side of the mountain of the first four people who died trying to.

"But there will never be another monument for any of the other people who died, because they don't want people climbing on the mountain, and then honoring them if they died trying.

"When you get closer to Uluru you will see there are many shallow caves in the mountain, these never show up in any of the pictures you seen, because all of those pictures are taken a long ways away.

"One of the things that made Uluru special to the Aboriginal is because there is an underground spring that fresh water flows from that the people and the animals around the area use.

"We will be stopping in a few minutes and I will lead you down some paths around the base of the mountain.

"Uluru was first named, Ayers Rock by the explorer who found it for his fiancée father.

"The explorer planned to be gone on his exploration for six months or a year at the most, but he was gone for two years and when he returned home. He found his fiancée had married someone else."

But the name, Ayers Rock stuck until the Aboriginals took control of the mountain then it reverted back to them.

The bus stopped and everyone got off the bus and followed Toby as he started walking around the base of the mountain.

Toby said, "Be careful as you walk along the trail, because we've had heavy rains for the last three days and you might slide off the trail."

They were certainly walking along some very wet areas and after they had walked about a quarter of a mile.

Toby walked up into one of the caves, where he pointed out some of the paintings made long ago by the Aboriginals.

You could also see where the walls in some area of the cave showed signs of smoke.

Toby explained the women used to cook in these caves and after hundreds of years; the wood smoke stained the cave walls.

They returned to the bus and drove to the other side of the mountain and Toby had the driver stop again and they took another walk and saw more caves and paintings.

After looking at these caves, one of Toby associates had been waiting for them in a small picnic area shelter with tea and cookies next to the small stream flowing from the mountain.

Uluru had much more to it them Sonny had expected. He thought it was just a huge hunk of solid rock sticking up in the middle of a desert.

But it had trees growing all along the base of it and small streams flow out from it.

After a thirty minutes drive, they returned back to their resort and found their rooms were ready and their luggage had been taken to their rooms.

The four of them took time to clean up and then they made their way to the dining room.

They had a very nice meal and did some shopping in the gift shop and went back to their rooms.

They were all ready for bed a short time after they got back to their rooms.

The next morning they had breakfast and spend time looking around the resort.

Next, they took the free shuttle bus and went over to the town center and the girls found several things they had to have, including getting all of them netting to go over their face and head to keep the fly's off of them.

Yesterday, they learned the Australian wave, which meant you continued to swat the flies away from your face, nose, eyes and ears all of the time.

They saw people who had been there for a few days wearing these nets and thought, boy that looks silly, wrong that meant they were a lot smarter than you where.

They found the resort spent a lot of money spraying for flies and other flying creatures, because they didn't have any of them around the whole resort area.

Their resort had one of the largest swimming pools they had ever seen in their lives.

With the greenest grass you would ever see, by looking around the area around the resorts, you didn't see anything that even looked like grass.

The last thing they had on their schedule was a bush dinner, and seeing the stars in the Southern Hemisphere, with a man who was an expert on the stars.

They boarded a bus and rode back out toward Uluru when it was at sundown so people could take pictures of the sunset on Uluru.

They could take pictures, but because the sky was so blue and the sky was so clear and without even one cloud. Their pictures didn't get the effect they expected by taking pictures of a sunset on Uluru.

They were told by one of the professional photographer with them that you need some clouds behind Uluru to get the best effect for your sundown pictures.

The pictures looked like Uluru, and the sun went down.

The picture takers were very disappointed with their pictures that night.

However, they were not disappointed, with their dinner or the star talker.

The four of them were seated at a table with four Brits who were wonderful dinner companions and they were feeling no pain with the wine they were drinking. They were all having a wonderful time.

It turned out to be a delight evening in every way and the star talker, started his talk by asking if anyone could point out the North Star and several people begin pointing at different stars.

Finally he said, "No, you can't point out the North Star, because it's not visible in The Southern Hemisphere."

The star talker had the most powerful light that any of them had ever seen in their life.

He could point his light directly at a star or planet and you had no problem following the light to the star or planet he was pointing his light at.

The next morning they had their breakfast and then they had to get their suitcases packed for their trip back to the Uluru Airport.

Their bus left at ten-thirty and their flight to Cairns was at one-thirty, so if the bus took exactly two hours for their trip to the airport, they would have only a one hour waiting time for their flight.

Well the trip took them two hours and a half, so they only had thirty minutes left to make their flight time.

When they arrived at the Uluru Airport everyone was hurrying off the bus and waiting for their luggage to be unloaded from the storage area from under the bus, although it seemed like it took forever, it only took about ten minutes to unload the luggage.

Finally, they had their two pieces of luggage and they began making their way to the counter to check in, there they found a big line because the two airport counter workers were working the flight to Cairns, but also to Sydney since both flights were scheduled at the same time.

After twenty-five minutes the four of them got checked in for their flight.

They tried to find someplace to sit down, but every seat was filled and had as many people standing up as there were sitting down.

However, there wasn't a plane on the ground for the people to load onto.

Ten minutes later, Sonny saw a plane on a final approach for landing at the airport.

Then people started rushing toward the gate to be ready to board.

An announcement was made over the public address system, "Flight 1444 from Sydney has just landing and will soon be parking at gate 2.

"Please clear gate area two, so the deplaning passengers can get through to claim their luggage.

Now the departing passengers began trying to move away from the area of gate two.

The plane from Sydney was now parked at gate two and people were going down the stairs from the plane.

The exiting passengers were now trying to make their way through the crowd of outgoing passengers.

Sonny beginning laughing and said, "It looks like a Chinese fire drill."

The four of them were standing up against the terminal's front windows and even there they were being brushed by people trying to get through the terminal and out to where they luggage would be delivered.

Another announcement over the public address system, "We will begin boarding the flight to Sydney in about fifteen minutes, please be patience we must re-fuel the aircraft before returning to Sydney."

Several of the Sydney passengers sat back down if they could find anywhere to sit.

Slowly, all of the arriving passengers beginning boarding their bus to go to the resorts at Uluru, about twenty minutes later.

Sonny saw the fuel truck moving away from the aircraft then another announcement was made, "We are now beginning the boarding process for all passengers traveling to Sydney."

The passengers begin streaming out of the terminal and up the stairs to enter the plane.

Gene said, "Look there another plane landing. I hope it ours, because as you all know, we are an hour late taken off for Cairns."

Jane said, "Yes, we know, if we don't leave pretty soon our ship is going to be leaving without us."

Betty Lovejoy, their Supreme Guide said, "Don't worry they're not going to leave twenty-one passengers in Cairns.

"I've been in contact with the ship and they know we are delayed. I am to call them back and let them know when our plane takes off.

"Now, if you folks were on a private tour and not on one of Supreme's tours that's a different story, they might only wait a few minutes.

"Then they would depart and it would be up to you to find your way to the next port to rejoin the ship."

Susan said, "Do you mean some passengers book their own tours and don't go on any of the Supreme Tour.

"I sure wouldn't want to do that and take the chance of getting left behind."

Betty replied, "Yes, some passengers do book private tours, over sixty percent of all passengers book their tours with Supreme.

"You know, some passengers never go on any tours, they just go for the trip and some just get off and walk around the area of where our ship docks."

Sonny said, "I guess I don't understand why some people never get off the ship."

Betty replied, "Normally, they have problems walking and just want to enjoy things they do on the ship."

Sonny said, "I guess it takes all kinds."

The announcement was made, "All Cairns passengers please board the plane now."

All of the Supreme passengers begin making their way to the plane and soon the plane's passengers were all aboard and the pilot announced, "We are ready for takeoff and we'll get you there as soon as we can.

"Sorry, for begin late, but we had a lot of storms we had to fly around en route to Uluru."

Three hours later, they landed in Cairns and the Supreme passenger's bus was waiting for them and it quickly took them to their ship.

They only delayed the ship's scheduled leaving time by just thirty minutes.

Sonny thought when they were still at the Uluru Airport; they would have to hold the ship up a lot longer than thirty minutes.

He was glad they didn't, for Donna's sake.

14

DNA Report from Kansas City

Donna was waiting for Sonny and Gene to give them the DNA Report she received from the Kansas City Police Department.

However, first she had to get her ship out of the Cairns Harbor and away from the Great Barrier Reef and out in the open sea before she could leave the bridge.

Yes, she had on board the local Cairns Pilot, but she was still in command of her ship and she could override any order the pilot might give, if she thought his order might put her ship in harm's way.

This pilot would stay on board, until they had cleared The Great Barrier Reef, then he would be dropped off near Coan, Australia.

Donna sent Sonny a message which read, *"I'm sorry, but I must postpone our dinner until tomorrow night, because I must stay on the bridge until we drop off our Cairns Pilot and after we leave the Great Barrier Reef.*

Love, Donna

Sonny read the note he found in their stateroom and said, "I've got a note from Donna that says we will have to postpone our dinner with her until tomorrow night.

"Seems like she has to stay on the bridge, until we get away from the Great Barrier Reef. I guess it's tricky to navigate through this area.

"So kids, we're on our own, which do you want to do?"

Jane said, "Let's go down to our regular table in the Dining Room, if that's OK with everyone else?"

Gene replied, "Sounds good to me."

Susan said, "OK, let's go."

The four of them made their way down to the Main Dining Room and found everyone else was there and now they had a new passenger assigned to the seat that Linda Goodyear had previously occupied.

They found that their new passenger had joined the ship in Sydney and her name was, Lou Ann Walker.

Lou Ann was a very pretty woman, probably thirty-four years old and was from Perth, Australia.

She was seated next to Lucky on one side of her and Sonny on the other side.

Lucky, was very busy flirting with the new addition to their table.

However, he stopped when the four of them sit down and gracefully introduced her to the four people who had just rejoined the ship from their trip to Uluru.

Lou Ann smiled and said, "Hello, did you have a wonderful time seeing Uluru?"

Since Sonny was seated next to her, he said, "It was a wonderful trip and we really enjoyed seeing Uluru.

"I have to say there was a lot more to it then I thought, with little caves and a spring with flowing water out of it forming a small stream."

Lou Ann said, "Yes, I think most people think, it just a big solid rock sticking up in the middle of nowhere."

Sonny replied, "Well I know that's what I thought. So how far are you going on this cruise?"

"I'm only going to Hong Kong.

"I have some work to do there, and I was tired of flying all the time, so I booked this cruise."

Jane asked, "What kind of work do you do?"

"I'm a fashion designer for one of those Paris Firms, you probably never heard of.

"We use a lot of factories in Hong Kong to actually manufacture our designs."

Susan asked, "What's the name of your Paris Firm?"

"Lou Ann's, it my own company and the reason you wouldn't know the firm's name, is because we will have the name of the company that actually sells the designs on our products, places like; Macy's, Penney's and Sears.

"Unlike the famous named Paris Designer's Houses, our products go to mass merchandisers.

Jane said, "I may have a lot of your designs, because I buy lots of my clothes from Macy's."

Lou Ann smiled and said, "Jane, you are wearing one of my dresses that I designed right now."

"Thank you for the design. I love this dress and I always get a lot of complements every time I wear it."

"I will say you look beautiful in your dress."

"Thank you."

Lucky said, "I would say all of you ladies always look beautiful."

Elizabeth Churchill said, "Lucky, you're always saying the nicest things, even if some of us don't think we're beautiful."

Lucky said in his most charming way, "Madam, all women are beautiful.

"Some are beautiful on the outside, but most are beautiful, where it really counts, on the inside."

By the end of dinner Lucky had invited Lou Ann to join him for a drink and dancing.

She thought about it for a little while and then agreed to join him after she went to her stateroom to answer an email from one of her clients.

After dinner Sonny; Jane; Gene and Susan went back to their staterooms because they had a long day traveling back from Uluru and they were pretty tuckered out.

The next morning a little past eight, there was a knock on Sonny and Jane's stateroom door.

Jane opened the door and saw Captain Donna waiting there.

Jane said, "Please come in, captain."

Donna entered the stateroom and Jane closed the door.

Donna said, "I'm sorry if it's a little early, but I wanted to get this DNA Report to Sonny."

Sonny came out of the bathroom and said, "Good morning Donna, so you received the DNA Report back from Kansas City?"

"Yes, I did."

Then Donna handed the report to Sonny and he quickly opened it and read it and said, "Well there goes my number one suspect for the murders.

"The DNA Report says the United States Army confirms the DNA from the hair we provided them is Lucky Jordan's.

"So we're back to square one."

Donna said, "Sorry, Sonny, but I thought you'd be happy to know that Lucky Jordan is who he says he is."

"Well I am, but I thought that someone else might have assumed his ID and was our killer.

"Now, I don't have any idea who this killer might be.

"Donna, I think you better provide us with the names of all of the women who are traveling by themselves or with another woman.

"I have no idea how we could keep watch over them, but it may at least give us a clue of who the murderer's next victim maybe.

"I told you before I sure wish you had security cameras in your hallways, so we could see who goes in and out of the staterooms."

Donna replied, "I don't think Supreme would approve of us doing that."

Sonny said, "Well it might help us to catch a killer, if we could rig up some cameras in the hallways.

"I always found working in the government, it's was always easier to ask for forgiveness, then to ask permission. Like I didn't know I couldn't do that."

Donna said, "All right Sonny. I guess you could talk with our video guys and see if he has any idea how it could be done.

"I just don't think we have anything in our video department that would work as a surveillance system for our hallways, but we can ask them."

"OK, Donna that would be great."

Donna said, "I let you have some breakfast and I'll check on when our video man is available, OK?"

"Certainly captain, whatever you say."

"Yes, Sonny, I'll call you later. When we can meet with our video man."

Donna left and Sonny called Gene to see if they were ready for breakfast,

Gene said, "We're ready whenever you two are."

Sonny replied, "We're out the door right now."

Jane and Sonny opened their door at the same time, Gene and Susan opened their stateroom door.

Sonny said, "I've got good news and bad news, DNA shows that Lucky Jordan is Lucky Jordan."

Gene replied, "Well, I'm like you. It's good news, that he is who he says he is and the bad news is he's no longer our prime suspect."

Sonny said, "Like I said, good news, bad news. So where do we go to find our killer?"

Gene replied, "Who in the hell knows?"

"Certainly not me, I have no idea where we go now."

The four of them finished their breakfast and returned to their staterooms and Sonny saw a light flashing on their telephone.

Pick up the phone and got a message from Donna that they had an appointment at eleven o'clock this morning in Donna's office with the ships video people.

Jane said, "Susan and I are going to the port talk at ten o'clock this morning to hear about the tours available for Papua, New Guinea."

Sonny replied, "We won't be here when you come back, we'll be in a meeting with Donna and her video people."

"OK, Sonny."

"Then we'll see you for lunch if you and Gene make it back by twelve, otherwise we'll see you when you get back."

15

Meeting with the Video People

Sonny and Gene went to Captain Donna's office a few minutes before eleven and Donna was busy visiting with her Executive Officer, JP Jones, about their fuel and the speed of the ship.

Donna said, "I want to hold the speed at 15 knots, so we save some fuel and we don't arrive in Papua New Guinea before eight a.m., that's our scheduled arrival time in port."

"No problem, captain.

"I agree if we get the weather their forecasting over the next few days, between New Guinea and Guam, we're going to need every drop of fuel we've got on board."

The captain said, "We are liable to be sucking every drop of fuel we've got to make it into Guam, if that weather is as bad as they say it's going to be.

"The other worry we got is we're going to have a lot passengers and crew seasick, let's hope the weather is not as bad as they forecast or we're going to be having a lot of people falling and getting hurt besides being seasick."

"OK, captain we'll do the best that we can do."

Donna said, "Angels can do no more. My dad had a habit of saying that."

"Thanks JP. I'm glad you agree with what we are planning on doing is the right thing."

"I certainly do, it's the best shot we've got to limp into Guam."

JP Jones left the captain's office and Donna turned her attention to Sonny and Gene and said, "Our video man, Toby Mc Guire will be here in just a couple of minutes."

Donna just finished her remark. When there was a knock on her door.

Donna yelled, "Come in."

Toby opened her office door and said, "Good morning captain, you wanted to see me."

"Good morning Toby, yes these gentlemen are doing the investigations of the two people who have been murdered on our ship.

Donna gestured toward Sonny and said, "This is Sonny Cousins and his partner, Gene Simpson.

"They wanted to ask you if you could set up surveillance cameras in all of our hallways."

Toby replied, "Well it's probably possible, if you had the equipment, but we don't have anything that would work as surveillance equipment."

Sonny asked, "If we could buy some equipment to do it. What would it take?"

Toby replied, "A lot more then I think the company would be willing to spend."

"We couldn't cover one of the ships hallways using one or two cameras, it would take at least four cameras, maybe six, we would have to have low light cameras since our hallways are so long and so dark."

"Then we would need monitors that could receive and recorders to capture every minute of the day."

"Last but not least, we would need power for all of the hallway cameras."

"As far as I know there aren't any power points in the hallways to tap into. So we would have to run power lines and install outlets to power the cameras."

"I would guess it would take maybe two or three weeks or more to install the complete system and then you need to have someplace to put the monitors."

"The area we work in is like a medium size closet, there's no way it could be installed in our area."

"Outside of these items, it wouldn't be any problem sitting up a surveillance system in this ship."

Sonny said, "I know they have cameras now that operate off of a battery, and they claim they would operate for more than a year."

"They say you can use them with your TV to see who's at your front door."

Toby replied, "Yes, they are used to cover an area of maybe six or seven feet, not hundreds of feet."

Sonny said, "I bow to your superior knowledge of cameras and surveillance equipment."

"I just knew it would be a big help if we could keep watch on who goes in and out of the staterooms."

"So, if we had another murder on the ship. We would be able see who went in and out of that stateroom."

Toby replied, "Yes sir. I can see where it could help you, but I don't see how we could possibly get a system sit up during this world cruise to do that."

Donna said, "No, neither do I."

Gene said, "Well, it was a good idea, but a lot of good ideas sometime can't be worked out."

Sonny replied, "I think this is one of those times."

Then someone knocked on the captain's door.

Donna said, "Come in."

In came Barbara White, Head of Hotels Operations into the captain's office.

Donna asked, "So what can I do for you this morning, Barbara?"

Barbara replied, "I'm sorry to tell you we've got another dead body."

"Ms. Lou Ann Walker, stateroom 8023, she joined the cruise in Sydney."

Sonny said, "My God, she another one. We meet her last night she was our new table mate."

"This is getting to be personal for Gene and me."

"He's killing women seated at our table."

Gene added, "Damn personal, she seemed like such a sweet young woman."

"We got to stop him from killing any more women."

Sonny said, "Donna, you were going to give me a list of women who were in rooms by themselves or two women traveling together in a room."

Donna replied, "I got the list right here, customer service printed out for me this morning."

Sonny said, "We better check out the body and the crime scene right now."

Donna picked up her phone and called Jack Taylor and said, "Jack, bring the fingerprint kit and meet me in stateroom 8023."

Jack replied, "Yes captain. I'll be right there.

"Do we have another victim?"

"I'm afraid so, bring Ted O'Shea with you."

"Right Captain, I'll bring him."

Donna; Sonny; Gene and Barbara White made their way to stateroom 8023 there they were meet by Jack Taylor and Bob Ford.

Jack said, "I've called Ted O'Shea and he said, "He would be here in a few minutes."

Barbara unlocked the door and the six of them entered the stateroom.

They saw the same sight they had seen twice before.

Lou Ann Walker body lay on the bed naked, with her panties stuck in her mouth and a champagne bottle stuck into her vagina.

Gene said, "That no good son-of-a-bitch. I hate him, whoever he is that doing this."

A few second later, Ted O'Shea knocked on the door and Barbara opened the door and let him in.

Ted took one look at the scene and said, "I don't believe it, it looks actually like the same pictures. I've taken twice times before.

"Doesn't this killer have any imagination at all, he only knows one thing to do when he kills these women, and he's got to really hate women."

Then Ted went to work taking his pictures of the murder scene.

Donna called the ship's doctor and asked him to come to stateroom 8023.

They had to wait a few minutes before the doctor arrived and pronounced Lou Ann dead, he established the time of her death was about 2:30 this morning.

The cause of death was strangulation.

Again, he took a blood sample to see if there was any sign of the victim being drugged.

Sonny and Gene searched the room to see if they could find anything that might give them a DNA sample.

They didn't think they found anything in the room that would help them.

Sonny found several fingerprints and after he finished gathering fingerprints.

Sonny gently removed the panties from her mouth and the Champagne bottle from Lou Ann's vagina.

They checked the bottle and found no fingerprints.

Gene took Lou Ann's fingerprints to be able to ID her prints from other prints they found in the room.

Then Gene had Barbara took him to fingerprint the room steward, so they could ID his prints.

Sonny said, "Donna, we need to move Lou Ann's body to the cold storage, until we reach a port where we could get an autopsy."

Donna replied, "We will be in Papua New Guinea tomorrow, but I wouldn't trust an autopsy there."

Sonny asked, "So where is our next port after that?"

Donna replied, "Guam."

Sonny said, "Since it's a United States Territory, they should have people there that could do a good autopsy.

"How long will it be before we arrive there?"

"Eight days."

"That's a long time Donna; it must be a long ways."

"It's more than a thousand nautical miles."

Sonny said, "You know Donna, this world is a big place."

"Yes I know Sonny. Our planet such have been called the water planet, instead of earth, because a lot more of it is covered with water than earth."

"Damn, Donna. I had no idea."

"Sonny, by the time you finish this world cruise you will have seen an awful lot of the oceans and seas that's on this earth."

16

Where can We Find Clues

Sonny said, "Gene, where can we find some clues about these three murders?"

"Partner, I'm sorry to say I don't have one good idea. Whoever is doing these murders is very good and very careful about leaving any clues.

"Normally, a serial killers wants you to know who they are, these killings are almost like ritually killings.

"The killer is like sending a message to women that he hates all women."

"Gene, we have to interview Lucky Jordan and asked him how long he was with Lou Ann Walker.

"Maybe, he saw someone watching them when the two of them were together.

"It could be this guy is jealous of how easy it is for Lucky to pick up these very good looking women or something like that."

"Sonny, it seems like the only common thing in all three of these murders are Lucky, and he is the last person to be with all three of them."

"I don't know how or why, but you're right, as far as we know Lucky Jordan was the last person to see these women alive, except for the guy who killed them.

"Gene, we need to find Lucky and talk with him before anything is announced that we've got another woman killed on this world cruise."

"Sonny, I think he's in the exercise room this time of day. I've seen him there when I was doing my walks."

"OK, Gene. I'll go see if he is in there and if he is. I'll bring him to the lounge on the tenth floor and we'll meet you there.

"I think it will look better if I go alone, so it doesn't look to other passengers that we are some kind of escort service."

"Got you, I'll go directly up to the lounge on the tenth floor and find us a quiet place to talk with Lucky."

Sonny took an elevator up to the ninth floor and walked to the exercise room and he saw Lucky walking on a treadmill.

Lucky looked up and saw Sonny and said, "Good morning Sonny, I haven't see you up here before."

"No, as a friend of my use to say, *I pay someone to do my exercise for me.*"

"Lucky, we need to talk with you about a problem we're having, if you have time."

"Sure, Sonny, I'm just finishing up right now. I'd be glad to try to help you with your problem, is it with your wife?"

"No, it's not with my wife, it's something else. I would rather be some place more private to talk."

Lucky stepped off of the treadmill and turned it off and said, "Where would you like to have this private conversation?"

"I thought we could go up to the lounge on deck ten. I know they are not opened yet with service, but I know we can use the area for sightseeing or for our conversation."

"Fine, that's no problem Sonny."

"Also, I've asked Gene to meet us there, because we both have the same problem."

"Well, Sonny I have no idea how I could help, but I'm always willing to try."

"Great."

Sonny and Lucky walked up the stairs to the tenth floor lounge and   found Gene waiting in the front of the lounge looking out in the distances.

Gene saw them coming toward him and said, "Good morning Lucky."

Sonny and Lucky sat down at the table Gene was seated out.

Then Lucky asked, "OK, gentlemen, how can I help you with this problem?"

Gene said, "Lucky, I know that you know that Sonny and I are retired Kansas City Homicide Detectives who are trying to help Captain Donna Morehouse and the security department with the murders that have been committed on the Golden Supreme."

Lucky said, "Yes, I know that you are involved in investigating the murders of the two women."

"So Sonny, are you interrogating me again?"

"No, Lucky, the fact is we had you down as our number one suspect, but we have taking you off of our list of suspects.

"However, if you're ready to make a confession that you killed three women, we'll be happy to take it."

"Don't you mean two women?"

"No, I mean three women. Lou Ann Walker was killed at about two thirty this morning."

"Oh, my God, she was such a sweet woman. How could someone kill her and these two other wonderful women?"

"We have no idea. The only thing we know is that in all three cases you were the last person that we know of that seen them alive, except for the killer.

"Now, you know why we need your help."

"I'll do whatever you want me to do and tell you everything I know."

Gene asked, "Lucky, how come you decided to take a trip around the world?"

"My doctor suggested that I take the trip to help me with a problem I have."

Sonny asked, "What kind of problem do you have?"

"Mental problems, guilt and have these three women killed on this cruise is not help me any."

Gene asked, "Guilt, what kind of guilt do you have?"

"Right now under the circumstance on this ship, I hate to say what my guilt is."

Sonny said, "Why, what kind of circumstance on this ship is causing you not to want to say what you guilt is all about."

With that question Lucky began crying and through his tears, he said, "I wasn't there when my wife was murdered.

"Someone broken into our home in Beverly Hills when our alarm system was turned off and whoever broke into our home killed my wife of three months."

"So where were you when she was killed?"

"I was with six of my men from my old company and we were visiting several wounded soldiers in the VA Hospital in Los Angeles at the time."

Sonny asked, "How long ago did this happen?"

"It was a little over two years ago. If I'd had been home, it would have never happened.

"There might have been someone killed, but it wouldn't have been my beautiful wife."

Gene said, "You think you could have stopped him?"

"Yes, I could have killed him. I always had a weapon handy, but my wife was afraid of guns. She wouldn't touch one.

"Besides, I'm a martial arts instructor. I doubt if I would have needed a gun to protect my wife."

Gene asked, "This happened over two years ago, did the Beverly Hills Police find any clues."

"No, they never found anything and the case is still open.

Sonny asked, "Lucky, what have you been doing these last two years?"

"Well, for some time I was just staying home and my folks threatened to have me committed to a mental hospital if I didn't see somebody to get some help?

"I finally agreed to see a shrink, and she has helped me. She was a very nice person, but she said if I didn't get out of this depression.

"She was gone to recommend to my parents to get me full time care in a new home.

"She convinced me to sell my home, and buy a new one and to move away from the memories of my wife's death."

Sonny asked, "Did that help you?"

"It helped some. Then she told me I should take a really long sea voyage and see if wouldn't help me keep my mind off of Cindy's murder.

"She told me relax, talk to people, have some drinks, go dancing.

"She said, get to know other people, listen to their stories and maybe you can find a new you.

"So what has happened? I took her advises and went on a world cruise and three very nice women have been killed, because of me."

Sonny asked, "Why would you say that, Lucky?"

"Why, all three of them had a drink and a conversation with me and then they were killed.

"Don't you think it must have something to do with me? I do."

Sonny said, "Yes, that's why you were our number one suspect. But now we don't think you had anything to do with the murders.

"Sonny, when we get to Guam. I think it would be best, if I fly back home and maybe the killings on the ship would stop."

Gene said, "Do you think your doctor would agree with you going home after only doing a small part of your world cruise?

Probably not, but if I wasn't on this ship maybe it would have saves these women's lives."

Sonny asked, "Why do you think these murders have anything to do with you?

"Did you have an affair with some guy's wife and her husband is out to get you connected to the murders?"

Lucky replied, "To the best of my knowledge. I've never had an affair with a married woman.

"In the past I had lots of girl friends, some were lovers, but none of them were ever married."

Gene said, "Maybe it one of your jilted lovers, who's killed your wife and these three women."

"I don't think so. Most all of the women that were my lovers, have kept in contact with me and most of their husbands are my friend.

"In spite what you may think. I never had that many lovers.

"I like women a lot, but most of the ladies were never my lovers, they usually left me for someone else, who at that time was more interested in getting married than I was.

"The only one I was interested in marrying, was my wife, Cindy and she was killed in our home."

Sonny asked, "Lucky, when you were with these women in the bar. Do you remember any one watching the two of you?"

"No, usually there are several other people in the lounge, but when I'm having a drink with a woman. I'm pay total attention to her.

"I'm not looking around to see who else is in the lounge. I'm there with one person and she's the only one I pay attention to."

Sonny said, "Yeah, Lucky, my wife would be really happy if I did that too."

That made Lucky almost smile, but he said nothing.

Sonny said, "Lucky, thanks for spending time with us.

"I'm very sorry to hear about you losing your wife that way."

Gene added, "Lucky, I want you to know we're doing everything that we can do to find the person responsible for killing these women.

"We're very sorry to hear about your wife's death."

Lucky got up and left walking away from them wiping new tears from his eyes.

Sonny and Gene went straight the captain's office and asked Donna to send a message to the Beverly Hills Police Department requesting all of the details of the murder of Mrs. Cindy Jordan that occurred about two years ago.

She was also to advise them, that they've have had three murders on board the ship and that her detectives believes they may be tied to the murder of Mrs. Jordan.

17

Beverly Hills Responses

Two days later, Donna received a copy of the full report on the murder of Mrs. Vernon Madison (Lucky) Jordan.

The email was thirty pages long including several pictures of the crime scene and the autopsy report on Mrs. Jordan's body.

Donna contacted Sonny and told him she had the report from the Beverly Hills Police Department.

Sonny and Gene came directly up to the Captain's office and as soon as they came in the door.

Donna handed the file to Sonny.

Sonny took one look at the file and said, "Those officers in Beverly Hills who investigated the case have done a great job.

"The case file was marked "open" still under investigation.

Sonny said, "Now I know why Lucky goes by his nickname, you haven't seen his real name yet, it's Vernon Madison Jordan."

Donna said, "Well my best friend's first name is Sonny, and it's not even a nickname."

Gene laughed and said, "Yeah, my best friend first name is Sonny too, have you ever heard of any man with Sonny as his actually first name in your life?

Sonny said, "I hope you two are through abusing me now."

Gene said, "I always thought it was your parents who wanted to abuse you."

Donna added, "It's amazing, you know Gene his folks actually love him."

Sonny said, "OK, if you two are finished. Let's get down to business."

Gene replied, "You're the one who started the conversation about people's names."

Sonny didn't say any more on the subject.

He was now busy thumbing to the back of the report to see the crime scene pictures and said, "Wow, it looks exactly like our victims.

"Mrs. Jordan was laying on her king sizes bed, naked with a pair of panties in her mouth and a champagne bottle inserted into her vagina."

Gene said, "It's the same pictures that our photographer took. The only thing different is the sizes of the bed and the size of the bedroom."

The autopsy report read exactly the same as the ones from their victims.

The cause of death was from strangulation, she was dead before the champagne bottle was inserted into the vagina.

If they sent copies of their pictures and their autopsy reports of their three victims to the police in Beverly Hills, they would certainly agree that the same person killed all four of the women.

Sonny said, "Gene, have you read in the police report yet, about who found Mrs. Jordan?"

"Yeah, Lucky, found her when he returned home along with his six buddies after they had returned from visiting wounded soldiers in the VA Hospital in Los Angeles.

"The men who were with him, all stated when they went into the house Sonny was calling for Cindy to come down, so they could all go out to dinner.

"Since, she didn't answer, he went upstairs calling her name and they said after he opened their bedroom door, they heard Lucky shout, oh my God, someone has killed Cindy.

"All six of the men rushed up stairs and found Lucky in a shocked condition, just standing at the door and saying over and over somebody killed my wife.

"A couple of men took Lucky down stairs and another one of the men called the police and none of them ever went inside the bedroom.

"When the police arrived, the seven men were sitting in a living room waiting for the police.

"Lucky was still completely out of it, after the police tried to question him they called an ambulance and they took him to the hospital."

Sonny said, "You know it's funny that his wife's murder would cause him to go into shock after all the combat he'd been through and having several of his men killed."

"Gene said, "Well maybe this was just too much for even him to stand.

Gene continued reading the autopsy report and said, "Cindy was two months pregnant."

Sonny said, "Do you think Lucky knew she was going to have a baby?"

Gene said, "I think we better ask him if he knew."

Sonny said, "Donna, we'll see you later, we need to talk with Lucky."

It didn't take long to find Lucky.

He was busy doing his exercises, as he did everyday at this time.

Sonny looked around, and at that moment no one but the three of them were in the room.

Lucky stopped riding the stationary bike and said, "Good morning, Sonny. Good morning, Gene.

"How are you two doing today?"

Sonny replied, "We wanted you to know we contacted the Beverly Hills Police Department and got the file on your wife's murder.

"We want to tell you something, and wanted to ask you something, which one do you want first?"

"What's your question?"

"Did you know your wife was going to have a baby, and how did you feel about it?"

"Yes, I knew and we were really excited about it, we're both thrilled.

"What did you want to tell me?"

Sonny replied, "We have looked at the pictures, the Beverly Hills Police Department took of the crime scene of your wife's murder.

"After looking at the picture of your wife's murder scene, we are certain the same person killed your wife and the three women on this ship."

"You mean these women were all violated the same way as Cindy?"

"I'm sorry to say they were."

"Oh my God, what kind of a sick bastard is he."

Gene said, "We certainly agree with that. That's why we have to catch him."

Lucky asked, "Do you think that every time I speak to a woman he's going to kill her."

Sonny replied, "We don't know. Just pay attention when you are talking to any woman in the lounge to see who might be watching you.

"There seems to be some connection to you and the lounge that he picks up on."

"OK, I'll try not to be talking to any women in the lounge again."

Sonny said, "Lucky, thank you for talking with us again.

"We're sorry to keep bringing up memories of your wife's murder, but we thought you would like to know that we think the killing of the three women on the ship was committed by the same person who killed your wife."

"Lucky, please watch for any man that seems to be watching you."

"We're getting ready to go shopping, just around the port for something to have from Papua New Guinea to go along with our collection of our world cruise."

"What are you doing here, Lucky?"

"I'm going on one of the Supreme' tours. I'm off to see the volcanoes, along with about thirty other people."

Gene said, "Lucky, try to enjoy the tour."

"Thanks, Gene. I'll see you two later."

Lucky went on his way to get ready to go on his tour.

Sonny and Gene went to their staterooms to meet Jane and Susan. Then the four of them went down to the third floor where the ramp was for them to leave the ship.

The four of them spent about two hours walking along the area just outside the secured port.

There, local people had items they made for sale, just laying on blankets on the ground or hanging on a fence.

They found out later these people use to have small little wooden stalls where they displayed their items in. These were all destroyed when one of the volcanoes erupted and wiped out everything around this whole area.

Both couples bought twice as much as they expected, because the prices were reasonable and the items were so unique.

Lucky and the thirty people going on the volcanoes tour boarded the buses to take them around to where the people could climb up the smoking volcanoes.

Betty Lovejoy was the Supreme guide for this tour, although they had a local guide, Sam who would do all of the presentations and guiding the people up the volcanoes.

When Betty boarded the bus for the trip to the volcanoes, she had to go to the back of the bus to find a seat and found a seat next to Lucky.

As they rode along the very bumping roads over to the volcanoes, Sam gave the people an idea of how bad, the last eruption of the volcanoes was to the area.

It had covered everything more than twenty miles away from the volcanoes with lava, rocks or fires.

Hundreds of people died and the gases from the volcano caused many other people to become ill.

Sam continued talking about the results from of that eruption that had totally changed the entire area around the port.

Many people left the area that could find a way to leave, but some people had to stay because they had no money or any place to go.

When they arrived at the volcano, Sam began leading all of the people up the side of the volcano.

Betty Lovejoy, job was to follow all of the people to make sure no one strayed away and got lost.

Lucky was trying his best to hang back from the crowd, but no matter where he went Betty was nearby.

Several of the people decided they were as close to the top of the smoking volcano as they wanted to get and begin turning to go back down the volcano back to the bus.

When they did, Betty stopped climbing and turned back to keep track of all of her people to be sure they didn't wander away to far and get lost.

Lucky saw one lady passed Betty, while Betty was helping an older gentleman with a cane get down a really slick area of the volcano.

Lucky thought to himself, why some passengers on this ship sign up for a tour that plainly says, *"This tour is not suitable for people who have problems walking or using a walker or other devices to walk"*.

Yet, here was this man, who probably had problems walking on a level sidewalk, trying to climb a volcano.

Lucky knew that he was just one of many people he had seen on the ship's tours with walkers and even wheelchairs who signed up for these types of tours.

Even though the description of the tour plainly gave a warning, the tour was not recommended for people who have difficulty walking.

Lucky keep watching the lady who passed Betty and saw she turned in the opposite direction away from where their bus was parked.

Lucky watched for a few more seconds and saw the lady was not turning around and continued going in the opposite direction of their bus and he hollered at the lady, but she couldn't hear him and now she was out of his sight.

Lucky decided he should try to find the lady and bring her back where their bus was parked.

Lucky passed Betty and the man with the cane and said, "Betty, I saw a lady went by you while you were helping this gentleman get down that really slick spot."

"She turned the wrong way and is going away from the bus. I'll go see if I can find her and bring her back to the bus."

Betty replied, "Thank you. I would appreciate it if you can bring her back to the bus."

Lucky left to try to stop the lady from going too much farther away from the bus.

It took him a few minutes to get down to the level of the volcano where he last saw the lady when she left his sight.

He continued to walk in the direction she had been walking.

Sometime later he saw her and she was quite a long ways from where he was. He tried to yell at her again, but she couldn't hear him.

Then he saw her slip and fall and she started sliding down the volcano and kept sliding.

Lucky saw she came to a stop much farther down the volcano and could see she wasn't moving any more, she was just laying there.

She continued laying there and when he got closer to her he yelled at her again.

This time, she heard him and said, "Help. Help me."

Lucky said loudly, "I'm coming to help you as fast as I can."

She didn't say anything else.

Lucky tried to hurry and found he begin sliding and had to work hard to keep himself up right.

He decided he couldn't go any faster than he was without falling and sliding down the volcano just like the lady did.

It took several more minutes before Lucky could get to where she was laying.

When Lucky got to where the woman was laying he asked, "How bad are you hurt?"

The woman said, "I don't know. I was afraid to try to get up before you got here. I wasn't sure I could get my balance. I didn't want to slide down the volcano anymore."

Lucky said, "I understand that. I almost took a slide down as I was trying to go faster to get over here to help you."

The woman said, "I glad you didn't fall coming to my rescue."

Lucky said, "Me too, my name is Lucky Jordan. What's your name?"

"I'm Aisha Charles."

Lucky said, "Aisha, I'm glad to meet you, let's see if we can get you up."

Lucky stood with his right leg downhill and his left leg up hill, then he reached his hands down to Aisha and she took hold of his hands.

Aisha first raised herself up on her knees, rested a moment and then tried to pull herself up with Lucky help.

When she was standing up with her feet spread apart. She tried to do the same as Lucky, as she was facing him with her left leg downhill and her right leg up hill.

She seemed to be standing pretty steady and said, "Lucky, you can let go of me now. I think I can stand up by myself now."

Lucky let go of Aisha's left hand and then her right hand.

They were now standing facing each other, suddenly Aisha left leg started sliding and Lucky reach out with both hands and grabbed her around her waist.

Aisha stopped sliding and then in a heartbeat. Both of them begin sliding down the volcano and then they were on the ground with Lucky lying on top of Aisha.

Then they started rolling together with their arms wrapped around each other and going down over and over and continued going down the volcano, until they were now at the base of the volcano.

When they final stopped, Aisha was laying on top of Lucky.

They lay there for a little while, before Aisha said, "Lucky, are you OK."

"I don't know I think so."

Aisha looked him in the eyes and said, "Thank you for rolling down the volcano with me."

Lucky smiled and said, "OK, I guess if you ever feel the need to roll down another volcano, just let me know. I'll be there for you."

Aisha rolled off of Lucky and got herself up and stood there waiting to see if Lucky could get up.

Lucky rolled over on his knees and used his hands to push himself up.

He took a step toward Aisha and said. "Aisha, I think we better try to make our way to the bus."

Lucky soon found the bus was making its way toward them.

Sam was the first one off the bus and came quickly up to them and asked how bad are you hurt, do you think anything is broke?"

Lucky replied, "I don't think so. I just got lots of bruises and cuts on my hands and I don't know where else."

Aisha said, "No sir, I don't think I have anything broken. Like Lucky, lots of small cuts and bruises."

Sam said, "I'm sorry you two got hurt."

Aisha replied, "It was my fault. I shouldn't have wandered off."

Sam said, "Well, we'll get both of you back to the ship and get you to the doctor."

Lucky and Aisha made their way to the bus and got on board and all the people on the bus were clapping their hands and one person said,

"Aisha, I see you found a quicker way down the volcano then the rest of us who had to walk all the way down."

Aisha replied, "Never could have done it without Lucky's help."

Someone else on the bus said, "Well, it looked like you two should have gotten a room the way you two rolled down that volcano."

Lucky replied, "I'm sure it would have been a lot easier on our bodies."

Another voice responded, "I'm sure it would have been a lot more fun."

Sam got on the bus and said, "I wanted to say. I do hope most of you found the trip to the volcano's interesting and you have a new appreciation of how much damage they can do."

"Thank you for coming to Papua New Guinea and hope you enjoy the rest of your cruise."

When they arrived at the ship, Betty Lovejoy came to the front of the bus and said, "I know everyone is anxious to get back on the ship, but I would appreciated it if you let me get the walking wounded back on the ship first and get them to sickbay."

Betty helped Aisha off of the bus and Lucky was right behind them and as soon as they checked onto the ship.

Betty took both of them directly to the ship's Doctor's office on the third floor."

By the time they walked all the way there. Aisha was beginning to hurt much worse and after the doctor examined her and had the nurse clean up several cuts and put medicine on them the doctor give her a shot for the pain.

Next, the Doctor went through the same thing with Lucky and the nurse did the same for him, cleaned up his cuts and putting medicine on his wounds and gave Lucky a shot for pain.

Before both of them left his office, Doctor Spears said, "Well you two have some fairly large cuts on your buttocks, so you may find it's not going to be comfortable sitting around for awhile."

They both thanked the doctor and his nurse for patching them up.

Betty had waited for them, to be sure they were both OK and well enough to stay on the ship and that they didn't need to go to the hospital.

Although they didn't need to go to the hospital they would need several days to recover?

That was good, because there wasn't a hospital in the little port they had docked in. They would have had to be flown to another city to get to a hospital.

Lucky said as he and Aisha left the doctor's office, "Goodbye, Papua New Guinea, we'll never forget you."

18

Next Stop Guam

Lucky and Aisha went directly to their staterooms and found they were both on the seventh floor.

Lucky was in stateroom 7024 and Aisha was in 7023. They said goodbye when they got off the elevator.

Lucky was going to his side of the ship and Aisha was walking to her side.

But before they had started walking down their hallways, Lucky, turned and said, "Aisha, some time on this trip, if you have time. I would love to take you to dinner at the Steak House Diner."

Aisha replied, "That would be lovely, but after I heal up some. Right now, I'm not sure I could sit down long enough to have a meal."

"Also, I would like to have my face looking somewhat normal, without all of the scratches and bruises."

"I don't think I have enough makeup with me to cover all of them."

Lucky smiled and said, "You can take all the time you need to get healed up."

"I'm not doing much better myself. I've never have enough makeup to cover up all of my flaws."

"I can't image you having too many flaws. You seem to be a pretty stand up guy. Maybe we can compare flaws, when we have dinner."

Lucky replied, "I can't wait to compare flaws."

Aisha then went on her way to her stateroom and Lucky to his.

Lucky smiled when he thought about Aisha. He realized he was actually smiling about something and without pretending he was happy, trying to please someone else."

In the deck above, Sonny, Jane, Gene and Susan were getting ready for another formal night.

Sonny said, "Jane, how many of these formal nights are we going to have on this world cruise? It seems like we have one every other day."

"Sonny, we don't have one every other day. I think we have one once a week."

"Jane, it seems like it oftener than that to me."

"They come way too often for me."

"Well, we don't have to go to everyone. We can go up to The Grand Buffet sometimes."

"Good. Next formal night, let's go upstairs."

"OK, Sonny. Right now, just get dressed, so we're ready when Gene and Susan are."

"OK love, if you promise we'll go upstairs on the next formal night."

"All right Sonny. I promise we will go up stairs on our next formal night."

Twenty minutes later they were both ready to meet Gene and Susan, they walked out of their door and saw that Gene and Susan were waiting for them.

The four of them went down to the Main Dining Room.

When they got to their table, they found everyone was all ready seated, except for them, Lucky and of course there was Lou Ann Walker's empty chair.

After they had been seated for a few minutes, Sonny said, "I wonder what's happened to Lucky?"

"I know these formal nights are right up his alley."

No one seemed to know.

After everyone had ordered their dinners, Betty Lovejoy stopped by their table and asked, "Has anyone seen Lucky?"

Sonny answered, "No, I was just asking if anyone knew what's happened to him. He always loves these formal nights."

Betty replied, "I was wondered how he was doing. The last time I saw him, I'd taken him to sickbay?"

Gene asked, "What was wrong with Lucky was he so sick, that you had to take him to the doctor?"

"No, but on our tour he fell a long ways down the side of the volcano."

Sonny said, "Lucky is pretty fit guy, what caused him to fall?"

Betty replied, "One of the women on the tour wandered away from the tour and he offered to go find her. When he found her, he found she had falling."

"As he was tried to help her get up, they both fell all the way down to the base of the volcano."

Sonny said, "Did they break anything from falling that far?"

"No, they just got lots of cuts and bruises."

"Tonight, I'm sure they are both in too much pain to come down for dinner, but I thought I would check to see if Lucky had made it here."

Gene asked, "Who was the woman he was trying to help?"

"A very nice young woman, her name is Aisha Charles."

Sonny said, "Thank you, Betty for stopping by. I'll check on Lucky in the morning, since this trip started we've gotten to be pretty good friends."

"Good, I hope you all have a wonderful dinner and a great evening."

"I'll be seeing you around the ship and if I can ever be of help to any of you, just let me know."

Betty walked away from their table and Sonny whispered to Gene, "We better get a watch on Aisha Charles. She could be our next victim."

Gene shook his head in agreement.

Dinner was very nice and when it was time for dessert, the music started playing and they had their Chef's parade for the Baked Alaskan Desert, with all of the diners waving their napkins as the chef and his staff went marching by their tables, proudly carrying trays of Baked Alaskan.

After they finished their dinners the four of them went to the Grand Show Room for tonight's presentation.

Sonny was having a hard time watching the show with his mind on Aisha Charles. He was certain that if the killer saw Aisha and Lucky together, he would surely go after her.

As soon as the show was over, Sonny said, "Gene, we need to find out what stateroom, Aisha Charles is in. We need to see if there's anyway we can keep a watch on it."

Gene replied, "I agree. Let's get the girls back to our rooms, find Captain Donna and get the number of Aisha Charles stateroom."

They went with Jane and Susan up to their rooms and Susan said, "Do you two boys have to go off and play detective again?"

"Jane and I are going to my stateroom and drink that bottle of white wine I have in the fridge."

Jane said, "Sounds like a great idea, let's do it."

Susan unlocked her door and the two of them went inside and Jane said, "See you boys later, when you two get through playing detectives."

Gene retorted, "We don't play detectives, we are detectives."

Susan shot back, "Yes dear, you are both, what did you call what you are, oh yeah, detectives."

Then Susan closed the door and left Gene and Sonny standing in the hallway.

Susan walked to the fridge and took out a small chilled bottle of white wine and poured each of them a glass full.

Jane had all ready sit down on the couch.

Susan moved a small table next to the couch so they had a place to sit their wine glasses and took a seat next to Jane.

Jane said, "Susan, you know we're proud of our husbands trying to find out who's killing these women."

"Yes, I know we are, but we have to keep them a little bit humble or their just impossible to live with."

They both took another sip of wine and Jane said, "You know that Lucky Jordan is a good looking son of a gun, there's a reason the girls go for him."

Susan replied, "Not only good looking, he's a charmer.

"You know Jane. Lucky has the knack of talking to you and you feel like you are the most important person in the whole world to him. It's unbelievable."

"I'm sure he doesn't have much of a problem charming the panties off of a girl in no time at all."

Jane said, "No, I'm sure he doesn't and obviously he takes really good care of himself."

"Jane, you have to remember, he's a lot younger then our husbands."

"Yes, he is Susan, a lot younger and a lot younger then we are."

"Damn Jane, using only a few words you really know how to shatter a girl's dreams."

They took another drink. Then they started talking about the latest emails they received from their kids today.

Sonny and Gene were waiting for Captain Donna in her office, after they were told by one of the crew that Captain Donna was on the bridge to check on the weather conditions for the night and would be back very soon.

They didn't have long to wait before Donna returned to her office.

When she arrived she greeted them and said, "You will have to wait a few minutes. I need to make an announcement."

Sonny and Gene both shook their heads, OK.

Donna sat down at her desk and turned around and picked up a microphone.

Pushed a button on the loudspeaker system and said, "Good evening ladies and gentlemen, this is Captain Donna."

"I'm sorry to interrupt your evening, but I need to advise you we are headed directly into a very large storm."

"The seas will be running high and the wind and blowing rain will be tossing our ship around."

"I have already had all of the outside doors locked."

"I'm advising all of you that have balconies, don't go out on your balconies."

"Walking will be difficult in the hallways and the stairways. Please be careful in your rooms, it's going to be a rock and roll night."

"The ship will be fine, but the increase of the motion of the ocean, can cause you to fall and break something. Please hold on to the hand rails in the hallways and stairways."

"The storm will pass by us around four-thirty or five tomorrow morning."

"Take care walking anywhere on the ship tonight, they do promise us a much better day tomorrow. Good night."

Donna turned around in her chair and asked, "So what's going on tonight?"

Sonny said, "We need to know which stateroom Aisha Charles is in, apparently she wandered away from the group when they were on a tour of the volcanoes."

"This happened while Betty Lovejoy was helping some older man and Lucky saw Aisha going off in the wrong direction."

"Lucky told Betty he would find her and bring her back to the rest of the tour group."

"Lucky fond her, but she had fallen and when Lucky tried to help her up, they both fell all the way down to the base of the volcano."

"We consider Aisha will be our killer's next victim."

"Sonny, the way you talk, it sounds like you believe the killer just follows Lucky Jordan around and kills every woman he talks to."

"Yes, Donna we think whoever this killer is has something that he's trying to get even with Lucky for or is jealous of him with his ability to attract women."

"Wow Sonny! I think I better get acquainted with your Lucky Jordan, if he's that wonderful with women."

"Only at your own risk, Donna, he's good looking; charming; a great dresser and as smooth as silk when he talking with women and he looks to be in great physical condition."

"OK Sonny, the way you describe him. I really have to meet Lucky Jordan; he sounds like he's the hottest thing on this ship."

"OK Donna. So what's Aisha Charles stateroom number?"

Donna went to her computer and pulled up Aisha Charles name and found her room number.

"Sonny, her stateroom number is 7023."

Gene said, "Lucky's in stateroom 7024 isn't that nice, she right next door to Lucky."

Donna replied, "No, she's not next door. She on the starboard side of the ship and Lucky is on the port side."

Sonny said, "That's too bad, because she might be a lot safer if she was next door to Lucky, he might be able to protect her."

"Lucky is a war hero, he was shot in the back twice and kept one of his men alive for three or four days, who was hurt worse than he was.

"Lucky, continued to fight off the enemy for several days by himself and at the same time keeping his buddy alive."

"Besides all of that, he's a martial arts instructor, so he could handle the killer all by himself."

Donna said, "Sonny, you're making him sound irresistibly."

"Sorry Donna, he's a lot younger then we are."

"That's all right Sonny. I've heard some men like older women."

Then Donna added, "I don't think you have to worry too much about tonight with the way this weather is going to be, it's going to be hard walking around the ship tonight.

"Even a killer would have a hard time getting around the ship tonight."

"In fact, you two better get back to your staterooms or you liable to get hurt."

"You know how us older folks are we have to be very careful of falling, because our bones aren't as strong as they use to be."

"OK Donna, we're carry our old bones back to our state rooms right now, won't we Gene?"

Donna smiled and said, "I want to meet Lucky Jordan, when things smooth out with this weather."

Sonny and Gene both said, "Good night Captain Donna, then they left her office and soon found out about holding on to the hand rails going down the stairs and down the hallway to their rooms.

It was rough and getting rougher every minute now. They could totally understand this motion of the ocean now thing now.

Several decks below them things were happening that they would not find out about until tomorrow.

Betty Lovejoy was wobbling along since the storm was pushing the ship around and just as she got to her room.

She saw someone in the hallway that wasn't a crew member and only crew members were allowed in this area of the ship.

Betty had inserted her key card into the lock and said, "Excuse me, are you lost?"

The person said, "Is this deck four?"

Betty started to answer when the ship took a big bounce and she went falling into her room and down onto the floor.

The person she saw in the hallway came into her room and turned on her lights.

Before she could recover and make her way up off of the floor.

The intruder had closed her stateroom door and before Betty could say anything more she felt his hands around her neck.

The intruder began choking her, she tried to struggle away, when she did the pressure on her throat was increased and her neck was being squeezed harder and harder.

Then everything went black for Betty.

Then the intruder pulled Betty's lifeless body over to her bed and carefully pulled her up onto her bed.

Next, he began taking off her clothes, one piece at a time and laying them neatly in a pile on the floor next to her bed.

When he had everything off except her pink panties, he slowly pulled them down and then off.

The intruder took the panties, got on the bed on his knees straddling her body; opened Betty's mouth as wide as he could and stuffed the panties down her throat as far as he could possibly get them.

Next, the intruder opened a black bag, took out an empty champagne bottle.

Then he spread opened her vagina as wide as he could get it and shoved the neck of the bottle into the vagina as far as he could.

Then he said, "This is what you like isn't it Lucky, as he gave the champagne bottle as hard of a push as he could in her vagina. That's what you have to have isn't it Sonny, see how you would like this one now."

Then before he got off the bed he hit the bottom of the champagne bottle one more time with his closed fist.

The intruder closed up his black bag, carefully looked over the room to be sure he had everything exactly the way he wanted it, walked to the door, turned off the lights and left.

19

Not Another One

The following morning Sonny and Jane were up and ready for breakfast.

Jane called Gene and Susan's stateroom to see if they were ready for breakfast and when Susan answered the phone and said, "Hello."

Jane asked, "You guys ready for breakfast?"

Susan replied, "No, we hardly got to sleep until sometime after five o'clock

this morning.

"Jane. If you're both ready for breakfast why don't you go on?

"That rocking and rolling of the ship wasn't anything different then us. We're rocking and rolling all over her bed until sometime after five this morning.

"I don't know how you two were able to sleep with all of that motion of the ocean, we sure didn't."

Jane replied, "You know I can lie down and go to sleep whenever I want to.

"Sonny, he never sleeps much anytime and he doesn't seem to need much sleep.

"So, we'll go to breakfast and see you two after while, get some rest and we'll see you later."

"Fine Jane, enjoy you're breakfast."

Sonny asked, "So, are they ready are not?"

"No, Susan said the ship's rocking around all night caused them not to get to sleep until sometime after five o'clock this morning.

"She said if we're ready to go, go."

"OK, then let's go. I need my coffee."

Sonny opened the door and the two of them went up for breakfast.

Before Sonny was finishing his last cup of coffee, he saw Captain Donna approaching their table.

Sonny saw she was coming directly to their table and said, "Good morning, captain. How was your night?"

"Long. I was on the bridge almost all night, but my night was better than this morning."

"I just got a call from our Head of Hotel Operation, Barbara White and she said we've got another one."

"Oh God, no, don't tell me we have another dead woman?"

"I'm so sorry to tell you Sonny."

Sonny said, "Please don't tell me it was, Aisha Charles."

Donna sat down at the table and then said quietly, "No, it was Betty Lovejoy."

"Oh God, she just came to our table at dinner last night checking to see if Lucky Jordan was able to come to dinner after getting hurt in a fall."

"As you may know Donna, Lucky wasn't at dinner last night.

"Betty said, she was sure he was hurting too much to come to dinner."

"One thing we know for sure is that Lucky and Betty Lovejoy were not at the casino lounge having a drink together last night."

"So the killer didn't see the two of them together there last night. Which breaks the pattern of where our killer picks his victims?

"I would have to guess he must have seen them together during the tour yesterday."

"Donna, I want a list of all of the passengers on Betty's tour yesterday."

Donna said, "I'll get it for you, but I'll have to get it from our Shore Tour Manager, Lee Douglas."

Sonny replied, "I'll finish my coffee and get Gene and come up to your office and then we'll check out the victim's room for any clues.

"Donna, it may take a little while. Gene didn't get much sleep last night too much as you sailors say, too much motion of the ocean."

Donna was leaving to go back to her office, but before she left.

Sonny said, "We need to get all of the usual investigation team together when Gene and I get to your office."

Donna replied, "I'll contact Jack Taylor and have him make arrangements to have everything ready by the time you come to my office."

"Thanks Donna, if it's going to be too long. I'll give you a call, but if I see that it's going to be a real long time. I'll come on to your office and do it all by myself with your people."

"OK, see you soon."

Donna returned to her office.

Sonny and Jane went back to their stateroom.

After they were there a little time, the telephone rang and it was Gene.

Sonny answered the phone and heard Gene say, "Good morning, well it's at least morning. It's not too good as far as I'm concerned man it was a rough night."

"So how are you two doing?"

Sonny replied, "Better than you are, you dressed yet?"

"Why, what do you two want to do today?"

"No, Gene it's not us two, it's going to be me and you."

"OK, so what are we doing?"

"Donna just told me we've got another dead body."

"My God, that crazy killer with all of those rough seas and he could still go around killing someone. Tell me wasn't it, Aisha Charles?"

"No, it was Betty Lovejoy."

"OK, Sonny I can be ready in about ten minutes."

"All right Gene, knock on the door when you're ready."

Ten minutes later Sonny heard a knock on the door.

Sonny gave Jane a kiss and said, "I love Jane. I'm sorry to keep running off trying to solve these murders."

"Sonny, it's what you do. You just can't help it. You have to help everybody who asked for your help.

"Susan and I will be just fine. I think there's a lecture on Guam today that we want to go to. Love you Sonny, please go catch that murderer."

"Gene and I are doing the best we can to get this creep."

Sonny opened the door and Gene and he were off to Captain Donnas' office.

When they arrived they found Jack Taylor, Bob Ford and Ted O'Shea waiting for them.

Captain Donna said, "I have several problems with the ship after the storm we had last night.

"I'm waiting for my chief engineer assessment of the damage to the ship. I'll be down after my meeting with him. You folks go ahead and do your thing."

Then the five of them headed to the third floor to Betty Lovejoy's cabin.

Arriving there Jack said, "Passengers are not allowed into the crew's quarters, so it's strange that a passenger would have been in this area.

"Normally, if one came into this area, one of the crew would have seen them and advised them of that rule and would have escorted them out of this area."

Gene said, "Maybe our killer is one of your crew."

Jack replied, "They could be of course, but Supreme screens everyone they employ pretty well. I guess someone could have beaten the system of Supreme checks. What cause's someone to start killing so many people?"

Sonny replied, "Generally, we found that someone who starts killing people and keeps killing them had something that sets them off of their normal behavior to kill someone.

"Then they keep killing people until they stop, because whatever the thing that caused them to start with was forgotten and they return to their normal self or they get caught.

"The ones' who stop on their own, may live for years and never kill anyone else or until whatever happened to them that sit them off in the first place, happens again, then they start killing people again.

"These are the ones that are really hard to catch. Otherwise, they just keep killing people."

Jack took out his key card, unlocked the door and with his rubber gloves on, turned on the lights.

Sonny and Gene stepped into the room after Jack stepped aside to let them in.

Sonny said, "I never wanted to see this scene again, but here it is. The same as the other three murders on this ship."

Gene said, "It's the very same scene, the woman is totally nude, her clothes are stacked neatly in a pile next to the bed everything but her panties, and they are of course, stuffed into her mouth.

"Then there's a champagne bottle's neck shoved up in her vagina.

"Without getting any closer to her, I can tell you she been strangulated and that's was the cause of her death."

Sonny added, "No fingerprints in the room and of course nothing that we can get DNA sample from."

Ted went to work taking his pictures of the crime scene and soon finished his work.

Ted said after he finished taking his pictures, "OK, I'll have the photos ready for you in about an hour.

"Jack, do you want me to bring them to your office or do you want to stop by and get them?"

"I'll get them after we are through here."

Sonny said, "Ted, we appreciate you taking the pictures of the crime scene for us."

"No problem Sonny, but to tell you the truth. I quit the police department, so I could take pictures of people who were alive.

"I'd had it taking pictures of victims, now you got me doing it again."

Gene said, "Ted, as soon as we find the guy that's killing these women. I'll tell him not to do anymore, because Ted is tired of taking pictures of dead people. OK, Ted?"

"Good, just hurry up and catch this guy will you."

Sonny said, "We'll work on that Ted."

Ted left the stateroom as Dr. Sam Spears was coming in."

Jack said, "Looks like it's the same as the other three women, Sam."

The doctor went to work checking over the body and after some period of time said, "Betty was strangled and she died around eleven o'clock last night.

Dr. Sam added, "Betty was a good friend of mine. I hope you find out who's killing these women and I hope he gets what's coming to him. I not a big believer in capital punishment, but I could make an exception in his case."

Sonny and Gene went through their normal steps of collecting all the fingerprints and looking for anything that might be something that could have any DNA on it.

Gene, this time was doing the fingerprints and Sonny was looking for anything that might give them a DNA clue.

Sonny was down on the floor beside the bed and saw a blond hair, just one strain about six inches long.

Sonny took his tweezers and picked up the hair and put it into a small plastic bag and then handed the bag to Jack and asked him to put down all of the information about where the hair was found.

After Sonny and Gene finished looking for any possible clue in the bedroom and the bathroom of Betty's stateroom, Sonny said, "Maybe this blond hair will give us a DNA sample of our killer."

Jack said, "Wouldn't that be wonderful."

Gene and Bob agreed.

Sonny said, "One thing we know is that blond hair didn't come from Betty and almost all of the room stewards are Asians, with very black hair."

Jack said, "If you are finished here. I'll have Betty's body moved to the cold storage, and have it placed next to body of Lou Ann Walker. Thank goodness, we'll be in Guam tomorrow and we'll have the bodies taken to the morgue to perform autopsies on them.

"I'll contact our Supreme Agent in Guam again to ask him to make arrangements for a second ambulance to pick up Betty's body, at the same time as they pick up, Ms. Walker's body.

"Also, I'll ask him to have someone from the police department pick up the hair to see if they can get any DNA off of it.

Sonny said, "Thanks Jack, we'll see you later."

Jack left to go to his office and Bob was waiting for the medical people to come to pick up Betty's body and take it to the cold storage unit.

Sonny and Gene went up to their staterooms and soon would be going for a very late lunch.

20

Welcome to Guam

Sonny, Gene and Jack Taylor met with the Guam Police Department Homicide Captain, Robert Cooper.

Jack, explained to Robert, that since Gene and Sonny were retired Kansas City homicide detectives they had been handling the investigation of the four women murdered on the ship since they left San Francisco.

Robert said, "I'm glad to meet all of you, frankly I never heard of anyone being murdered on a cruise ship before."

Jack replied, "I've been working security on cruise ships for over twenty years and neither had I. Not until this cruise.

"Murder investigations, is not in my job description either."

Robert laughed and said, "I wouldn't think so."

Sonny asked, "Did Jack give you the one clue we found from the last victim's murder scene?"

Robert replied, "Yes, he did and I've had one of my men take it to the lab to see if they can get a DNA sample and asked the lab to put a rush on testing it for you.

"Jack, what time is your ship set to leave port?"

"Five o'clock."

Robert said, "I would think they could get a DNA sample off of it by then.

However, I doubt if that would be enough time to cross check it through the data base, but I've asked them to do the best they can for you."

Sonny said, "Thank you Robert, do you have any idea how long it will be before they will have any results back on the autopsies?"

"Well you know these doctors, you can't rush them, but I'm guessing they would have you the reports late tomorrow or the following morning.

"I will say our man does a very thorough job."

Sonny said, "Thank you Robert. We hope to meet you again one day, and when we had time to really visit with you about your work here in Guam."

"Well, I'd certainly like to hear about your experiences in Kansas City. I'd guess you had more work in a week, and then we do in a year."

"Yeah, we never ran out of work, it's not as bad as somewhere like Chicago or LA, but bad enough.

"Sometime in Kansas City we could run into some of the Mafia killings, those were always fun."

Gene added, "We can tell you they usually went unsolved. We hope we don't have to say that in these four killings."

Jack said, "We hope we don't have any more of our people killed by this madman."

Sonny said, "That goes for Gene and me too. Four people killed of this cruise is four too many.

"We and our wives were looking for some excitement, but people getting killed on our world cruise, wasn't in our plans."

Jack said, "No it wasn't what the security department was established for by Supreme Cruise Line either."

Robert replied, "No sir, I doubt that any of the cruise lines expect to have their security people handling one murder much less four on them on one cruise."

Jack retorted, "Murder, is way above my pay grade."

That made Sonny, Gene and Robert begin laughing out loud.

Finally, Gene said, "Jack, maybe you can get Supreme to increase your budget and your salary as long as these murders go unsolved."

Jack replied, "I'll talk to Captain Donna about that."

Robert asked, "You have a woman for your captain. I've never heard of any of the cruise lines having a woman captain."

Jack replied, "Well she the best captain I ever served with. I'll tell you for sure."

"Before joining Supreme she was a captain in the navy in charge of carrier task force."

"That woman is as cool as anyone I ever worked with and I've been working cruise ships for over twenty years."

"Her officers love her and all of the rest of her crew adore her. If they got anymore navy women captains' like Captain Donna, then Supreme should hire them."

Jack, thanked Robert for his help and said, "Maybe sometime if you would like to take a little trip around your islands and then onto Tahiti. I'd be happy to get you and your wife a pass to take one of the cruises at no cost."

"Course you would have to pay for your plane fares back home to Guam. Unless, I could find another Supreme ship traveling to Guam, then I could put you on it."

Robert thanked him and said "I might take you up on that one day."

Jack replied, "Don't wait too long they may retire me if we can't catch this killer soon."

The three of them said good bye to Robert and re boarded the ship.

When Sonny and Gene returned to their staterooms, they asked Jane and Susan if they would like to g o shopping in Guam.

The answer of course was *"yes"* they were ready to go shopping.

Jane said, "We're women aren't we, yes we want to go shopping."

Sonny replied, "Gene and I thought you might, so we found we can take a shuttle bus into town at no cost and the bus drops us off at Guam's largest shopping center."

Gene added, "We can take time to have lunch there too."

The four of them quickly made their way to where the shuttle bus picked up and dropped off passengers and crew members, to travel to and from the ship to the shopping mall.

They only had to wait a few minutes before one of the shuttle buses arrived.

They rode the bus to the shopping mall and Susan said, "If this is Guam's biggest mall. I wondered where the rest of it has gone to."

Sonny spotted a Wendy's and said, "I'm wanting some Wendy's Chili, how about the rest of you?"

The other three agreed, so it was a short walk across the parking lot and they all ordered chili and large chocolate frosties.

They took a seat to wait for their order to be ready. They didn't have to long to wait before Sonny's named was called letting them know their order was ready.

Sonny and Gene picked up their orders and returned to the table where Jane and Susan were waiting.

It didn't take the four of them long to finish off their chili and quickly get to their frosties.

When they finished their ice cream treat. Jane said, "Boy, it's good to have just a simple good old American fast food after all the various types of food we've been eating on the ship."

Sonny added, "Yeah, I know we have lots of good meals on the ship, but it nice to have a real taste of home and we've got a lot of meals left to have on the ship until the world cruise is over."

Susan asked, "So, does that mean you're ready to get off of the ship and go home?"

Sonny replied, "Are you out of your mind, we're all doing this world cruise.

"We've been talking about doing it for the last ten years, we said when we retired we'd do a world cruise."

Gene added, "I know it hasn't been exactly like we planned, with the four murders, but we're still committed to catching this killer and finishing our world cruise, aren't we Sonny."

Jane said, "Damn, right we are. We not quitting because these murders are interfering with some of our plans.

"Besides, I know Sonny and Gene wouldn't never leave without finding this nut that killing these women."

Susan said, "Just asking."

Then the four of them started laughing and all of the people in the restaurant turned to see if they could see what was so funny.

They got up from their table, deposited their used chili cups and their frosty cups into the waste container and walked back to the mall.

Here they went into a small shop in the mall. Which had just about everything you could think of from local souvenirs to suntan lotion and a little bit of everything in between?

Jane and Sonny begin picking up differ things and soon Sonny had to get a basket to carry all of the things.

Jane found some makeup she thought she needed. Sonny got some Aloe Lotion, candy, peanuts and more candy.

Sonny wasn't sure of all the things Jane kept putting into the basket.

By the time they checked out it the bill was over eighty dollars.

Sonny paid the cashier and she put all of their treasures in a large plastic bag.

Gene and Susan were ready to check out at the same time and their plastic bag full of stuff was over fifty dollars.

They walked around the mall for a few minutes and decided they were ready to go back to the ship.

On the shuttle ride back to the ship, Gene asked, "So what did you two buy at the store?"

Sonny looked to Jane she just shrugged her shoulders, indicating she didn't know what they bought, so he replied, "Darn if we know. I only know we spend over eighty dollars for whatever it was that we bought."

"How about you and Susan, what did you buy?

Gene answered, "I think we must have the same things you got, but we only spent a little over fifty dollars worth of it in our plastic bag."

Jane said, "You know what, we bought things because we were in an America kind of store and we haven't been in one for a long time and it was fun seeing names of things we knew."

"So we kept picking up items and putting them in our basket and they filled up our plastic bag."

"It made us happy to buy things; we actually knew what it was we're buying."

As soon as they got back to the ship, Sonny saw Jack waiting for them, but first they would have to be logged back onto the ship. Then they had to clear the ship's security screening.

They had to be cleared through the x-ray machine for their bag of goodies and pass through the security metal detector.

When they finished these tasks, Jack was waiting for them just passed the security check point.

Sonny said, "Jane, you and Susan might as well go on up to our rooms, because I see Jack Taylor is waiting for Gene and me."

Jane and Susan went on past and took their new bags of goodies they bought at the mall.

Sonny and Gene went too met with Jack.

Jack said to Sonny and Gene, "We got some information from the Guam Police Department on the DNA of the hair you found at the crime scene."

"They said the hair was of a type of rayon material that is used to make wigs."

Gene said, "Maybe our killer wears a wig because he's bald, so no one would recognize him when he's killing women."

Sonny said, "Or it was left by one of the entertainers who had the room before Betty.

"I don't remember seeing any blond men on this ship, do you Gene?"

Gene replied, "No, there's plenty of blond women, but no men, most of the men have gray or white hair,

"I'd say most of the women had help of becoming blonds from the beauty shop."

Jack said, "What if our killer is a woman?"

Sonny replied, "I've never considered a women, could be our killer, had you Gene?"

"No, never gave it a though, that our killer could be a woman. That might explain how easy some those woman opened their door and let them into their room."

Sonny paused and said, "Maybe the killer is pretty smart by placing a champagne bottle neck into the vagina of his victim to throw us off.

"Doing this we would think, which we have, it's a man who hated women that was killing them.

"Well I would say it has certainly worked so far.

"Jack, I think Gene and I need some time to think about this new theory.

"You know, Jack, you may have hit on the right idea about who our killer is."

Sonny and Gene went up to their staterooms and Sonny said, "Do you want to come to my room or do you want to meet in yours?"

Gene answered, "Let's see what our wives are doing before we decide."

"Right, Gene."

Both of them went into their rooms and Sonny found Jane looking at the Supreme Daily News, this little information guide available every night.

Jane looked up from the paper and said, "Sonny, do you want to go down to see a movie that coming on in a few minutes?"

"No, I can't.

"Gene and I have to work on a new possibility of who our murderer is."

Jane replied, "OK, then Susan and I are going so you two can work on finding your murderer."

Jane opened the door and stepped over to the stateroom next door and knocked on the door and Susan and Gene were both standing just inside.

Susan said, "I know Jane, we're going to the movie while the boys are working on their new theory of who the murderer is."

Jane replied, "OK, Susan, let's go. I don't want to be late and miss the first part of the movie."

Jane and Susan started off to see the movie, as Gene went into Jane and Sonny room to work with Sonny on finding the killer.

Sonny and Gene discussed several ideas on how they might discover who the murderer was and why Lucky Jordan always seemed to be the key, as why these women were targeted.

Sonny, finally said, "If it's a woman killing these women, what would it have to do with Lucky?"

Gene said, "Maybe it's someone that Lucky rejected, that's doing the murders."

Sonny added, "Well I guess that would make sense, but how would they know he was taking a world cruise, unless it was something that happened lately.

"Lucky, told us that he had been in a deep depression and his doctor suggested he take this trip, you don't think the doctor would be doing these murders do you?"

"I doubt it. I would think if she was on the ship Lucky would have recognized her by now. This ship isn't that big and on a trip this long you would have had to seen her at least once.

"The only other thing I can think of Gene, is, if it's a woman he rejected that's killing these women. She must have really changed her appearance for Lucky not to have recognized her.

"He looks over every woman pretty well, from top to bottom and everything in between."

"Well Sonny, Lucky certainly does that. I think we have to talk to Lucky again to see what he thinks about the possibility that it's some woman he rejected at sometime, that's killing these women."

"OK Gene, let's go see if we can find Lucky."

21

Another Meeting with Lucky

It didn't take long to find Lucky he was in the casino, playing a slot machine.

When he saw Sonny and Gene, he could tell they were looking for him.

His last play on the machine was just completing its spin, bells started ringing and lights flashing. He just hit the jack pot for $4,500.00.

Lucky said, "I guess it was time for me to quit playing, as he pushed the button on the machine to cash out and transfer his winnings to his cruise card."

Gene said, "I guess we know how you got the nickname, Lucky, by just the way you finished your last play on the slot machine."

"I normal do pretty good gambling, maybe I'm not as lucky in my life."

"So, guys what's up today, that you're looking for me?"

Gene replied, "We had a new idea of who the killer might be and wanted to talk to you about it."

"OK, where would you like to go for our talk?"

Sonny looked around and saw that there was no one in the casino lounge and said, "Why don't we sit down over in corner, since there no one in the bar and it's not open at this time of day."

Lucky replied, "Sounds OK, to me."

The three of them went over to a table in the corner of the bar and sit down around a small table.

Lucky asked, "OK, what's your new idea of who the killer might be, unless you think, it's me again."

Sonny answered, "No, we don't think it's you. We're thinking it might be a woman who's committing these murders."

Lucky said, "Well, that's a different idea all right. What makes you think it might be a woman."

Sonny said, "For one thing, the way the murderer has gained entrance to the women's staterooms. There no evidence that the killer forced his way into any of their staterooms. In every case, it seems the women opened her door and let the killer in."

Lucky said, "I didn't know that."

Gene said, "No, you wouldn't have known that, because we never said anything about it to you before.

"Lucky, we are wondering if at sometime in the past you rejected a woman who resented you rejecting her so much. That she became so angry, that she wants to try to get back at you for rejecting her for someone else. Including your wife?"

Lucky replied, "Wow, I can't think of any woman that I ever had a relationship with that would have felt bad enough about breaking up with me that she would do anything like killing my wife and these other women."

Sonny said, "Lucky, I know you love women, but did you ever have an affair with another man?"

"You've got to be kidding me, an affair with a man! No way man, I have enough trouble with women."

"Sorry Lucky, I had to ask."

"It's all right. I understand you have to probe ever possibility."

Sonny said, "Lucky, somehow, someway all of the murders seemed to happen to women you have been seen with, ever since we have been on this ship."

"I don't know why, I haven't really been involved with any of the women who have been killed. I had a drink with three of them in this bar, but that's all.

"Betty Lovejoy, the only time I was ever even near her was when she was our guide on the tour of the volcanoes. Even there, I never got closer to her than probably six or eight feet, while we were climbing the volcano.

"That was when Betty was helping an older man and I saw a women, Aisha Charles headed off in the wrong direction, away from our bus. I told Betty I would find her and bring her back to the bus."

"The next time I saw Betty, was when the bus found, Aisha and me lying at the base of volcano."

"When the bus arrived back at the ship. Betty asked everyone to wait until Aisha and I got off of the bus and she took us directly to sickbay."

"The last time I saw Betty, was when Aisha and I were coming out of the doctor's exam rooms. She was waiting to see if we would have to leave the ship and go to a hospital."

"Since the doctor cleared us, to stay on the ship. Betty went on her way and I never saw her again."

"Sonny, I know you told me that night at dinner, Betty came by to see if I had made it for dinner. But she never came to my room or called to check on me."

Sonny said, "I don't know anything else to ask you right now. Wait, do you think you could help us look after Aisha Charles, if someone was trying to kill her?"

"I'm sure I would be happy to help look after her, but I don't know how I could do it."

Sonny said, "I think I have an idea, but I need to talk to Captain Donna first, OK, Lucky?"

"Well, just let me know how I could help you look after her."

"Lucky, I'll call you or find you, after I've talked to the captain."

"OK, Sonny. I'll wait to hear from you."

Sonny and Gene left to go up to the captain's office and found her in her office and Sonny said, "Donna, I have an idea of a way to try to keep Aisha Charles from becoming our next victim."

"How's that, Sonny?"

"Well it depends, if you have staterooms that have adjoining doors."

"We do have a few of the family suites that have adjoining doors. I'd have to check to see if they are all occupied.

"I'll call Barbara White, and ask her what we have."

Donna called Barbara and asked her if they had any family suite available.

Barbara told her that they could have one by move one of their guests.

Donna asked her if they could give the passenger in that stateroom an upgrade.

Barbara told her no, but they could move the passenger into one of her open min-suite.

Donna asked her to move the passenger to another min-suite and tell them, they needed to do some work on the pipes running through their stateroom.

Barbara said, "OK captain we'll have the rooms available in two to three hours. She said the units were on the eighth floor, staterooms 8047 and 8049.

Sonny said, "That will be great, if we put Aisha Charles in 8049 and Lucky in 8047, she would be between Lucky and my stateroom. Maybe between the two of us, we can keep Aisha alive."

"One more thing Donna, do you think your people could put an emergency alarm signal from Aisha room to both Lucky's and my room, so Aisha could signal us, if she was in danger?"

Donna replied, "I think our people could do that without too much of a problem. I'll call my chief electrical engineer, to see what he can do."

Sonny said, "Great, I think that would be a great step to help us keep her alive. Gene and I will be looking for Lucky and Aisha, to let them know what's happening and why."

Donna said, "You don't have to do that. I can have them paged, and ask them to come to the reception desk, and you two can be waiting there for them."

"You can use an office there to talk with both of them."

Gene said, "Great idea Donna, we'll go on down to the reception desk and wait for them. Can you give us about ten minutes, so we can be sure we're there to talk with them?"

"No problem Gene, it will take me a few minutes to be sure they have an office that you can use to meet with them at reception."

Sonny and Gene left Dona's office to go down to the reception desk.

They had been there for several minutes when they heard a voice over the ship's loudspeakers system say, "Would the following passengers please come to the reception desk as soon as possible, Ms. Aisha Charles and Mr. Lucky Jordan."

Only a few minutes past, before Lucky came up to the reception desk and asked, "They just paged me to come to the reception desk. How can I help you?"

The clerk at the desk pointed at Sonny and Gene and said, "These gentlemen would like to have a word with you, sir."

Lucky hadn't notice Sonny and Gene sitting on the other side of the reception area. He walked over to them and said, "OK, what's up?"

Gene said, "We want to have a meeting with you and Aisha Charles, if that's OK?"

"No problem, for me."

Gene replied, "Good, why don't you and I wait for Aisha, in the office over there, while Sonny waits here for her."

"OK Gene, no problem."

Gene and Lucky went into the office and closed the door, while Sonny continued to wait for Aisha to arrive.

After about ten minutes passed and Aisha hadn't appeared the clerk asked, "Mr. Cousins, should I page her again?"

Sonny said, "Yes, please page her again, thank you."

The clerk paged saying, "Ms. Aisha Charles please come to the front desk as soon as possible."

Sonny thanked the clerk and sat back down to wait for Aisha to show up.

After another five minute waiting a young woman walked up to the reception desk and said, "I'm Aisha Charles, you were paging me."

The desk clerk said, "Yes, Ms. Charles, the gentleman sitting over there is looking for you."

Sonny heard Aisha tell the desk clerk her name. Then Sonny began walking over to the desk to meet her, as Aisha turned to see who was looking for her.

Sonny said, "Ms. Charles, my name is Sonny Cousins and I need to speak to you for a few minutes, if I may."

Aisha replied, "Can you please tell me what you need to talk with me about?"

Sonny said, "I would be happy to do that, but I think it would be better if we met with my partner, Gene Simpson and Lucky Jordan. Please come with me into the office over there."

"OK, but are you sure you have the right person that you want to talk to?"

"Yes, Ms. Charles, you are the one we need to speak to. We'll try not to take too much of your time."

Sonny took a couple of steps toward the office door then turned around to see if Ms. Charles was following him.

She was.

Sonny opened the office door and Aisha could see Lucky and another man waiting there.

After the two of them went inside the office, Sonny closed the door.

Then he said, "Ms. Charles, you know, Lucky Jordan, and this is my partner, Gene Simpson and we are working for the captain trying to find who killed four women on this ship.

"Gene and I are recently retired homicide detectives with the Kansas City Police Department. Captain Morehouse and I have known each other since we were born into this world."

Aisha asked "So, what does all of this have to do with me?"

Sonny replied, "Well, Ms. Charles, we are concerned you might become the next victim of this serial killer."

"Why would you think that?"

Lucky spoke up and said, "Aisha, I'm afraid it has to do with me coming to find you, to bring you back to the bus and the two of us falling down the volcano together."

"Lucky, why would that cause me to become a victim of some crazy serial killer?"

Sonny replied, before Lucky could speak, "Let me try to explain the reason we think you might be on the killer list of potential victims."

"Please do?"

"These killings seem to have something to do with Lucky Jordan, since each time one of the women who have been murdered have had some kind of relations with Lucky."

"Well, I haven't had any kind of relationship with Mr. Jordan."

"None, except that you two falling down the volcano together from what Mr. Jordan told us. Three of the victims, had only had drinks in one of the ship's bar with Mr. Jordan, and as far as we know he had no other involvement with these women.

"His only contact with Betty Lovejoy was that she was the Supreme Tour Guide on your volcano tour and the one to take you two to sickbay to treat both of you after your fall."

"So what do you want me to do, get off the ship in the next port and fly home, just because he tried to help me get back to the bus?"

"No, we don't want you to get off the ship at the next port, what we want to do, is to keep you alive."

"Well that's sounds like a good idea, so what do you want me to do?"

"The first thing we want you to do is to move to a different stateroom. We have arranged to move you to stateroom 8049, which is next door to me and my wife's room and we want to move Mr. Jordan to stateroom 8047, which is an adjoining stateroom to your new stateroom."

"What does adjoining staterooms mean?"

"Ms. Charles, an adjoining stateroom means they have doors which could be opened between the rooms."

"You don't know it yet, but Lucky Jordan is a highly decorated Special Forces veteran and a martial arts instructor."

"We are also having an alarm signal, set up in your new stateroom, between both Lucky's stateroom and mine."

"Sonny, you're really serious about thinking someone is going to try to kill me, because I fell down a volcano with Lucky Jordan and went to sickbay with him?"

Sonny replied, "We're very serious."

Then Gene said, "Lucky, what do you think, could you help keep Ms. Charles be safe."

"I could and I will, if she feels comfortable enough having me in an adjoining room."

Sonny said, "Aisha, to make sure this works we have to put Lucky in an adjoining stateroom but, you would have to feel safe enough, that he's there to look out for you.

You would have to be willing to leave your adjoining door unlocked, so he could get into your room, if you were in any danger."

Aisha replied, "I don't know Lucky very well, but I know he certainly tried to keep me from getting hurt on the volcano. Based on that, I would be willing to leave my adjoining door unlocked."

Lucky said, "Aisha, I would be honored to try to make sure no one harms you in any way on my watch. I think it only fair to tell you that Sonny and Gene thinks the man who killed these women on the ship, also murdered my wife in our home in Beverly Hills, two and half years ago."

"She was killed, while I and six of my buddies were visited wounded veterans in the Los Angeles VA Hospital."

Aisha replied, "OK, Lucky, I understand why you would offer to help look after me so you might be able to catch the man who killed your wife.

"So, when do you want me to move, Sonny?"

"Right now would be good, but the ships staff will move both of you after you have a few minutes to get your things kind of organized for them. One other thing, don't give out your stateroom number to anyone on the ship and that goes for both of you. We will also instruct the reception desk and the telephone operators not to give your stateroom numbers out to anyone."

Two hours later with the help of the Supreme staff, both Lucky and Aisha had all of their belongings moved and put away in their new staterooms.

After the Supreme people left her stateroom. Aisha unlocked and opened the connecting door between Lucky's and her stateroom.

She could plainly see that, Lucky's connecting door was closed as she had been told it would remain, unless she had some kind of a problem.

Aisha heard a knock on her stateroom door. She went to the door and looked through the peek hole and saw it was Sonny Cousins and a maintenance man.

She then opened the door to let them into her stateroom.

Sonny said, "Aisha, this is Tucker Brown and he will be installing your signaling device."

Aisha stood aside and let Sonny and Tucker inside her stateroom.

Tucker said, "I won't take me very long to get your security system set up."

Then Tucker picked up her telephone and connected some wires from a small square plastic box, with a red button in the center of the top of the plastic box, into the base of the telephone.

Then Tucker said, "Captain Cousins, that's all we need to do here. I'll just need to go over to Stateroom 8047 and to your suite and attach the buzzer to the telephone lines. Then we will need to come back here and give the red button a little push to make sure it's works like it should."

Sonny and Tucker left Aisha stateroom and went next door to Lucky's stateroom. There Tucker quickly connected a bell to the base of the telephone.

Then Sonny and Tucker went into Sonny's stateroom and connected a bell to his telephone.

The last thing Tucker had to do now was press the alarm button on Aisha's telephone to be sure both bell would ring if the button was pushed.

Sonny told Lucky, that they were ready to test the alarm system from Aisha's room to his and Sonny's stateroom.

Tucker knocked on Aisha's stateroom door and she opened the door to let him into her stateroom.

Tucker said, "I just need to check to be sure your alarm system works, like it is design to operate."

Tucker pushed the alarm button and both Lucky and Sonny quickly came to Aisha's stateroom.

Lucky came through the connecting door between his stateroom and Aisha's stateroom and Sonny was knocking on Aisha's stateroom door.

Tucker said, "Well, I guess that was a good enough test on the security system, we know it works OK."

Aisha opened her stateroom door to let Sonny in and Sonny saw that Lucky was already standing in the room ready to handle any problem.

Sonny said, "Thank you Tucker, you did a good job of getting an alarm system sit up, for Ms. Charles stateroom."

"No problem, I was glad I could do it. If there isn't anything else I can do for you. I'll get back to my other jobs."

Sonny replied, "No, that's all I can think of, thanks again for your help."

Tucker left the stateroom and Aisha's said, "Well, I guess you two could get to my aid, pretty fast using this system. I have to say, I've never got two men to my aid, that quick in my life."

Sonny laughed and said, "I doubt that you ever had much of a problem getting men to help you, anytime you asked for help."

Aisha responded, "Well I've tried not to ask for too much help in my life, but of course, I've never been in a position where someone was trying to kill me before either.

"Thank you Sonny. Lucky thank you too, it's really appreciated that you are both trying to look after me."

22

The Autopsy Reports from Guam

Three days later Donna received the autopsies reports from the Guam Police Department on the bodies of Ann Walker and Betty Lovejoy.

As soon as she got the autopsies reports she telephoned Sonny to have him and Gene to come up to her office to read them.

The autopsies reports read just like the ones of the first two victims, death by strangulation, no semen in the vagina of either victim, no DNA sample found on either of the victims.

In other words, there wasn't any new evidence that would help them find the killer of these women.

Donna said, "Sonny, what can you do now, without any more leads to work with."

"I don't have any more ideas, how about you Gene?"

"The only thing I know to do right now is keep studying the passengers to see if we could get a clue that one of them might be our killer."

Sonny said, "With 3,225 passengers that could be a lot of studying to see if one of them somehow showed some type of hostility toward women."

Donna said, "My personal experience taught me that most men can show hostility toward women."

Sonny asked, "You mean Donna that you've had personal experiences in your life that lots of men have shown hostility to you?"

Sorry to say, yes I had coming up in the ranks, since a lot of older men resented having a woman in the navy to begin with and then being of equal rank they couldn't stand it."

"Then again a lot of senior officers didn't like women being in their officer core and you can believe me. I got ever crappy assignment they could give me. I really don't know how I made it through some days. I just wouldn't give up."

Gene said, "Donna, that's what we have to do to find our killer, we can never give up."

Sonny piped in, "That's right Donna we never give up."

Donna said," We will be in Singapore in a few days and we have several of our passengers getting off the ship there."

Sonny asked, "I didn't know that you could just take part of the world cruise."

Donna replied, "Yes, passengers can just take segments of the world cruise, there are seven segments on this world cruise."

Gene asked, "So Donna, what are the seven segments of this world cruise?"

"The first segment was San Francisco to Sydney, we are in the second segment right now, from Sydney to Singapore, the third segment is from, Singapore to Dubai, fourth segment from Dubai to Lisbon, fifth segment Lisbon to Rio de Janeiro, sixth segment Rio de Janeiro to Lima and the last or seventh segment, is from Lima to San Francisco."

Sonny asked, "So Donna, how many people will be getting off the ship in Singapore?"

Donna checked her passenger list on her computer and found that 160 people would be leaving the ship in Singapore.

Then she said, "We're having 160 passengers leaving the ship in Singapore and 148 new passengers joining us there."

Gene said, "Maybe this time our killer might get off the ship. In many ways that would be good, except if he does we won't have a chance to catch him."

Sonny replied, "I, for one wouldn't be happy if the killer got off the ship, since we would have failed to find him.

"After killing four women on this ship I don't want him to get away, we owe it to these ladies to find him."

Gene said, "OK, then, Sonny let's get started studying passengers to find our killer."

Sonny replied, "Well if you're waiting for me there no time like the present to get started.

"We'll see you later, Donna."

Sonny and Gene made their way to ship's exercise room and found it was almost empty at this time of day.

Sonny asked the exercise room attendant what time did most of the people come to do their exercises?

She told him that most of the regulars came between six to nine in the mornings.

Sonny thanked her and Gene and he left to go to the main deck where most of the various actives went on.

Arriving on the main deck they found some people were playing bridge, others were having dance lessons, some of the women were making quilts or other sewing projects, but the biggest number of people were attending a port lecture.

Sonny and Gene took seats near the back of the room to listen to Lee Douglas, Shore Tour Director telling about things to see and do in Singapore.

At the end of the talk Sonny and Gene continued to stay seated as they watch the people who had been attending the talk filing out of the room.

They saw Aisha Charles walking out of the room talking with a woman they didn't know.

The two women seemed to be deep in conversation, which as they passed by Sonny heard the unknown woman say, she couldn't decide what one of the tours she wanted to go on.

The woman with Aisha was probably five foot eight in height and of medium built and well dressed in sports clothes.

Gene said, "I would have to say the woman with Aisha was one of our beauty shops blondes and I'd guess she spent a lot of her time doing exercise, since she looks like she in great shape."

Sonny asked, "Did you notice her hands?"

"No Sonny, what should have I noticed about her hands?"

"She had very long fingers and her nails look like she just came from having them done at the Spa."

Gene replied, "I'm sure lots of the women have their nails done at the Spa."

Sonny said, "If we go up to the Spa, we could find out who the woman is, because anyone who we see with Aisha, we need to find out everything we can about them."

"OK, I agree we need to find out who she is and all the information we can obtain about her. Let's go up to the Spa and ask them who she is."

Sonny and Gene went up to the Spa and spoke with the manicurist, who said yes, she certainly remembered who the lady was they described

Her name was Veronica King. Her stateroom was 6066 and the reason the manicurist could remember her so quickly, was the woman gave her a $50 tip for doing her nails this morning and every time she had her nails done.

The manicurist said, "Veronica, is one of the nicest customer we have, she is always saying such nice things to all of us who work here."

Three other people who worked at the Spa agreed, they all said she is truly one of the nicest person's that we have that comes to the Spa.

When Sonny and Gene left the Spa they went directly to customer service and found Alvin, who they had worked with before and asked him to give them all of the information that they had on Veronica King in stateroom 6066.

Alvin went to his computer and looked up Veronica King, after he found her name, he said, "Veronica King is from Los Angeles, California.

"She's 37 years old, born in Los Angeles, single, serviced in the US Army for six years, honorable discharged, wounded in Afghanistan, totally recovered after many months in several VA Hospitals and she is currently unemployed."

Alvin said, "That's all the information we have on Veronica King."

Gene said, "I wonder how she has the money to take this world cruise?"

Sonny replied, "Good question, maybe she has a rich uncle or rich boyfriend who wanted her out of his life for awhile.

"Alvin, two more questions for you. The first one, is do you have her home address, second question, does she have a credit card on file that you use to charge for her monthly charges on the ship.

"Sorry, Alvin, a third question I have for you is, do you have a copy of her passport."

Alvin looked at the computer screen and replied, "Yes, I have her home address, its 4878 Valley View Drive, Los Angeles, CA 90906, her credit card on file is an American Express Platinum Card and her passport number is 8899776666."

Sonny said, "Thank you Alvin. We appreciate your help."

Sonny and Gene left and went up to their rooms. When they arrived there Sonny said, "I going to sent an email to the Kansas City police chief and ask him to see what he can find out about Veronica King."

The following day Sonny received a message back from the KC police chief about Veronica King it read. Very little information on her prior to her inheriting her parents' estate two years ago after they were both killed in a car wreck in Los Angeles.

Veronica served six years in the US Army and was wounded in Afghanistan and was in several VA Hospital prior to her being discharged from the army.

She inherited stock, property, and interest in several businesses that used her father's inventions in their business. He had several patents used in the computer industry. Estimate value of her inheritance is over thirty million dollars.

She recently bought a new home in Los Angeles the address is 4878 Valley View Drive, Los Angeles, CA 90906.

Sonny telephoned Gene and told him what the chief had replied to his email yesterday about Veronica King.

Gene said, "Well, I guess we know how she could afford to take a trip around the world without any problem."

Sonny replied, "Not any problem buying a ticket that's for sure."

Gene answered, "It must be nice not to have to struggle to do anything you ever wanted to do."

"I've told you many times before Gene, you should have never blowing out that knee you would have had all those millions playing basketball."

"Yeah Sonny, but I wouldn't have had you as my best friend, you'd have been too poor."

Sonny laughed and said, "Too bad you're right, you would of have to have somebody like Michael Jordan as your best friend."

"Let me think about that, you or Michael Jordan as my best friend, tough choice!"

23

Visiting Singapore

The next day they arrived in Singapore and Sonny, Jane, Gene and Susan were going on tours on their day in Singapore. The ship would be in docked in Singapore until late that night and depart about midnight.

Sonny had read and heard about a famous old hotel in Singapore, where many of the famous writers from years long ago spend lots of their time in a hotel called the Raffles. It seems they made the Raffles their home, and he wanted to see it.

Plus, the Long Bar at the Raffles was where their bartender invented a drink called the Singapore Sling. Sonny thought it would be neat to go to the hotel and each of them have a Singapore Sling at the Long Bar and then have dinner at the hotel.

Their tour would take them to the Singapore Zoo for Breakfast with the Orangutans, the National Orchid Garden, and a Driving Tour of Central Singapore and to the Top of Mt. Faber and then Chinatown.

They left the ship at eight am and boarded a bus, along with about another thirty of the ship's passengers going to the Singapore Zoo. The local guide who joined them this morning told them the Singapore Zoo was one of the top rate Zoo's in the world and one of the first zoo's to ever have very large spaces for all of their animals

The trip took over an hour to get to their destination and when they arrived there, the driver parked as close to the entrance gate to the zoo as he could.

Everyone got off the bus as quickly as they could and begin walking to the restaurant area of the zoo after they reached the entrance gate of the zoo their Supreme Tour Guide, Jean Evans, had tickets for each one of them so they could quickly pass through the entrance gate.

After they were inside the zoo, the group continued to walk for another fifteen or twenty minutes before they reached the zoo's cafeteria, there the staff was ready for their group, they were quickly seated around several tables.

While they were being seated the woman who was seating them, told them as soon as they were ready, they could help themselves to their breakfast.

The lines at the serving areas quickly filled up and Sonny said, "Jane, why don't you and Susan go ahead and fill your plates. Gene and I will wait for you and stay at the table and watch your purses.

"You know we take a lot longer filling our plates, since we eat so much more then you two do."

Jane replied, "OK, you two stay, get us coffee and orange juice and we'll fill our plates."

Jane and Susan left the table to get their food, as Sonny and Gene waited.

Soon a waitress came by their table with coffee and water.

Sonny asked the waitress for coffee and water for the four of them and asked if they could please get four glasses of orange juice.

The waitress poured their coffee and water and told him she would be back with four glasses of orange juice for them.

Sonny thanked her and she left, just after she left. Jane and Susan returned to their table with their plates full of food.

Gene said, "Your plates of food sure looks good."

Susan replied, "They got a lot of good choices, we only made it through the first serving table."

Jane added, "Yes, they have three food serving tables set up for our breakfast, lots of choices."

Sonny said, OK, Gene lets gets some of the food before there isn't anything left."

Sonny and Gene made their way to the first serving table and by the time they were at the end of the first serving table both of their plates were full.

As the four of them were eating their breakfast, a young man with a microphone appeared a little ways from their table and said, "Good morning ladies and gentlemen.

"My name is Roger and I'm your host for this morning's breakfast with the Orangutans.

"Right now, I'm going to ask one of our special families of Orangutans to join us for breakfast."

Roger said, "Where is my Orangutan family? Oh, I see you coming, come on down and have breakfast with us."

A male Orangutan came down next to Roger and Roger put his hand out and the male Orangutan placed his hand in Roger's hand.

Roger said, "So, where is your mate and your little one?"

The male Orangutan turned his head and looked back at the area where he had just come and you could see a female Orangutan with a young one next to her coming over a big rock.

Roger said to the male, "You better go help mommy bring your baby here for breakfast."

The male let loose of Roger's hand and gracefully climbed up to where the female and baby were, then the three of them came down and sit in an area just above where Roger was standing.

The three of them looked at Roger, then Roger and another man begin giving the three of them some kind of food and the Orangutans continued to sit and have their breakfast.

Roger told the audience if you would like to have your picture taken with them, you can come here and we will take your picture with the Orangutan family.

Jane and Susan both said, "We want our picture with the Orangutans."

So Sonny and Gene dutifully got up and joined the girls as they got in line to have their pictures taken with the Orangutan family.

As they waited in line for their pictures with the Orangutans, they heard Roger telling about the problem the Orangutans are having in the wild today because in the areas that was once their natural home has been destroyed by men harvesting their trees and building homes in their areas of their world.

Roger said "The Orangutan's DNA is a 97% match to human's DNA, only the chimpanzee with a 99% DNA match to human's DNA is closer."

Jane said, "Sonny, now I know way you are always wanting to monkey around."

Sonny, Susan and Gene laughed at her statement.

Then the woman who was taking the pictures, told Sonny and Jane they were next to have their picture taken with the Orangutan's.

Another woman who was helping the photographer, positioned Sonny and Jane in front of the Orangutan family and the photographer took their picture.

Gene and Susan were next soon the four of them would have a souvenir of their breakfast with an Orangutan family, as soon as they paid their twenty Singapore Dollars for each picture.

They were told they could pick up their pictures at the photographer's booth as they were exiting the zoo.

After breakfast, they took a tram ride that took them all around the very large zoo. This trip took them an hour.

They still had time to walk around some of the areas that they had the most interest in. They were scheduled to meet back at the bus at 12:30.

They walked back to where the elephants were and saw several elephants playing in the water and they seemed to be having a great time doing it.

As they were making their way back to the exit, they came by an exhibit of Dinosaurs. They found it was very well done, using man made models of the various Dinosaurs and they were placed in areas of trees and bushes.

As you walked through the exhibit these Dinosaurs would move and make you think they were alive.

A few times when the four of them walked along, the two women were not the only ones who jumped, when suddenly a large head moved out over their heads or something moved in the bushes as they walked by.

After they finished walking through the Dinosaur jungle they begin their trek back to the bus.

When they arrived at the photographer booth they paid for their pictures, boarded the bus and were very happy they had the experience at the Singapore Zoo.

Their next stop would be the National Orchid Garden. They found there were more than a thousand different orchid plants growing in this beautiful Orchid Garden.

Everything was well displayed, clean and neat unlike any place else they would see on their world trip.

Their local guide explained why that was in Singapore. She said Singapore is known as a fine city, because they will charge you a fine for everything.

Throwing trash on the street; driving too fast or driving too slow; walking across the streets, you name it they have a fine for it.

She told them you can't have chewing gum in Singapore, you will be paying a fine and god help you if you have any kind of drugs, the penalty is death!

Gene said after hearing all of this, "Singapore is a beautiful place to visit, but I don't think I would want to live here."

Sonny replied, "Well one thing for sure, the drug problem in the USA would certainly drop fast if the penalty for having drugs was death.

If that was the case we wouldn't have had to be concerned about arresting people a second, third, fourth and how many more times for drugs if they executed the people after we arrested them and they were convicted in court the first time."

Mary said, "Sonny, do you really think we should have that kind of law in America?"

"No."

Susan said, "Well I wish we didn't have the drug problem that we have, but so many people get hooked on drugs when they are very young and have no idea of what kind of problems they will have in the future."

Gene said, "OK, let's enjoy our time in Singapore and not try to change the way they run their city. They can run it the way they want to without any of our help."

They arrived back at bus and climbed back onto the bus and found their seats and sat down and they were ready for their next stop in Singapore.

After their guide, Jean Evans accounted for all her folks they were off to Mount Faber.

When they arrived there, their local guide said, "We will be here for only about twenty minutes.

"Mount Faber is one of the highest points in the city and you will have a great view of the city and the harbors below you.

They also saw a sky lift, something like a ski lift that came from somewhere down in the city and then it turned around at the top of Mount Faber without stopping and went back down to where ever it started from.

They saw a lot of people riding the lift and seemed to be enjoying the view and the ride.

They walked around a short time and were back on the bus waiting for their guide and the rest of the passengers to get back on the bus.

Their next destination was the tour of the business area of the city. As they were driven around the city center, they saw the Raffles Hotel next they made a stop at the Singapore China Town.

They were told they had about thirty minutes at this stop. Mary and Susan both found several pieces of clothes they bought at a very reasonable price, OK, they were very cheap.

Sonny and Gene tagged along behind them and while the girls were finding more treasures.

Sonny saw at one of the booths what looked like some very old US Silver Dollars.

Sonny always liked the idea of collecting coins, but never had the money to pursue actually collecting coins. He asked the Chinese Gentleman how much he wanted for the coins he was told five US Dollars for five coins.

That meant that Sonny would be buying silver dollars for five US Dollars, so he paid the man the five dollars, in one dollar bills.

Sonny picked out the oldest coins he could find, out of the little basket that the coins were in. The man placed the coins in a small plastic bag and Sonny put them in his pocket.

Sonny thought when he got home he would talk to a friend who owned a coin shop about how much these coins would be worth today.

It was soon time to load back on the bus to go back to the ship since the tour would be finished.

After they were on the bus, they decided they would get a taxi and go back to the city and to the Raffles Hotel for their Singapore Slings and dinner.

They returned to the ship and they went back to their staterooms and dressed in better clothing to go to the Raffles Hotel.

They got a taxi from the ship to the hotel and made their way to the Long Bar, except it was closed for remodeling, so they went to the bar in the Billiard's Room.

They were shown to table for four people and they were given a drink menu and saw the price was $32 for a Singapore Sling. Unlike most of the countries they would be traveling to the exchange rate between a US Dollar and a Singapore Dollar was almost the same.

However, Sonny was determined to have his Singapore Sling, so when their waiter came to their table they all ordered the Raffles famous Singapore Sling.

They soon had their drinks and a large bowl of peanuts in the shell, while they waited for their drinks they read the story about how this drink came about.

It seems in 1915 women having a glass of whiskey in public was not considered the proper thing, so a Raffles bartender invented a drink that the ladies could order in public which would kind of look like they were have a glass of Lemonade and the Singapore Sling was invented.

The ladies loved it and it soon became a popular drink for both men and women.

Their Singapore Slings cost them $32 a person but all four of them enjoyed their drink, and it made it extra special having their Singapore Slings where the drink was invented 102 years ago.

They finished their day in Singapore by having dinner at the Writers Grill, where famous writers like Noel Coward; Rudyard Kipling; ate while living at the hotel.

Again, it was very expensive but certainly a real change from eating on the ship day after day. They found that almost every famous actor in the world had at one time been a guest at the Raffles Hotel, such as: John Wayne; Charlie Chaplin; Clark Gable; Grace Kelly; Gary Cooper and Royalty from all around the world.

In short, it was the place to stay in Singapore.

They took a taxi back to the ship and Sonny and Gene both said it was a wonderful day they got to spend with their wives and not even thinking about women being murdered on the ship.

A few minutes after midnight Captain Donna, along with the local pilot steered the Golden Supreme out of the Singapore Harbor and soon after clearing the harbor they dropped off the Singapore Pilot and then her ship would be bound for Cochin, India.

24

Going to the Taj Mahal

They were scheduled to be in Cochin, India in four days, there they would leave the ship and fly to Delhi from Delhi they would take a fast train to Agra to see the Taj Mahal.

To return to the ship, they would return to Delhi by bus then fly to Mumbai. In Mumbai, they would rejoin the Golden Supreme and then be heading to its next stop, Dubai.

The four of them decided to attend the port talk by the Shore Tour Director, Lee Douglas, who was very good at giving a helpful information about each port they would be visiting.

Lee had been to every port they would be visiting and probably on every tour offered by Supreme, since he had been doing this for over twenty-five years. They were soon doing the things Lee told them about their tour.

In Cochin they were taken on a windshield tour of the city and they make a stop to see local fishermen at the fish market using a device called a Chinese Fishing Net to catch fish.

The Chinese introduced this system to the world centuries ago, but they no longer used them, now these nets were only used in India.

The tourists got an opportunity to help use this special devices to help the fishermen catch some fish.

The local fishermen actually got the tourists to help them pull up some very long ropes, which had several very large rocks attached to the ropes used to hold the net under water.

When the tourists pulled the large rocks up, the net followed out of the water as the weight of the rocks helped pull the net out of the water.

Once the net was out of the water, two local fishermen took the fish caught in the net and put them into large containers to be sold right here at the fish market.

Sonny thought it was a pretty slick move by the local fishermen to let the tourist work at pulling up their nets and helping them catch fish for them to sell later.

Anyway, all of the tourists thought it was great fun and had an opportunity to do something that they couldn't have done any other place in the world.

Soon the tour of the City of Cochin was finished and the bus took them to the airport to begin their quest to see the Taj Mahal.

When they got to the airport and the Supreme Staff was ready to hand out the plane tickets to each of the ninety-two passengers and the four Supreme staff who would be traveling with the passengers on this tour it was pure chaos.

The four Supreme Staff members didn't know any of the passengers traveling on this tour, since they had just joined the crew in Singapore this morning and they couldn't pronounce the passengers names correctly.

Everyone was crowed into an area half the size needed for this many people and the announcements being broadcast over the public addresses system, was also drowning out the staff members voices trying to call out the name of the people on the tickets.

Finally, two of the passengers nearest to the two staff members told them to give them the tickets and they would call out the passenger's name on the tickets.

Since the two staff members were from Serbia and most of the passengers were from the USA, the two American's were able to begin getting the tickets to the right people.

Sonny was now beginning to understand what one of the Indian guides said, "It's India."

Soon the four friends from Kansas City traveling on this trip would completely understand the word *Chaos* was just another name for *India*.

What should have taken maybe 30 to 40 minutes to hand out everyone their plane tickets took well over an hour?

OK, now they had to go through security, another surprise, the women had to go through one line and the men, through another.

Of course the women's line took two to three times longer to go through than the men.

Sonny, thought the security stations, such be like what he thought public toilets for women should be.

They should have twice the number of security stations as the men did and they should have at least twice the number of toilet stalls as the men did.

It was hard to believe, but finally all of the passengers made it through security and to the departure gate.

They were probably there for less than fifteen minutes before they started loading the plane and the 96 Supreme passengers were scattered through -out the plane, with almost none of the couples seated next to each other.

Gene and Susan seats were located in the middle of the plane and they were able to load through the front door of the plane. Their seats were about three rows apart with both of them in middle seats.

Sonny though with Gene's long legs, he certainly wasn't going to be a happy camper for a three hour plus flight.

Sonny and Mary were in the back of the plane, Sonny's seat was a window seat on one side of the aisle, and Mary had a middle seat on the other side of the aisle and three rows ahead of Sonny's.

Finally, the plane was completely load with its crew; passengers and luggage and it was ready for take- off and away they went into the air and on their way to Delhi.

Three hours and fifteen minutes later, their miserable crammed flight came to an end, as the pilot landed in Delhi. The pilot taxied the plane to a parking space some way away from the terminal.

Everyone started getting out of the plane going down stairways at the front and back of the plane all of the passengers had to board buses to be taken to the terminals.

When Sonny made it down the stairway, he could see they were quite a ways from the terminal.

Sonny was waiting at the bottom of the stairway for Mary and she soon caught up with him.

As they begin walking to the buses, they saw Gene and Susan were already getting on a bus to take them from the plane's parking area to the terminal.

Before Sonny and Mary made it to Gene and Susan's bus, the buses' doors closed and drove away on its way to the terminal.

Sonny and Mary quickly changed directions and got onto the next bus, it was as crowded as the plane, but at least the trip to the terminal was much shorter.

Arriving at the terminal, Sonny and Mary saw Gene and Susan waiting for them as when they entered the terminal.

The four of them, begin walking to catch up with other Supreme Passengers going out of the secure area of the airport.

As soon as they left the secure area of the airport their Supreme Guide, Jane Evans was waiting for them to direct them to a location in the terminal that she wanted them to wait until she had all thirty passengers in her group.

When all of her people were there, they would load onto a bus and be taken on a windshield tour of New Delhi and then to their hotel.

When Jean had all of her group, which was Group 2, out of three groups on the Taj Mahal tour they would all walk to their bus as a group

After they begin walking, they found their bus was some distance from the terminal.

When Jean had been waiting for all of her group, the local Indian guide for Group 2 of the Taj Mahal tour arrived to help her get her people to the bus.

They would soon find he was a very knowledgeable on everything about the area and he would be staying with Group 2, until they left Delhi on their flight to Mumbai.

There they would rejoin their ship to continue on their world cruise.

Now that all members of Group 2 had arrived, Jean and her local Indian Guide begin leading all of them to their bus.

The walk took them about twenty minutes, before they got to the waiting bus and soon everyone was on the bus.

When each of them arrived at the bus the bus driver placed a garland of Marigold's around each of the pilgrim's neck.

The bus began making its way out of the parking lot and into the traffic bound for New Delhi.

After everyone had an opportunity to get settled in their seats, Jean picked up the bus's microphone and introduced their Indian guide for their tour of the Taj Mahal, his name was, Sunsil.

Jean gave the microphone to Sunsil and he began to explain that the airport was quite a ways out of New Delhi and this was rush hour.

He said, "You can see the traffic coming out of the city is much greater than the traffic going into the city at this time of day.

"Many of the people who work in the government offices live outside of New Delhi. They can get a much larger and nicer home out of the city for the what they would have to pay if they bought a home in New Delhi.

"He added however in a few minutes we will have another major highway merging with our highway and it will cause us to be slowed down a lot."

Truer words would never be spoken, when they begin to merger with the other highway, the traffic was dead stopped and the a snail would be passing them if he was in a race with their bus.

The bus crawled along with the other traffic and there was everything on the road from cars, trucks, motorcycles, scooters, bicycles, people walking and even a three wheeled bicycle with two passengers sitting in small compartment with a man propel the people down the road.

The highway was a four lane road but in some of the areas of the road there were as many as six vehicles of various types occupying the four lanes.

It was apparent to Sonny, that the main device used on all of the vehicles in India, were their horns, even their bus driver was constantly honking his horn, along with all of the other vehicles on the highway.

Sunsil said, "Before your stay in India is over you will have full knowledge of the term OMG!"

Finally, their bus managed to get off of the highway and onto one of the city streets.

The traffic was less, but the traffic signals were plentiful and now they had many more people walking in the street or dashing across the streets in between vehicles.

Sonny, watched in fear for the people just running across streets, these people seemed to be without any thought for their own safety.

Sunsil continued to tell the visitors about the various statues as they passed by them, most of the statues were people Sonny never knew who they were but when they passed by several statues of Mohandas K. Gandhi and Jawaharlal Nehru, even Sonny recognized their names and who they were.

Sunsil, commented on all of the many of the government buildings as they drove past them, including the Prime Minister's residence, India's Arch of Triumph and a new stainless steel Mosque which was shaped like a Lotus Blossom, they were all very beautiful.

Sunsil said, "New Delhi has laws completely different than any other city in India, no cows are permitted to roam around the streets.

You will also see that the streets are very clean and without trash blowing around everywhere as you will see in Old Delhi and Agra.

They also passed by the many embassies as they made their way to the hotel. Sonny saw the Embassies of Russia; Iran; Turkey; the United States; United Kingdom and many other countries.

All were very beautiful and their grounds were maintained beautifully. Very impressive it was as impressive as the ones in Washington D.C.

When they finally arrived at their hotel, all of the pilgrims were exhausted as they had to be up at four am to be ready to make the trip to visit the Taj Mahal.

The first thing they encountered when they arrived at the entrance to the hotel was two very large iron gates covering the entrance to the hotel parking lot.

A few minutes passed before the gates sung open and then their bus was met by hotel security people, who took a long pole device with a large mirror and a light on the end of the pole and slide it under the bus checking to be sure no bombs were under the bus.

After the security people cleared the bus, the driver pull the bus up to the front door of the Sheraton Hotel and the passengers began to get off the bus.

Then each passenger than had to pass through an electronic security device just like the ones used by airports around the world.

Then finally the pilgrims were allowed inside the hotel were each one was given a dot on their forehead as the symbol of the Hindu Religion.

Their hotel rooms were previously assigned and the Supreme Guide for their group Jean Evans took the key cards and begin calling out the names of the guests, one by one everyone soon had their card keys for their room.

When Jean handed out the key cards she told them dinner was sit up in a banquet room and each of them would be getting a wake up call at four am to be sure everyone was ready for their train trip to Agra to visit the Taj Mahal.

Sonny; Jane; Gene and Susan were all on the same floor so they quickly got an elevator up to their floor, dropped off their luggage in their rooms and make a quick potty stop before the four of them heading down for dinner.

Everyone, but Sonny enjoyed the Indian Dinner but since Sonny hated curry, his dinner was bread and butter, and as much fruit as he could find.

Soon everyone in their group finished their dinner and was on their way to get as much sleep as they could before they had to be up again at four am.

Jane, set the alarm on her little travel clock for three thirty because she didn't want to have to be rushed so much, since they were to be on the bus at five am.

Sonny was having his usual problem of getting to sleep but Jane was asleep almost before her head hit the pillow.

Sonny was jealous of her ability to get to sleep, so fast when he was still awake at twelve thirty. Jane had been asleep for over two hours as he was tossing and turning trying to get to sleep.

Jane always told him his problem must be a guilty conscious that kept him awake so long.

He thought if that's what it was, too bad he didn't remember have that much fun in his life or that he had been that bad.

Although some of the people he had arrested for murder had been executed for their crime.

Finally, he made it asleep before the alarm on Jane's clock went off at three-thirty.

25

The Visit to the Taj Mahal

Jane's travel clock's alarm began ringing at three thirty, just as Sonny was really beginning to be in deep sleep.

Jane reached for her clock and turned off the alarm as Sonny rolled over and started to get up when he realized that Jane was getting up.

So he rolled back over and would be content to lie in bed for another thirty minutes, while Jane had time to go to the bathroom and have her shower.

Well he didn't make it for thirty minutes when he realized he hadn't made them coffee. He was pleased they had a small sink in the entrance area of their room; with a coffee pot and an adequate supply of coffee and sweeter.

Sonny filled the coffee pot with water and plugged the power plug into an outlet and turned the coffee pot on, then took the two coffee cups, torn opened the packets of instant coffee and put the coffee into the cups and a packet of sweetener in Jane's cup.

The water came to a boil in only a couple of minutes, then the coffee pot automatically shut off then Sonny poured the hot water into the cups.

Sonny stirred the coffee around in each of the cups as Jane came out of the bathroom and said, "Good boy, you've got coffee ready."

Sonny replied, "Of course I do, it's my job everyday to be sure my love's coffee is ready for her when she's ready for it."

"Thank you love, you do a good job of it every morning, it's appreciated. You know I got to have my coffee to start my day."

"Jane, you are very welcome. I'm glad I can do something for you, since you do so much for me."

Sonny went into the bathroom and took a very quick shower, dried off and blew his hair dry, combed it, then put on his hair spray to keep it from blowing away with the slight breath of air.

Shaved and got himself dressed and was soon ready to go, just as Jane was finishing doing her makeup and they were both ready for the day.

They left their room and made their way downstairs and found their breakfast was been prepared to be boxed up and given to them on the train.

They were able to get another cup of coffee and by that time they were joined by Gene and Susan.

Their local guide, Sunsil said, "They would have different buses this morning to take them to the train station.

"Because after our driver brought them from the airport and drove them around the city last night. He dropped everyone off at the hotel he drove his bus to Agra so he could meet our train when we arrive there this morning."

"Sunsil also said, "Our bus driver will drive us around in Agra, then bring us back to New Delhi and to the hotel for the night and then pick us up at the hotel the next morning to take us to Old Delhi, then to the airport for your flight to Mumbai.

"I see that all of my people for bus two are here. So this morning we have a new driver and bus to take us to the train station, so let's get loaded and be on our way to the train station."

Soon all of his people were on the bus and on their way to the train station and they would soon be followed by the other people on bus one and three.

The trip to the train station was much easier than the trip that had during rush hour last night to their hotel.

They were soon ready to get out of the bus and walk about three blocks to the train station, which was as close to the station as the bus could get.

Sonny was surprised to see how many people were at the train station and either waiting for their train or meeting someone coming on a train.

There were people begging on the streets and other people trying to sell things to the people going to the train station.

Sunsil advised them to keep looking down and don't make eye contact with people trying to sell you something and never let them put whatever they are selling into your hands, because they considered the item sold, if you have it in your hand.

The sights and sounds of the city were overwhelming to them and the dirt and trash all around them was something none of them were used to seeing.

The various classes of people from beggars, business people, women, dressed in all types of clothing, women with babies or small children asking for money, disfigured men who were missing hands or parts of legs, all of these people were very difficult for Sonny to ignore.

He would have like to help all of these people looking for a handouts, but there would be no end to them in a country with one and half billion people.

Finally, Sonny knew he had to do what Sunsil told them to do, keep his eyes down to the walkway and keep going to the railroad station.

Eventual, all ninety two of the tourists and their guides made it to the train station and to the track where their train would be arriving.

The Supreme Guides handed out tickets for each of the passengers and they would be located throughout the various train cars.

Sonny Jane, Gene and Susan were all in the same car and at least the couples had seats next to each other, unlike their plane seats.

Their train arrived on time and all of them boarded the train and found their seats, a few minutes later, young boys began passing out the boxes with their breakfast made by the hotel.

They had all been told not to buy any food from anywhere except where Supreme had made arrangements for their meals they were told it was too risking for them to eat food that who know how it had been handled and prepared.

Sonny was sure if he bought anything except where Supreme arranged for their food, he was certain to get sick, he didn't do will with any kind of strange food.

The breakfast supplied by the hotel was fine, except there wasn't nearly enough of it for Sonny, since breakfast was his big meal for the day.

Jane gave him half of her breakfast, which would hold him until lunchtime, he hoped.

They didn't realize their train was one of the fast trains in India, they arrived in Agra in just a little more than an hour, that was even after making one short stop on the way there.

Everyone quickly got off the train and they soon saw Sunsil standing with a Supreme number two sign, they all made their way to where he was standing soon all of their group was gathered around him.

He then lead them to bus two, which was waiting with the door open and their driver standing at the bottom of the stairs ready to help anyone who might require help getting on the bus.

They were off as soon as everyone was on board and the driver drove them to a very large Hindu Temple, there everyone was off the bus and Sunsil took the ones who wanted to go inside the Temple with him, he advised them that everyone had to remove their shoes and leave them outside.

Sonny remained outside because he didn't think he could get his shoes back on, without somewhere to either sit down or get his feet up and have a shoe horn to help him.

Sonny found plenty of things to look at, as the monks were selling firecrackers and what appeared to be bundles of money.

Then the people would take over their bundle of money and the firecrackers to two other monks, who were stationed at a large what appeared to be a giant fireplace.

These monks would take the bundles of money and put it on the fire and at the same time they would sit off the firecrackers to get the attention of the saints for the people's sacrifices.

Before too long the tour group was back on the bus headed for the Taj Mahal and driving through streets with ever kind of vehicle that the world knew about driving along with them and in Agra, and unlike New Delhi, the sacred cows were walking or lying on the streets.

The vehicles had to make their way around them. Sonny had no idea how all of this traffic could possibly get anywhere but they did.

One thing for sure in India, the horns on the vehicles were the most used device that their vehicle had. It was honk and honk and honk.

Sonny had no idea how the driver did it, but they were soon at a location where the bus could park as close as the bus could get to the Taj Mahal.

Everyone got off the bus and began following Sunsil and his bus two sign and after walking ten or fifteen minutes. They arrived at the entrance to the Taj Mahal.

Here they waited, until the Supreme Guides picked up their tickets for their entrance into the Taj Mahal.

Tickets were dispensed to all of the passengers and Sunsil begin lining up his people to get them all inside the gate to see the object of every person in their group's purpose for making this special trip, *"The Taj Mahal."*

They would soon have the opportunity to have their first view of it.

Sonny and Jane kind of held their breath until they made it through the gate and caught their first look at the gleaming white Taj Mahal.

It didn't disappoint them it was everything they had hoped it would be it was breath taking beautiful.

As soon as all of the people from bus two made it inside the gate. Sunsil begin positioning all of them to stand on a high walking area, there he had a photographer waiting to take a group picture using the Taj Mahal as the background for their group picture.

The photographer quickly took several photos of the group.

After the photographer finished taking their group picture, Sunsil announced they would each be getting a copy of the picture at no cost at the end of today's tour.

Sonny asked the photographer how much he would charge them to take several photos of him and Jane during their stay at the Taj Mahal.

The photographer told them he would charge them fifty US Dollars and this price would also include an album with them in several poses, along with some special pictures of the Taj Mahal that he had taken at different times of the day of the Taj Mahal.

Sonny agreed to his price and the photographer beginning taking lots of pictures of Sonny and Jane with several different poses and at many different locations on the Taj Mahal grounds.

Sonny had no idea how many he picture he took of them, but Sonny knew he took a lot.

Sonny and Jane saw that everything about the gardens of the Taj Mahal was beautifully maintained.

Sonny had no doubt in his mind that this was the cleanest and best maintained place in all of India.

Sonny, Jane, Gene and Susan made it up to the place where they would soon actually be going inside the Taj Mahal, but first they needed to buy some shoe covers to go over their shoes, so their shoes wouldn't mark up the floors.

They found many of the Indian people simply went barefooted through the Taj Mahal.

The cost for the shoe covers wasn't much, one US Dollar for two pairs of the foot covers, which looked like they were clear plastic shower caps.

The four of them put their foot covers on and walked up the stairs to go inside the Tal Mahal and when they got to the doors.

Guards were working trying to maintain some kind of order to the crush of people trying to get through the doors.

The guards had their hands full, as people were coming from two sides to get through the same two small doors.

They finally made it through the doors, although it took them several tries to make it since people pushed and shoved themselves through the doors in front of them.

American's, unlike what most of the world might think, Americans were generally not pushy in a crowd.

When they got inside, they had to walk only one way through the entire building, the first thing they walked passed, was what you would think was the crypts of Emperor Shan Jahan and Mumtaz Mahal, however their bodies are actually entombed below these false crypts.

Sonny figured by hiding their real tombs below was to keep tomb raiders from being able to disturb their bodies.

They learn a lot about the Taj Mahal, such as it took twenty-two years to build it and was built as a loving monument from Shan Jahan to his love, Mumtaz, Mumtaz died shortly after giving birth to her fourteen baby.

Seeing the Taj Mahal was the main reason Jane wanted to make the world cruise. She saw it and wasn't disappointed it was everything she hoped it would be.

They were told the crowd was light today compared to the crowds on the weekends, when anywhere from twenty-five thousand to as many as fifty thousand people might be here on a weekend.

Sonny was concerned that their photographer hadn't found them to give them their pictures and collect his fifty US Dollars.

When Sonny said something about it to Sunsil, Sunsil, told him not to worry he would find them and Sonny would get his pictures.

They only had one more stop in Agra and that was for lunch and they drove about maybe a mile or two before the bus turned into a gated restaurant and the gates opened as the bus approached the gates, the bus drove inside the fenced property.

Sunsil said, "You may leave your things in the bus, because it will be locked and you can all come into the restaurant for a nice lunch."

Everyone got off the bus and the driver locked the bus as soon as all of his passengers went inside the restaurant.

Sunsil was right as always, their lunch was ready and waiting for them at their tables and after they finished their lunch, everyone was looking for the toilets before they got back on the bus for their trip back to New Delhi.

When Sonny returned from the restroom he saw his photographer waiting in the lobby of the restaurant, of course Sunsil was right their photographer found him and several other people that he had taken pictures of at the Taj Mahal.

The photographer smiled and handed Sonny an album with his and Jane pictures, along with several other pictures the photographer had taken during times when there weren't any people in the pictures of the Taj Mahal at all.

Jane arrived just at that moment and Sonny handed the album to her, she approved and Sonny paid the photographer his fifty US Dollars.

Sonny and Jane stood aside and looked the pictures over very carefully and Sonny said to Jane, "The man did a great job. I've going to give him a ten dollar tip."

Jane agreed and Sonny walked over to the photographer and said, "Thank you, we think you did a great job."

Then Sonny handed him a ten dollar bill.

The photographer looked at the ten dollar bill and said, "Thank you. It was my pleasure working with both of you."

Sonny and Jane went directly to the bus, since many of the other passengers had already made their way to the bus, including Gene and Susan.

Jane said to Susan, "You have to see our pictures the photographer took of us at the Taj Mahal."

Jane handed the photo album to Susan who looked it over and said to Jane, "I'm sorry we didn't have the guy take a bunch of pictures of Gene and me there too.

"It's too late now, but at least we got the group picture."

The bus was now on its way back to New Delhi, they would have an opportunity to get a better view of the India countryside riding on the bus instead of their fast train where everything outside the windows was kind of a streak.

Sonny was surprised to see how much open land there was available with small farms dotting the countryside and lots of very small coal mines.

They also saw a lot of wind powered turbines producing electricity, as they drove through the countryside.

Sunsil told them India was depending on producing much of their electric in the future using wind power and planned that in five years they would produce sixty percent of their electricity with wind power.

The fast little train ride from Delhi to Agra, in just over an hour was replaced by more than a four hour trip on the bus back from Agra to Delhi.

When they got back to New Delhi it was almost the same time that they had arrived there last night and they were back in the rush hour traffic again.

By the time they made it to their hotel and went through the hotel security procedures it was after eight o'clock.

Sunsil told them dinner would be ready for them in the same room as it was last night and they would be getting their wake up call at four am again tomorrow morning.

Their bus would pick them up at five thirty in the morning to travel to Old Delhi to take a ride in the human powered three wheel bicycles through the streets of Old Delhi and then visit some of the markets before their flight to Mumbai.

Dinner for everyone was just fine, except Sonny who wouldn't eat anything but bread and butter and fruit, since he wouldn't eat the India food. He didn't like the spices they use to favorite their dishes.

He ate a lot of watermelon and apples and Sonny thought the bread was just great, everyone to their own taste.

The same drill for the third day in a row, Jane was up at three-thirty and in the shower and Sonny was making coffee.

When Jane was out of the shower, Sonny took a quick shower and before it was four thirty they were both ready to go.

The difference this morning was that the restaurant was going to open at five this morning for them, so they would have the opportunity to have breakfast before they left the hotel.

A few minutes before five, Sonny and Jane were waiting along with a couple of other folks from their group for the restaurant to open.

About five minutes after five the restaurant opened and Sonny and Jane picked a table for four and a waiter brought them some coffee and water.

They decided to go ahead and get something to eat, instead of waiting for Gene and Susan too arrive.

Jane told Sonny to go ahead and she would wait and hold their table and watch for Gene and Susan.

Sonny filled his plate with eggs and wheat toast and another plate with watermelon and cantaloupe.

Gene and Susan still hadn't made an appearance in the restaurant when Sonny returned to the table.

So Jane made her way over to where the food was and filled her plate and returned back to their table.

Sonny had been waiting for Jane, before he started eating and after she returned Jane gave a short prayer for them.

After she finished her prayer, she saw Gene and Susan coming through the restaurant door and Gene saw Sonny and Jane at the table.

Gene and Susan made their way over to Sonny and Jane's table and Gene said, "Good Morning to you folks.

"How's breakfast Sonny, did you find something you would eat besides bread and watermelon?"

"Yes, I did, they had some very good fried eggs and of course toast and my watermelon."

Susan said, "How's the coffee Jane?"

"It's better than the instant coffee we had in our room that's for sure."

Sonny said, "You guys better get something to eat, we're going to have to leave this place in about twenty minutes."

Gene replied, "OK, you don't have to tell me twice to get food, because the way this trip has gone. I know for sure they never plan to fed us, unlike the ship where there always food available."

Gene and Susan quickly filled their plates and were back at the table just as the waiter was finishing filling their coffee cups and their water glasses.

Sonny asked, "Jane, are you through with everything in our room, if you are I'll go get our bag and check out at the front desk?"

Jane replied, "Yes, I'm ready to go. I packed up all of my things in our suitcase, but take a look around the room and the bathroom to be sure I didn't leave anything,"

"Yes dear. I'll take one last look to be sure we have everything out of both rooms."

"Good boy, I'll see you in the lobby after Gene and Susan finish their breakfast."

Sonny took the elevator up to their floor and went into their room and checked the rooms over and he found Jane had indeed packed up everything.

He closed the suitcase and locked it and was on his way back to the lobby.

When he arrived at the lobby he didn't see Jane, Gene or Susan anywhere in the lobby yet, so he went to the front desk and returned their key cards. They asked him if they had anything from the min bar.

Sonny told them no, they didn't have anything from the min bar.

Sonny found an area in the lobby with enough seating for the four of them and sat down to wait.

A few minutes passed and Jane and Susan joined him, while Gene went upstairs to get his and Susan's suitcase.

A short time later Gene returned with their suitcase and he dropped off his key cards at the front desk and the four of them were ready to go.

Sonny saw Sunsil walking through the lobby encouraging all of his bus two people to get on the bus, but before Sunsil came to where they were seated.

The four of them begin walking to the front door of the hotel to board their bus. When they arrived at their bus the driver was taking suitcases and putting them in the compartment under the bus.

Sonny and Gene gave their suitcases to the driver as Jane and Susan got on the bus to find them four seats that were close together.

When Sonny and Gene got on the bus they found where the girls were sitting and took seats next to their wives.

Not long after they were seated Sunsil did a quick check to be sure all of his people were on the bus and found they were all aboard.

A couple of people in the front of the bus shouted, our Supreme Guide, Jean Evans isn't on the bus!"

Sunsil replied, "No, she's not on the bus, she's gone ahead to the airport to get everyone's boarding pass. That way, when we get to the airport, the boarding passes can be quickly hand out to everyone."

Then Sunsil told the bus driver we are ready to go.

The bus driver drove out of the hotel's gated parking lot and was soon in the morning traffic on his way to Old Delhi.

Traffic in Old Delhi was a lot different than the traffic in New Delhi, the streets were much narrower and the cows wandered down the streets and some plod down in the middle of the street and the traffic had to find its way around them.

One thing was for sure, there were still as many people and vehicles in Old Delhi as in New Delhi and Sonny, Mary, Gene and Susan was soon going to enjoying the experience of being right in the middle of all of the traffic riding in one of those three wheeled bikes powered by a human.

Their bus pulled into an area where there was probably close to a hundred of these bikes and Sunsil said for everyone to get out of the bus and find one of the bikes and a driver and get ready to take a ride in one of these wonderful old vehicles to see an very old fort in the heart of the city.

Gene and Susan stopped at one of the better looking bikes and the driver showed them how to get into the seat.

Gene long legs didn't have very much room for them to even stay inside the bike carriage.

The ship's photographer was taking pictures as the people were getting into their seats.

Sonny and Jane took the vehicle next to Gene and Susan's bike and the driver helped Jane to get seated, then he helped Sonny with directions on how to get into the vehicle.

Sonny didn't think it was going to be easy to do and he was right.

However, he make it inside the carriage, just as the ship's photographer came by and took their picture crammed inside this little ancient form of transportation.

After all of the people in bus two, were loaded the driver of Sonny and Jane's vehicle who must have been in charge of all of the drivers in their group, because he signaled to all of the other drivers to form a line and after they were in formation.

They all started onto the street headed for the old fort.

Their driver was a young man who told them he had three children and he had been working with the bikes, since he was fifteen or sixteen years old, some of the drivers looked to be in their late fifties, but all of them had slim bodies and strong legs.

The whole group were now strung out over an area of a couple of blocks long and every once in awhile their driver would race up ahead and tell some of the drivers to get up closer to the pack, then he would fall back to be the last bike in the pack.

When the lead driver of the pack started across an intersection he just pulled out in front of the trucks, cars and buses and the rest of the bikes followed right behind him and after traveling several blocks the lead driver turned his bike into what looked to be an alleyway.

However, they found out later it was one of the oldest streets in Old Delhi.

When Sonny and Jane's bike got into the old street, they saw lots of activities going on, there were men making the garlands of marigolds, men cooking some kind of meat, women carrying all kind of different types of clothes, men making some type of wooden beads.

There was also a large variety of dogs, cats and goats roaming along the street.

This street looked to be ancient, except for the mass of power lines hanging from high on the buildings, theses lines were without any junction boxes or any covering over the wires.

It was a reminisce of a picture Sonny had seen of the power lines in Vietnam, where a large number of power lines, along with huge circles of wire were hanging down from all of the buildings.

The power lines looked actually like the picture he saw of the ones in Vietnam.

When they reached the end of the street they came to the old fort, there their driver said, "This is the oldest fort in this part of India and it's still in use today and we are not allowed to go inside the old fort."

Then the driver turned his bike around next to the fort and started back out the old street and then began making his way back to where they started their bike trip from.

Traffic was even heavier now and when they got across from the parking area where their bus was parked and their driver saw that all of his group had made it safely across this four lane road.

He pulled his bike directly in front of a very large bus that was busy blasting its horn at their bike and sliding his wheels trying to keep from hitting them.

Sonny and Jane were both saying to their self *"Oh My God"* we're going to die here on the streets of Old Delhi.

However, they made it into the parking lot and the driver never let on that it was any big deal, like he did it that way every day.

They paid their driver and got onto their bus, as quickly as possible and slide into their seats and said to each other, OK we've had that experience once and once was enough.

The bus stopped at one of the open markets and Sunsil told everyone they would be staying here only fifteen minutes.

Sonny and Jane stayed on the bus and skipped another shopping experience.

Fifteen minutes pasted and everyone was back on the bus and they were on their way to the airport to fly to Mumbai.

When they arrived at the airport Sunsil said goodbye and hoped everyone enjoyed their tour of the Taj Mahal.

Everyone gave Sunsil, round applauses for a job well done and each of the tourists gave Sunsil a nice tip for making their trip to the Taj Mahal a wonderful experience.

Jean Evans, who had been waiting in the parking lot for her people on bus number two, boarded the bus and handed each person their boarding pass.

Making it some much easier for everyone to get their boarding passes without all the problems they had in Cochin airport.

No one was checking any luggage, so now they only needed to get through security and to their departure gate.

The airport in New Delhi, security was the same as it was in Cochin with the women passing through one area and the men through another.

The only good thing was they had more security stations for the women in New Delhi. However, it still took twice as long for Jane and Susan to get through security as Sonny and Gene did.

They soon found their way to their departure gate and found a seating area where all four of them could sit down to wait for their plane.

Again, none of them were seated together, but they were happy just to get on the plane to go back to their ship.

The flight time was shorter from New Delhi to Mumbai, than it was from Cochin to New Delhi, which made all of them happier.

When they arrived in Mumbai they had buses waiting to take them on another windshield tour of the City of Mumbai.

Sonny wasn't fond of the new name of Bombay. He had always dreamed about traveling to the mystery city called, Bombay, the name Mumbai, only sounded like someone was muttering some mumbo jumbo.

By the time everyone traveling on bus two got on board, all they could think about was getting back to the ship.

Everyone thought another windshield city tour wasn't wanted or needed at this time, however, wanting it or not, they were getting the windshield tour of Mumbai.

Sonny had to admit seeing the beautiful Victoria Railroad Station was very interesting even thought it was no longer used as a railroad station and seeing the Gate of India, built for King George and Queen Elizabeth arrival in India, was also very interesting and historic.

At that time King George was also the King of India as well as the King of England.

Mumbai was the money and commerce capital of India and its buildings showed it.

It is the largest population of any city in India with over fourteen million people and growing, our local guide said if they counted all of the areas around the city it would probably be over fifteen million.

Finally, the dreaded windshield tour of Mumbai was over and their bus pulled up in front of their ship and everyone was glad they went to see the Taj Mahal and happy to be back home again.

Sonny, Jane, Gene and Susan were thrilled to get back home to their min suites.

26

Dubai and Pirates

Sonny and Gene met for breakfast the following day, while their wives were doing their exercise class.

Sonny said, "It was good to get away from the ship and to have the opportunity not spending all of our time trying to figure out who killed our four women wasn't it."

Gene replied, "Yes it was. I guess being away from the ship for those three days probably gave us a glimpse of what our world cruise would have been like, if we hadn't been caught up in investigating four murders.

"It was nice not to be thinking about who killed four of our fellow passengers, while they were on their vacations, wasn't it.

"You know Sonny, of course us being involved in investigating those four murders, is all your fault."

"My fault, I didn't kill those four women."

"Of course you didn't kill those four women, but you had to grow up with the captain and you just had to help her find the killer, didn't you?"

"OK, you got me there, but it wasn't my fault I grew up next door to Donna, it's our parent's fault, they're the ones who bought houses next door to each other and had children."

"You know Sonny you sound just like some of the guys we've arrested, it wasn't their fault they took a hatchet and wacked their wife in the head fifty times; it was their parents fault.

"Their daddies spanked them too hard and too often or their mother never corrected them when they did something wrong, the poor things, they just didn't understand about something being right or wrong."

1

"OK Gene, it's all my fault I got us into this mess of trying to help find the killer of our four women."

"That's good Sonny, I'm glad we're clear about that."

"So what do you think we can do now about trying to find out who our killer is?"

"How in the hell do I know, maybe we could just ask him to kill someone else and leave us a clue or two, so then maybe we could find him."

"Well Sonny, I think that's the best idea we've had so far on how to find this guy, ask him to leave us a clue or better yet two clues as to who he is."

"Gene, you know what I really worry about in this case, is the guy is going to get off this ship somewhere before we find him and leave him free to doing it all over again on another ship."

"You're right Sonny, the guy could get off at one of these ports and we would never find him."

"Gene, I'm pretty sure we have the big ace in this deck of cards that we been dealt and it's Lucky Jordan.

"Somehow Lucky, is still the key to these murders and we just don't know how to use this key."

"You're right, Sonny somehow Lucky is the big ace in this deck and he's scheduled to be on this cruise until we return to San Francisco."

"Gene, everything always comes back to Lucky, his wife being killed and all four the women killed on this ship had been seen with Lucky, even when it seems like it was only for a brief moment."

"Somebody, has a real problem with Lucky, either they are trying to get him arrested as being the one who murders these women, or they're in love with him and don't want him to have any other woman."

"Sonny, if it is somebody who's in love with him then maybe we've been looking for a man, but maybe it's a woman who killing these women."

"Yes Gene, it could be a woman, but if it is, it would break from every woman killer we've ever had experience with."

"A woman whose method of killing a victim by strangulation is something I never heard of."

"Women who kill someone use knifes, guns, poison, hatchets, heavy objects to strike their victims in the head, push victims down stairs, strangulation never."

"You've got a good point Sonny, but maybe this woman has really strong hands."

"I guess it's possible Gene, so I guess we better start looking for women on this ship who have very strong hands.

"We sure don't have anything else to go on in these murders."

"How many days will it take our ship to get to Dubai, do you know Sonny?"

"I think Jane said we would have four days to rested up before we got to Dubai."

"OK Sonny, let's spend four days looking for women with very large strong hands."

Sonny and Gene left the Grand Buffet and returned to their staterooms and by that time their wives had finished their exercise class.

Sonny asked, "So how did your exercise class go this morning?"

"Well, it went all right except missing three days of doing exercises and now restarting them again has left Susan and me pretty tried."

"I'm sorry to hear that, but Gene and I have an assignment for you and Susan."

"An assignment, what kind of an assignment do you have for us?"

"We want you two to help us find our killer."

"Just what do you want us to do?"

"We want you to look for any woman who looks like they have very strong hands."

"We think maybe our killer is a woman, if she is, it would be something we've never heard of before, a woman who strangulated their victims to death."

"OK, so we find some women who look like they have very strong hands what do you want us to do about it?"

"You don't have to do anything you just tell us her name."

"OK, you've never asked me to help you find a murderer before, but I guess I was always working or looking after babies."

"But, I'll do it. I'll look for woman with very strong hands."

Five mornings later, the Golden Supreme arrived in the port of Dubai and was just coming into the harbor.

Sonny, Jane, Gene and Susan were just finishing their breakfast at the Grand Buffet.

All four got up from the table and went to the windows on the starboard side of the Grand Buffet and they could see in the distances a lot of very tall buildings.

They were scheduled to go on a tour at ten o'clock this morning to see the tallest building in the world and a windshield tour of the city. Plus a couple of stops at large shopping centers and a large mosque.

They went back to their staterooms and picked up their cameras and Sonny and Gene both opened their room safes and got additional money out to take with them for their tour.

They thought who knows what their wives might see in these shopping centers that they might want to buy.

They made their way down to the Grand Show Room, where they would meet to join with other passengers going on the same tour as they were.

After they arrived they found their tour would be the first tour leaving the ship today and among the other passengers going on their tour, were Lucky Jordan and Aisha Charles.

There were a total of fifty people going on this tour. The tour would be using two buses, with twenty-eight people in bus one and twenty-two people in bus two.

For once the four of them were going on bus one as well as Lucky and Aisha were also on bus one.

Tour one was now leaving to join their Supreme Guide, Jean Evans, the same lady the four of them were with on their India trip.

Sonny said, "Good, I'm glad we are on Jean's bus, she a good guide and she will certainly look after us."

The group was following Jean as she made her way off of the ship and led then directly to their bus.

Lucky was sitting at the back of the bus and Aisha was sitting in the first row with another woman, that none of the four knew who she was.

The bus was soon loaded and made its way to the world's tallest building, they had to park several blocks away from the entrance to the building.

Jean had all the passengers get off the bus and follow her to the entrance to tallest building named, Burj Khalifa which was 209 stories high and measured 828 meters high or 2,717 feet in height, almost twice as tall as the next tallest build in the world.

The elevators in the building were as smooth and fast as some elevators that Sonny had ridden on just going up ten floors.

All in all everyone were enjoyed seeing and going up in the Burj Khalilfa building.

When they were waiting for their turn to ride in the elevators, a photographer took each couples picture.

They were told when they came back down they could get a copy of their picture as they were leaving the building.

Everything about the visit to the tallest building in the world pleased them except for one thing, there was some very fine dust in the air limiting their view.

The one thing Jane thought by going up in the building would give her the opportunity to see the man made Palm Island, since they wouldn't have any other way of seeing the island from the air.

It was hard to believe, but you could hardly see down to the ground directly below them in this building with this fine dust in the air.

OK, they finished looking around and buying some things in the gift shop at the top and they were ready to go back down and needed to be at the meeting place Jean had told them that would be their meeting place.

Each of the couples bought their picture and added it to the things they bought at the gift shop at the top.

It wasn't long until everyone in Jean's tour group was at the meeting place and Jean led them out of the building in a total different direction than the one they came into the building to rejoin their bus.

Jean said, "The next stop we will make is at one of the largest shopping center in the world, it's called the Dubai Mall it has 3.77 million square feet."

Sonny, Jane, Gene and Susan could have spent hours looking around this mall it had everything you could ever want to find or to buy in this world.

However, they didn't buy one thing.

They met the rest of their tour group at Jean's assigned location and then they were off to visit the next mall.

This mall was the Mall of the Emirates. This mall was the one Sonny was looking forward to seeing. In this mall you could go snow skiing in Dubai, oh yes you can, just right inside the Mall of the Emirates at anytime of the year.

The world in Dubai is whatever the sheiks can dream up in their heads, they can find some way to build it. If you can conceive it, they can find the money to build it.

Sonny's one word for Dubai is: *Unbelievable!*

They even have the old ship, Queen Elizabeth sitting in the dock they haven't decided what to do with it yet, a hotel, a floating restaurant, they don't know but they had to have it.

They were scheduled to leave Dubai tonight. However there was a change in the departure time to six am tomorrow morning.

That evening after dinner Sonny and Jane were leaving the Main Dining Room when they met Captain Donna Morehouse.

Sonny asked Donna why the delay in her departure time was put off until six am tomorrow morning?

Donna looked Sonny straight in the eyes and said, "Pirates."

Sonny and Jane both started laughing.

Donna said, "That's the reason we are being delayed, pirates. Pirates took a large tanker this afternoon off the coast of Yemen and our military escort can't be ready to meet us until tomorrow early afternoon."

"So we have been ordered to remain in port until six am tomorrow morning."

Sonny said, "For goodness sake Donna, you have women being murdered on your ship and now you got pirates, what else will you have for entertainment for us on this trip."

Donna replied, "I don't know yet we'll try to think of something, so you don't get bored."

Jane said, "Please don't think of anything else, murders and pirates should be plenty."

The next morning a few minutes after eight am, Captain Donna began speaking over the ships loudspeaker system.

She said, "Good Morning Ladies and Gentlemen, this is Captain Morehouse speaking and in two hours we will be having a pirate drill, most of this drill will involve the crew."

"What it means for all passengers when you hear *this is a pirate drill* you will be asked to close your curtains in your room and go outside in the hallway and take a seat on the floor with your back against the wall next to your stateroom.

"This is necessary for us to account for every passenger on the ship."

"All of the ship's crew have their assignments which, includes accounting for all of our passengers."

"Tonight all outside lights will be turned off and stay off throughout the night and they will stay that way until we are out of the Suez Canal."

"No one is to be outside on their balcony or on any open desk on this ship at nighttime."

"During the pirate drill. All services will be suspended, because each and every member of the crew have their assignment to carry out."

"The nighttime restrictions will remain in effect until we leave the Suez Canal."

"We will start the pirate drill at ten am, thank you all for listening to this important announcement."

Ten o'clock came and the Captain beginning speaking, "This is a pirate drill all crew members go to your assigned positions."

"All passengers close your drapes and go to the hallway and sit with your back against the wall next to your room."

"This is a pirate drill all crew members go to your assigned positions."

"All passengers return to your staterooms and close your drapes and take a seat outside your stateroom with you back against the wall."

"*Warning: Warning!* This is a pirate drill."

Sonny and Jane calmly closed their drapes and went outside their stateroom door into the hallway and took a seat next to their cabin door with their backs against the wall.

They were soon joined by Gene and Susan, they sat down next to their stateroom door and Gene asked, "Do we have any idea how long this drill is going to last?"

Sonny replied, "I have no idea. I didn't know they had such a thing on cruise ships."

About that time Lucky Jordan came out of his stateroom and took a seat outside his door."

A few seconds pasted and Aisha Charles came out of her stateroom and sat down next to Lucky."

Aisha said, "Hi, how's everyone doing sitting on the floor in a hallway?"

Sonny replied, "I can tell you one thing, my knees sure don't like it."

Jane said, "Well if you do more walking and exercising they might do a lot better."

Sonny replied, "I'm sure you're right love, however I been paying a guy to do my exercising for me. I guess he's not working at it hard enough."

Everyone sitting in the hallway laughed, than Jane said, "I don't think that's the way it works dear."

Sonny shot back a reply: "Damn, now you tell me. You mean I've been wasting my money?"

Lucky had to get into this act, so he said, "Listen, maybe you've hired the wrong man to do your exercise for you."

"You should hire me, than I'm sure I would be better off getting paid for doing all of the exercises that I do. Instead of just doing it for myself, then I would have more money."

That made all of them laugh, especially Sonny.

However, their playful mood changed when their cabin steward came down the hallway with a clip board checking off names of all the passengers sitting in the hallway.

He quickly checked off all of the passengers sitting outside their rooms and when he came to a stateroom that didn't have the passengers sitting outside their stateroom.

He knocked on the door and then took his master key card and opened the door and found the occupants of that stateroom inside, he asked them why they were not outside their room sitting of the floor.

Sonny heard the man say, "I think this whole thing about pirates is ridiculous, whoever heard of pirates in the twenty first century."

They heard their steward replied, "Sir, three days ago only a short distances from our direction of travel. Pirates took a tanker and are hold the crew as hostages until the ship's owner pay the pirates several million dollars."

"That why the captain is having pirate drills and why we sat waiting overnight in Dubai until we could get a military escort and make arrangements for satellite tracking of our ship through these waters and this will continue until we are safely out of the Suez Canal."

"Now do you understand why the pirate drills sir? If you were in your room with the glass sliding doors, you would be an easy target for the pirates."

The passenger replied, "Well why didn't they tell us that in the first place, then we would have been sitting outside our room."

"I don't know sir. I'm only a room steward, who only knows how to follow my captain's orders."

Then the steward left the room, as the two folks who stayed inside their stateroom came out and sit down on the floor next to their door.

Probably another ten minutes pasted before the captain announced over the loudspeaker, "The pirate drill has been successfully completed and all passengers and crew member have been accounted for and we will now resume all normal activities."

"Thank you for your cooperation during this drill."

After the pirate drill was completed the rest of the day past by quickly and it was time to go down to dinner in the Grand Dining Room.

It would be the first time the four of them would be having dinner in the Grand Dining Room since they returned from their trip to the Taj Mahal.

Arriving at the entrance to the dining room they were met by their waiter, Vesko, who told them some things have changed with their seating arrangements, since they last had dinner in the dining room.

He took then to the same area that had been sitting in since they left San Francisco.

Sonny asked, "Vesko, why the change?"

The waiter replied, "Your four English friends left the ship in Dubai and they decided to change your table to a round table and you will only have six people at your table now."

"The four of you; and Mr. Lucky and Miss Aisha, all six of you will be going all the way back to San Francisco."

Sonny said, "That's great Vesko, with a round table we will be able to hear everyone's conversation."

"All of us are going all the way to San Francisco, so how about you Vesko are you going to be with us all the way?"

"No, I will be going home to Serbia when we get to Rio de Janeiro."

Jane said, "Vesko, why don't you stay with us, it's not going to the same without you."

"I can't Miss Jane, I will have been gone for nine months when we get to Rio, and my mommy wants me to come home. I'm the only child she has, so I need to go home."

The four of them took a seat around their table; and they were soon joined by Lucky and a few minutes later, Aisha arrived.

All six of them decided they were very happy with their new table,

Now no one would be left out of the conversation as it was when they ten people were at the larger table.

Everyone loved Vesko, he made dinner lots of fun and if you want something special. He would get it for you. If you want four desserts, you got four desserts.

They would all really miss their waiter, Vesko when he left them to go home.

They would not be in port in Aqaba, Jordan for seven days more days.

After they finished their dinner, the six of them went to the Grand Show Room for tonight's show.

After the show was over the six of them went to their rooms and everyone made sure their drapes were closed and no lights were on their balconies.

27

Aqaba and Petra

They arrived around six in the morning at the Port of Aqaba, by eight am they had all cleared customs and immigrations.

Now, all of the passengers would be ready to go on their tours, all six of the table mates; Sonny, Jane, Gene, Susan, Lucky and Aisha were going to see Petra.

Sonny, had seen pictures of it all of his life and he was really looking forward to seeing Petra for himself.

They left the ship and traveled by bus for almost two hours, before reaching the entrance to the lost city of Petra.

At the entrance, they followed their Supreme Guide, Charles Johnson for almost a half mile before they entered a narrow gorge called the Siq, which turned out to be the actual entrance to Petra.

They walked through this gorge for about five miles before they reached the lost city of Petra.

It was everything, Sonny had hoped to see, here was the ancient city carved into red sandstone, unlike any other place on earth.

They were told the city was built around 100 AD; and that the city had several monuments located around the city, but the one that was most impressive to Sonny was called Khazneh.

It was a tomb carved into the cliff face of a sandstone mountain, a mountain called Jebel Knubtha.

After spending as much time looking at Petra as any of them wanted to see, the six of them made their way back through the Siq and finally back to their bus for their ride back to Aqaba.

Lucky, was by far the best of the walkers of the group, he of course was much younger than everyone but, Aisha.

He had had to spend lots of time walking, after being shot twice in his back in Afghanistan.

The bullets had glanced off of his spine near his spinal cord, which required him to do lots of physical rehabilitation to regain his strength and to be able to walk again.

He kept up doing his exercises, as part of his recovery after he was released from the hospital, and still continued to do them after he was considered to be fully recovered.

Now it had become part of his everyday routine.

Lucky, made sure he watched after Aisha, he helped her keep her balance several times. As she struggled through the heavy sand coming and going back through the Siq.

Aisha wasn't the only one who had problems walking through the sand, several times Jane almost fell and Sonny had plenty of trouble walking through the sand as well.

The truth was it would have been a real struggle for all of them to walk ten miles on good sidewalks. It wasn't something any of them did every day.

The only good thing was, they all did it, and they were all happy that they had made it.

After they had finished the hard part of the tour, they were now on the way to have lunch.

Aisha and Lucky were sitting near the back of the bus together and Lucky asked her about her life.

Aisha said, "I'm a farmer's daughter, my father owns a large farm in Iowa, near Iowa City. I went to school in Iowa City and stayed at home until I left to go to Iowa State University in Ames, because I wanted an engineering degree.

"I studied engineering and got my masters degree, after completing my degrees at Iowa State. I started working for a consulting engineering company in Chicago and went on an assignment in Brazil.

"I was in a car accident in Brazil and it has taken me a long time to recover. I survived the crash. However, my supervisor who was driving the car was killed."

"My company suggested that I take this cruise, before coming back to work and they even paid for my trip."

Lucky said, "That's very nice of your company to do that. How long were you in the hospital?"

"Three months, a month in San Paulo and two months in Chicago, before my doctor's would release me to a nursing home."

"How long were you in a nursing home, Aisha?"

"A year and a half and I had to relearn how to do everything. The accident had affected the part of my brain that communicates to my body."

"It took months before I was able to speak and then I had to learn how to make my arms and legs move.

"In other words, I had no control over any part of my body functions."

"It was months after I was in the nursing home, before I could speak or feed myself and many more months before I could sit up or begin to be able to walk."

"I was totally depending on someone else to do everything for me."

"It was awful, my mind worked OK, but it was impossible for me to tell anyone that I could think or what I needed."

"The company had us covered by special international insurance. It was in effect anytime we were working out of the country."

"Because of my age when the accident happened "I was paid more than seven million dollars by the insurance company for pain and injuries."

"They thought I would never recover enough to be able to work again and I would spend the rest of my life in a nursing home."

"But here, I am. Maybe not as good as new, but I' m here."

"I can tell you it wasn't worth the money to get hurt that bad and be in the position I was in for all those months, being totally unable to do anything for myself."

Lucky said, "Kid, you've had a tough go, but you look like you are doing OK now, do you still have lots of pain?"

"No, I don't. I'm lucky that way. They say I may have pain when I get older."

"Aisha, you are a very beautiful woman. I don't think I would tell too many men about your settlement, you're liable to end up falling for some gold digger."

"How about you Lucky, are you a gold digger, would you be interested in me because I had a little money?"

"Aisha, I'm interested in you even if you didn't have two nickels to rub together, as I said, you are a very beautiful woman."

"Right now, my biggest job is to help keep you alive, until we finish this world cruise."

"And then Lucky, if you keep me alive, would you be interested in me?"

"Aisha, as I said I'm very interested in you right now. But I don't have a very good track record with the beautiful woman that I loved."

"Sonny told you, someone killed my wife when I went with some of my men while we were visiting wounded soldiers in a VA hospital."

"I don't want that to happen to you."

"If you were my husband, I would have been right with you visiting those soldiers, because I wouldn't let you out of my sight."

"Lucky, you're beautiful. I think I've already fallen in love with you."

"After we rolled down that volcano together, I can't stop thinking about you."

"Aisha, OK I understand that, since I haven't stopped thinking about you either, but we need to be careful to not let this get out of hand."

"At least not until they find the person that's killing these women."

"OK, Lucky. I'll do my best not to let things get out of control. I've never felt this way before in my life."

Then Aisha, kissed Lucky's hand and said, "I'll try my best, not to let myself get killed because of you."

Lucky replied, "Dammed good of you, not to let yourself get killed, because of me.

"However, I'm the one, who is supposed to be making sure you don't get killed."

Aisha looked longing into Lucky's big blue eyes and said, "Then Lucky, I expect you to do your job."

At that time the bus pulled into a unpaved parking lot with lots of potholes and the rear tires dropped into the biggest pothole in the parking lot directly under the bus where Aisha and Lucky were sitting.

The impact threw Aisha right over into Lucky's lap.

Lucky quickly grabbed Aisha to keep her from falling on the floor.

Then Lucky pulled Aisha up and was holding her in his arms when the bus came to a sudden stop.

Charles Johnson, their tour guide said, "I hope everyone is OK after the crash landing our bus driver made at our lunch stop."

"Does anyone need any help and is everyone OK after the crash, if so let's get off the bus and have some lunch before heading back to our ship."

Lucky asked Aisha if she was all right?

She said, "Just a little shook up, I think I'm going to have some more bruises.

"But I'm really OK, let's join the others and have some lunch, after all of the walking we've done. I'm hungry."

Sonny, Jane, Gene and Susan, as well as everyone else on the bus were banged around when the bus hit the big pothole in the parking lot, but at least none of them got knocked out of their seats like Aisha did.

Everyone began getting out of the bus and making their way into the restaurant and Lucky and Aisha were following at the rear of the rest of their group.

One inside the restaurant, Lucky saw Sonny motioning to him for him and Aisha to join them at their table.

Lucky shook his head to indicate that he saw Sonny motioning to them.

Lucky then directed Aisha to walk over to where Sonny and their table mates were seated.

The six of them were seated at a table for six people, so it was like the way the six of them were seated on the ship for their meals.

The big difference, sitting at this table was that no one was going to bring them anything to eat, just something to drink.

It was a self service buffet, so one by one each of the couples went to get their food.

Lucky and Aisha was the last couple to make the trip to the food bars.

Jane remarked, as Lucky and Aisha were sitting down with their plates of food, "You two make a darling couple, don't you think Susan?"

Hearing what Jane said about Lucky and Aisha, as they were sitting down caused both of them to grin and their faces turned a bright red.

Then they heard Susan say, "They certainly do, they make an adorable couple."

As if the faces of Lucky and Aisha weren't red enough already, both of their faces got even redder hearing Susan response to Jane's comment.

Lucky looked at Aisha face and he knew his face must be as red as hers, and he felt like a kid of sixteen again, being kidded by his friends about a girl he liked.

Lucky couldn't help it. Lucky did felt like Aisha was his first girl friend. He hadn't felt that way about anyone in a long time, not even his wife.

No, it didn't make any sense, maybe it was because he was suppose to be looking out for her, like he had to do when he had his first girl friend in high school. There were so many boys who liked to tease his girl friend, because they knew they could make her cry. Young boys could be really mean at that age.

So Lucky had lots of fights, these fights were normally quick, one punch and the other boy ran away.

The teasing stopped, after Lucky down the biggest kid in their class with one big uppercut to the jaw, the guy got up spitting out teeth and that ended the teasing of Lucky's girlfriend.

However, that one caused his folks to have to pay for replacing a couple of front teeth, but actually Lucky was the one who had to pay.

He repaid, by working for his dad enough hours to pay back his dad for what he had paid for two new front teeth.

It took Lucky several hours of work, to pay his dad back, that's what happens when you're only making a buck an hour it takes a lot of hours.

From that day, on Lucky and Aisha were almost always to gather.

Lucky was doing his part to be sure that Aisha stayed alive, he hardly let her out of his sight, and Aisha was thrilled and happy about it.

28

Aisha Makes a New Friend

Aisha would continue her work out in the exercise room every day around ten o'clock and after seeing a woman there for several days she said, "Hi, my name is, Aisha Charles.

"I've seen you here every day at the same time I come to do my work out, what's your name?"

The woman in a very soft low voice answered, "Veronica King."

Aisha said, "I know I've seen you on the ship several times, but you don't seem like you are enjoying your cruise much."

"No, it probably doesn't look like I am, I'm shy around strangers. I haven't been seeing very many people, since I got out of the hospital and rehab."

"Oh my god, I've just in the process of recovering from a car accident myself. It's taken me two years to get this far, what was your problem?"

"Some men shot me in Afghanistan."

"Veronica, where you in the army there or where you an aid worker?"

"No, I wasn't an aid worker, I was in the in the United States Army, like lots of people over there, our unit got hit by a surprise attack."

"I was wounded pretty badly, but I made it back to the states alive. Unlike a lot of soldiers I knew."

"Veronica, I'm so sorry you were wounded, but at least you look like you are doing OK now."

"Yes, I am. Right now I'm trying to get over a broken heart."

"The man you were in love with. Was he a soldier and got killed in Afghanistan?"

"No, he was wounded, but when he came home, he married somebody else."

"I'm sorry."

"Me too, but I don't ever want to talk about it again with you, and I hope you won't say anything about it to your friends."

"Trust me, I won't ever say anything about it, to my friends that I've made of this trip."

"That's good Aisha. Let's talk about sometime else, like I see you with a good looking man all the time, did you just meet him on the cruise."

"Yes, I'm crazy about him. I've never felt like this before."

"I have to ask, are you sure he feels the same way as you do."

"Yes, I know he does, he's told me so."

"Well the reason I asked, is because I'd seen him with several other women on the ship, are you really sure he's in love with you?"

"Yes, I am Veronica. I'm very sure. You have no idea what he doing for me."

"So, what's he doing for you?"

"I'm sorry, it's something I can't talk about and I've promised I would never say anything about it."

"It sounds pretty strange, that he doing something that so important to you, yet you can't tell anyone about it."

"Sorry, Veronica, I just can't break my promise."

"OK, I understand.

"I just never heard of someone doing something for someone that they couldn't tell what it was."

"Let's drop this subject. "

"Veronica, you know what we could do is to get some voodoo dolls that look like your ex boyfriend's wife and stick pins in them, maybe that would make you feel better."

"Aisha, you are a funny girl, I really like you."

"Good, I like you too Veronica. I've got to go now, so I can get my shower and get dressed for lunch with my feller."

"See you here tomorrow, try to forget about that guy and have a great day. See you."

Aisha left the exercise room and went directly to her room.

Quickly, showered and dressed for lunch, she was just going to have time enough to do her hair and make-up before Lucky would be knocking on her door.

She just finished putting on her lipstick, when she heard a knock on her door.

She rushed to the door and opened it and sure enough, Lucky was there.

Aisha asked him to come in and Lucky came into the room and took hold of her arm and pulled her up close to him and gave her a kiss on the lips.

It was their first kiss and she was ready for more, he was holding her very close to him, then Lucky said, "Good morning Aisha, how's my love this morning?"

"Ready for another kiss, that's how I am."

Lucky wasn't about to refuse her. He gently leaned down and gave her a very long slow kiss.

When he pulled his lips away from hers, she said, "Maybe one more liked that one please, before we go to lunch."

Lucky leaned his lips back down on her lips and gently begin kissing her and continued to apply more pressure on her lips.

Until it was as hard a kiss as he had ever kissed any woman in his life and continued holding the kiss for as long as he could, before he moved his lips away from hers.

When he was able to take a deep breath he said, ""Darling, I think we had better go to lunch, before lunch is forgotten."

Aisha replied, "I could miss my lunch, if you would make love to me."

Lucky said, "Are you sure, that's what you want?"

"Yes, that's what I want."

"Then my love, if that's what you really want, then that's what you'll have, you'll always be able to get whatever you want from me."

Lucky begin kissing her again and at the same time, he began pulling her skirt up and putting a hand between her legs.

He could feel wetness, beginning to form on the crotch of her panties, as he continued kissing her and running his fingers around the edge of her panties.

Then he put his fingers inside her panties and started pulling her panties down by the crotch and continued until her panties were now half way down her legs.

Suddenly, he stopped and said, "We better put your *"Privacy Please sign"* on the door, so no one interrupts us."

Lucky continued holding Aisha, with one arm around her, while he used his other hand to slightly open the door, and put the *"Privacy Please"* sign over the door knob.

As Lucky was saying that, Aisha stepped out of her sandals, and gently kicked them away from where she was standing.

Then he said, "Where was I? Oh I know."

As he put his hand back under her skirt and begin gently and slowly stoking between her legs again.

Aisha reached down and took hold of Lucky's belt buckle; unfastened his belt; then unbuttoned his pants and they fell to the floor, his pants where now around his ankles.

Then Lucky said, "I think it's time we get serious about making love, as he reached over her head with both hands, put his hands under the inside of her sweater and pulled it up and off, then threw it on the couch, he unfastened her bra; pulled it off, threw it on her sweater, then pulled her skirt down, and last, he finished pulling her panties down.

They were now down at her feet, she stepped out of them, kicking them aside and now she was completely naked, standing in front of Lucky and looking into his eyes.

Lucky stepped back to take a good look at Aisha's naked body and said, "My love, you're beautiful."

Then he began taking his clothes off as Aisha sat down on her bed to watch.

Lucky took off his shoes and socks, since his pants were already around his ankles; he pulled them off and laid them aside, took off his shirt, then pulled down his briefs and kicked them away.

Aisha reached out to touch his naked body, than he got on the bed with her.

They spent the rest of the afternoon exploring each other's body and making love; they continued making love until both of them were happy, satisfied and completely exhausted.

After both of them were totally exhausted, Lucky and Aisha continued to lie on her bed and hold each other until they both fell asleep.

Almost two hours pasted, before Lucky woke up and realized he had fallen asleep and looked to see what time it was.

It was almost four o'clock in the afternoon and by that time he had moved slightly away from Aisha and she woke up too.

She said, "What's the matter Lucky?"

"Nothing's the matter, it's wonderful.

"I woke up and wondered what time it was and surprised to see it was almost four o'clock."

"Are you hungry, Lucky?"

"No, I'm to full of love for you right now to think about food."

Aisha said, "I'm pretty sore and full of something wet between my legs right at the moment."

"Did I hurt you Aisha?"

"No, well yes, it kind of hurt when you first got into me, but pretty quick, it felt so good. I never wanted you to stop doing it."

"I'm sorry if I hurt you. I'd never want to hurt you in any way."

"The only way you could really hurt me, would be if you weren't in my life. Will you be in my life, after we finish this cruise, or will I just be the woman you cared about while we're on this cruise?"

"Aisha, I honestly believe you will be in my life as long as I live. I have the strongest love for you that I've ever felt for anyone in my life."

"How about, how you felt about your wife?"

"Believe me I loved her. It almost killed me, when she was murdered, but somehow the way I feel about you is different, don't ask how. I don't know how, or why, it's just different, it something I can't explain.

"I just know I love you, it happened so quickly, it almost knocked me off my feet."

Aisha said, "Yeah, I noticed your laying naked on my bed."

Lucky laughed, "Yes, I am. I'm not too sure how I got here, but you're laying naked on your bed right beside me.

"The last thing I remembered was I was giving you a kiss before we were going to lunch.

"Yet here I am, naked as jaybird lying next to you, whom I might add, is also as naked as that jaybird, except you're a lot better to look at naked than I am."

Aisha looked at Lucky's naked body and said, "I guess it depends on whose eyes is doing the looking, your naked body looks pretty good to me."

Lucky reached over and pulled Aisha on top of him and softly kissed her, then said, "I love you so much Aisha."

Aisha looked into his eyes and replied, "I'm so in love with you. I don't know what to do about it. I never was in love before; you will have to help me know what I need to do to keep you. I never want to let you out of my life."

"Darling Aisha, the only thing you have to do to keep me, is keep loving me and I'll be there."

"Do you promise Lucky, you have to promise me, that you will keep loving me?"

"Aisha, I promise you, I will always love you and I will for as long as I live."

"OK, Lucky. Now that I have your promise, you have to let me go into the bathroom, and then I need to take a shower, so you can take me to dinner."

"All right my love, you can go to the bathroom and I'll go over to my room, take my shower and get myself dressed for dinner and met you here at five fifteen.

"Is that a deal my love?"

"Deal, put it here." As she moved her lips close to Lucky's and kissed him. Then she was off the bed and quickly hurried into the bathroom.

Lucky, gather up his clothes and put on enough of them to go out into the hallway to make the trip next door to his stateroom.

Aisha and Lucky were both on cloud nine and feeling no pain, well maybe Aisha had some pain, since she had never had sexual intercourse before, but it was a good kind of pain.

Neither of them could hurry fast enough to be sure they were ready to be on-time for their dinner date.

Promptly at five fifteen. Lucky was knocking on Aisha's door.

She was standing near the door, because couldn't wait to see Lucky. She opened the door and Lucky said, "There stands the lady I love, would you like to go to dinner with me?"

"Would I, something kept me from lunch today, but I will say it was the most wonderful thing that I ever had to miss my lunch before in my life."

Lucky said, "I know, how that is, the same thing happened to me, missed lunch but oh what I had was better than any lunch I ever had in my life."

Aisha came out of her room and the two of them locked arm and arm went down the stairs to the Main Dining Room.

There they saw Sonny, Jane, Gene and Susan sitting at their table waiting for them.

All four of them saw, the biggest two smiling faces on the ship that day.

Sonny said, "I'd have to say that you two look like you had a much better day than anybody else on this ship, those smiles are million dollar smiles."

Aisha blushed like she had never blushed in her life and Lucky said, "Well we certainly did have a wonderful afternoon."

Then Lucky looked at Aisha and both of them smiled bigger and brighter than Aisha's flushed face.

Then Gene said, "We better all sitting back down and have dinner, before whatever happened to them, happens to us."

Lucky and Aisha just looked into each other's eyes and smiled even more.

29

Transiting the Suez Canal

Captain Donna would be kept busy for the next several days after they left Aqaba, until they passed through the Suez Canal, while being shadowed by an American warship, protected them, in case of a pirate attack and at the same time she had to be getting ready to transiting the Suez Canal.

She hadn't talked to Sonny for a couple of weeks, she hadn't seen him since he and Gene and their wives left the ship to go the Taj Mahal.

Donna was happy that they no more of her women passengers had been murdered.

She was beginning to wonder if the murderer had got off the ship at either Hong Kong or Dubai, since there hadn't been any one else murdered for several weeks.

She was certainly happy about that fact.

Donna found out that since her ship was the only passenger ship going through the Suez Canal at this time, her ship would be lead ship of a convey of thirty five ships.

She saw as her ship approached the entrance to the canal, several ships laying at anchor waiting for her ship to pass along with the other ships that were all ready following her.

The ships following her were all part of her thirty-five ship convey that were following in a line and after the last one of these ships passed, the ones at anchor, they would take their place in the convey in their assigned position, and would continue in this line until they all passed through the Suez Canal.

When they passed out of the canal each of the ships would go on their way to their destinations.

Donna was en route to the island of Crete, where they would arrive tomorrow morning.

Sonny, Jane, Gene and Susan spent most of their day outside on their balconies looking at the landscape around the Suez Canal.

They couldn't believe the number of military garrisons and guard towers built along the canal that appeared to have been built not too long ago.

They had been told that the large sand hills located on the eastern side of the canal had only been built over the last thirty or so years, to help keep people from firing at the ships and to slow down any vehicle which might be trying to reach the canal.

Sonny thought that before these large sand hills had been built, he could now understand how in the movie, *"Lawrence of Arabia"*, that Lawrence could be walking in the middle of a desert.

Then Lawrence suddenly saw the top of a large ship, which appeared like it was going through the desert sand.

In fact, the Suez Canal was just a big ditch carved out of the sand to form the canal.

Sonny had never been able to forget that scene from the movie.

Sonny and Gene made their way to Donna's office to see if anything had happened on the murders of the four women that they didn't know about, since they had been away from the ship.

Donna was glad to report that no more women had been murdered or nothing had come in from any of the police departments, since she had seen them last.

Donna said, "Sonny, do you think our murderer might have gotten off the ship at either Hong Kong or Dubai?"

"I have no idea of course, maybe he's just in one of those times when he's not aggregated, so he not in the right mood to kill anybody else.

"I hate to say it, but I hope he hasn't got off the ship, because I would, well Gene and I would like to catch, whoever it is that's killed these very nice women.

"Isn't that right Gene?"

"Yes, that's right Sonny, I'd hate to think he's gotten away."

Donna said, "Well I hope, he doesn't kill anymore of my passengers."

Sonny replied, "I can certainly agree with that. Let's hope, if he tries' to kill anyone else it's the person we have sit up to protect, Aisha Charles.

"The way Lucky looks at Aisha. I would hate to be the one trying to kill her."

"Plus, if Lucky thinks it's the man who murdered his wife. I'm not sure there be enough left of the guy for us to bury at sea."

Donna asked, "Sonny, do you think Lucky is in love with Aisha?"

"Yes, if not, he one of the greatest actors in the world that's not working in Hollywood, he certainly got all of us believing he is, isn't that right Gene?"

"I would say if he's not in love with her, I wouldn't have a guess of what else he could be feeling about the woman. He's got all the right characteristics of a man in love."

Donna said, "Damn, I've missed out on another one, just because you wouldn't bring him up here and introduce him to me."

Sonny said, "OK, Donna I know, that I've saved you from another heart break."

"I know you have to get back to your captain's duties now. See you later."

Sonny and Gene left her office and Gene said, "You know Sonny, I think Donna really wanted to meet Lucky, how come you never brought him up to meet her."

"Easy, I was protecting her. She would have falling for him, just like all the rest of the women do."

"I didn't want to loss our captain you know the killer might have killed her."

"OK Sonny, you're joking with me aren't you?"

"Partly, I wouldn't want Donna to get hurt falling for Lucky, he's way too young for her."

"So Sonny, when did you decide that you should be the one to decide who someone should fall in love with?"

"Only when it is my best friend that I'm looking out for."

"OK, do you have something you want to tell me, that you're in love with Donna?"

"Gene, I've always loved her, but not the way you're implying. She like my little sister. I've always looked after her."

"Maybe you haven't noticed, but she a pretty grown up woman, perhaps you should let her make her own decisions for god sake, she a captain of a ship and a captain in the navy."

"She's seems to have been making it pretty well, without too much of your help for a lot of years."

Sonny replied, "Yes dad, I think you're right. I should keep my nose out of other people's business, even my best friends."

"OK son, I'm glad you understand that. Now, we better catch up with our wives so we know what we are supposed to be doing next."

It took about three hours to go through the canal and for Sonny it was one of the many places that Sonny really wanted to see.

It did surprise him, how much construction was going on near the canal, he had always thought the canal was just a canal through the sand, but now there were huge construction projects under way on the east side of the canal that looked like hundreds of apartments or condo being built.

As they were exiting the canal, they were informed that a new container port was under construction at this site and when finished would be one of the largest in the world.

Sonny couldn't understand what is was going to be used for, but he could certainly see that it was going to be huge.

He was also impressed with the Friendship Bridge, it was a huge beautiful bridge built by the Japanese's and must have cost billions of dollars to build.

The length of the raised approaches up to the bridge must have been at least a half a mile or more on each side of the bridge and the bridge was high enough to let the tallest ships in the world under it.

The bridge was also completely closed when a ship was passing under it. This was to be sure that no terrorists could throw something down onto a ship and damage it.

Sonny also saw that at several points along the canal there were ferry boats to take cars, trucks, buses and people across the canal from one side to the other.

These ferry had to make their run across the canal between the ships traveling the canal.

The income from the canal was almost the total income that the government of Egypt these days, so they had to protect it at all cost.

30

Visiting Europe Was Hard Work

Their first port of call in Europe was Crete; Sonny, Jane, Gene and Susan tour of Crete, included visiting Knossos; Palace of Minos; and the Minoan relics at the Archaeological Museum in Iraklion.

They all were impressed with the way the royalty lived in 3000 B. C.

However, they were shocked to see the mountain tops in the central part of the island were all covered with snow in early April.

The idea of snow on one of the Greece Islands just didn't fit any of their ideas of one of the beautiful Greece Islands in the Mediterranean Sea that could have mountains that were over 8,000 feet high with snow on top of it.

However, the girls soon found some wonderful small shops and they were happy with their new treasures.

OK. The girls were happy with their first port of call in Europe.

They would be making a new port almost every day or every other while they were in the Mediterranean.

The question would soon become, do we have to get off the ship again today?

The next stop was Sicily, there they only took one tour and it was a drive through the countryside and up into the mountains.

Where at one time one of the civilizations had built a town and a fort, on the highest mountain which made it impossible for invaders coming from the sea to attack and overtake the people living there before they could be ready for an attack.

If someone tried to attack them they had all of the advantage being higher than their attackers and plenty of food and water available for them.

At this site, they also visited a Roman Theater built into the mountainside where plays and meetings were held and one very large church was left which still had several of its walls still standing after many centuries.

OK, they had done Sicily, next, Rome.

Here the four of them, took tours to the Vatican, they saw the Fountain of Neptune, the Colosseum, the Pantheon, the Roman Forum and the awful traffic of Rome.

All in all, it was more than any of them could take in the two days they were there.

They would be getting a little break after they left Rome, because they would need two days of travel, before the ship made it to their next stop, Barcelona.

OK, they had a day on the ship to rest before they reached Barcelona, but it passed by quickly, now they were docked in Barcelona.

They found on their tour that the city was founded in 230 B. C, by a Carthaginian Leader, Hamilcar Barca, and he named the city after himself calling it, Barcino.

They visited the Barcelona Cathedral, built on a high hill in the city. The building of the cathedral started in the late 1200's. Plus, in Barcelona they visited the Sagrada Familia Basilica, the Palo de la Musica Catalana, Picasso Museum, Torres Glories and the port where Columbus set sail and sailed into the new world.

They also walked the famous street, the Las Ramblas and yes it was very busy with lots of tourists and they found out later pickpockets.

At least none of them had any problem and they didn't hear about any of their shipmates having a problem with the pickpockets.

The four of them now understood, the phrase, *"ABC"*, because anytime you visit any of the old cities around the world. You go to so many churches or cathedrals, that everyone soon learns the phrase *"ABC"*; meaning; *"Another Bloody Cathedral"*.

The four explorers made their way back to their ship and arriving there they all had to take a nap before dinner.

Seeing all of these places in Europe was beginning to take its toil on the four of them. They were all very happy that they would have three days on the ship before they arrived in Lisbon.

They did all make it to dinner, that evening and were glad to see Lucky and Aisha.

Sonny asked, "Did you two go on any tours today?"

Aisha replied, "We did go on a couple of tours, but we spent a lot of the day at the Picasso Museum, we were just trying to decide if we liked his art or did we think it was really art.

"However, after several hours they said they still were not sure of what it was all about."

Lucky added, "I know his work sold for a lot of money, but some of it is certainly not the kind of art I would enjoy."

"I like my pictures to look more like a photo, then there's absolutely no question of what it is."

Gene said, "You know what they say, *"Art like beauty, is in the eyes of the beholder."*

Lucky replied, "I guess I've just never had an eye for art then. I know what kind of pictures, I like."

Sonny said, "There once was an old joke about a woman whose face was so misshaped. That one day there was a man who sat up a blind date for his friend with this woman."

"The day after the date his friend said to the man, my date was a very nice woman, but I didn't care much for how the ladies face looked, it was kind of misshaped."

"The man who had sat up the date snapped back, "Either you like Picasso or you don't."

All of them kind of laughed, but they weren't sure they liked the idea of making fun of someone who had a misshaped face.

However, Aisha said, "I enjoyed seeing the museum at least I can say I had the opportunity to see the Picasso Museum in Barcelona."

Lucky replied, "Yes you did, and so did I. I would never do it again, ever."

This got laughs from all of the rest of his table mates.

After dinner the six of them went to the live show, tonight they were having performances by a group of Spanish musicians and dancers.

The show was lively and indeed entertaining.

As the six of them were on their way back to their rooms, a woman they met said hello to Aisha.

Aisha responded, "Hello Veronica. How are you?"

The woman responded, "Just fine. I've been missing you at the exercise room."

"I know, we've been going on tours, but I'll be back soon."

"Good, see you later."

After the woman was gone, Lucky asked, "Who was that woman you spoke to?"

"Oh, her name is Veronica King and we met doing our exercises."

"Huh, she reminds me of someone I've met, but I don't have any idea who it was."

Aisha replied, "Oh, probably one of your old girl friends."

"I don't think so, but she sure does look like someone I knew."

Sonny and Gene both were interested in who that person was too.

Sonny asked, "Lucky, you don't have any idea who that woman is?"

"No, but I'm telling you, she sure reminds me of somebody I've met or knew. You know what I think it was, it was her eyes that seemed so familiar, yes it was the eyes."

Sonny asked, "Aisha, what do you know about this woman?"

"Not much, we met in the exercise room and we do our exercises at the same time."

"She said she got on the ship in LA and was trying to get over a man, who broke her heart. That's about all I know about her, except she's normally there at the same time, I am every day."

Sonny said, Thanks, we'll look into her."

Aisha said, "Oh, I do remember one other thing she said."

"She said she was recovering from being wounded in Afghanistan. She said she had been serving in the army over there."

Lucky replied, "Well maybe I saw her in one of the hospitals, when I was being cared for, or when I was visiting wound soldiers in one of the VA Hospitals."

"I've see a lot of wounded vets, not too many women, but there are certainly are some theses days."

Sonny said, "Gene and I will check on her tomorrow."

The following morning Sonny and Gene met with Captain Donna and Sonny asked her to send a request to the Beverly Hills Police Department and ask them to run a check on a woman named, Veronica King of Los Angeles.

Sonny said, "Tell them that she maybe a suspect in our four murders on the ship and maybe the person who killed Mrs. Jordan."

Donna said, "I'll do it, but do you really think a woman killed my four women?"

Sonny replied, "We don't know, but she seems to be interested in Aisha and Lucky Jordan said there was something about her that's seemed familiar to him about her."

"We know it's not much, but we just need to find out what we can about her. Frankly, it's more of a lead than we had so far on this case."

"We do know, she got on the ship in LA, so she been here all the time our women were killed."

Donna said, "OK, I'll send a message to the chief of police in Beverly Hills and ask him to give us any information they can find out about Veronica King."

Sonny thanked her and asked her to contact him or Gene as soon as she got anything back from Beverly Hills.

Donna told them she was having a meeting in a few minutes with her staff to determine everything they would be needing, while they were in the port in Lisbon.

She said, "After we leave Lisbon, we wouldn't be able to get any supplies until we arrived in Fortaleza, Brazil, then they would get additional supplies when they reached Rio de Janeiro.

The ship would be at sea for two full days, and reach Lisbon on the morning of the third day.

It was now morning of the second day, after Sonny and Gene met with Captain Donna.

She called Sonny to come to her office, that she had a message back from the Beverly Hills Police Department with information on Veronica King.

Sonny and Gene hurried to Donna's office and she asked them to come in after Sonny knocked on her office door.

Donna handed Sonny the message she received from the Beverly Hills Police Department on Veronica King.

Sonny said, "It sure looks like a short message."

Sonny read the message out loud, "Veronica Kay King lives at 2000 Beach Drive, Long Beach, California, she is thirty-six years old, she was discharged from the US Army, nine months ago; after serving in the army for six years and she has a one hundred percent disability pension from the army.

Her military record says she was wounded in Afghanistan and was hospitalized for over two years, due to complications with her recovery.

"When discharged, she was a staff sergeant, after being discharge from the service she worked as a cashier for a service station near her home in Long Beach for about four months prior to leaving her job to go on a world cruise.

"There is no record that she has ever been arrested or could we find any more information on where she was born or on her parents or where she attended school.

"She received a GED diploma while serving in the army.

"Prior to her army service, we can find no information on her parents or any other information about her, prior to her military service."

"Gene, apparently the information we got form our police chief in Kansas City is more up to date than we got from the Beverly Hills Police Department and from Alvin at the front desk here on the ship.

"They didn't give us any information about her inheriting thirty million dollars or her new LA address."

Sonny said, "It still looks like we got a mystery woman."

Gene replied, "It pretty hard to believe in this day and age, that you can't find anymore more information on her life than what the Beverly Hills police found."

"It sounds like she just dropped in out of the sky one day and joined the army."

Sonny replied, "There something fishy about what's going on about her records."

"You know Gene, I've heard that in some cases, when you're in the military and you were a government spy or working for the CIA, sometimes they seal the records of that person and it's not available to anyone."

Gene said, "One thing I know is, I don't think we would get much more information directly from her if we interrogated her."

Sonny replied, "I don't think so either, Gene, if she was someone who worked as a spy or for the CIA. I'd doubt we'd get any information from her."

"I think we will just have to keep an eye on her."

Donna asked, "Have you ever had anybody before that you couldn't get any more information on them that they came up with?"

Both Sonny and Gene said, "No, no, and no."

Donna said, "Well, I guess you better keep a close eye on her."

Sonny said, "With Lucky's help, we will."

The third day after they left Barcelona they arrived in Lisbon, where the four friends had one big tour one day and another tour the second day that they were in port.

On their first tour they visited, the Praca do Comerico, the Ribeira Palace; National Museum of Ancient Art, and Belem Palace.

By the time they returned to the ship the four friends felt like they could understand how Portugal was such a power in the world for some many years.

OK, it was now day two in Lisbon and their tour today included, Lisbon Cathedral, Castle Almourol, and wine and a short show of Portuguese music and songs, the songs were dark and sad, were called Fedo.

The learned that Fedo music begin in Lisbon, sometime in the 1820's, the woman who sung these songs was dressed in all Black including her gloves and the four friends listened and wondered how something so sad and dark remained so popular in Portugal after all these years.

The songs were sad to them, and they couldn't understand one word of Portuguese.

They also learned the Portuguese were the great navigators of the oceans, including Henry the Navigator, who promoted explorations of the cost of West Africa and helped Portugal claim several countries in Africa. Which they controlled until after the Second World War.

Interesting to them, was that he sent out more than fifty expeditions to many parts of Africa and his efforts and work helped with the development of maps, geography, navigation, and math, but he never went on one of these expeditions himself.

The Portuguese maps were held as valuable documents and they understood that if Portuguese captain gave or sold a copy of one of these maps to anyone from some other country the punishment was death.

OK, the four friends had done Lisbon and Europe.

Now, they were leaving Europe in the morning and their ship would be taking them south west to South America.

31

On Their Way to South America

The next morning the Golden Supreme left Lisbon on her way to South America, her next stop would be in Fortaleza, Brazil, this segment of their trip would take seven days.

The passengers would be able to get off the ship in Fortaleza, for only ten hours; tours would be Scuba diving at a state park; a windshield tour of the city, with stops at a couple of malls; or a trip to the Acqario Ceara Aquarium, the third largest aquarium in the world.

Or on your own for sunbathing and swimming on one of the beautiful beaches, located not far from where their ship would be docked.

Sonny, Jane, Gene and Susan, decided they would go on the tour to see the Acqario Ceara Aquarium.

However, there were seven days at sea to rest and get ready for their tour in Fortaleza. Which all four of them were ready for the time to relax and rest up for their adventures in South America?

Lucky and Aisha were also looking forward to have a lot of time together over their seven days at sea.

Both of them continued to do their daily exercises, just not at the same time, Lucky liked to do his very early in the morning.

Aisha, well, she liked to do hers a little later in the day, like around nine thirty or ten.

So they didn't see each other until lunch, which they always plan to meet at twelve thirty each day whenever they were on the ship.

Aisha new friend, Veronica was always in the exercise room everyday Aisha was there.

They had lots of conversations about their lives and their months spend in hospitals and rehabilitation over the past two years.

The two of them bonded very well with their shared experiences of injury and recovery.

Veronica told Aisha how she owed her life to one soldier that she served with and he had stayed with her when she was wounded, until help finally came to rescues both of them.

"I would do anything for him, all he would have to do was ask."

"I'm sorry to say he doesn't see me anymore he's gone out of my life."

Aisha said, "Well that's too bad. I'm sorry to hear that, maybe he's been kept to busy with the army."

Veronica replied, "No, he's not in the army anymore. He's moved on into other things now."

"Well, maybe he just wants to forget about serving in Afghanistan and everything that happened to him there."

Veronica replied, "No, I think he just doesn't want to see me."

"You know Veronica, sometimes it's better to move on. I know I've had to do that a few times in my life."

"I think it's worked out for the best, because now I've found the man I want to spend the rest of my life with."

Veronica asked, "Do you mean, Lucky Jordan?"

"Yes, I'm crazy in love with him and he loves me."

"Aisha, are you sure he loves you, it seems to me, he loves every woman he has ever had a chance to."

"You don't know Lucky, he's not like that at all. I know he was married once and his wife was killed by some mad man."

"Lucky's been having a terrible time recovery from that shock."

"He told you his wife was murdered by a mad man?"

"No, he didn't say the murderer was a mad man. I just used that phrase, don't you think anyone that kills someone is mad, you know, not right mentally."

"Yes, I guess that's right. I guess they must be mixed up in their mind and don't know what they are doing."

Aisha said, "Well it time for me to go. I'll see you in the morning. Have a great day, Veronica."

"OK love, see you and you have a great day too."

Aisha left the exercises room and as soon as she left, Veronica began following her and keeping out of Aisha sight.

Aisha hurried down the stairs from the eleventh floor, and was soon at the eighth floor and she began walking down the hall and never saw Veronica.

"When Aisha reached her room, she took out her cruise card; unlocked the door at her stateroom; number 8049.

Veronica saw which stateroom Aisha went into and walked past her room, now she knew which stateroom Aisha was in.

Aisha took her shower, fixed her hair; did her make-up; dressed and was ready to go to lunch with Lucky whenever he knocked on her door.

She had time to read the little daily newspaper, put out each day by the ship on news from the USA.

Aisha thought it was a very nice service the ship provided; she also knew the ship provided the same service each day for the passengers from Britain; Australia and Canada.

These papers were certainly not like receiving a regular newspaper at home, but they did cover the major new stories from each of these countries.

She finished reading the news from home and was putting the paper in her trash can when she heard a knock on her door, she rushed to open the door and there stood Lucky.

Lucky said, "Good afternoon my love, how are you today?"

"Well, I'd be better if I had a kiss for the day."

Lucky replied, "Your wish is my command."

Lucky reached out and took Aisha into his arms and gave her a nice warm kiss on her lips.

After kissing her, Aisha said, "You would do anything, I'd ask you to do."

"Of course I would."

"OK, I'll remember that forever, so don't you ever forget it."

"Aisha, would you like to have lunch?"

"Love to, so let's go."

"Where would you like to have your lunch?"

"At the English pub."

"OK."

The two of them went up to the English Pub and on their arrival Aisha saw her friend Veronica and she asked her if they could join her.

Veronica replied, "Certainly, love to have you two join me."

"Thanks Veronica, I don't think you've met my boyfriend, Lucky Jordan, have you?"

"No, of course every single lady on this ship knows his name, he the best looking single man on the ship."

Lucky said, "How do you do. I know who you are, your Aisha's friend, Veronica King. You two met in the exercise room."

"That's right, we met there and I really enjoy talking with Aisha while we're doing our exercises."

They sat down at Veronica's table and were soon enjoying their fish and chips and a glass of white wine."

Veronica asked, "So Lucky, are you enjoying your world cruise?"

"Well, I certainly am, since I've met Aisha. We're kind of helping each other enjoy our cruise. I wasn't enjoying it much until Aisha and I hooked up, now it's a blast.

"How about you Veronica?"

"Well, looking at the two of you together. I'd have to say, not nearly as much as you two. But I have moments, when I am enjoying my cruise.

"Right now, I'm looking forward to visiting South America. I used to dream about coming to Rio and lying on Copacabana Beach and seeing Sugar loaf Mountain and the Christ of the Andes statue."

Lucky said, "You sound like a travel agent selling Rio."

Veronica laughed and said, "Well, I'm really looking forward to seeing someplace that I've always wanted to go to and that place is Rio."

Aisha said, "I guess in about ten days you're going to have your chance to be in Rio and see it all."

"Boy, I'm looking forward to seeing it all."

A waiter came to their table and Lucky ordered all of them another glass of white wine.

The waiter brought them three more glasses of white wine.

Lucky asked the waiter, to please give him the charges for the wine and Lucky gave the waiter his cruise card.

When the three of them finished their second glass of wine Veronica said, "Now I see why all the women on this ship are crazy about you Lucky, you're so good looking and you buy them wine, you've got to be a keeper."

"Aisha, you better keep a close watch on your fellow or one of these gals will be moving in on your man."

Aisha said, "You can tell all of them, they better keep away from Lucky. I intend to keep him for the rest of his life."

Veronica thought to herself, *or your life.*

The three of them got up from the table and Lucky said, "Veronica, I was very glad to meet you after hearing Aisha talk about you all the time, she thinks you're a special friend."

"Well, I feel the same way about her. She tells me you were in the army over in Afghanistan. We'll have to talk about it sometime did she tell you I was wounded there myself?"

"Veronica, to tell you the truth I'd rather talk about anything else. I'm doing my best to forget about the time I spent there. I lost too many of my men there."

"How long where you there, Lucky?"

"Too long, can we change the subject, please Veronica?"

"Sure, no problem Lucky. It was nice to meet you."

"It was nice to meet you too Veronica, we'll see you later."

Lucky and Aisha got on the elevator and Veronica went up the stairs on her way to the open deck.

Aisha asked, "Lucky, I'm sorry I didn't think Veronica would want to talk about Afghanistan. I didn't know you felt that way. Sorry."

"It's OK, Aisha, like I said to her. I lost too many men over there."

"I love you Lucky, say is Lucky your real name or is it a nickname?"

"It's a nickname my name is Vernon Madison Jordan. I've been called Lucky, since I was about three years old, my father called me Lucky and told me it was because I was so lucky to have my mom and him for my parents."

"Then he said it was because everything I tried to do came so easy for me; school; grades; sports; and so many friends, he declared I was just lucky in life."

"I didn't think I was so lucky in Afghanistan, when I lost nine men in my platoon in one battle and had another seven of my men wounded, not counting myself."

"That's not lucky?"

"Lucky, was it really your fault these men were killed and wounded?"

"No, it was a surprise attack, we were told by headquarters there weren't any hostiles in the area, but they were there, lying in wait as we were crossing the mountain."

"How did you get hurt?"

"I was in the front of my platoon, along with my scouts, when we were cut off from the rest of my platoon."

"The rest of the company was behind us, we were the advance unit looking for any hostiles that might have been missed by an earlier scouting party."

"One of my men fell to my left and was dead, another one was hit on my right. He was wounded really badly and the two of us were trapped away from the rest of my platoon and most of them made it back to our company."

"So the man who was hurt bad was next to me. We were on a little ridge higher than the people who attacked us and they kept trying to come up to finish us off and I kept shooting at them."

"By now it was dark, so I couldn't tell if I had killed them or even hit one of them."

"I had bandaged my man wounds and kept pressure on the wound as much as I could and gave him a shot for the pain."

"I was so busy trying to keep him alive and shooting at anyone who tried to come up over the ridge."

"I don't know I had two slugs in my back, but after a long time I begin to feel weak and the pain in my back."

"Several mornings came and days went by then one morning my company advanced up to my position and when one of my men tried to help me up. I couldn't stand, so they had my wounded man and me put on a chopper and taken back to a hospital area."

"My man survived, and both of us, along with five of my other men made it back to the USA for treatment and rehab."

"I got a discharge from the army, and here I am."

"That's some story."

"I've seen the scars on your back and they looked awful close to your spinal cord."

"Yes, the doctor said about another quarter of an inch and I wouldn't be walking, but I'm OK now."

"Lucky, I'm so glad you are. I love you."

"I love you with all my heart Aisha."

Six days later the Golden Supreme arrived in Fortaleza, Brazil and Sonny, Mary, Gene and Susan had booked the tour to visit the Acqario Ceara Aquarium.

Lucky and Aisha were going scuba diving at a state park, Lucky asked Sonny if he and Gene and their wives would like to join them?

Sonny said, "No, I want to live to finish my world cruise and I haven't the slightest desire to be eaten by some big fish."

Lucky just laughed and said, "I think where we will be scuba diving, the fish would only tickle your toes, they won't be big enough to eat you."

"Well at my age you don't want to take any chances."

Lucky just laughed again and replied, "OK, but you'll be missing out a good time."

"I'm sure we will have a great time, just looking at the fish behind the glass walls at the aquamarine and we won't have to get wet to see them either."

"OK grandpa you go see the fish in the glass bottles and we'll be swimming with them."

"OK, you kids go and have a great time and us old people will be waddling around those big fish tanks."

All the tour groups were being called one at a time and the first tour of course was the scuba diving tour and the last one was the aquamarine tour.

By the time the four friends got off the ship, the tour bus for the scuba tour was long gone.

Gene said, "You know why Lucky wanted us to go with them don't you Sonny?"

"No, why did he want us to go with them scuba diving?

"Easy my old friend, he wanted to see our sagging old bodies in swimsuits. That's why."

"So you think he just wanted a good laugh?"

"I think so, he certainly looks in great shape and he's up bright and early everyday walking the track and doing his exercises."

"Well he wouldn't have been disappointed, because my old body is pretty saggy these days."

"Well partner, mines not much better."

Jane and Susan said, "Those old bodies are still good enough for us."

Sonny said, "Thanks, Jane."

Gene added, "Well mines old, but it's still working."

Susan said, "It working good enough for me."

"Thanks." Gene said.

Jane said, "Yours too Sonny, it's still works good enough for me."

Sonny replied, "Thanks Jane."

The four of them enjoyed the aquamarine it was the biggest and best aquamarine that they had ever seen.

They were amazed at the size of some of the sharks, they saw one great white shark that must have been close to twenty feet long and was the largest fish at the aquamarine and the one that got the most attention by the people visiting the aquamarine.

Sonny said, "If I went scuba diving that's the fish that I would find or the one that found me, that's for sure.

"No thanks, I'll stay on the big ships and wouldn't go into the ocean."

When the tour was over their bus arrived back at the ship at the same time as the bus with the folks who had been doing the scuba diving.

As they were getting off the bus. Sonny saw one of the people getting off the scuba tour bus had a large bandage on their head.

Soon after Sonny, Jane, Gene and Susan were off their bus they saw two more of the scuba drivers had bandages on their head.

Arriving back on the ship Sonny saw Lucky and Aisha and Sonny asked them, "What happened on your scuba diving trip that got three of the drivers hurt?"

Lucky answered, "They got caught in an undertow and banged them into a huge rock."

Aisha said, "If it hadn't been for Lucky they would have probably drowned."

Lucky said, "I'm sure they would have made it all right. I just helped to get them up and away from the undertow and back to the boat we were diving from."

Aisha said, "No, they would have drowned. Lucky went down two more times after he got the first person to the boat and brought each one back to the boat."

"The last one Lucky had to resuscitate him when he got him back to the boat or he would have been gone."

Sonny said, "It's a good thing we didn't go with you, you would have probably had to resuscitate four of us."

Aisha said, "The people he got back to the boat certainly knows Lucky is a hero."

"They were still thanking him when the bus returned to the ship, all of them thanked him for saving their lives."

Sonny asked, "Where were the people who operated the scuba diving boat, didn't they help."

Lucky replied, "They were busy helping other people, because there were several other folks who got swept down in the undertow."

Aisha said, "Lucky got the three people who went down and hit their heads on the big rock. I'm sure Lucky was a stronger swimmer than the people with the boat, two of them were young girls and the man with the boat was a lot older and not as fit as Lucky."

Lucky said, "I was just lucky to be able to get them up, the last man was pretty heavy and I couldn't have been able to get him in the boat my myself."

"It took me in the water and two younger guys in the boat to get him on the boat."

Sonny said, "I'm glad you were there to help Lucky, you're a good man."

Lucky smiled and said, "Try not to let that get around you'll ruin my reputation as a bad boy, one that picks up every pretty girl on the ship."

Aisha said, "Not any more, big guy, you're my man, no more picking up all the pretty girls you'll have to settle for just one, me."

Lucky had a very big smile on his face and replied, "Yes ma'am."

That night after Captain Donna heard about Lucky saving three of her passengers while scuba diving she invited him and Aisha to dinner.

She also invited the other folks who were seated at their regular dining room table to join them.

When Lucky and Aisha went to the Steak House for dinner that evening they were surprised that the captain had also invited Sonny, Jane, Gene and Susan to join them.

The captain had a private dining room sit up for them and had Vesko and his helper, Linda serving their dinner.

Captain Donna hadn't official met Lucky or Aisha before. Although she was sure she had shaken hands with both of them sometime at one of her champagne parties.

Where all of the passengers are invited and the captain and her officers greet ever passenger.

Captain Donna said when Lucky and Aisha come into the private dining room, "Good evening. I very happy to meet both of you. I'm Captain Donna Morehouse."

Sonny was standing next to Captain Donna and said, "Donna, I'm pleased to introduce you to Lucky Jordan and Aisha Charles."

Donna said, "On behalf of Supreme Ship Lines Lucky, I want to thank you very much for saving three of my passengers today.'

"I don't often have the opportunity to host a dinner for a hero on my ship but you are certainly a hero saving three lives today from drowning. Thank you and I hope you enjoy your dinner."

"I hope you don't mind share your special dinner with your regular table mates."

Lucky replied, "No, Aisha and I are always happy to be with our friends and it's very nice that you have Vesko and Linda here with us, we think they are very special."

Sonny said, "Their very special to all of us, now if you could only keep Vesko from leaving us in Rio, we certainly would appreciate that."

Donna replied, "I'll see what I can do about it."

Then Donna said, "Aisha, I understand you were there in the scuba diving adventure this afternoon, did you have any problem?"

"No ma'am, Lucky, quickly got me back to our boat when he saw what was happening.

"I was able to get back on the boat by myself while the people from the diving company, were working on getting several other people out of the water."

"Lucky went deep to get the people who hit their heads on the big rock."

Donna said, "Well I very happy you were save and the three people that Lucky saved have all been checked out by the ship's doctor and he reports they will all will recover quickly."

"Shall we all take a seat at the table now?"

Lucky replied, "Yes, thank you Captain Donna. I'm ready to have a seat and looking forward to wonderful dinner."

Donna said, "Good our chef has selected some very special steaks for everyone tonight and has promised a wonderful dessert."

Lucky replied, "It sounds wonderful to me, the food on the ship has been fantastic."

Donna said, "Our chef will be pleased to hear that, they all try so hard to please everyone, it's one of the toughest jobs on the ship."

The dinner was spectacular and all the guests enjoyed it, it would have been hard not to have enjoyed it.

The only complaint at the end of the dinner was they all wish they could have been able to eat more.

32

Welcome to Rio

Veronica was now at her dream destination and she signed up for two tours, since the ship would be in port in Rio for two full days.

Her first tour would take her to the top of Corcovado Mountain, which rises 2,329 feet high to see the Christ the Redeemer Statue; with a windshield tour of Rio, on the way to the Corcovado Train Station.

Reaching the train station, she would be taking the cog train and would be traveling through the Tijuca Rainforest to the top of Corcovado Mountain, where the statue of Christ, raises 98 feet high and has out stretched arms that are 92 feet wide.

Veronica learned by listening to the lecture about the tours offered by Supreme Ship Lines on Rio, that the Christ the Redeemer Statue is considered as one of the New Seven Wonders of the World.

After her visit to the Christ the Redeemer Statue, her tour would take her to see Sugarloaf Mountain. She learned during the lecture that Sugarloaf Mountain stands 1,299 feet above the Guanabara Harbor located on a peninsula that juts out into the South Atlantic Ocean.

To reach the top of Sugarloaf Mountain it's necessary to take a cable car from the base of Morro da Babilonia, with a stop going and coming at Moro da Urca, which is 722 feet high, here the passengers must leave the cable car then take a second cable car to reach the summit of Sugarloaf Mountain and she would have to do the same thing in reverse going back down to the base.

On her second day in Rio, she was going to go to two beaches, first Ipanema Beach and the second stop would be at the Copacabana Beach. She would be spending three hours at each beach.

She had been waiting a long time to see the Copacabana Beach, because she had been waiting to lie on that beach ever since she was twelve years old.

Everything she had ever heard about Copacabana Beach was it was the utopia of beaches, prefect sand; wonderful water; and lots of beautiful girls and boys. It was heaven right here on earth.

The people at Supreme Lines did tours very well, after spending an hour and a half traveling on the bus for their windshield tour of the city they arrived at Corcovado Rail Station.

A lady with the company that operated the trains boarded the bus when it stopped. She passed through the bus giving each of the tourists a train ticket and told them to be sure to hold on to your ticket, because you will need your ticket for the return train trip back down the mountain.

Veronica didn't know that people could walk up to top of Corcovado Mountain and sometimes the walkers decided they wanted to go back down and they tried to get a free ride on the train, thus the reason you had to hold onto your ticket for your return trip back down the mountain on the train.

It was a beautiful day and when they reached the top of the mountain the sight of Rio and the surrounding area was beautiful. The South Atlantic Ocean was breath taking and she thought she could see their ship in the harbor.

Veronica took picture after picture of the statue and of the view from the mountain and a young man who was watching her taking all the pictures asked her if she would like him to take a picture of her by the statue.

She told him, she would certainly appreciate it if he didn't mind, of course he didn't he'd asked her if she would like for him to do it. So the young man took several pictures of her with the statue and with her looking out toward the city below.

Veronica asked him if he would mind if she took his picture, no he didn't, so she had him stand next to the statue and took his picture.

After she took his picture, a group of people who he had obviously been with yelled, "Manuel."

The young man turned to his friends and replied, "OK, I'm coming."

Veronica said, "Thank you for taking my picture Manuel, it was appreciated."

Manuel smiled and said, "You're welcome ma'am. Have a wonderful stay in Rio."

Manuel turned and rejoined his friends and they started down the path to walk back down the mountain.

Standing at the base of the statue made Veronica feel like she was very small, it was hard to explain how she felt about been here, she had wanted to be standing here for a very long time and thought she never would.

She made a stop at the gift shop and purchased a Christ the Redeemer Statue then bought a Coke and looked around the sights of the mountains on the backside of the statue.

Veronica made a quick stop at the toilet before making her way to the train station for her trip back down to the base of the mountain. There her bus would be waiting for her and the rest of her fellow passengers on this tour.

Once the cog train made it down, she saw some of the other ship's passengers that came with her on the bus.

She asked a man standing there with his wife, if he had seen their bus yet?

He told her no, they hadn't seen the bus but he knew their local guide wasn't down from the top of the mountain yet either.

He told her, I guess we will just have to wait until our guide and our bus shows up.

He said there were some benches over in the parking lot and he thought some of our people were waiting there.

He suggested they might as well go there, so they would have a place to sit down and wait for their guide and their bus.

Veronica agreed and the three of them started walking to the benches where some of their folks were sitting waiting for their bus.

By the time they made it to the area of the benches, the three of them had introduced them self, the man name was Curley Brown.

His wife's name was Sherry, they were from Beaumont, Texas and Veronica told them her name was Veronica King, from Los Angeles, California.

The three of them had a nice conversation about their trip on the Golden Supreme, it seems the Brown's joined the cruise in Lisbon and when Veronica told then she started her trip in San Francisco they were surprised.

They wanted to know how she could be on a ship for that many days.

She explained to them, that she had been concerned about that before she started her trip, but told them there were so many things to do on the ship and she had enjoyed going to all the different ports the ship had visited.

Their wait was soon rewarded only about fifteen minutes passed before their local guide arrived, along with the rest of the people who were on their tour.

The guide took out her phone and called the bus driver and told him everyone was here and they were ready to go to Sugarloaf Mountain.

No one knew where their bus was parked, but they recognized it coming up the road and it soon pulling up in front of the people and were ready to load them.

The bus driver stops the bus and the people filed onto the bus and took the same seats they had on the way from the ship.

In a very few minutes everyone was on the bus and it was on its way to Sugarloaf Mountain.

Twenty minutes later they arrived at Morro da Babilonia, the base of the cable car they would be riding up to Mora da Urca. There they would get out of the cable car and take a second cable car on up to the summit of Sugarloaf Mountain.

Before everyone got off the bus, the local guide told them that a James Bond movie, called Moonraker was shot here using the cable cars in the most exciting scene of the movie.

Again, when the bus arrived a representative from the cable car operator came onto the bus and handed out tickets to each of the passengers.

Veronica thought Supreme certainly knew how to do tours the right way.

Before all of the guests left the bus, the local guide told them, they were all to be back on the bus by four thirty.

She said the bus would be parked in this same location.

Then the cable car representative led all of them to the cable cars and they were put at the head of the line and when the next car arrived and after all of the passengers got off the cable car.

All of them were able to get into one cable car and traveled to the first stop, there they an option. They could either spend time there or they could take a second cable car onto the summit of Sugarloaf Mountain.

Veronica chose to spend time at Mora da Urca, their first stop on the way to the summit of Sugarloaf Mountain.

There she took lots of pictures of the beaches and the buildings lying out in front of her like a little toy town, she thought she could tell there were people on the beaches, but she was up so high above the beaches she wasn't sure.

After spending some fifteen minutes taking pictures and looking around Mora da Urca, Veronica decided she better get on the next cable car and go on to the top of Sugarloaf Mountain.

She made her way to the cable car platform and when a cable car arrived there, she waited for the people to get off then she got on the car to make the trip on to the top of Sugarloaf.

Veronica wasn't happy to look down from the cable car, since there was only two other people in this car. She could see how far the cable car was up in the air from the ocean down below her. Veronica was afraid of heights so this trip was making her very nervous.

She had to remind herself they had been operating these cable cars since 1912 and she had read they redid the system in 1972 and increased the size of the cars from 22 people to be able to hold 75 people.

Arriving at the summit, she was very happy to get out of the cable car and stand on very firm ground.

Again, she spend a long time taking pictures in every direction that she could see, that meant she could see in every direction. She even got pictures of some of the huge tankers in the ocean which were either coming into port or leaving.

Since it was kind of windy, Veronica decided she had taken enough pictures and she returned to the cable car platform to wait for the next car to go back down to the bus.

She didn't have long to wait, she got on the next car and made sure she looked straight ahead and never down. She got off one cable car and on the next one which took her back to the base where her trip began.

Veronica still had almost an hour before it was time for her to be back on the bus, so she went into very large gift store, looked around and wound up buying a amethyst and gold necklace and a pair of matching amethyst and gold ear rings.

Veronica again met Curly and Sherry Brown as they were walking to the bus and Curly asked if she was traveling on the trip by herself.

Veronica said, "Yes, I am. I thought when I booked the trip I would be traveling with my new husband, but he married someone else."

Sherry said, "Oh my, I'm so sorry dear. I can't even start to think how terrible that must be."

"It was pretty awful, it broke my heart. However, now I believe it was for the best."

"Veronica if there is anything I can do to help you please let me know."

"Sherry, that's very sweet of you, but when something like that happens to you, you're the only one that can make yourself get over it.

"I'm much better now and I know this trip has helped me tremendously, it's giving me the chance to reflect on my own life and on the things I could have done better, if I had tried harder."

"Veronica, I understand that you blame yourself for him marrying someone else, but the true is that normally in these kinds of situations there more than one person to blame, maybe in this situation there's a third person."

"Thank you Sherry, for your kind words. However in this case, I'm afraid it was entirely my fault. I just lacked something he needed."

"So sorry my dear, there's still a lot of men out there and their one of them looking for someone like you."

By that time they had reached the bus and the conversation ended. Which Veronica was happy about, she felt like she had already said too much.

The next day Veronica was ready to go early, she couldn't wait to get to the Copacabana Beach, yes she knew she had three hours to spend at Ipanema Beach but then they would be taking her to the place, she had dreamed about being for a long time.

She had on her one piece red swim suit and she turned around and looked at herself in the full length mirror on her closet door. She turned slowly around and thought to herself, I look pretty hot in this swim suit.

She had shaved her legs this morning and under her arms and put lotion on her legs and rubbed the lotion in very well.

Before she went to the beach she would put suntan lotion on her legs, arms, breast area and her face. Her skin didn't like too much sun, she knew she burned easily.

Her tour bus was leaving at eight thirty and it would take them almost thirty minutes before they reached Ipanema Beach and the tour bus would be picking the tour group up at noon.

The guide for today told her it would take them about fifteen minutes to get to Copacabana Beach from Ipanema Beach and then the bus would be picking them up sometime between three thirty and four o'clock to bring them back to the ship.

The guide explained they couldn't be sure of the exact time, because they would be there to pick them up was because the traffic at that time of day was very heavy.

Veronica checked the time and saw it was eight fifteen, so she made her way to the assembly area for all the people who would be going on the beach tour.

She gathered up all of the things she thought she would need for the day and put it into the very nice large bag that Supreme had given all the passengers who were traveling of the complete world cruise, when they boarded the ship in San Francisco.

She had; sunscreen lotion; sunglasses; a large beach towel; two bottles of water; a small purse with about fifty dollars in it and her comb and a tube of lipstick.

She thought that should do it and she was surprised it all fit into her Supreme bag.

She was wearing a short white wrap over her swim suit and after she had the wrap on she had to check it out in the mirror.

She left her room and went to the tour assembly area to wait for her tour to be called and was surprised to see Aisha and Lucky there.

Aisha was wearing a white wrap that looked a lot like the one she was wearing and Lucky had on a pair of white shorts and a Supreme blue t-shirt with the words *"world cruise"* printed on the front of the t-shirt and a silk-screen picture on the back of his t-shirt of the *"Supreme 2017 world cruise route."*

As soon as Aisha saw Veronica she came over with Lucky following along behind her and Aisha said, "Hi Veronica, I glad to see you are going on the beach tours. Lucky and I are going to, please stay with us today so you have someone to be with."

Veronica replied, "OK. I'd be happy to do that, if it all right with Lucky."

Lucky quickly replied, "Certainly, I would be glad to have you go with us, it's a beautiful day and the water should be wonderful and I'm really looking forward to seeing these beaches.

"Besides, having two beautiful women with me will make me feel pretty special."

Aisha said, "Yeah, I'm sure Lucky is happy to be going with two women. Plus, he's all ready told me he'll be looking for that *"girl"* on Ipanema."

Veronica smiled and replied, "I doubt that, I think he's pretty happy with the girl he's with right now, that's what I think."

Lucky said, "I'm glad you said that Veronica. I keep telling her how much I love her, but she acts like she doesn't believe it."

Veronica was going to say something about Lucky's statement, but before she could they called their tour, so the three of them heading to their bus and following their guide for the day.

As they were leaving the ship they meet Sonny, Jane, Gene and Susan and Lucky asked, "So where are the four of you going?

'Are you going on the beach tour today?"

Sonny replied, "No we're going to see. The Christ the Redeemer Statue and to Sugarloaf."

Veronica replied as they pasted by them, "Their great. I did them yesterday."

Sonny said, "Good, you folks have a great day at the beach, see you later."

Just at that moment the four of them arrived at their bus as Lucky, Aisha and Veronica went by them on the way to their bus.

The thirty minute ride turned into a forty five minute ride to reach Ipanema Beach, but they finally made it through all of the traffic and the guide told them since we're late getting here, we will not leave here until twelve thirty.

She told them that their bus will return to pick them up right here at twelve thirty and then they would travel on to Copacabana Beach.

Lucky, Aisha and Veronica got off the bus and soon found a nice spot to lay their towels and bags down.

Aisha took off her wrap and she was wearing her two piece gold bikini.

Veronica thought the suit didn't leave much for anyone to have to have any imagination of what she had, everything was pretty well exposed right out there for anyone to see.

Lucky pulled off his t-shirt and took off his white shorts and was standing there near Aisha and Veronica in his dark blue swimsuit.

Veronica thought he looked like she had hoped he would. Now, she knew he did.

Veronica hesitated to remove her wrap, but she did and tossed it down on her towel.

Aisha said, "Veronica you look pretty hot in that suit, we'll have to watch out for you, some of those hot blood Brazilians will be trying to steal you away."

Veronica replied, "Well if they look as good as your guy, I'd be happy to let them."

Lucky and Aisha both laughed and Aisha said, "Good luck, I got the good looking one and I'm keeping him."

Veronica said, "I don't blame you, if he was mine, I'd hang on to him."

Lucky and Aisha took off hand in hand and went down to the water and both begin to swim out from the beach.

Veronica lay down on her towel on her back and checked the time to know when to turn over and work on a tan on her back.

Before too long Lucky and Aisha returned to where Veronica was and told her the water was wonderful and she should try it.

She told them, maybe later she would, but right now she wanted to work on her tan.

The three of them spent time lying in the sun and Lucky kept put lotion on Aisha and his self and said, "Veronica would you like for me to put some lotion on you."

She replied, "It would be very nice, if you did."

Lucky put lotion on each of his hands and began to slowly rub it onto her back and her shoulders, than he did each of her arms and the exposed upper part of her breast.

When he finished those areas, he began rubbing lotion on Veronica's legs. He was slowly rubbing it on each of her legs all the way from her feet up to the bottom of her swim suit.

It was almost too much for Veronica, feeling Lucky's hands rubbing up between her legs.

Her body was becoming too excited from his touch and said, "Thank you Lucky, that was very nice, but I think it's enough lotion for now."

"No problem Veronica, if you need some more, just tell me and I rub some more lotion on you. We don't want you to get sunburned."

"Thank you Lucky, no I don't want to get sunburned."

Lucky said, "You know girls. I keep looking for that *"girl"* from Ipanema, but I think I with the best two looking girls on Ipanema."

"Veronica replied, "We're glad you think so, aren't we Aisha?"

"All I have to say is, he better think that."

Lucky retorted, "It's no doubt, you two women are without a doubt, the best looking women on this beach."

With that remark Aisha picked up a bottle of drinking water and poured it out on Lucky's head."

Lucky shook the water off of his head, as he was laughing loudly and said, "What's the matter, didn't you think that sounded sincere enough."

Veronica responded, "No, it didn't sound sincere at all."

Lucky said, "I'm sorry ladies. I was very sincere it was probably was just the way I said it."

Aisha answered, "I'd say you're generally a pretty smooth talker, however I'm I think you maybe you could have sounded a lot more sincere with that statement."

Before anything else was said by any one of these three people.

The Supreme guide came walking by them and said, "OK, folks it's time to go to the bus."

Lucky, Aisha and Veronica quickly gathered up their things, at the same time the girls put on their wraps and Lucky pulled on his white shorts and put his t-shirt on.

They soon caught up with their guide and got to where the bus would be picking them up just before the bus pulled into the parking lot.

The Supreme guide counted the people who were on her tour and found all of her people were there and she told the bus driver we're ready to go.

For once the traffic was lighter than expected and their bus soon pulled into a parking lot near Copacabana Beach but before they tour group got off the bus the guide told them to be back to the bus by three thirty.

Then their guide led her tour group over to Copacabana Beach.

Lucky, Aisha and Veronica soon found a nice place to spread out their towels and three of them again took of their cover ups off and were ready to enjoy the beach and the water.

Lucky and Aisha went into the water again and Veronica lay down on her towel, fulfilling the dream she'd had since she was twelve years old, lying on Copacabana Beach in Rio.

When Lucky and Aisha returned from their swim, Lucky again applied lotion on him and Aisha.

When he finished putting the lotion on both of them he looked at Veronica and said, "Veronica, you're getting sunburned. I'll get some more lotion on you before it gets any worse."

Lucky didn't wait for a response from Veronica, he began putting lotion on her back and neck then asked her to turn over so he could do her front.

He quickly got lotion on her shoulders and her exposed breast area and then begins with her feet and legs.

This time when Lucky was rubbing her legs up to the bottom of her swimsuit, she didn't say anything, she simply laid there and enjoyed it when he was rubbing up the inside her legs all the way up to her swimsuit.

To soon the day was over, and the three of them made their way back to the bus and as they were getting back on their tour bus, Veronica said to Aisha, "Now I could die and be satisfied that I accomplished all the things I wanted to do all of my life."

Aisha replied, "You're kidding aren't you Veronica?"

"No, I'm not kidding. I wanted to lay on Copacabana Beach as long as I can remember."

33

Going to Buenos Aires

Captain Donna had her ship resupplied with all the food and fuel they would need to take them to Buenos Aires. She had been in contact with the local Supreme agent in Buenos Aires and told him they would be arriving there in three days.

Donna told him she would be in contact with him again the day before they arrived in Buenos Aires and would send him a list of the supplies that day that they would require during their stop there.

Sonny and Gene met with Captain Donna and told her at least it has been several months since the killer killed anymore women.

Donna asked, "Sonny, do you think he's gotten off on the ship?"

"I truthfully don't know Donna. We'd hope to catch him before he got off the ship, but if he did, we're pretty sure we would never know who the killer was."

Gene added, "I guess the best thing that's happened, is that we haven't had any more victims."

Donna said, "Amen to that, I think if we had one more. My replacement would have been flown in at my next port of call and I'd been on my way home to Hutchinson, Kansas."

They finished their conversation with Donna, went back to their rooms and they like so many other passengers were busy recharging getting ready for tours at their next port of call.

That evening at dinner the six regular table mates were gathered at their regular table and were not happy that they didn't get to say goodbye to Vesko, he was the favorite of all of them and they knew their dinners would never be the same without him.

Lucky said, "Well, I'm very sorry Vesko isn't with us anymore, but I have to share some news with my friends."

Sonny said, "OK, share it."

Which made Lucky laugh loudly and he got up from his chair and said, "I've asked Aisha to be my wife and she has accepted."

What do you think about that?"

Sonny said, "I think it wonderful."

Aisha was beaming and her face was as red as the swimsuit she was wearing yesterday.

Gene said, "Aisha, are you sure you want to marry Lucky?"

She replied, "I'm sure. I'm very sure."

Jane said, "That's wonderful, so when are you two going to get married?"

Lucky replied, "We're going to get married on the ship, we're going to ask Captain Donna to marry us."

Sonny said, "Wow, that should be something? Does Donna have the power to marry somebody?"

Gene said, "Good god, Sonny, the captain of a ship in international waters can damn well do anything she wants, she like god out here."

"OK, I just wanted to look out for Aisha. I didn't want Lucky pulling a fast one on her."

Susan said, "I think Aisha can do a pretty good job of looking out for herself, after all, she got the most eligible bachelor on this ship, to ask her to marry him.

'Half the women on this ship would throw their husbands overboard if Lucky would have asked them to marry him."

Gene asked, "Does that include you, Susan?"

"I don't know, he didn't ask me."

That got a real laugh from everyone at the table, except Gene and he said, "Well what if he asked you?"

Susan replied, "Darling, you know I wouldn't trade you for two Luck's, maybe three."

All the people at the table were laughing so hard, it made everyone in the dining room wondering what in the world was going on."

Sonny told the replacement waiter for Vesko, Ronald. "Please bring us two bottles of champagne, so we can celebrate the upcoming wedding of Lucky and Aisha."

Ronald soon brought two bottles of champagne and six cold glasses and opened the bottles.

Soon everyone at their table was busy toasting the bridal couple.

The night was happy and gay at their table and before long everyone in the dining room knew about Sonny and Aisha getting married.

The news spread quickly through out the ship and soon it got all the way to Captain Donna and she heard she would be performing a wedding soon.

One of the men at Veronica's dinner table returned from the men's room and asked if everyone had heard the news about Lucky Jordan and Aisha Charles, they were going to get married on the ship.

Everyone at Veronica's table were talking about them getting married and one of the ladies at the table asked Veronica what she thought about then getting married.

Veronica said, "You know Aisha is my dear friend and I will say I very happy for both of them, Aisha is such a sweet girl and I think Lucky is lucky to get her to marry him."

One of the other ladies at Veronica's table said, "Well most of the women I know on this ship would say Aisha is the lucky one to get a hunk like Lucky, he's hot stuff."

Her husband looked at her and said nothing.

When the woman saw her husband's look she said, "Well darling he is."

After dinner, Veronica saw Lucky and Aisha holding hands when they left the dining room and she follow behind then for awhile then went to her room.

When Veronica was in her room, she waited until it was a little before midnight and she left her room and walked directly to Aisha room and softly knocked on her door.

Aisha had just got ready for bed and had her night gown on and was in the process of taking her panties off when she heard the knock on her door.

Aisha cautiously went over to her door and looked through the peep hole of her door and was surprised when she saw Veronica's face looking at the door.

Aisha thought about it for a moment, but opened the door and let Veronica inside her room.

Veronica said, "I just heard the news about you and Lucky getting married."

"Yes, Veronica he asked me to marry him today and I told him, I would."

"Veronica why do you have on a blonde wig and white gloves?"

"Because, I can't let you marry Lucky, he's the man I love and he wouldn't have me."

"Veronica, I don't understand what you're saying."

Aisha back up to her bed and Veronica dropped a large black bag she was carrying and a empty champagne bottle rolled out of the floor.

Veronica reached both of her hands around Aisha neck hands and pushed her down on her bed.

As Veronica was pushing Aisha down on her bed, Aisha hand found the button on her bedside table.

Then Aisha was on her back on the bed with Veronica straddling her with both of her hands around Aisha neck choking her.

Veronica was making the grip on Aisha neck tighter and tighter, suddenly Veronica's hands were pulled away from her neck.

Aisha was coughing and choking and she saw Lucky had pulled Veronica off the bed and was fighting with her.

Veronica shoved an elbow hard into Lucky's ribs and it surprised him and he let go of Veronica and she turned quickly and kicked him hard and he fell back again the wall.

Then the door of Aisha room burst open and Sonny was there.

When Veronica saw that she had both Lucky and Sonny in Aisha's room.

Veronica pulled a small automatic gun out of her jacket pocket and fired a shot, but just before she fired her gun.

Sonny had jumped onto the bed and pushed Aisha off of the bed and onto the floor.

The bullet grazed Sonny's head and went into the headboard of the bed.

Before Veronica could pull the trigger again, Lucky hit her in the head with a champagne bottle he found on the floor.

Sonny jumped off the bed and grabbed Veronica as she was falling to the floor and gently laid her down on the floor.

Sonny looked up and saw Lucky was helping Aisha up from the floor where he had pushed her away from the gun fire.

Lucky said, "Aisha, are you all right honey?"

It took a minute for Aisha to answer, then she said, "I'm all right my neck hurts and I hit my head on the wall when Sonny pushed me off the bed, but it will be OK."

Sonny said, "Lucky called the front desk and tell them that Sonny Cousins said it's an emergency, contact the captain and have her come to room 8049 and bring a photographer; the doctor and the chief of security."

Lucky picked up the telephone and called the front desk and told them what Sonny had asked him to do.

Sonny was listening to Veronica's heart and heard nothing, he checked her pulse, nothing and she wasn't breathing.

Sonny said, "She dead. That blow to her head killed her."

Sonny added, "Thank you Lucky, she would have killed Aisha and me if you hadn't hit her in the head when you did.

"She was despaired she couldn't let you marry Aisha."

"Sonny asked "Lucky, how come you didn't tell us you knew her?"

"I didn't know her. I never saw her before in my life, until I met her with Aisha."

"Well, she certainly knew you."

"Well, I don't know how she knew me."

Sonny said, "Never mind that. We'll get into that later, how are you doing Aisha?"

"My neck is really hurting and I think. I'm going to throw up. Seeing poor Veronica lying dead on my bedroom floor isn't helping any.

"Lucky, she said before she started choking me that she loved you but you wouldn't have her, so why do you keep saying you never knew her."

"I'm telling you Aisha, I never saw that woman in my life, until I met her on the ship when you introduce her to me."

Sonny said, "Lucky, maybe it was a one night stand with her."

"I don't know what I'm going to do to convince you two. I've never seen Veronica in my life before meeting her on this ship."

Fortunately for Lucky, Captain Donna, Dr. Spears, Jack Taylor and Ted O'Shea all arrived at the room at that moment.

Donna said, "Sonny, you got our killer?"

"Actually Lucky got our killer for us. We need to get lots of pictures of this room."

"But first Doctor Spears, would you check Miss Aisha over. I'm sorry to say the killer had her by the neck before we got here."

Doctor Spears took a quick look at Aisha's neck and said, "I happy to say the killer didn't crush any of your seven cervical vertebra in your neck, your necks is going to be sore for a few days, but you're going to be all right.

"I'd say they saved you just in time."

"Let me check the woman on the floor."

Doctor Spears went over to Veronica's body and checked her head and said the blow to her head was enough to kill her it had crushed the Cranium into the brain.

The doctor said he would do a quick examine of her body to see if there was any additional damage to her.

The doctor glanced over at Sonny and said, "Sonny, what's happened to you, you've got blood running down the right side of your head?'

"It's nothing. I guess the bullet that Veronica fired at Aisha grazed my head."

"Let me take a look at it anyway."

Doctor Spears put on his rubber gloves and had Sonny sit down on a chair so he could examine the wound.

The doctor said, "It's not too deep. I'll get it cleaned up and put some medicine and a bandage on it."

He took out a bottle of alcohol and some medium size pads and cleaned off the blood and then put some type of medicine on a bandage and taped it on Sonny's head.

Doctor Spears said, "I'd say you were really lucky, another inch or maybe less and we would have had a major problem trying to keep you alive."

The doctor said, "Well now, I'll take a look at our killer's body."

Captain Donna said, "Before you do that doctor. I want to tell Aisha how sorry we are that someone tried to kill you, but I'm glad Sonny's idea worked and kept you alive."

"Lucky thank you, Sonny told me you saved him and Aisha from being shot, thanks for saving both of them."

"Aisha, would you like to come and stay in my quarters for the night, until we can sort this all out?"

"Yes, thank you captain. I would like to do that."

Aisha put on a robe and the two of them left the stateroom to go up to the captain's quarters.

Doctor Spears said, "OK, now that they are gone. I will take a look at the killer's body to see if she had an additional injures."

The doctor began to make an exam of Veronica's body.

The doctor said, "Well she certainly has a lot of scars on her body and oh my god; she has a penis; but no testicles, the scrotum is missing, it looks as if she/he may have had a prior injury and they were removed, since there is a lot of scar tissue in this area."

"I'm going to check her/his breast; well the mammary glands are real enough, perhaps he has been going through the process of having a sex change.

"That may explain the growth of the mammary glands, although I'm not an expert on sex change procedures. I don't think they would normally remove the scrotum and the testicles until they were ready to remove the penis and construct the vagina."

"I think this person must have had a serve injury in the scrotum area and they found it necessary to remove it and the testicles."

"I don't think there anything else I can do here. I'll write up a report of her/his death, the time of dead and the cause of death."

"Jack, you can remove the body whenever you're ready."

Dr. Spears said, "Good night."

Sonny said, "Jack can you take some fingerprints from our killer and tomorrow we'll send them to my friend, the chief of police of Kansas City."

Jack said, "I'll take care of getting the body moved to cold storage and we'll get the killers fingerprints, so they can be sent off tomorrow."

The director of security picked up Veronica's gun and placed in a plastic bag and left the room to take care of getting the body moved out of the room and to take the fingerprints.

Sonny said, "Lucky, thank you for saving both of us, Veronica was going to kill both of us, you do know that don't you."

"Lucky, I don't know if you can get any rest or not, but I wish you go could try to get some and tomorrow we'll sort this all out."

"Between us, we'll figure out why this person was so in love with you that she was willing to kill five women."

"I know she succeed in killing five of them and if it hadn't been for you, she would have killed Aisha."

"OK Sonny, I'm going back to my room and try to figure out whom, this person was that claims to have been so much in love with me that she would kill women."

Sonny said, "I'm going to close the connecting door, so we keep this room locked up until we get everything we need for these four murder cases."

Lucky left the room and closed his connecting door and Sonny closed the other door."

During all this time, Ted O'Shea had been waiting to take his pictures and he wanted to get them before Veronica's body was moved.

Sonny said, "I hope this is the last pictures you have to take of dead bodies on this trip."

Ted replied, "If isn't, I think I'll go back to work for a police department, then I know that's the kind of pictures. I'll be taking."

Sonny said, "Good night Ted, thanks for all your help."

34

Finally Some Answers

Gene knocked on Sonny and Jane's stateroom door the next morning and Jane answered the door and said, "Well Gene, you missed all the action last night."

"What do you mean I missed all the action, you and Sonny have a big fight last night?"

Gene just finished saying that as Sonny came out of the bathroom and Gene saw the bandage on the right side of his head and it was soaked with blood.

Gene said, "My god Sonny what happened to your head, did you fall from drink too much champagne last night?"

Jane said, "No, Sonny didn't fall he got shot."

"You have to be kidding, Sonny how did you get shot?"

Sonny head was hurting pretty bad at that moment and said, "Veronica shot me, but it's OK. "

"Lucky killed her by hitting her in the head with a champagne bottle she had brought to deposit into Aisha's vagina after she had killed her."

"Is Aisha all right?"

"She is, she managed to ring her danger bell, and so Lucky and I stopped Veronica from killing her."

"Why didn't you call me?"

"I didn't have time it was all over in less than five minutes. I wasn't really keeping time, but I'm sure Veronica managed to attack and choke Aisha and Lucky got her off of her."

"I pushed Aisha off the bed and Veronica shot at Aisha and hit me and Lucky crowned her with the champagne bottle."

"However, we've got a lot more work to do on this case. We're going to find out a lot more about Veronica, she had a penis, so we think he was in the process of getting a sex change and maybe that why her military record had so little information about her past."

Gene said, "Well we never had a case like this in all the year we worked homicide in Kansas City."

"You're right Gene we never had some one that killed five women to keep them away from the man she loved, maybe one woman, but never five, four on the ship and Lucky's wife.

"She tried to kill the sixth one after she found out Lucky was going to marry Aisha.

"Gene, you know the topper to this case, Lucky still claims he never knew this woman before Aisha introduced her to him."

Jane said, "Maybe, Lucky had so many women, he just couldn't remember Veronica."

Sonny replied, "Maybe, but I think the way you said he had so many women kind of intimating he had sex with so many women. I think he would have remembered one that had a penis."

"Lucky is a pretty observed fellow, I think he would have remembered that detail."

Gene and Mary both laughed and Gene said, "You're right. I'm sure he would have remembered that small detail."

"So how do you explain it that he insist he's never meet her?"

"I don't know Gene, but maybe when we search Veronica's room we may have a better clue as to way Lucky didn't recognize her."

Up in the captain's quarters Aisha was just getting up in the captain's guest room. She put on her robe and made a stop in the bathroom. Then she went out of the bathroom to see if she could find Captain Donna.

Aisha was rubbing her sore neck, she soon found Captain Donna drinking a cup of coffee in her office.

Captain Donna said, "Good morning Aisha, how's your neck?"

"Well it's sore, but not too bad, my head a little sore from hitting the bedroom wall when Sonny pushed me off the bed and I found a bruise on my butt from hitting that wall."

"However, unlike Veronica I'm alive, thanks to Lucky and Sonny. My little hurts will go away soon."

"You know captain. I can't help but think of something Veronica told Lucky and me after we had the day at the beaches in Rio. She said *"now I can die happy, after lying on the Copacabana Beach and seeing the Cross of the Redeemer."*

Captain Donna said, "That's kind of pathetic, don't you think?"

"It is, but somehow, as much as I liked her. I can't feel too sorry for her. She tried to kill me and apparently she murdered four other women on your ship."

"Captain Donna, the one thing I don't understand is that she told me, she loved Lucky, but he rejected her."

"Yet he claims he has no idea of who she is."

"Aisha, I wouldn't be too quick to judge Lucky, maybe there a reason he doesn't remember who she is."

"I can tell you Donna, I mean Captain Donna, and it better be a damn good reason why he couldn't remember her."

"I've promised to marry him, so how many other women will be showing up in the future says they loved him, but he doesn't even know who they are."

"Lucky said after I told him. I'd received a seven million dollars settlement that I'd better watch out telling too many men that or some gold digger would be after me for my money."

Donna said, "What did you say to him then?"

"I asked him if he was after my money."

"OK, Aisha then what did he tell you?"

"He said, I was beautiful and he would be after me if I didn't have two nickels to rub together."

"Then I don't think you have to be too worried about a lot of women coming after him after you're married."

"Yesterday, I thought Lucky was just being nice to Veronica, when he offered to put sun screen lotion on her at the beach."

"Aisha, I think Lucky is nice and I think after what you went through last night you've got a right to be concerned."

"It is all right to just call me, Donna but as an older woman I would tell you it's been my experience that you should be sure of something before you decide what's true when you're dealing with a man."

"I've found sometimes when something seems so straight forward to a woman it may be not be to a man."

"I guess we better find you some clothes to wear. I'd guess you don't want to go the whole day with wearing your gown and robe."

"I'll call Sonny and have him take you to get some clothes out of your room and then we'll see if we can find you some new accommodations."

"Sonny Cousins is my best friend, he has been since we were five years old, he's my big brother, since our parents were best friends and we were both only children. He a very good guy and he will look after you."

Donna called and got Sonny on the phone and asked him to take Aisha to get some clothes to wear today and she would make arrangements to have the rest of her things moved to a new stateroom."

Sonny and Gene came to Donna's office and took Aisha down to her stateroom, Veronica's body had been removed and things were being cleaned up and a new head board had all ready been put in place and the one with the bullet hole had been taken out of the stateroom.

Aisha took a quick shower and told Sonny and Gene. "It was all right, they didn't need to stay there."

Now, Sonny and Gene were assured that Aisha was doing all right.

Sonny and Gene made their way to Veronica's stateroom and begin searching for a clue of as to who she was and why couldn't Lucky recognize her.

If she was so much in love with him, that she killed four people on the ship it was probably certain she was the one that killed his wife. If that wasn't enough, then she tried to kill Aisha last night.

They begin to search the room for answers to these questions.

Gene looked in Veronica's closet and found a box of medical records and military records, along with a trove full of pictures.

After Gene and Sonny spent five minutes looking at the pictures and her military and medical records, Sonny said, "Gene, we need to take all this stuff up to Donna's office and have a meeting with the three of us and have Donna contact Aisha, Lucky, Jack Taylor and Doctor Spears to join us to discuss what we've found in Veronica's room."

Gene agreed, so Sonny called Donna and asked her to have all of the people come to a meeting in her office.

Thirty minutes later, all of the people Sonny asked to attend the meeting were gathered around Donna's conference table.

Donna said, "Sonny, you asked for this meeting, so what's it all about?"

Sonny said, "Gene and I searched Veronica's room to see if we could find any information as to why Veronica claimed to be so much in love with Lucky that she would kill five people."

"What Gene and I found was all of her military and medical records. These documents along with hand written notes, Veronica wrote give us all of the information we were looking for."

Sonny took a picture from the box of pictures they found in her room and handed it to Lucky.

Sonny asked, "Lucky, do you know who this is a picture of."

"Sure I do, it was one of the men in my platoon. It's Tony Longstreet. He's the one that was wounded that I took care of for three days in Afghanistan before we were rescued. So, what does that mean?"

"Lucky, that's Tony Longstreet after a lot of plastic surgery. We have pictures of the various procures he had to go through to become Veronica."

"Her or his military records shows that when Tony was wounded in Afghanistan one of his wounds required removal of his testicles and his scrotum.

"His penis was injured but at the time they were able to repair it.

"After Tony was back in the US, did you ever go to see him, when he was in a VA hospital, Lucky?"

"Yes, I did. I saw him several times?"

"Lucky did he ever tell you he loved you?"

"Yes he did. I remember him saying that. I told him I loved him too, but I liked women a lot more."

"When you been through what we went through in Afghanistan. You form a bond with all of your buddies. I guess other people wouldn't understand that, unless you been through combat. I loved all my men."

Sonny said, "We found Veronica's diary, saying she would do anything to have you for her own and she was sorry to have to kill your wife and any other woman that you might become interested in."

"She said she knew what you wanted and liked, so she was going to get it for you a vagina, if you would have just giving her time."

Sonny added, "Well, Tony Longstreet was deeply in love with you and was willing to go through a sex change to have you for him/her self."

"Then while he was having all of these surgeries, apparently, he found out you got married, he snapped."

"His medical records from his Beverly Hills Plastic Surgeon indicated he was to have his final surgery to remove his penis and built a vagina a month after this cruise ended."

"I'll pass around these pictures of all of the surgeries on his face and pictures as his breast developed from the shots he took."

Lucky looked at the pictures and after all of this soaked in, he said, "I'll be damned. I saved his life in Afghanistan and he comes back and kills five women and try's to kill Aisha.

"Something all wrong with this, I tried to do something good by saving Tony and what were the results. The person I saved killed five women, and in the end, I had to kill him myself."

Aisha along with all the others who looked at the pictures of what Tony looked like before and then what Veronica looked like after the transformation from all of her plastic surgeries, little wonder Lucky couldn't recognize her.

Now they understood why Lucky wouldn't have recognized Veronica and why he kept saying he didn't know her.

Aisha reached for Lucky's hand and he took her hand and Aisha said, "Lucky, I'm so sorry for doubting you, when you said you didn't know who Veronica was. I'm so sorry."

"I love you."

35

The Happier World Cruise

Lucky and Aisha talked to Captain Donna about getting married and she told them she would be please to marry them.

They told Donna, they would like to have their parents at their wedding and Donna asked them when they wanted to get married, well of course, as soon as possible.

Donna suggested then, they should have their folks meet them in Valparaiso, Chile. She said they would probably have to fly into Santiago from the US and then get ground transportation on to Valparaiso.

Donna told them the ship would be there in two weeks and we have several passengers who will be leaving the ship there, so we will have several min suites available for your parents.

Lucky and Aisha agreed they would wait to get married until their folks could be with them and they would have the wedding soon after their ship left Valparaiso.

Both of them thought it was going to be a long two weeks.

Captain Donna talked to Barbara White, head of hotel operations and found they had one of the large suites available for the balance of their trip all the way back to San Francisco.

Aisha had been staying in Donna's guest room ever since Veronica attacked her and most of her things were still in her old min suite.

Donna said, "Aisha, I've made arrangements to have all of your things moved to the owner's suite on deck nine."

Then she handed Aisha two key cards for the suite.

Donna said, "I thought you and Lucky should have the best we have, with all that you two have gone through on this voyage. Consider it, your first wedding gift."

"Oh, thank you Donna, you've been so wonderful to me. I know Lucky is going to appreciate it too."

"Aisha, I want to wish you lots of happiness in your married life."

"Thank you so much, you are just too kind Donna."

Donna then said, "I must go to a meeting with my senior staff now."

Donna left her office to go to her conference room, where her staff was waiting for her.

Aisha also left, to see her new quarters and when she arrived she found several room stewards unpacking her things and putting them away in the closets and in the several drawers in her very large suite.

Her new room steward said, "Ma'am, I'm sure you will probably want to rearrange your things, but right now we just wanted to get everything out of your old quarters into the owner's suite for you."

Aisha thanked them for bringing all of her things to her new suite and putting everything away and said, "I know I had some things in my safe there, you didn't bring those did you?"

The steward replied, "No ma'am, we don't have access to safes, you will have to get those things yourself. If you need help bringing them to your new quarters, I'd be happy to help."

"No thank you, there not too much in the safe. So I wouldn't need your help to do that, but thank you."

That morning while this was going on Lucky was busy on his own errand. He went to the ship's jewelry store and after an hour looking at engagement rings for Aisha he made his decision on the one he wanted to buy for her.

Finally, he decided on what he thought would be the best one for Aisha it was a solitaire two carat diamond, set in a gold princess style ring.

They had matching wedding bands for both the bride and groom with the engagement ring, but Lucky thought he wanted to have Aisha decide of the wedding bands.

Lucky bought the ring for his princess, although he wasn't sure what a princess style ring was, but it sounded good. The jewelry store placed the ring in a lovely blue box for him.

Lucky paid for his purchase and then he was off to find Aisha, to give her, her ring.

It didn't take long to find her, as he was walking past her old suite he saw the door standing open and Aisha closing up the safe.

Lucky hadn't been in that room, since he killed Veronica there.

He didn't go into the room, but asked, "Aisha, what are you doing in here?"

Aisha turned and saw Lucky in the hallway and said, "They've moved me into a new suite and I'm just getting my things out of the safe."

"Can I help you move your things honey?"

"No, everything has been moved by the ship's people, except what I had in my safe. Can you come and see my new digs, Lucky."

"Of course I can. I was just on my way to find you. So where is your new room?"

Aisha played it cool, she said, "Come with me, and I'll show you my new quarters."

They left and took an elevator up to the ninth floor and Aisha guided Lucky to her new room.

She opened the door and gracefully invited him into her new suite.

She showed him her new living room, with a large screen TV; dining area; two bathrooms and one very large bedroom, with a second TV and a whole wall of closets and drawers."

Lucky gave a whistle and said, "Wow, who do you know to get a suite like this?"

Aisha shrugged her shoulders, grinned and said, "Who else, the captain."

"Of course you do."

Aisha said, "Actually, it's not just my suite, it's our suite for after we are married. I'm just occupying it by myself until we're married.

"Captain Donna, told me it's was our first wedding present. Lucky, Donna is so nice, I love her."

"Not more than you love me do you?"

"Of course not Lucky, why would you even say that?"

"Good, then I have something I want to say to you. Please, sit down on your new couch."

Aisha said, "Yes sir."

She sat down on the couch and Lucky got down on one knee and said, "Aisha, would you do me the honor of becoming my wife?"

At the same time he saying that, he opened up the pretty blue box and the sun was shining brightly through the window onto that beautiful diamond and it sparkled like the sun it's self.

Aisha replied, "Yes my darling. I would be honored to marry you."

Lucky took the ring out of the box and slipped it on her ring finger on her left hand.

Then took he took her in his arms, gave her a very tender loving kiss.

After the kiss, Aisha had to inspect her new diamond ring and she was flashing the reflecting sun off of her diamond all around the room. The ring was beautiful and she loved it and told Lucky it's perfect.

Later that afternoon they went to the jewelry store and bought the two wedding bands that matched her diamond engagement ring.

The next three weeks would prove to be a very long wait for these two, even thought their ship made it into port in Buenos Aires, a very interesting exciting city.

As Sonny, Jane, Gene and Susan were leaving the ship to go on their tour in Buenos Aires. Sonny saw a hearse was waiting to pick up Veronica's body.

Captain Donna had gotten in touch with Veronica's cousin. She was the person Veronica listed as her emergency contact.

Veronica's cousin, Joan King told Donna, she would make arrangements through the American Embassy to have Veronica's body brought home for burial in the family plot in Beverly Hills.

Sonny would find out when he returned home that Joan King was the only heir that of Veronica. She would be the one to inherited what was left of the thirty million dollars Veronica had from selling her father's property.

However, now Sonny, Jane, Gene and Susan were off to enjoy seeing the sights of Buenos Aires.

Sonny couldn't believe the size of Avenue 9 of July, the widest boulevard in the world, at an amazing 425 feet wide.

America may have the White House, but Buenos Aires has the pink house, it is the executive mansion and office of the President of Argentina. Although they were told by their guide, the president actually lives in Qunita de Olivos.

The four of them laughed out loud when their guide said the pink house was painted baby pink, considered the most emblematic building in Buenos Aires.

However, they all agreed it was beautiful to look at.

Their next stop was the Plaza de Mayo and they were told it was the sight of the May 25, 1810 of the beginning of the revolution that gained independence of Argentine from Spain.

They saw the Obelisk, built in 1936 to commemorate the four hundredth year of the founding of the City of Buenos Aires.

Their guide told them it had suffered a lot of vandalizes over the years and once the city had even voted to tear it down but there decision was overruled by the federal government and the Obelisk was made a national monument and now has a fence around it.

Their last stop was the girl's favorite, Florida Street, the elegant shopping street in downtown Buenos Aires had been a pedestrian avenue since 1971 and was just over a mile long. She told them some part of the street had been just for pedestrians since 1913.

The four of them found Lucky and Aisha as they were looking around, Aisha was in the process of looking for a wedding dress and if she couldn't find a dress here she would never be able to find one before their wedding.

Sonny got one big surprise when they were talking to them. Lucky asked Sonny to be the best man at his wedding and Aisha said she had asked Donna to be her maiden of honor, but Donna said she would love to, but she was performing the wedding.

She suggested Aisha should ask Jane to be her maid of honor.

Aisha did ask Jane and she accepted. She said she would be honored to be her maid of honor.

Now, Jane had to have a dress for the wedding. Since this was the last stop of their cruise before the wedding that they could really shop it.

Aisha asked Jane to come with her and help her find her wedding dress and then they would find one for her at the same time.

Lucky and Sonny had no problem with what they would wear for the wedding they had their tuxes, so the men had it easy.

Jane said, "Men are so lucky, they never have to worry about what they're going to wear."

Lucky looked at Sonny, then they both smiled and jointly said, "That's right dear, whatever you say."

Sonny, Gene and Susan left Lucky, Aisha and Jane to join their tour group at the appointed time.

Sonny told their guide Jane was shopping and would return to the ship with two of their other passengers.

Sonny, Gene and Susan made it back to ship three hours before the shoppers returned.

However, the other three made it back in time for dinner and in plenty of time, before it was time to sail away from Buenos Aires.

The most important thing that happened that day was the bride and her maid of honor had their wedding dresses.

Next, the ship would be traveling to Antarctic and when they arrived there.

They found that they couldn't get off the ship, because under agreement with the International Association of Antarctic Tour Operators, their ship was too large to allow passengers off.

The maximum number of passengers any cruise ship could land on the Antarctic was 100 people.

However, what they were able to do was to have a wonder opportunity to observe the numerous birds; penguins and whales off the coast.

It was a great experience, to at least view this very forbidding looking land and it was plenty cold enough for the four friends being out of the deck of the ship, with every piece of warm clothing they could find.

They used to think it got cold in Kansas City and this it was the warmest time of the year in Antarctic.

Sonny thought my God. I'd hate to be here when it was the coldest time of the year.

They cruised around the Antarctic for a day before they left to be on their way to their next stop, Valparaiso, Chile.

36

Ships Bells Ringing for The Wedding

Time passed slowly for the couple waiting for their wedding, while the rest of the ships passengers were enjoying the many on board ship experiences.

The other passengers were enjoying activities such as instructions in ballroom dancing; learning knitting; exercise classes; the casino; bingo; playing bridge; making new friends; the nightly live shows; computer classes; meeting of veterans; reading books; playing computer games; visiting the numerous bars; demonstrations of ice and vegetable carving; lectures on sights to see in your next port and additional lectures on a variety of other subjects; and watching TV and movies or simply the opportunity to rest and relax and watch the world go by from your stateroom window.

In other words there was never a shortage of things you could get involved with on your cruise you could join in or not, and of course the favorite thing of almost everyone of board was eating. There was never a shortage of things to eat and several places to do it.

However, if you were counting the days to your wedding, none of these things were as important as making the days go by quicker.

Lucky and Aisha now wished they hadn't invited their parents to their wedding but on the other hand they were glad they did.

Aisha hadn't been married before and her mother and father always assumed they would be at her wedding and they were delight she was getting married.

Lucky's parents had been so concerned about him after his first wife was murdered that they were thrilled he had found a someone that gave him something to live for, they were concerned he might take his own life.

Lucky and Aisha were spending as much time as they could together and really getting to know each other likes and dislikes. They shared experiences they had in their life and talked about their schools and about the friends they grew up with and where they had traveled.

Aisha had a hard time talking about her accident when she was working in Brazil and had dreading the two stops there, but having Lucky with her helped and she never told him how much she dreaded going there.

If it hadn't been for her relationship with Lucky, she would have just stayed on the ship during their two stops in Brazil.

However, being with Lucky, she not only made the stops but she enjoyed them. Life was far better sharing places with someone that you loved.

The other thing the two of them decided was they would not have sexual relations until they were married, sometimes Aisha thought, oh that such an old fashion idea. But they stuck to their decision, no sex!

Days pasted by slowly, oh so slowly, but one day when Aisha woke it was the day their ship would be arriving in Valparaiso.

There, hers and Lucky's parents would be meeting them and the day after they left Valparaiso. The two of them would be getting married. She could hardly wait.

Captain Donna kept busy each time they arrived or left a port she was on the bridge directing the whole procedure then was when her ship was most in danger of hitting something or getting hit.

Docking her ship was like maneuvering a building that was almost a 1,000 feet long it just didn't stop on dime like a car would traveling at a very slow pace like her ship was.

Everything had to be exact, one false move or one wrong turn could mean a damaged ship or worse wiping out a dock.

Donna was truly the master of her ship years of navy experience with all sizes of ship made her the expert.

Most people like her when they retired from the navy would not have chosen to be a captain of a cruise ship. They would have taken their pension and sit on a beach somewhere, but Donna loved people and loved being a sailor.

If she had stayed must longer in the navy and earned another promotion she would have been given a desk in Washington. So she retired, so she could keep sailing.

Again, her ship was docked without any problem and her passengers would soon be able to get off of her ship and she knew two people who were looking forward to see their parents come aboard.

It was afternoon before the parents of Lucky and Aisha arrived at the dock and boarded the ship and they were certainly ready to see their children.

As soon as they came aboard the ship Lucky and Aisha were standing by waiting for them.

Their parents came aboard together and Lucky hugged his mother and gave her a kiss and then his father.

Aisha was busy doing the same with her parents and then Aisha was introduced to Lucky's parents and Lucky was introduced to her parents.

Lucky said to his parents, "I would like to introduce you to, Aisha."

Lucky's mother Helen said, "Oh we knew who she is, we meet her parents in Dallas and the four of us have been talking nonstop ever since then.

With that Aisha father, Will said, "Lucky, I'm very happy to meet you, I'm soon to be your father-in-law and my wife, Nancy will be your mother-in- law, and you know what they say about mother-in-laws.

Lucky laughed at Will gave him a big hug, than Nancy gave him a hug and a kiss and said, "Welcome to our family."

Lucky's father, Charles said, "Aisha, you're even pretty than your mother and father told us. Honey you're beautiful and my son is lucky to find you."

Aisha replied, "Thank you, and the true is Lucky did find me and I've been causing him trouble ever since."

Then the four of them continued talking and suddenly Captain Donna arrived and Lucky said, "Folks I would like to introduce you to our Captain Donna Morehouse."

Aisha father, Will said, "You're the captain of this ship, the one that going to marry our daughter to Lucky?"

Donna smiled and said, "Yes sir. I'm the one who has the pleasure of marrying your daughter to Lucky Jordan."

"I swear I never had a good looking captain that looked like you when I was in the navy."

Donna replied, "That's funny I never had any good looking men like you when I was in the navy."

Will said, "You're in the navy, captain?"

"More than twenty years."

Lucky said, "Mr. Charles, I understand Captain Donna's last command in the navy was the captain of an aircraft carrier task force."

Will said, "I guess you've earned your stripes, being a captain of a carrier ma'am."

Donna replied, "Thank you Mr. Charles, for your navy service. I was here just to welcome all of you aboard. I'm looking forward to doing the best I can with your daughter's wedding Mr. Charles."

Will said, "I'm sure you're going to do a wonderful job captain."

Donna replied, "I certainly intent to do my best."

Lucky and Aisha helped to get their parents comfortable in their min suites.

The ship's staff had already taken their suitcases to the staterooms, so they were already there when they got to their staterooms.

Aisha told her parents that she was so glad to see them and they both told her how much being in love must be helping her, because she looked so much better than when she left to go on the cruise.

Both of them told her how much they enjoyed meet Lucky's parents, they told her they were sure helpful to get around when we got to Chile.

Her dad said, "I doubt that we would have got here if we hadn't been with Charles, he sure knows how to get around in a foreign country."

Aisha said, "I'm sure you would have made it, but I think Lucky's dad has done a lot of traveling when he was running his business."

Her dad asked, "Do you know what kind of business his dad had?"

Aisha answered, "I don't know dad, but I think he was very successful doing it."

Aisha mother, Nancy said, "Do you have everything ready for your wedding dear?"

"I hope so, one thing we don't have to worry about, is a bunch of people coming to the wedding."

Will said, "That's good Aisha, we won't have to hear all about what you should have done from your Aunt Mattie."

Nancy said, "Will don't be picking on your sister, Mattie. She knows a lot, about weddings."

Will replied, "Hell yes. She should know, as many of them that she had."

Aisha trying to change the subject said, "It so good to have you here for my wedding. I know it's hard to get away from the farm."

Will said, "We decided to let the farm take care of its self. We've signed up to go all the way back to Los Angeles with you, to make sure Lucky treats you right."

Nancy said, "Will, you know when we found out our daughter was getting married on the ship. We decided to actually take a vacation for those few weeks, since we would already be here."

"That's good mom, I'm glad you could get away and have sometime away from the farm."

"We need it, your father not getting any younger and I'm trying to get him to sell the farm and retire somewhere close to where you're going to live."

"You know what mom, Lucky and I have never talked about where we were going to living after we're married and finish this cruise."

Dad said, "Well it would be good thing to talk about pretty soon, what kind of work he does, to make a living?"

Aisha replied, "You know dad we never talked about that either."

"You know daughter. I think there a few things you two should talk over with Lucky before he becomes your husband."

"Your right dad, but the true is. I don't really care where we live or what kind of work he does, just as long as we're together and he loves me."

Nancy said, "You're right Aisha, those are the most important things. The rest is just details."

Will added, "Details yes, but some of us always had to worry about those details."

"I know dear, but the details can't replace being together with someone you love and they love you."

Will replied, "Women! I'll never understand women."

"No dear, you won't, but I love you just the same."

In a stateroom not far away a lot of the same questions were being asked by Lucky's parents.

Lucky was luckier, because he quickly said he didn't care where they were going to live and he could do his investing, from wherever they were in the world.

He said he would always have enough income for them to live on unless all of the companies he had stock in went out of business.

Thanks to getting a little money from his grandparents, which he invested and turn a little amount of money into a lot of money.

Plus he had his military disability check every month.

The next day everything was ready for Lucky and Aisha wedding and the captain had directed her staff to construct a wedding chapel in the lounge on the tenth deck and fill it with flowers and make it as romantic as possible.

Further, she charged the food and drink department to prepare a masterful lunch with plenty of bottles of champagne.

When the bridal party arrived at the lounge on the tenth deck, they thought they may have left the ship, as there was now a white chapel in this space complete with a sign outside the open doors that read;"*Wedding today of Ms. Aisha Charles to Mr. Lucky Jordan.*"

The photographer had began taking photos of the bridal party and their guests as soon as they arrived an entered the wedding chapel.

Inside the chapel where white pews with beautiful flowers attached to both ends of the pews.

The chapel had stained glass windows on the side wall and extra large stained glass window at the back of the alter, along with baskets of flowers and a large cross placed in the front of the large window.

Captain Donna Morehouse was dressed in her all white navy dress uniform complete with her naval rank and a chest full of ribbons and medals and was standing at the altar at the front of the chapel.

The entertainment department wasn't left out of the fun. Music was playing as the wedding party arrived and their guests. Two ushers seated the guests and then the organist beginning playing the wedding march.

The grooms' mother and father were seated and next the usher seated the mother of the bride.

The music continued and Sonny and Lucky came down the aisle and took their place, next Jane came down the aisle and the last the bride and her father.

The wedding service conducted by Captain Donna went along beautifully and at the end of the ceremony they had the traditional wedding at the end of the marriage the ceremony kiss between Lucky and Aisha.

Then Captain Donna said, "Ladies and gentlemen. I have the honor to introduce you to Mr. and Mrs. Lucky Jordan.

The wedding party left the chapel and made their way over to what had now became an outdoor French restaurant, except it was inside the ship.

The champagne began to flow and everyone was congratulating the bride and groom with everyone praising the job the captain and her staff had done with the wedding.

The entertainment continued with both a male and female singing duets and solo's and dancing began after they had they finished their marvelous lunch.

After the meal and as the champagne continued flowing and the music continued the bride and groom quietly slipped away to their large suite to begin their honeymoon.

37

The Last Leg Home

Sonny said, "Jane, do you know, that now that we've left Valparaiso we're on the last leg of our world cruise."

"We've only have one more big thing to do, as far as I'm concerned, and that's to go to Machu Picchu. We got about six days until we get to Lima. There we'll be leaving the ship to fly to Cusco and on to Machu Picchu."

"It doesn't seem possible that we're all ready turning north and on the last leg of our world cruise, we're traveling north headed back in the direction of San Francisco."

"The time has gone by so much quicker than I ever thought it would, it's been a great trip."

"The only thing that would have made it better is if we wouldn't of had four women murdered on the trip."

"Jane, I guess we really had five people killed, when you count Veronica King. That poor person was so off of her mind. I don't think she even realized what she was doing."

"She was so in love with Lucky she couldn't thinking about right and wrong. She only had one think on her mind and that was to make Lucky her own and nothing was going to stand in her way, nothing."

"She was going to do whatever she had to do to fulfill her dream."

"Sonny, I want you to know how much I really enjoyed our cruise. I'm so glad you and Gene wanted to do it when we retired, even with the pirate drills, bad weather and the murders. It was a trip of a life time."

"The other thing, I was so happy about was to get to know your best friend, Donna Morehouse. Donna is a very sweet accomplished woman, the kind of woman, I truly respect."

"The only thing about Donna is that I'm ashamed of you for not keeping in contact with her over all of these years."

"However, maybe if you did. Since I'd never met her I might have worried you were really in love with her and not with me."

Sonny laughed and said, "It seems I was going to be in trouble with you, whichever way."

"Sonny, you're always in trouble with me, but I love you so much I always forgive you, sometimes you don't even know you're in trouble, do you?"

"No ma'am. I never do."

Gene called and asked if they were ready to go to breakfast?

They were, and the four of them were soon on their way to the Grand Buffet.

The four days passed quickly by and the four friends arrived in Lima and were on their way to Machu Picchu.

The first flew from Lima to Cusco and checked into a hotel in downtown, than they were taken on a walking tour of the city.

They had an excellent local guide and as they continued Sonny began to get ill, then Jane. They couldn't understand why they didn't feel good.

Finally, their guide, Victor said you're having problems with the altitude its over 12,000 feet high here, one of the reason we stay her for a day is to help people adjust to the elevation.

Victor took them to a restaurant where they were scheduled to have lunch and had the waiter bring them glasses of special coca leaf tea, which is said to help with altitude sickness, they drank their tea and then had lunch and they began to feel better, much better.

While they were relaxing and resting in the restaurant their guide, Victor took Jane's camera and took over thirty pictures of the cathedral and pictures of several buildings sin the center of town and few inside the ruins of old Spanish buildings, that were left from when Spain ruled Peru.

Victor said, "The area in Cusco has had people living here since 1,300 B.C. and it was the capital of Inca Empire in the 1,400's. The Inca's had roads built to Cusco from all of their empire."

"This afternoon, we're going to visit were the Inca built a city in the shape of a puma, which was large fort, called Sacsahuaman, Victor said for tourist it was pronounced, *Sexy Woman.*"

The Inca called this place the Royal House of the Sun. Many of the Inca religious ceremonies were held there. It was an enormous place much larger than Stonehenge it took over 70 years and 20,000 men to build it.

When they finished touring Sacsahuaman, they boarded two large step vans and through the Sacred Valley which was indescribably beautiful. Looking at the Andes they decided they went a long ways up in the air.

They drove several miles on paved highway and then the driver turned off of the highway onto a dirt muddy road with holes so large in some places in the road you would have thought the van might not be able to pull itself out of them.

The driver continued on until everyone in the van thought their driver must be completely lost.

Suddenly the road made a sharp turn to the right, but their driver continued straight until he pulled up in front of two very large beautifully carved doors.

The driver honked his horn and the doors opened and he drove into a huge resort. Several uniformed staff members of the resort were standing at attention, there to welcome them.

The driver opened the door and one member of the staff boarded the bus and welcomed us and told us as we got off the bus a member of the staff would give us a room key and direction to our room.

By the time Sonny, Jane, Gene and Susan were out of the van, a porter was waiting for them with their room keys and after they identified their luggage, he left to deliver it to their room.

This was a magnificent resort: it had swimming pools; spa; a movie theater; chapel; several shops with local treasures and alpacas grazing on the lawn.

They were served at a very nice dinner at one long table which seated all twenty-four people on the tour plus their guides.

Early the next morning they loaded back on their vans and drove quite a ways to Olianta Train Station, where they boarded a train and traveled on it for an hour and half to a village called Agues Calientes, it was end of the line and located near Machu Picchu.

In fact you could call it the gateway to Machu Picchu.

Their train had traveled alongside the Urubamba River it looked like a chocolate brown river, churning over huge boulders which had fallen from the mountains.

They were told this river would travel to become part of the Amazon River.

Arriving at Auges Calientes, the community seemed only to have a train station; some small restaurants; tourist knickknacks shops and the large rushing river flowing by it, in addition to some small hotels or tourist camps.

The four friends thought the river looked like the quickest rushing chocolate river that any of them had ever seen, because none of them had ever seen a river that looked like chocolate before.

Their train had ran along this river for several miles and when they arrived at the little village's train station and got off the train, the sound of the river rushing through the mountains was unbelievable.

You could hardly hear talking if they weren't standing next to you.

OK, they made it this close to Machu Picchu, so now what do they do?

They soon found out, Victor led them to a bus station and all of the Supreme Tourists, were soon on buses taking them up a winding narrow dirt, muddy road, since they had a hard rain last night or earlier this morning.

Later, they found out there were twenty hairpin curves, barley wide enough for their bus.

However, the curves were slightly wider and when you meet another bus, the buses had to pull their right wheels off the road onto just a little bit of ground and pull their larger mirrors in to have just enough room for the buses to slowly pass by each other.

Yes, they had to live through passing like this forty times on this trip.

Sonny hopes their driver was really good and the same went for the drivers of the buses they met.

Sonny, said, I'll be happier, when we're coming down the mountain and we're the bus that next to the mountain, not where we are now, with nothing but air and a huge drop off of the mountain, on our way up to Machu Picchu.

They held their breath until they finally made it to a large parking area and they were here. Hurray! Plus they were still alive and about to see the second one of the new seven wonders of the world, Machu Picchu.

It was everything they hoped it would be, layers of on layers of buildings, the work it took to build this place without modern equipment had to have taken enormous number of people and years to build.

Each row of buildings was on made man plateau wide enough to have some fairly large buildings, in addition to plateaus for farming vegetables.

No one had known anything about this place for centuries, until an American Explorer, by the name of Hiram Bingham on an expedition for Yale University and National Geographic in 1911, found Machu Picchu. While he was looking for another Inca lost site, which turned out to be about thirty miles away from here.

Yale and National Geographic did the restoration of Machu Picchu, than it was turned over to the government of Peru to take care of it.

They had lunch at the Sanctuary Lodge and then retraced their trip back to the resort where they were in the night before. The same bus ride back down the mountain, than on the train back to Olianta, and their vans back to the resort.

The next morning, they rode in their vans back to Cusco to the airport and flew back to Lima, then took another flight from Lima to Guayaquil, Ecuador.

There, they were met by a bus, which took all of the Machu Picchu tourists back to their ship and were given a quick windshield tour of the City of Guayaquil.

They made it back in time for a late dinner in the Grand Buffet and soon all the weary travelers were on their way to their staterooms and soon were in bed.

One thing all of them knew was, tomorrow morning they would not be getting up at four in the morning, as they had been doing for the past three days.

Later that evening the Golden Supreme sailed out of Guayaquil en route to San Juan Del Sur, Nicaragua.

Their six dinner table had now been expanded back to a table for ten, with Aisha and Lucky's parents joining them at dinner.

Lucky and Aisha were enjoying their honeymoon, even if their parents were traveling with them. They were just so happy that they found each other, so they were glad to share the time with their parents.

It also gives the opportunity for Aisha to get acquainted with Lucky's parents and Lucky to have time with her parents.

Amazingly, the six of them got along very well with each other, with all of them having totally different lives and life experiences.

Maybe that was the reason that they blended so well. Knowing people that everything about their lives was so much different than their own, it gave each of them a new appreciation of how different people's lives were lived from

their own.

When their ship arrived in San Juan Del Sur, all ten of the new friends were booked on the same tour, visiting the volcanoes and Lake Nicaragua.

Lucky said, "Aisha, honey were not climbing any volcanoes. That's how I got into big trouble the last time we did."

Aisha replied, "Trouble, is that what you call me?"

"Absolutely, not my love. Never!"

"So, explain what kind of trouble did we get into the last time we climbed a volcano?"

"Aisha, don't you remember, we both wound up in sick bay."

Sonny pipe up and said, "Lucky, you think you're going to get by with that explanation of what you said."

Lucky responded, "Well, I thought it was the truth."

Aisha said, "Good try boy, but that don't cut it."

Lucky said, "Well it's the truth Aisha. We did both wind up in sick bay, then I feel in love with you and we got married, isn't that right love?"

Aisha flashed her million dollar smile at Lucky and said, "That's right darling and don't you forget it."

The local guide said, "OK, everyone please get in the bus and we will be on our way to see the volcanoes and Lake Nicaragua."

The ten of them boarded the bus and were soon on their way to Masaya Volcano National Park.

Arriving there they saw the steam spewing from the Masaya Volcano named *"the mouth of hell"* by the Spanish conquerors. None of the ten wanted to climb this volcano.

Their guide told them, Lake Nicaragua was home to many rare species of animals including fresh water sharks, the only place in the world that has them.

The lake was almost one hundred miles long and forty-five miles wide and when the Spanish arrived in the area they thought they had found an ocean.

All of the tourists enjoyed their day, the weather was warm, but not too hot and only Lucky and Aisha had ever been this close to a volcano before.

The next stop their ship would make would be La Paz, Mexico, when the ship docked it was in an industrial port area, theirs was the only cruise ship there and it was a several mile bus ride to get to the city.

Here the ten of them visited the Cathedral de Nuestra Senora de la Paz and located in the heart of the city. It was a big change from the other cathedrals that the six world travelers has seen, it wasn't as big or gaudy as the ones they had see in the other parts of the world.

They enjoyed seeing it, do to its California mission style architecture, along with seeing the paintings and statues dedicated to the Virgin Mary.

The last thing they saw was a glass blowing studio; here they had a demonstration of the special technique of blending different colors to make amazing pieces, plus the opportunity to buy several beautiful pieces, which all of the women did.

Their ship sailed out of La Paz, Mexico later that afternoon, their next stop Los Angeles, California USA.

Sonny, Jane, Gene and Susan were talking later that evening and Sonny said, "I don't know about what you think the highlights of our world cruise was, but to me the four that stood out was: Uluru; the Taj Mahal; Suez Canal and Machu Picchu.

"I certainly enjoyed something in every port we visited and we have made two very special friends on this voyage, Lucky and Aisha."

Gene replied, "Sonny, I think you've got it right, these four things would be my pick and Supreme did them up right, all in all, everything about the cruise was great.

"We certainly could have done without having four women murdered and killing poor Veronica was a pity."

Jane agreed with Sonny's pick but she added one of mine was getting to know Captain Donna Jean Morehouse, she's truly a wonderful person and she's got us all around this great big beautiful earth."

Susan added, "I agree with all of you, but I loved all the wonderful souvenirs of everyplace we been and all the pictures the ship photographers took and our videos of all the places we've been.

"The smarts thing we did, was to buy the entire package when we first got on board, they tell me now the price has almost doubled, on this package since we started our trip."

Sonny said, "Good, we did one thing right, buying the pictures and video package when we first boarded the ship."

A few days later they arrived in Los Angeles and the ten friends did the tour of the Universal Studios and the visit to the TCL Chinese Theater.

All of their group enjoyed seeing Universal Studios and Aisha folks loved going to the Chinese Theater, although they would always continue to call it Grauman's Chinese Theater, because of all the years that they had seen it of TV it was always called Grauman's.

Now, they were truly on the last leg of their world cruise when they left LA and were on their way back to where they started their cruise from.

There was one last big captains cocktail party and during the party, Captain Morehouse introduced a gentleman from Supreme Cruise Line, Executive Vice President, Robert Vincent.

Everyone gave Mr. Vincent a nice round of applause when Donna introduced him.

Mr. Vincent asked the audience what they thought about Captain Donna, the audience clapped their hands and many yelled out, she's the best, we love her.

Mr. Vincent thanked everyone for their enthusiastic response for their captain.

He continued on with his speech and said, "I would like to ask the following passengers to please come forward, Mr. Sonny Cousins; Mr. Gene Simpson and Mr. Lucky Jordan."

Sonny got up from the table where he was sitting and begin walking up to where Mr. Vincent was standing and Gene and Lucky followed right behind Sonny.

Mr. Vincent said, "I'm sure many of you folks who have been on this world cruise for a long time have meet Sonny; Gene and Lucky at sometime.

"Many of you who joined the cruise later probably don't know about the problem we had on our ship, but we have four women murdered on our cruise."

There was a noticeable gasp in the audience hearing about women being murdered on the ship.

Mr. Vincent continued on, "Sonny Cousins and Gene Simpson are recently retired homicide detectives from the police department in Kansas City.

"Mr. Lucky Jordan severed in the army in Afghanistan and is a martial arts instructor.

"These gentlemen are responsible for stopping the murders on this ship and bring the guilty person to justice.

"I'm here on behalf of Supreme Cruise Line to personally thank them for their service and present them with a Golden Lifetime Pass for them and a guest to take any cruise they want to take for the rest of their life on Supreme Cruise Line."

Big applause from the audience.

Sonny looked at Gene and Lucky and finally Gene pointed at Sonny to go talk for them.

Sonny said, "Somehow, I just got appointed as the spokes person for the three of us. I'm not sure why."

The audience heard Gene say, "Because you always do all the talking."

Lots of laughter from the audience at Gene's statement.

Sonny continued, "OK. So I'm always doing the talking, then I just want to say for the three of us, thank you Mr. Vincent. I know we all certainly appreciate the Golden tickets, but now I'll never be able to keep my wife and me at home anymore."

Big applause from the audience.

Mr. Vincent handed a Golden Printed Lifetime Pass to each of the three men.

Mr. Vincent said, "I want to tell you one more thing about your, Captain Donna.

"I've asked her to marry me when we return to San Francisco and she said yes."

Then Captain Donna joined Robert Vincent and thanked him for presenting the Golden Passes to Sonny, Gene and Lucky.

That ended the speeches and everyone rushed to congratulate Donna and Robert on their news.

After things settled down, Donna and Robert came over to Sonny and the friends table and said, "Sonny, I'm sorry I didn't get to tell you before Robert made the announcement about us getting married.

"He'd asked me before I started on this world cruise. I'd told him I'd let him know when my trip was over."

"Sonny since you're my best friend and have been all my life. I want you to my attendant at my wedding, will you do it."

"Of course. I'd be honored too.

"Robert, I have to tell you're getting a wonderful person for your wife."

"I certainly know that, my first wife died a few years ago and when I met Donna. I fell for her, just seeing her the first time.

"She can do anything. She just took one of our ships around the world. Maybe she can help me with three daughters to learn that they can do whatever they want to with their lives."

Sonny said, "I'm sure she can inspire them to be whatever they want, just like she has herself.

"OK, Donna when are you two planning on getting married?"

"Sonny, I would have to say it would be a couple of months. I'll need to take Robert home to Hutchinson to meet my parents.

"He'll need to let his girls have some notice that their dad is going to get married. I'm sure they will need a little time to get to know me too.

"Sonny, when we have a date. I'll call and give you a couple of week's notice, if that's all right."

Jane said, "That's all right Donna. I'll see to it that Sonny is there to be your, what do you called it when a man is your maiden of honor."

Donna replied, "Damn if I know. I guess he will be *my man of honor.*"

Everyone laughed loudly at that.

Gene said, "I have this picture in my mind of Sonny as, *a man of honor* for the bride, does he have to wear white?"

Donna replied, "Great question. I guess we'll have a couple of months to figure it out."

A few days later it was time to say farewell to all of their new friends that they made on their world cruise.

They knew Lucky and Aisha would always remain in their circle of lifetime friends and would see them when it was time for Donna's wedding.

Saying goodbye wasn't easy for any of them, but Sonny, Mary, Gene and Susan knew it was time for them to fly back home to Kansas City and wait for Donna's call for Sonny's next great adventure.

THE END